Praise for *New York Times* bestselling author

"Expert storytelling ... the romance between A... is compelling novel p... ers will be sad to leave ..."
—*Publishers Weekly* on *Wild Wicked Scot* (starred review)

"London's writing bubbles with high emotion. Her blend of playful humor and sincerity imbues her heroines with incredible appeal, and readers will delight as their unconventional tactics create rambling paths to happiness."
—*Publishers Weekly* on *The Devil Takes a Bride* (starred review)

"This tale of scandal and passion is perfect for readers who like to see bad girls win, but still love the feeling of a society romance, and London nicely sets up future books starring Honor's sisters."
—*Publishers Weekly* on *The Trouble with Honor*

"This series starter brims with delightful humor and charm."
—*RT Book Reviews* on *The Trouble with Honor*

"Julia London writes vibrant, emotional stories and sexy, richly drawn characters."
—*New York Times* bestselling author Madeline Hunter

JULIA LONDON

SINFUL SCOTTISH LAIRD

HQN™

HQN™

ISBN-13: 978-0-373-78990-0

Recycling programs
for this product may
not exist in your area.

Sinful Scottish Laird

Copyright © 2017 by Dinah Dinwiddie

This edition published by arrangement with Harlequin Books S.A.

For questions and comments about the quality of this book,
please contact us at CustomerService@Harlequin.com.

® and TM are trademarks of Harlequin Enterprises Limited or its
corporate affiliates. Trademarks indicated with ® are registered in the
United States Patent and Trademark Office, the Canadian Intellectual
Property Office and in other countries.

www.HQNBooks.com

Printed in U.S.A.

For Attadale Gardens, the lovely Highland estate in Wester Ross, on the shores of Lochcarron, where I had the great pleasure of writing a portion of this book. The estate serves as the inspiration for my fictional Arrandale. A special thanks to the Laird of Attadale, who is not a strong, muscular man with dark eyes, wearing a kilt, but the lovely Joanna Macpherson. She and her husband could not have been more welcoming or their gardens more beautiful.

CHAPTER ONE

Scottish Highlands, 1742
Balhaire

THE COACH GROANED and shuddered along a nearly impassable road, tossing its inhabitants across the benches and back against the squabs. The young Lord Chatwick's complexion had turned gray, and he rested listlessly against the wall.

"My poor darling," crooned his mother, Daisy, Lady Chatwick, as she stroked his hair.

"I said from the beginning such aggressive travel would make the child ill. I pray we see a quick recovery from him."

This sunny observation was made by Daisy's cousin Miss Belinda Hainsworth.

"I'm well when the coach isn't moving," moaned Ellis.

"Dear boy, you *think* you are," Belinda said and smiled sadly, as if Ellis had been made feebleminded by the travel and didn't know his own feelings. She glanced at Daisy. "Is it not too late to turn back and spare us all?"

Too late? Yes, it was too late! They'd been traveling for an eternity and were only miles from their destination. "Too late," Daisy said and closed her eyes.

She would explode, she thought. Shatter into a million bits of furious fatigue. Almost three weeks in transit, from London to Liverpool, then sailing up the coast through rough seas to Scotland, and then the relentless plodding past hovels made of peat and mud, past people in strange dress with small cattle and barking dogs, through miles and miles of empty landscape with a young son made ill by the motion of travel, a gloomy cousin, and no place for them to rest except the occasional mean inn.

It had been wretched.

"You look piqued, Daisy."

Daisy opened her eyes; Belinda was studying her, her head cocked to one side. "Yes, I am. I am sick to death of riding in this coach," Daisy fussed. "And I will be much relieved when I can remove these blasted stays." She pressed a hand against her side with a heavy sigh, feeling the stays of her corset digging into her ribs.

At that very moment, the coach shuddered violently and sank hard to the right, and the stays dug deeper into Daisy's side. Her son landed on top of her with an *oomph*, and Belinda was thrown against the wall of the coach with a cry of alarm.

"For heaven's sake," Daisy said, breathless.

"Madam!" someone shouted from outside the coach; the door swung open. "Are you unharmed?"

"We're fine. Is it a wheel?"

"It is indeed," her escort, Sir Nevis, said as he lifted her son out of the coach.

"What shall we do?" Belinda asked as she carefully backed out of the coach. "We haven't the proper tools to repair it. We'll be forced to camp here!"

"We shall endeavor to repair it," Sir Nevis said as he extended his hand to help Daisy down.

She stepped gingerly onto terra firma and adjusted her corset as best she could without removing her gown and clawing the damn thing from her body, then joined Sir Nevis to have a look. A spoke had broken, and the wheel was bowing. The driver and his helper were quickly releasing the horses from their traces.

"We must elevate the coach to keep the wheel from snapping," Sir Nevis said. He looked to the three men they'd hired at port to escort them to Auchenard. Gordons, he'd said. A mighty clan, he'd said. Daisy didn't know how mighty the Gordons were, but she hadn't liked the look of these three from the start. They were as thin as reeds, their clothing worn and filthy, and they looked at her like little boys staring at sweetmeats in the shop window. They were fond of whisky, and if they spoke English, she couldn't say—they rarely uttered a word, and when they did, their accents were so heavy that she couldn't make anything out. Now, they stood aside, eyeing the broken spoke with disinclination.

"Madam, if you and his lordship would take shelter beneath those trees," Sir Nevis said, nodding to a stand a few feet from the coach. "This might take some time."

Might? Daisy sighed wearily. She was not new to the world of coach travel and rather imagined it would take all day. She looked around them. It was a sun-drenched day, the air uncomfortably warm. Even the plumes atop their coach were wilting. There was no shelter, nothing but miles and miles of empty rolling hills and swarms of midges as far as one could see.

Ellis had dipped down to examine a rock. At least some pink had returned to his complexion; she was thankful for that. "See, Mamma," he said, and held up a rock. "It's pyrite."

"Is it?" she asked, leaning over to peer at a rock that was yellowish in color. "So it is," she agreed, although she had no idea what sort of rock it was. She looked back over her shoulder at her retinue—three servants and a tutor; Sir Nevis and his man, Mr. Bellows, who had accompanied them from London along with the two drivers; a pair of wagons under Mr. Green's care, loaded with boxes and trunks that carried their things; and a smaller chaise in which Mrs. Green and the housemaid rode.

It was as if she were leading a band of gypsies across the Highlands.

A movement at the lake caught her eye, and Daisy noticed the Gordons at the shore. Well, yes, of course, they should swim, the poor things. Perhaps wash a bit of the dirt off them while her men toiled in the hot sun to repair the wheel. How much had they paid for that trio of scoundrels?

"We can't possibly be forced to camp here," Belinda said, fanning herself. "There is no shelter! We leave ourselves open to marauders and thieves."

"Belinda, for God's sake, will you *stop*," Daisy said wearily. "I have listened to your complaints until I can bear it no more. There is nothing to be done for our predicament. We are here. We will not die. We will not be harmed. We will not be set upon by thieves!"

All those years ago when Daisy had been a new bride, with her mother gone and no one to advise her, she'd promised her maternal aunt on her deathbed that she would look after Belinda. Of course she would—Daisy loved her childhood playmate. She'd just never realized how doleful her cousin could be until she was under her roof.

Belinda said nothing to Daisy's rebuke. In fact, she seemed to be staring at something behind Daisy. With exasperation, Daisy drawled, "What is it *now*? Marauders?" She turned around to see what had captured Belinda's attention, and her heart sank to her toes—five figures in highland dress were galloping down the hill toward them.

"Not marauders," Belinda said, her voice trembling. "*Smugglers.* I've heard it said they hide in these hills."

And with that remark, the air was snatched cleanly from Daisy's lungs.

There was a sudden and collective cry of alarm

as the rest of Daisy's entourage noticed the riders. It was as if someone had fired several rounds into their midst; people ran, grabbed up their things as they raced to hide behind the wagons.

"Lady Chatwick!" Sir Nevis shouted. "Take shelter in the chaise!"

He had drawn his sword, and together with Mr. Bellows, stood with his legs braced apart, facing the intruders, prepared for battle. Belinda was already moving, grabbing at Ellis's arm as he lined up the rocks he'd collected and dragging him toward the chaise.

But Daisy? She didn't move. She was too stunned to move. Utterly paralyzed with fear and exhilaration, on the verge of screaming in terror or laughing hysterically at the absurdity of it all—of course they would be set upon by highland thieves! This was precisely the disaster Belinda had predicted all along.

Something about the notion of disaster made her move; she whirled about to summon the three Gordons, but they were no longer on the shores of the lake. They had fled. Fled! Her heart leaped to her throat, and she whipped back around…almost expecting the Gordons to have joined the riders.

The Highlanders had slowed their mounts, approaching with caution now. One of them—a woman, it appeared—spurred her palfrey to lope ahead of the others. Roving bands of thieves were not led by women, were they? Perhaps, then, this was not what it seemed.

The bark of gunfire startled Daisy so badly that

she dropped to all fours on the ground before realizing that Mr. Bellows was the one who had fired his musket. But his aim had erred, and the shot pinged off a tree to the right of the band of Highlanders.

One of the riders abruptly spurred his mount forward, catching the palfrey's bridle before the woman rode headlong into buckshot, and reined her to a hard stop. "For God's sake, put down your weapon!" he roared in English. "Bloody hell, lad, you might kill someone, aye?"

Mr. Bellows aimed his gun at the man. "We've no use for highwaymen or Jacobites, sir! If you do not ride on, I will aim for the spot between your eyes!"

Daisy found her feet and hurried forward with the vague intention of seeking shelter inside the listing coach. But she paused at the driver's seat and peered over the footrest as another of the men rode forward to meet the first and spoke in the language of the Scots.

The first man answered, his voice low and soft. Whatever he said prompted two of his companions to laugh. But *he* did not laugh. He sat tall and stoic on that horse, his mien fiercely proud, his gaze shrewd and locked on Sir Nevis and Mr. Bellows. He looked to be a head taller than the others. He was broad shouldered and square jawed, with thick auburn hair that he'd tied at his nape. His appearance was so rugged, so overwhelmingly masculine, that Daisy's blood raced in her veins in a mix of absolute terror and fascination. He looked stronger than any man she'd ever seen, as if he alone might have been responsible for carving these hills from the granite landscape.

Something sharp and hot waved through Daisy, making it impossible to breathe, much less move.

He spoke to the woman, who clearly did not care for what he said, judging by the way she jerked her gaze to him and responded in a heated tone.

"Do as I tell you, lass," he said, his voice unnervingly calm. "Fearful men fire without warning and without aim."

The woman muttered under her breath, but she turned the palfrey about and put herself behind the other three men.

Now the man nudged his horse forward, his gaze still fixed on Mr. Bellows and his gun.

"Come no closer!" Mr. Bellows warned him, then looked around. "Gordon, where are you? Why do you not do something?" he shouted.

The man chuckled. "The Gordons willna help you now, lad." One of the riders muttered something that made the others laugh. They weren't the least bit afraid of Mr. Bellows's gun or the fact that they were outnumbered, Daisy realized with a slam of her heart against her ribs. They were...*amused*.

Like a cat, the man's attention suddenly shifted to his left; Daisy followed his gaze and noticed that the drivers had crept around one of the wagons, both holding muskets. He sighed loudly as the drivers both leveled their sights on him. "We're no' highwaymen," he said brusquely. "Put down your guns, aye? I donna care to kill you on what's been a bonny afternoon thus far." He swung off his horse; everyone in Daisy's party took a step backward.

But not her, because Daisy had clearly lost her fool mind. She was keenly aware that she ought to be seeking shelter, hiding Ellis, finding something with which to defend herself…but she couldn't tear her eyes away from the perfect physical specimen of a man. A bolt of feral desire shot down her spine, unlike anything she'd ever felt, as she studied him standing there, his weight cocked on one hip as he yanked his gloves from his hands. He wasn't handsome in a conventional way. His looks were fine enough, she supposed, but it was *him* that enthralled her—his presence, his carriage and the veritable confidence that exuded from him.

He was wearing the plaid about him, and his legs, Lord in heaven, his legs shaped by sinewy muscle, were covered in a sort of red-and-white plaid pair of stockings, tied just below his knee with garters. He *was* tall, but not overly so, and lean, but burly, too. He was clean shaven, yet his hair appeared untamed, even tied at his nape as it was. He was so calm, so unruffled—he projected palpable power.

Had she been any other place, Daisy might have fanned herself. As it was, she was on the verge of swooning. She was astonished by her physical response to this man who, for all she knew, was a murderer, a smuggler, a thief—but damn her, in that frenzied moment of lust and fear, she could not think

of a single other time she had been so completely enthralled by one man.

Now that he'd removed his gloves and tucked
them into the plaid somewhere, he moved with great
ease toward Mr. Bellows as Sir Nevis circled around,
his sword raised, prepared to attack.

"*Mi Diah*, look around you, aye?" the Scotsman
said. "Does a lady and gentlemen in leather boots
rob coaches? *Here?* Where scarcely anyone resides?"
He swept a thick arm to indicate the vast, untouched
land around them. "We are no' Jacobites, nor high-
wayman. But if we were, we'd shadow the road to
Inverness. No' this seldom used road."

That seemed like a perfectly reasonable explanation to Daisy. Wasn't it? She wanted to believe him,
but her nerves, always so pragmatic, warned her that
this entire situation might be planned. Perhaps the
Gordons led them here so that these men could rob
them. Now her heart began to pound with the possibility of danger, her palms dampening, her breath
shortening. And yet she didn't hide—she slipped
around the coach while Mr. Bellows nervously kept
his gun sighted on the man.

"We are charged with the protection of Lady
Chatwick and her son, and we will not hesitate to
give our lives if necessary, sir! Do not come closer!"
Mr. Bellows's hand shook.

If these Scots were in cahoots with those rotten
Gordons, her party would be outnumbered at any
moment. She was struck cold with the image of doz-

ens of them coming down from the hills to pillage them, just as Belinda had predicted.

"We mean only to help, aye?" the Scotsman said. His voice wasn't as heavily accented as the Gordons. In fact, his speech sounded as it was tinged with a bit of an English accent.

He lifted his hands shoulder high to show he was unarmed. "We've no desire to harm you; I give you my word as a Highlander and a gentleman." He didn't tremble, didn't seem to be the least bit concerned. He seemed only impatient, as if he wished this meeting to be done.

"You expect us to believe it?" Mr. Bellows snapped.

"There is no' a man among us who is inclined to haul so many boxes and trunks down the road."

One of the riders behind the Scotsman spoke in the Scots language, and when he did, Mr. Bellows made the mistake of looking at him. In the space of no more than a moment, the Scotsman lunged so quickly for the barrel of the musket that Daisy couldn't help but sound a yelp of alarm. He yanked it cleanly from Mr. Bellows's hands and twirled it around in one movement to train it on him. "You'll tell your companions to put away their firearms now, aye?" he asked, his voice deadly in its calm.

Daisy believed she would be bargaining for her son's safety at any moment and frantically thought what to do. Should she find him and run for the lake? She glanced toward the chaise where Ellis was hiding, and saw Mr. Green furtively begin to lift his musket and take aim. Mr. Green, her grounds-

keeper, who'd likely never before fired on another
man. "No!" she cried out inadvertently, the desperate sound of her voice startling her. "All of you! Do
as he says, sir, *please*."

The Scotsman did not take his eyes from Sir
Nevis. "Heed your lady."

"I urge you, madam, put yourself in the coach!"
Sir Nevis shouted.

"If these men intended to rob us, would they not
have already done it?" she asked, tripping over the
traces of the chaise as she picked her way around the
coach, desperate to avert a crisis. "Would not our
hired men have interceded? I think he speaks true."

"Ah, a voice of reason, then," the Scotsman drawled.

There was no reason in Daisy at all—she had
no idea what these men intended and spoke only
with the frantic hope of avoiding bloodshed. "Please,
Sir Nevis, tell your men to lower their sights," she
begged. "We want no trouble here."

Sir Nevis jutted out his chin, but he turned slightly
and nodded at the other men, and slowly, suspiciously, they lowered their guns.

The Scotsman smirked, then twirled the musket
in one hand so that the butt was facing away from
him and handed it to Mr. Bellows. "Now…might we
help you repair the wheel?" he asked as if the ten-
sion had not just simmered so menacingly between
them. As if none of them had, only moments before,
feared for their lives.

"That is not necessary," Sir Nevis said stiffly.

The Scotsman shrugged indifferently. "Aye, then.

We've no desire to toil under the hot summer sun." He turned as if he meant to depart, but he caught sight of Daisy and he hesitated, his eyes locking on hers.

Daisy's breath quickened; her first instinct was to step back, to run. Her second instinct overruled the first, however, for he had a pair of astoundingly blue eyes. Cerulean blue. She was moving without thought, stepping away from the coach as she nervously pressed her damp palms to the front of her gown.

His heated gaze slowly traveled the length of her, his eyes like a pair of torches, singeing her skin as he took in every bit of her gown and the tips of the shoes that peeked out from beneath her hem. Then up again, to her bosom, where he unabashedly lingered, and finally to her face.

Daisy self-consciously brushed her cheek with the back of her hand, wondering if she looked dirty or worn.

He continued to stare at her so boldly and unapologetically that Daisy couldn't help but smile uneasily. "Ah...th-thank you for your offer," she stammered. What the devil was she to say in this situation?

He stared at her.

"Madam, I must insist that you return to the chaise with your lady to wait," Sir Nevis begged her.

"Yes, I will," she assured him, but she made no move to do so, not even when she heard Belinda call for her. She simply could not look away from the Scotsman.

"Who are you?" he suddenly demanded.

"Me?" she asked stupidly, but then she remembered herself and stepped forward, her hand extended, and sank into a curtsy with the vague idea that if all else failed, perhaps civility might work. "I beg your pardon. I am Lady Chatwick." She glanced up, her hand still extended. The Scotsman scowled down at her. He showed no inclination to take her hand.

Daisy self-consciously rose. She'd never seen eyes so blue, she was certain of it—the very color of an early spring day. "I do so appreciate your offer of assistance. We've come a very long way and have not seen roads as bad as these."

His gaze narrowed menacingly, and he took a step toward her. And another. He tilted his head to one side, studying her, as if she were a creature he'd never seen before. "What is an English noblewoman doing in these hills?" he demanded, his voice tinged with suspicion.

"We are to Auchenard," she said. "It is a lodge—"

"Aye, I know what it is," he said. "No one goes to Auchenard now but rutting stags. What business have you there?"

She was slightly taken aback by his crass comment. "Ah…well, Auchenard belongs to my son now. I thought he should see it."

He frowned as if he didn't believe her. His gaze fell to her lips, and there it lingered.

Daisy's blood fired and flooded her cheeks. She

nervously touched a curl at her nape. "I beg your pardon, but might I know your name?"

He slowly lifted his gaze. "Arrandale."

"Arrandale," she repeated.

He took another sudden step forward, and now he stood so close that she had to tilt her head back to look up at him.

"Stand back!" Sir Nevis shouted, but the Scotsman ignored him.

Daisy's heart was seizing madly in her chest. She could clearly see the emerging shadow of a dark beard and the dark lashes that framed his eyes. And the nick of a scar at the bridge of his nose, another one on his jawline. She looked at his mouth, too, the dark plum of his lips.

"You should no' have come here," he said quietly. "This country is no' safe for *Sassenach* women and children. Repair your wheel, turn about and head for the sea."

Daisy blinked. "I beg your pardon, but we've—"

He abruptly turned his back on her and strode to his horse, swinging himself up onto its back. He said something to the others, and, just like that, they rode away, in the direction from which Daisy and her party had labored all day.

It seemed several moments before Daisy could breathe. She exchanged a wide-eyed look with Sir Nevis, who at last instructed the others. "To the wheel," he said. "Make haste."

"What has happened?" Belinda's voice cried out behind Daisy. "Where have they gone?"

"Be thankful they have gone and left your purse and your virtue intact, madam," Sir Nevis said darkly and whirled about, marching to assist in the repair of the wheel.

Daisy felt Belinda's hand on her back. "You are shaking," she said. "Calm yourself, Daisy. They've gone—you're quite safe for the moment."

Daisy wasn't shaking with fear. She was shaking because she had never in her life been so bewitched by a man.

CHAPTER TWO

MORE THAN TWO hours after the Scotsman and his group had left them deserted on the road, the wheel repaired as best it could be, Daisy and her party began the arduous progress east once more.

As they bumped along, her heart still fluttered a little. She couldn't rid herself of the image of that man. She listened idly to Belinda, who hugged the small window, peering out at the landscape, remarking on the vast emptiness and dangers lurking, but Daisy thought of him.

"I'd not be the least surprised were we attacked by those wild men," Belinda said, shuddering.

"They didn't seem so very wild in the end, did they?" Daisy asked. She thought of the warnings her friends had given her before she'd departed for Scotland. She'd invited several ladies over for tea. "What trouble you'll find there, what with all the traitors among them," Lady Dinsmore had cried. "You can't go! I've heard they slaughter the English."

"They're savages," Lady Whitcomb had added gravely. "They have been unnaturally influenced by the Stuarts and are quite impossibly untrustworthy! You won't be safe for a moment among them—

everyone knows the greatest prize is an English-woman."

Daisy didn't share their pessimistic view. She'd been married to a man who was himself a Scot by blood, and he had never given her any reason to believe she should fear them. Then again, she'd never seen a Scot like the one she'd encountered today.

Neither had Belinda apparently, for her head snapped around, her brows almost to her hairline. "I thank the good Lord we escaped unharmed!"

Ellis lifted his head and looked at his mother, an expression of worry on his face. Daisy smiled reassuringly and hugged him to her side. "We are safe, darling."

She'd often privately wondered if she'd done something while she carried the boy to produce such a fretful, fearful child. What else could explain it? He was nine years old and had never wanted for anything, had no outward ailments to speak of, and yet he was so timid. Their London physician had warned Daisy a few years ago that her son suffered from a weak constitution. "No doubt he shall be sickly all his life," he'd said as he'd closed his bag.

That news was not what Daisy had expected, and she'd looked at him with confusion. "*Sickly?* What do you mean?"

"Just that." The physician had no regard for her, much less Ellis, who was old enough to understand what he'd said.

"Do you mean he will have a chronic ague?" Daisy had asked, for certainly that particular winter, it had seemed her son was perpetually ill. And then she'd led the physician from Ellis's bedside and whispered, "Or something worse?"

The physician had shrugged and said absently, "One never knows how these things will manifest themselves."

"I beg your pardon, sir, but that is why I sent for you," she'd said impatiently. "So that you might explain to me what his illness is and how it may manifest itself."

"Lady Chatwick." The physician had sighed, as if she was testing his patience, then had said quite loudly, "You will not understand the nuances of the boy's medical constitution. You must trust me when I tell you that he will never be a robust lad."

Ellis had burst into tears as one might expect having just heard such a callous delivery about the state of one's health. Daisy had known then that the physician meant only to collect his fee and didn't care a whit for her son. "Then we have a problem, sir, for I don't trust you at all," she'd said, then called for the butler to dispatch the good doctor.

When she'd complained of his demeanor later that evening, her husband had chastised *her* for being disrespectful to the doctor.

Nevertheless, Daisy refused to believe the man's prediction of Ellis's future. Frankly, her son's health was the second reason Daisy had undertaken what had become an increasingly dangerous journey north.

Robert was the first reason. If Robert had only

reached her in time, this travel might well have been avoided.

She mindlessly touched his letter, kept safe in the pocket of her gown. *I will come with great haste as soon as my commission has ended,* he'd written her.

But not soon enough, as it turned out.

"If they don't find us now, they'll surely find us at this lodge," Belinda warned, settling back against the squabs, still intent on worrying them all.

"We are perfectly safe," Daisy said, and tried to convey a warning to her cousin with her expression, which, naturally, Belinda did not notice. Daisy smiled and squeezed Ellis's knee. "Pay Cousin Belinda no mind, darling. It's been a trying day for us all."

"I am not unreasonable in my concern," Belinda said. "We were all of us frightened by those dangerous men."

"Need I remind you that those dangerous men offered to repair our wheel?" Daisy asked, then impulsively covered Ellis's ears with her hands and leaned forward, whispering, "Forget that now, darling. Did you not *see* the gentleman? He was so… *alluring*."

Belinda blinked. "The Scotsman? *Alluring?* Daisy!" She gasped, clearly appalled. "What is the matter with you? Scotsmen are *not* alluring. They are traitors to the Crown!"

Were she not so exhausted, Daisy would have argued that Belinda was not acquainted with any Scotsmen, and, therefore, couldn't know if they were all or any of them Jacobites. Instead she was disappointed that Belinda had not noticed the man's allure. She could not share in the observation of how a man with his extraordinary presence could be found on an abandoned road in what seemed the most remote region of the earth. With a sigh, she let go of Ellis's ears and turned her gaze to the grimy window as Belinda began to speculate if they would be forced to camp on the road tonight.

He'd been so utterly unexpected. Daisy flushed again, thinking about the Scotsman. Oh, but she was a hopeless cause. Quite possibly even mad! She shuddered to think how foolishly beguiled she'd been, particularly in the face of what could have been terrible danger. She'd long been an admirer of healthy men, but this...*this* bordered on lunacy.

And yet...she hoped she might see him again one day. She would very much like to make him smile, to see the light she was certain could be coaxed from those blue eyes under the right circumstances. She quivered a little, imagining just how she might.

Oh yes, she was mad—completely and utterly mad.

This tendency to fantasy was something that had been slowly building in Daisy since her husband's death more than two years ago. She'd since dabbled liberally in the art of flirtation in salons across Mayfair, had imagined any number of handsome gentlemen in varying degrees of compromise, so much so that now that tendency often felt impossible to control. The truth was that Daisy very much missed a man's touch.

Her husband, Clive, had been robust when her marriage was arranged, but he'd contracted a wasting illness soon after Ellis's birth. In the last years of his life, he'd suffered gravely, too sick to be a father, too sick to care for her as a husband ought. Now, at nine and twenty, Daisy felt desire flowing in the vast physical wasteland of her life like a river that had overrun its banks.

Her steady stream of suitors since Clive's death were the raging storm waters that fed that river.

But the Scotsman was not a suitor, and she thought of him in an entirely different light. She closed her eyes and imagined being kidnapped by him, carried off on the back of his horse, tossed onto a bed high in some rustic castle. She imagined his large hands on her body. She imagined resisting him at first, then succumbing to his expert touch. She imagined feeling his body, hot and thick inside her, and those blue eyes boring into her as she found her release.

Daisy shifted uncomfortably.

"Are you all right?" Belinda asked.

Poof. In an instant, the image of him disappeared. "Pardon?" Daisy's cheeks warmed as she shifted again. "Yes, I'm fine."

"Is it your stays?" Belinda asked sympathetically. "Stays can be quite dangerous, you know," she said, launching into conjecture about the dangers of corsets.

Daisy sank into the squabs and resolved not to

think of the stranger again. She would think of London, of all the reasons she'd been so determined to leave.

Ah yes, that stream of suitors.

Her husband's will had made London unbearable for her. It was no secret to the gentlemen bachelors about town that Lord Chatwick's widow must remarry within three years of his death or risk forfeiting her son's inheritance.

Clive had explained this to Daisy from his deathbed. "You must understand, darling. I should not like to see you refuse to marry again and deplete Ellis's inheritance to live as you like. You will rely on Bishop Craig to help you find a suitable match. He will see to it that the man you agree to marry will ensure Ellis's education in the finest institutions and will possess the proper connections for Ellis when he reaches his majority."

Daisy had been horrified by his unexpected edict. She could scarcely embrace her husband's looming death, much less the plans he'd made for her for after he'd gone. "I can look after him, Clive," she'd said. "I am his mother—of *course* I will."

Her husband had lost a moment in a fit of coughing, then patted her hand. "You will do as I decide, Daisy. I trust you to understand."

But she didn't understand. She would never understand.

Daisy and Clive's match had been made on the basis of compatible fortunes and family interests. He was fifteen years her senior, and Daisy had been his second wife, his first having been lost in childbirth along with the child. It was the sort of match she'd been brought up to expect, and she'd been somewhat prepared for it. Duty first, wasn't that what had been drummed into her?

But something miraculous had happened in that first year—she'd discovered affection for Clive. She'd been a steadfast and true companion, and she'd given him a son. She'd remained at his bedside when other women might have sought diversion elsewhere, and she'd held his hand when he felt searing pain rack his body. She'd been the wife she had promised him she would be.

And for her devotion, in the last weeks of his life, he'd made his final wishes known to her. Plans he'd already made. None of them included any regard for her.

Daisy had felt used and unimportant. As her husband lay dying, she'd realized that she was and always would be nothing more than a conduit to provide a son and then bring that son to his majority. That was her worth to Clive. Her feelings, her wants, were irrelevant to him.

As Daisy had struggled to keep her bitterness from coloring the days and weeks following his death, word of his final wishes began to whisper through the salons of Mayfair. The Chatwick fortune was up for bidding!

In fairness, Daisy had enjoyed the attention at first—it was a welcome change after caring for a sickly husband for so many years. She quickly became one of the most sought-after women in London…but, as it was readily apparent to everyone, not for herself. She was a widow with a fortune and a deadline for remarriage, and that was like raw meat to lions as far as the bachelors of the Quality were concerned. She could hardly keep them from her door.

As time ticked by, and the vultures flocked around her, Daisy began to distrust the intentions of anyone who came calling. She felt suffocated by it all and began to question her own instincts. Bishop Craig made the situation all the more intolerable as he began to negotiate on her behalf—without her knowledge—with men she scarcely knew. Her pleas to him to stop fell on deaf ears. "Your husband put his trust in me, Lady Chatwick. I will not let him down in this."

There was nothing she could do, and Daisy had all but resigned herself to her fate. But then, five months ago, as if delivered on the wings of angels, came the letter from Robert Spivey. *Rob.*

Rob was now a captain in the Royal British Navy. She really didn't know more about him than that, for it had been a little more than eleven years since she'd last seen him. She'd imagined he was married and surely had children of his own. She thought that he'd forgotten her altogether. Eleven years was a lifetime in loves lost, wasn't it?

Well, she'd not forgotten him. He'd been her first love, her deepest love and her only real love.

Ah, but they'd been so young when they'd met,

so hopelessly idealistic. They'd dreamed of a future together—nothing terribly magnificent, mind you, but one that suited two people consumed with each other and with love. A future that had room for only the two of them.

Lord, how naive she'd been then! She used to daydream of how they would live: in a thatched-roof cottage with window boxes filled with flowers. They would have children, too—robust, healthy children—who would run among the fields of heather. She would have a garden, and take great pride in it, entering her flowers and fruits in the village festivals. At night, she and Robert would lie in bed beside each other, listening to the sounds of their children slumbering, their dogs in their corners. And they would make love, sweetly, gently, reverently.

What silly dreams. She'd always known her path, and no amount of wishing could change it. Daisy was the only surviving child of two elderly parents, and she was the shiny bauble they dangled before titled and wealthy men. She'd known since she was a girl that she would be married to a fine family, that her marriage would consolidate fortunes and land and forge important connections. But then she'd met Robert, and she had foolishly believed that if two people truly loved each other, they would find a way to be together.

In the eyes of her parents and society, however, Robert wasn't good enough for her. He'd even warned her he wasn't, so much more present in the truth of their affair than she'd been. He knew that because he didn't have a title, or any wealth to speak of, and was merely the son of a country vicar, her parents would never agree to a marriage. It was true—while she was dreaming of her idyllic life with Robert, her parents were striking the marriage bargain with Clive. Daisy's fate had been sealed before she even knew what was in the offing.

When she found out, she'd begged Robert to elope with her, but Robert, always the voice of reason, had refused. "I would never dishonor you in that way, Daisy," he'd said gallantly.

She'd argued with him. "Dishonor me! Take me from here, please! You love me—how can you let me go?"

But let her go he had. "You must accept it," he'd said.

Wasn't it funny that those were the exact words Clive would utter to her from his deathbed many years later? *You must accept it.*

Robert Spivey's family had managed to arrange a commission in the Royal Navy and he'd left Nottinghamshire without even saying goodbye to her. He had forced her to accept it.

Daisy was older and wiser now, and she was determined that she'd not merely accept these things in her life. She wouldn't accept that an old bishop would tell her who and when she had to marry. She wouldn't accept that one of the most important decisions of her life had been tainted with a fortune that followed her everywhere she went.

And then, the letter had come. *It is with sadness*

and grave concern that I have received the news of your husband's passing, he'd written. *Long have I kept you in my heart, Daisy. I will not lose you to another man again...*

He'd written that he was sailing soon, but that his commission in the Royal Navy would end this year, and at such time, he hoped she would welcome his call to her in London.

Daisy had been astounded. Heartened. How was it possible that after all these years, her love for Robert could burn so brightly? And yet, she could feel it, along with all the hope gurgling in her. Unfortunately, he did not say when he might come to London. What did *this year* mean? Tomorrow? In six months' time? That would be too late for Daisy.

She had to give Robert time to reach her and thereby put an end to the madness around her. And the only way to do that was to escape London for a time.

She had discussed the letter and her predicament with her good friend, Lady Beckinsal, who had urged her to go, to give the poor man time to end his commission and come to London to save her before Bishop Craig forced her into an unhappy marriage. *"If he comes so soon as the summer, simply tell your butler to ask if he'd like word sent to you. He will wait for your reply if he still esteems you,"* she'd said with great assurance.

A knock on the coach ceiling from above startled Daisy from her rumination; Belinda opened the little hatch to the driver as Daisy sat up, wincing as her stays dug into her ribs once again.

"Milady, Auchenard just ahead," the driver called down. The coach was slowing, turning right.

Daisy braced her arms against the wall of the coach and peered out the dusty window. It was so filthy she could scarcely see, but she could make out a tower above a high wall. The vegetation next to the road was so overgrown that she couldn't see much else. There was no livestock, no cattle, no sheep—nothing but untended meadow and forest.

A few moments later, the coach shuddered to a stop. Ellis pushed himself up and crowded in next to Daisy, peering out the window. "Is this it, Mamma?"

"It is."

The coach door swung open; Ellis kicked the step down and then practically leaped out of the coach with more vigor than Daisy had seen from him in days. She followed her son, shook out her skirts and put her hands to her back as she gazed at the structure before her.

Belinda stumbled out after her, knocking into Daisy and catching herself with one hand on her shoulder. "Oh *dear*," she said as she, too, gazed up.

"Oh dear" was the kindest thing that might be said. The old hunting lodge was much larger than what Daisy had expected, really—it looked more like a medieval castle. The stone was dark and weathered, and ivy ran unchecked and wild over half of it. Long tendrils of it danced in the early-evening breeze. There were two towers anchoring the struc-

ture on either end. The windows—a few boarded—
were dark and looked as if they hadn't been cleaned
in years. There were numerous chimneys, at least
two of them crumbling, and there was no smoke
rising from any of them. Auchenard seemed completely deserted.

"I thought a caretaker looked after it," Daisy said,
baffled. This had not been cared for in the least—if
anything, it had been abandoned.

"Ah, there you are!" The front door, large and
wooden and battered by weather, opened, and her
late mother's brother, Uncle Alfonso, strode toward
Daisy as the other chaise and the wagons pulled in
to the drive. His full head of gray hair was tied in a
queue, and his tall, slender frame was clad in a manner she'd never seen—he'd shed his coat, rolled up
his sleeves and was wearing a leather apron. "At last!
I thought you'd never come!" he sang out, smiling.
"Ellis, my boy, come and give your old uncle a hug."

Mr. Rowley, the longtime Chatwick butler, and a
slightly smaller version of Uncle Alfonso, appeared
at the door. He was dressed like her uncle, but he
was also covered in dust.

He bowed. "Milady."

Uncle Alfonso and Rowley had come a fortnight
ahead of Daisy and the rest to make the lodge in-
habitable for them all. By the look of things, that had
been a greater task than they'd all assumed.

"How very happy we are to see you both!" Daisy
exclaimed. "It's been such a dreadful journey, I de-
spaired we'd arrive at all."

"I had begun to worry," Uncle Alfonso said as he bent to kiss Belinda's cheek. "You must be exhausted. We'll feed you well, but first come and stretch your legs and have a look at your Highland hunting lodge," he said as he tousled Ellis's hair. "It's not as bad as it appears on first sight."

Oh, but it was every inch as bad as it appeared at first sight.

The interior of the lodge was just as deteriorated as the outside. The floors were covered with a thick layer of dust; Alfonso's and Rowley's footfalls could be seen quite plainly across the hall. The air stank of stale chimneys and damp peat. The cut stones that formed the walls were so thick that it was quite cold inside. Daisy supposed that the hearths must be lit every day to keep the chill at bay. And it was dark, in part because broken windows had been covered, and in part because there were no candles.

The lodge was archaic. It was nothing like the sun-dappled rooms at Chatwick Hall with their damask draperies and Aubusson carpets, marble floors and French furnishings. It was nothing like the bright and open townhome in Mayfair.

And yet, in spite of its decaying appearance, Daisy could see the rustic charm…but it would take the work of an army to dig it out.

When they had completed the tour, Uncle Alfonso led them to what he said was the great room. The ceilings, held up by thick beams, soared high overhead. He pushed aside some heavy velvet drapes, kicking up a cloud of dust that set them all to sneezing. When Daisy opened her eyes, she was greeted with an unexpectedly beautiful view of a lake at the bottom of a gentle green slope. Mist curled up from its surface in the day's gloaming, and the hills beyond created a backdrop of dark green, gold and purple. She smiled with delight.

"All that you see belongs to you, darling," her uncle said.

"Really? All of it?"

"All of it," he confirmed. "It's lovely, isn't it?"

"There is so much work to be done," Belinda said, folding her arms. "I don't know where you think you'll find the labor for it."

"If we can't find the labor, we will do it ourselves," Daisy said and turned to her uncle. "Was there not a caretaker after all?"

"Oh, there was a caretaker, all right," he said. "But I rather think he was far more concerned with his next drink than with Auchenard. You'd do as well to leave the place to sit empty than to have it cared for by the likes of this fellow."

Daisy sighed wearily. She hated dealing with servants who did not want to work for their wages. "What do you think of our hunting lodge, darling?" she asked her son.

Ellis frowned thoughtfully. *Always so serious!*

"There is a room at the top of the tower that is ideal for stargazing," Uncle Alfonso offered.

Ellis blinked. "Can you see all of them? Can you see Orion from there?"

"Orion," Uncle Alfonso repeated curiously.

"The ship's captain taught Ellis a thing or two about navigation during our voyage," Daisy explained.

"Yes, I'm sure you can see it," Uncle Alfonso assured him.

"Perhaps Ellis and Belinda would like to find their rooms," Daisy suggested to Rowley. "Belinda, will you please settle Ellis? Uncle and I have some things we must discuss."

"Let me first have a word with Sir Nevis," her uncle said, following Belinda and Ellis from the room.

Daisy stood a moment, listening to the sound of her uncle's boots echoing down the stone hallway. When she was certain she was alone, she fell onto a settee that was still covered with a dust cloth and propped her feet on a chair. She was bone weary and wanted nothing more than to sleep in a decent bed. She closed her eyes and let her mind drift to the lake, and the hills beyond…and to the startlingly blue eyes of a Scotsman. She imagined him once again with his hands on her—this time, in that decent bed—his touch reverent, his gaze soft.

How long she was in that state, she didn't know, but she was awakened by the sound of chuckling.

Daisy opened one eye. Her uncle was standing before her, his arms folded over his apron, smiling with amusement at her lack of decorum.

"Do you blame me?" she asked, forcing herself up with a push. "It's been a wretched journey."

"Yes, I suppose it has." He walked to the sideboard and poured two glasses of wine. He returned and handed her one.

Daisy yawned, then sipped the wine. She wrinkled her nose.

Uncle Alfonso shrugged. "It was all that could be found in the fishing village."

"This place is a shambles, Uncle," she said morosely. "Belinda is right—it will require so much work! How will we ever put it to rights?"

Uncle Alfonso rubbed his eyes a moment. "I don't know," he said. He wandered with his wine to the windows and gazed out at the sun sinking behind the hills.

Daisy pushed herself to her feet and joined him there. "Can we find workers?"

"A few, I should think," he said with a shrug. "I'll have Sir Nevis scout about on the morrow. But it will require our concerted effort, darling." He put his arm around her shoulders. "By that, I mean *all* of us."

She smiled lopsidedly. "Are you suggesting that I indulge in labor?" she asked with mock astonishment.

"We'll need all hands."

Daisy kissed her uncle's cheek, then stepped away and began to release her hair from its pins. "Belinda won't stand for it, you know. But frankly I'd like nothing better. I'm weary of sitting about all day with nothing to occupy me but gossip and needlework." She would not let on that she was cowed by the state of the lodge; she would keep the fears gurgling in her belly to herself.

"Shall I send for Mr. MacNally, the supposed caretaker?" he asked.

She needed to address the issue of the caretaker, quite obviously, but at the moment, all Daisy cared about was that she was exhausted, and she needed a bath, and she was desperate to free herself from these stays. "On the morrow," she said, and mustered a smile.

She was not going to think about the shambles that surrounded her just for now. Instead she'd let thoughts of the Scotsman occupy her thoughts and would try not to look too closely at the disrepair and the foreign surroundings.

CHAPTER THREE

THE SOUND OF Fabienne's barking brought Cailean's head up from his task. He lived alone at Arrandale—he was almost single-handedly constructing his home—but rarely did anyone come by that was not hired on to help put up a roof or lay a floor. Today, however, he was expecting his brother Aulay—but he would be arriving by boat, up the loch. He would be bringing the wine and tea they'd recently brought in from France…without registering their cargo with the tax authorities.

All the more reason to be suspicious of whoever was now at his front door. He strode forward, grabbing up a musket on his way.

"Arrandale!" he heard someone shout as he neared the door. He pulled it open and swung the musket up onto his shoulder, sighting the man standing there.

Padraig MacNally threw his hands up and stumbled backward, almost tripping over Fabienne, whose tail was swishing madly, so pleased that someone had come to call.

"What do you want?" Cailean demanded gruffly.

MacNally began to prattle in Gaelic, something

about a foreigner and the years of his life devoted to serving others with no reward for it.

With a groan of exasperation, Cailean lowered his gun. "For God's sake, take a breath, lad. I donna understand a word of it."

MacNally paused. He drew a deep breath. He said, in Gaelic again, "A lady has come and released me from service!" He took a cautious step forward, nervously rubbed his hand under his nose. His plaid was filthy, and from a distance of a few feet, Cailean could smell whisky on him. That was not surprising— everyone knew that the MacNallys of this glen were drunkards. "I'm without situation!"

"Aye, and whose fault is that?" Cailean sighed.

"I've looked after Auchenard for fourteen years!" he wailed.

"Looked after it? The place is a pile of rocks."

"The old man refused to send money for repairs," he insisted, seemingly on the verge of tears. "What was I to do? There was naught I could do, laird! I need your help," he said, clasping his dirty hands together and shaking them at Cailean. *"Please."*

"Aye, and what can I do, then?" Cailean asked, annoyed. MacNally was not a member of the Mackenzie clan, and he didn't like him being here. The man could not be trusted, and Aulay would be arriving at any moment with their goods. They would store it here until they were ready to sell it. Which meant when they were certain no one was in pursuit of them for having "forgotten" to declare their cargo with the authorities.

"I tried to reason with her, but my English isn't very good," MacNally begged. "And she *talks*, laird. She talks without a breath so that a man can't say what he might."

Diah.

He thought of the woman he'd met on the road yesterday. The one who had looked at him as if he were a beefsteak and she a starving orphan. She'd not been at Auchenard for as much as a day and had let go the man who'd kept a watchful eye on a property all but abandoned?

That was the way of the English—or *Sassenach*, as they referred to them here. They seemed to appear out of the mist to take this or that, to demand change to a way of life that had been known in these hills for hundreds of years. But of all the English reavers Cailean knew, none of them were quite as striking as this one. Her eyes were shaped like those of a wily cat, the color of them as green as new pears. She had a fine figure, too—frankly, she was beautiful.

She'd been quite a surprise to him, in truth, and Cailean was not a man who was easily surprised. But with rumors swirling fast and furious about another attempt to restore a Stuart to the throne, tensions were quite high between Highlanders who disagreed about it, and between Scot and Englishman. For a beautiful English lady to suddenly appear in the Highlands was an invitation for trouble.

Aye, she was surprising and beautiful—and unforgivingly, unacceptably English. Poor MacNally was no match for them.

"Aye, then. Wait there," Cailean said. He stepped inside, slammed the door and marched across his half-finished house toward the back to leave his brother a note.

As MacNally was on foot, they walked the mile or so to Auchenard. They came through the woods, emerging near the drive. Weeds had sprung up among the gravel, and as they neared the lodge, Cailean could see the windows were unwashed, the lawn overgrown. Cailean paused and looked pointedly at MacNally.

MacNally read his expression quite accurately. "I'll put it to rights, laird. I will."

Cailean grunted at that and continued on. He didn't believe it for a moment, but MacNally was not his worry.

He strode up to the front door and rapped loudly. Several moments passed before a man wearing shirt-sleeves and a leather apron answered the door. "Sir?"

"Lady Chatwick," Cailean said.

The man blinked. He looked at MacNally, then at Cailean. "Who...who may I say is calling?" he asked uneasily.

"The laird of Arrandale."

The man seemed shocked. He hesitated, casting a disapproving look over MacNally.

"Be quick about it, lad," Cailean said impatiently. "I havena all day for this."

The man's throat bobbed with a swallow. He nodded and disappeared into the dark and dank foyer of the lodge.

Several moments passed. Cailean could hear male voices, and then a sudden and collective footfall. It sounded as if an army were advancing on the door, but there appeared only the lady, the butler and two other men. One of the men was familiar to Cailean—he'd brandished a sword yesterday. The other man was a stranger to him.

Lady Chatwick, who led them, looked worried as she approached the door, but when she saw him standing there, a peculiar thing happened. A smile lit her face so suddenly and so sunnily that it startled him. "*You* again," she exclaimed, and her voice was full of...*delight*?

She should not be delighted to see him, and Cailean eyed her suspiciously. She was dressed plainly, her hair tied up under a cap. Her slender neck was unadorned, and he could faintly see the pulse of her heart in the hollow of her throat.

He looked away from her neck, shifted his weight onto his hip. "Aye," he said impatiently.

Her smiled deepened. What was she doing, smiling at him like that? He didn't like it—it unbalanced him. She should not be smiling at him; she should be trembling in her silly little boots.

"I beg your pardon," she said, touching a wayward strand of hair. "We've only just arrived, as you know, and I'm afraid we're not ready to receive callers. I had hoped to be here a week earlier, but the journey was so *arduous* from London that we were delayed. First the rough sea, then all these *hills*."

Why was she nattering? "These hills," he said

brusquely, "is why the area is called the Highlands. One might have expected it. And I've no' come to call."

Her green eyes widened with surprise. And then she laughed, the sound of it soft and light in that cluster of men. "I thank you for not couching your opinion in poetic phrases, sir. Of course you are right—I should have expected it."

Just then a lad pushed his way through and latched onto her skirts, staring up at Cailean with trepidation. "Ah, there you are, darling." She turned slightly, put her hands on lad's shoulders and moved him to stand in front of her. "May I introduce my family? My uncle, Mr. Alfonso Kimberly," she said gesturing to the taller of the two men. "And of course, Sir Nevis you have met," she said, her eyes twinkling with amusement.

Sir Nevis stood with his hand on the hilt of his sword. Both men glared at him with wariness, as if he were the intruder here. Cailean grunted at them. He didn't care who they were, was not interested in introductions.

"And my son, Lord Chatwick."

The lad stepped back into her, practically hiding in the folds of her skirt, but she gently pushed him out again. He looked to be about seven or eight years old, slight and pale, his blond hair sticking to his head. Cailean wondered if the lad was ill.

"Ellis, might you bow to the gentleman?"

The lad clasped his hands behind his back and bowed woodenly. "How do you do."

"Latha math," Cailean said absently.

The lad blinked up at him.

"I said, 'Good day, lad.' Have you no' heard a Highlander speak?"

"I thought you might be English," his mother said.

"English!" he very nearly bellowed. By God, he looked nothing like an Englishman! He was wearing trews, for God's sake. *"No,"* he said gruffly, feeling slightly injured by the insult.

"Well, it's not as bad as *that*, being English," she chirped and gave him a lopsided little twinkle of a smile.

It was at *least* as bad as that. "I am a Scot," he said stiffly.

She pulled the lad to stand in front of her again, putting her arms over his shoulders and holding him there. "You must admit you do *sound* a bit English," she pointed out.

What was happening here? He'd come to speak to her about MacNally's employment, not about the manner of his speech. As it was, MacNally was looking at him with horror. Cailean could imagine how the story would travel up and down the glen and evolve somehow into one of his being sympathetic to the English or some such nonsense. Tongues in this glen wagged with the force of gale winds. "My mother is English," he bit out.

"Is she, indeed?" Lady Chatwick said happily. "Who is—"

"I've no' come for pleasantries, madam," he said

curtly, cutting her off. "MacNally tells me you've released him from service."

"Perhaps I ought to discuss this with the gentleman," her uncle said, moving to stand beside her.

"Oh no, that's not necessary," she said pleasantly. "I think the gentleman means no harm."

Of course he meant no bloody harm, but how could she possibly know what he meant? He was a dangerous man when he wanted to be, and he thought perhaps he ought to point that out...but she was talking again.

"I did indeed release Mr. MacNally from service," she said, with a gracious incline of her head, as if she was accepting his praise. "I thought it imperative that I do so, as I explained to him. Did I not explain it, Mr. MacNally? I think we might all agree there are certain expectations when one employs another as an agent in their stead."

MacNally looked at Cailean. "Do you see?" he asked in Gaelic. "She says so many words, and with much haste."

Cailean ignored him. "The man has been caretaker here for nigh on fourteen years."

"It is true that he has been employed as the caretaker here for that long...but somewhere along the way he quite forgot to take care of it." She looked meaningfully at the broken window over her shoulder.

"I had no money," MacNally said in Gaelic, understanding more than he was apparently willing to admit.

"He informs me your husband did no' provide the funds for repairs, aye?"

"Did he, indeed?" she murmured, and one finely sculpted golden brow lifted above the other. "My husband has been dead for more than two years. *I* have not received any requests for funds to repair Auchenard, and yet I've seen to it that Mr. MacNally's stipend has been sent to him with unfailing regularity." The second delicate golden brow rose to meet the first in a direct challenge to Cailean to disagree.

That subtle challenge stirred something old and unpracticed inside Cailean. He looked away from her green eyes, glanced at MacNally and asked in Gaelic, "Is this true? You've not asked for the funds?"

"How was I to know to ask for funds?" he returned nervously. "No one has come round."

Now Cailean glared down at MacNally. "Yet you've managed to put your hands on the stipend. Surely you know from where *that* has come."

MacNally shrugged, scratched his scraggly beard and looked off contemplatively at the hills. "Did the best I could, I did," he said defensively.

"Pardon? What does he say?" the lady asked politely.

Cailean had a sudden intuition and glared at MacNally. He asked in Gaelic, "Have you been making whisky here?"

MacNally colored.

Cailean responded with a colorful string of curse words. It was dangerous enough that he and Aulay were storing as much wine and tea as they were at Arrandale. But to have an illegal distillery on land an Englishman owned was reckless. "You're lucky you have your fool head," he snapped. "Off with you now. Go to Balhaire and see if there is work for you, but leave here at once before the authorities are summoned."

At the mention of authorities, MacNally did not hesitate to stumble away.

Cailean looked at Lady Chatwick and the men behind her. She was smiling. They were not. "I beg your pardon," he managed to say. "It appears we have bothered you unnecessarily."

"There is no need to apologize," she said, her eyes twinkling with delight once more. *Diah*, she acted as if this were all some sort of lark. He turned to go.

"My lord! May I inquire…from where did you come, exactly?"

Cailean paused. He slowly turned back to look at her and the two men behind her. Why did she ask him that? He was suspicious—after all, he was a Scot whose English grandfather had been tried for treason. He was also a man who practiced the fine art of smuggling goods into his country, outrunning British naval ships on at least a dozen occasions. He'd not put it past the English authorities to install a well-bred lady to spy, to root out the smuggling they'd failed so miserably to catch thus far. He was therefore not inclined to answer any questions posed by her.

She seemed to sense his distrust. She turned her son about and sent him into the lodge, then hopped out of the doorway and onto the flagstones. "I'm curious," she said and leaned against a pillar that held up the portico, her fingers skirting across her décolletage, drawing his eye to the creamy skin swelling above her bodice. He slowly lifted his gaze, and she smiled. "Is it a secret?"

Was she *trifling* with him?

She clucked her tongue and smiled again. "It's just that you seem unduly suspicious. I ask only because you rode away yesterday and I never expected to see you again. And yet here you are."

"You willna see me again," he assured her.

"No? A pity, that."

Her smile turned sultry, and Cailean's pulse leaped a beat or two. He was astounded by her cheek, really. He rarely met a woman so bold, and, by God, he was from Scotland—he knew more than a few bold women. "Aye, you willna. And for that you may thank your saints and pray others leave you be."

"What others?"

Now she was being ridiculous. "Are you daft, then?" he asked disdainfully. "You shouldna be here at all."

"Why?"

Good God, she *was* daft. Utterly addlepated. "Because we donna care for *Sassenach* here. I should think someone would have told you before you made such an *arduous* journey," he drawled.

"Sassenach..." she repeated thoughtfully. "What does that mean, precisely? Does it mean ladies?"

Her smile deepened into dimples. She was amusing herself.

"It means *English*."

"Come in, milady," Sir Nevis warned her. "Let him go."

The incredibly cheeky woman ignored the man. She stood there, tracing that invisible line across the swell of porcelain skin, smooth and pale, considering Cailean.

She looked delicate. Fragile. Completely unprepared for a man like him. An appearance that belied the things that came out of her mouth. What sort of highborn woman flirted so blatantly with a stranger? What sort of woman trifled with a stranger twice her size? And yet she was not the first Englishwoman he'd known to behave in that manner, and the sudden, unwanted image of another delicate rose who'd once held his heart in her hands flooded his thoughts.

He tensed. He took a step forward. "Are you so foolish, Lady Chatwick? There is no' a Scot in these hills who will want you and your kind here, and yet you behave as if you're attending a garden party, aye?"

She laughed softly. "Oh, I assure you, sir—this is no garden party. There's no garden! I am determined to have one, however, because I do find the landscape quite lovely—the scenery is unsurpassed." Her eyes brazenly flicked over the length of him, and she grinned, saucily touching the corner of her mouth with her tongue.

That unpracticed part of him was rousing from its slumber.

"Won't you tell me from where you came?"

Impatience and disbelief radiated hotly through him now. He had stayed longer than he'd intended, and he was not going to stand here and be interrogated by her. "Good day, madam," he said coldly and turned about, striding away.

"Good day, sir! You must come again to Auchenard!" she called after him. "We'll have a garden party if you like!" She laughed gaily at that.

Unbelievable.

Cailean fumed on the long walk to Arrandale, exasperated he'd been put on his heels by the Englishwoman, astounded that it had happened before he knew it, and amazed by her cheek. *Och*, she was barmy, that was what. And bonny. A barmy, bonny woman—the worst sort to have underfoot.

Funny how a long, hot summer could be made suddenly interesting in the space of a single day.

CHAPTER FOUR

July 28—One of the chimneys must be rebuilt, which Uncle assures me that he and Mr. Green will know how to do, but I don't care for him to be on the roof. He has ignored me thus far and urges me to keep my thoughts to what must be done inside. My thoughts will be much crowded, then, for there are many repairs to be done. Every day we discover something new, which sends Belinda into fits of panic. I have assured her that we will manage, but I confess I spoke with far more conviction than I felt. Ellis is fearful of the deep shadows in the lodge, which cannot be avoided due to the lack of proper windows. But he is happy that he can see the night's sky so clearly from his room and is busily charting the stars under Mr. Tuttle's tutelage. The poor boy sneezes quite a lot, and Belinda fears the dust will make him ill. She is quite concerned there is no real village to purchase sundries and frets that she didn't bring with her enough paints for her artwork, which she is very keen to begin when the repairs have all been made.

I know that Belinda and Ellis are not happy with the lodge, and I do so hate that I was clearly wrong to bring them to such a disagreeable place.

The Scotsman came in defense of Mr. Mac-Nally. He does not care for me, I think it quite obvious, for he does not smile at all and did not find me the least bit humorous. His face is a lovely shade of brown, as if he has been often in the sun. It rather makes the blue of his eyes that much brighter and the plum of his lips that much darker.

I rather like it here in a strange way. It is quiet, and the landscape unmarred. I should think that it would be a lovely place to live, if one could live without society.

IT WAS TRUE that Daisy felt quite badly for having dragged her household here. She'd known the lodge was remote and had been uninhabited for a time—but she'd not been prepared for just how remote and how uninhabited. Because she hadn't given the matter proper attention when her husband's agent tried to explain it to her.

The truth about Auchenard was buried in the papers that he'd wanted to review with her shortly after Clive's death. At the time, Daisy had found the discussion of a remote hunting lodge so dreadfully tedious that she could scarcely keep her eyes open. She'd been exhausted from the details of Clive's funeral, and Scotland had seemed as far removed from her as the moon. Moreover, the estate had existed for the purpose of hunting—an activity that held no interest for her whatsoever. She had not paid the matter any heed.

Not until she had needed someplace to which to escape.

And now? More than once Daisy had considered putting her son back in the coach and returning to England, no matter how exhausted they all were.

On their first tour of the lodge, she'd been appalled by what they'd found in the lodge—a dim interior, deteriorating furnishings. And the decor! Turkeys and stag heads seemed to lurk around every corner.

"Well, then," she'd said when they'd seen it all. "There is nothing to be done now but begin work." She'd said it confidently, as if her occupation was that of a woman who routinely walked into deteriorating hunting lodges and rejuvenated them. "We will muster our little army and work, shall we?"

"Assuming none of us is made ill," Belinda had said darkly from beneath the lace handkerchief she kept pressed to her nose and face.

In that moment, the prospect of defeat before Belinda was enough to spur Daisy into turning this lodge into a highland jewel.

In the days that followed, Daisy worked as hard as anyone to restore the lodge. She and her household polished and scrubbed, tore down old wall hangings, washed windows and sashes, and carted out unsuitable furnishings. Carpets were dragged outside and beaten, mattresses turned, linens placed on beds. Sir Nevis, who meant to return to England after a week, scouted the area while they worked, and returned with a craftsman to repair the windows. He also returned with information about Balhaire, the large Mackenzie estate and small village where sundries—and, thankfully, paints—could be purchased.

But as the days progressed, Ellis looked more and more disheartened. He and his tutor wandered about looking a bit lost. Ellis was curious to inspect their surroundings, but Daisy would not allow them to venture far from the lodge...the Scotsman's warnings of others had made her a bit fearful.

She tried to engage Ellis with the lodge itself, but the boy, like any nine-year-old, did not want to beat carpets. So Daisy urged him to continue his star charting. That occupied him until they had charted all that they could. She then commanded him to help her clean windows, but he tired easily.

When Daisy wasn't struggling to please her son, she toiled from morning to sundown in a manner she'd never experienced in her life.

At first Rowley, Uncle Alfonso and Belinda had tried to dissuade her from it. Great ladies did not beat carpets, they said. Great ladies did not scrub floors. But Daisy ignored their protests—she found the work oddly soothing. There were too many thoughts that plagued her when she was left idle, such as whom she'd be forced to marry, and how the days of her freedom were relentlessly ticking away. Whether or not Rob would reach her in time, what was wrong with her son that he was so fragile, and how cake-headed she'd been to think a journey to the northern part of Scotland could possibly be a good idea, and, of course, what a terrible thing she'd done, dragging her family here.

Yes, she preferred the labor to her thoughts. At the end of each day, she ached with the physical exertion, but the ache was not unpleasant.

But there were times, when she couldn't keep her thoughts from her head, that Daisy felt a gnawing anger with her late husband. Clive had forced her into this untenable situation, and her feelings about it had not changed with time. She felt betrayed by the man she had respected and revered and tried to love. She'd been a dutiful wife—how could he have had so little regard for her? How could he believe she would jeopardize her own son's future for her own pleasure?

Sadly, the answers to these questions were buried with Clive.

By the end of their first fortnight at Auchenard, Daisy could see that the old lodge was beginning to emerge, and she was proud of the work they'd done. She began to notice less the repairs that had yet to be made and more of the vistas that surrounded the lodge. It was possible to gaze out at the lake and the hills beyond and forget her worries.

When she was satisfied with the work on the interior, Daisy turned her attention to the garden. Or what she assumed had been a garden at some point. Whatever it might have been, it was overgrown.

Vines as thick as her arm crawled up walls and a fountain, and weeds had invaded what surely once had been a manicured lawn. She'd donned a leather apron and old straw hat she'd found in the stables. She'd cut vines and pulled weeds until her hands were rough. She crawled into bed at the end of those days and slept like the dead.

Belinda complained that the sun was freckling her skin and turning her color. Daisy didn't care.

Each morning she rose with the dawn light, pulled a shawl around her shoulders and sat at the bank of windows that overlooked the lake from the master bedchamber. She'd open them to the cool morning mist, withdraw her diary from a drawer in the desk and make note of the previous day.

She pressed flowers into the book, as well as the leaves of a tree she'd never seen before, and had sketched the tree beside it. She'd drawn pictures of boats sliding by on the lake, of a red stag she saw one morning standing just beyond the walls, staring at the lodge.

Yesterday, Daisy had uncovered an arch in the stone wall that bordered the garden. She dipped her quill into the inkwell to record it—but a movement outside her window caught her eye.

The mist was settling in over the top of the garden, yet she could plainly see a dog sniffing about in a space she'd cleared. Not just any dog, either— it was enormous, at least twice as tall as any dog she'd ever seen, with wiry, coarse fur. She wondered if it was wild. She stood up, pulled her Kashmir shawl tightly around her and leaned across the desk to have a better look. "Where did you come from?" she murmured.

The dog put its snout to the ground and inched toward the one rosebush she'd managed to save.

Daisy hurried out of her room, down the stairs and the wide corridor that led to the great room and outside.

When she reached the garden, she slowed, tiptoeing through the gate, her bare feet on cool, wet earth that slipped in between her toes.

The dog's head snapped up as Daisy moved deeper into the garden. It lifted its snout in the air, nostrils working to catch her scent. Daisy froze. The dog didn't seem afraid of her, only curious.

She took another step, and the dog crouched down, as if it meant to flee. "Don't go," she whispered, slowly squatting down and holding out her hand. "Come."

The dog stood alert, its tail high, watching her warily.

She looked around for something to entice it. There was nothing but a battered rose, and she reached for it, breaking it off at the stem and wincing when a thorn pierced her thumb. She crushed the petals in her hand and held them out. "Come," she said again.

This time the dog slunk forward, its nose working, every muscle taut. It kept slinking forward until it could touch Daisy, its nose to her hand. A bitch,

Daisy noticed. She uncurled her fingers and revealed the crushed petals in her palm.

The bitch sniffed at the flowers, licked them, and then allowed Daisy to scratch behind her ears. But when she'd inspected the petals and found them wanting, she touched her snout to Daisy's arm, then loped away, disappearing through a patch in the hedge...through what Daisy had believed was a stone wall until this very moment.

She followed the dog's path, pushing back against the overgrowth of vegetation, and discovered a crumbling crack in the wall. The stones had fallen away, leaving a gap of about a foot. She stepped over the pile of stones, pushed away the leggy and tangled vines of the clematis and squeezed through the opening, popping out the other side into a meadow.

She steadied herself and looked around. She caught sight of the dog loping lazily away...toward a man on an enormous horse. Daisy's heart leaped with fear when she saw him, and in her head all of Belinda's warnings about dangerous Scotsmen began to sound. She unthinkingly took a step backward, bumping into the wall. Just as she meant to squeeze through the hole and flee to the lodge, she realized that the man was familiar.

He suddenly reined his horse about and started toward her, the long strides of his mount eating up the ground with ease.

Perhaps she would prove all of Belinda's fears true in the next few moments, but Daisy didn't flee; she pulled her shawl more tightly around her as the man slowed his horse and pulled to a sharp halt before her. His horse jumped around a bit, wanting to carry on. Daisy's heart raced with fear that she would be trampled by the horse, until she realized that the man kept a steady hand on the beast, and the horse would come no nearer to her. She looked up at the rider, her heart pounding.

The Scotsman's gaze was locked on her, and Daisy's heart began to flutter so badly that she could not recall his name. *Oh dear, what was it? Avondale?*

His inspection slowly moved over her, studying her, his expression one of mild surprise. That was the moment Daisy remembered that she was wearing bedclothes, and her hair, uncombed, was draped over her shoulders. She felt the heat of self-consciousness rise up in her cheeks.

"Madainn mhath."

He towered above her in sinewy masculinity, and Daisy's mind emptied of all rational thought other than how much she wanted to touch him. "Good morning, Lord Avondale."

He shifted in his saddle. "Arrandale."

Ah, yes. That was it. She winced apologetically and thought the better of explaining that her heart was pounding so hard in her chest that she couldn't think of his name. "I beg your pardon," she said and curtsied. "My lord Arrandale." She rose up, drew her breath and released her hard grip on the shawl. It would not do to seem timid in the presence of a man like him.

God in heaven, he was even more dazzling than

she'd recalled. He wore the plaid today, and his bare knees and a bit of his powerful thigh were exposed to her. She imagined touching that thigh, and how hard it would feel…and a salacious little shiver ran down her spine.

He was frowning at her, as if he knew what she was thinking.

"I saw your dog," she blurted, trying to explain herself, and nodded in the canine's direction. "She was in my garden."

Arrandale glanced briefly at the dog, who had come loping back to them, her nose to the ground. But his gaze quickly moved over Daisy again. He looked at her as if he'd never seen a woman in her bedclothes and bare feet. He cocked his head. "Has something happened, then? Has the lodge burned? Have you been raided?"

Had something happened? Her heart had been invigorated and hammered in her chest—that was all. "No."

"No?" He lifted his gaze to her eyes. "It's no' often one sees the lady of the house standing in a meadow in her bedclothes, aye?" He arched a brow as if he expected her to disagree.

"You think I'm a bit mad."

"No' a bit. Completely. And a wee bit daft, as you might recall."

He said it so calmly, his manner so matter-of-fact, that Daisy laughed with surprise. "Do you find my appearance so scandalous?" she asked, her smile deepening as she brazenly opened her shawl to reveal her nightgown.

His horse jerked at the tight hold Arrandale had on him, and he adjusted his grip, giving the horse a bit more of his head but still holding him back. "You want me to find it scandalous, aye?"

She laughed with incredulity, the way a girl laughs when she finds a boy attractive. The gentlemen she sparred with in London never seemed to understand her motives, but she rather thought this Scotsman understood her motives very well.

"You enjoy trifling with gentlemen," he remarked, as if to agree with her thoughts.

"Trifling! I am not trifling with you, my lord—I chased your dog out of my garden."

A corner of his mouth tipped up in a vaguely droll smile. "Ah yes, the *garden*," he said. "No need to deny it. I'm no' offended."

Daisy's laughter was inexplicable, but it was spilling uncontrollably out of her now. "You are a very disagreeable man, sir," she said cheerfully.

"Me?"

"You're certainly the first gentleman to complain of flirting. But do you honestly believe that I rushed out here into the meadow just after dawn on the slim hope that you might be riding by? Do you think I came out in here in my bedclothes merely to *trifle* with you?"

He leaned over the neck of his horse and looked her directly in the eye. "I donna think you came out here with that intention. But I think you leave no opportunity for it untouched."

He might have hoped to offend her with that remark, but it really only spurred her to trifle with him more. "Indeed? And what precisely do you see that leads you to such an outrageous conclusion?"

"The color in your cheeks," he said, gesturing to her face. "The light in your eye."

"Perhaps the color in my cheek comes from the sun. And the light in my eye is a result of the mist lifting."

"Aye, and perhaps you leave your shoulder bare because the air is warm," he suggested.

Daisy looked down. She hadn't realized her nightgown had slid off her shoulder. She very slowly and deliberately pulled it up. "*That* was inadvertent."

Arrandale snorted. "Donna mistake me for naive," he said, as if speaking to a child. "I am well acquainted with women, aye?"

Goodness, but he seemed quite proud of that. "Ah, you are acquainted with *women*," she repeated as if this were a revelation to her. "You grace me with your superior knowledge of them," she said and curtsied daintily, holding out one corner of her nightgown as she dipped, aware that he was probably being treated to a view of the swell of her breasts. Frankly, the thought of it gave her a thrill. She was so unlike herself! She'd never flaunted her figure like this. As she rose up, she liked that his blue eyes had turned a bit stormy, as if something was brewing in him. "But as you know women, so do I know men. You said I would never see you again, and yet here you are. *I* know that when a man appears in a meadow beside a lady's abode, riding about when he clearly has no destination in mind, he means to encounter her one way or the other." She smiled pertly.

Arrandale's smile was so slow and so wolfish that she felt it trickle down to her toes. "You speak like a man."

"Why should it be only the provenance of men to speak directly? Must women speak only when addressed, and never flirt, and only agree with everything you say?"

He arched a brow. "How cynical of you, Lady Chatwick. I didna say I disapproved of it, did I? As it happens, I donna care for the demure wee English flowers. I prefer women who lust for life. Nonetheless... I have no interest in engaging you in a flirtation."

Daisy's eyes widened with surprise. No one had ever said such a thing to her, *especially* not since Clive died. "I beg your pardon," she said flatly, suddenly annoyed with his lack of decorum and his dismissal.

Arrandale's smile deepened at her irritation. "I suspect it comes as a great shock that you are no' roundly esteemed by all members of the male sex. But you are no'." He tipped his hat to her. "*Latha math*, Lady Chatwick. I'll leave you to return to your rooms to dress." He reined his horse about and, with a whistle for his dog, galloped away.

Daisy stared at his departing back as he and his

massive horse and massive dog bounded across the meadow.

There went a man who wasn't afraid to offend her. Who refused to flatter her. Who did not feign infatuation so that might lust after her purse. And as annoyed as she was with him at the moment for rebuffing her, Daisy couldn't help but admire him a very tiny bit.

Damn Scotsman.

She returned to her rooms and resumed her seat at the window, where she recorded her encounter with Lord Arrandale in her diary, biting back a smile as she recalled what he'd said: *I suspect it comes as a great shock...*

He was right. It did.

She pressed one of the rose petals she'd held out to his dog into her diary.

CHAPTER FIVE

THE WIND HAD shifted from the north, bringing with it cool air that gave hope the long summer would soon be over. The freshness of it invigorated Cailean; he rode with gusto on his favorite horse, Odin, galloping down the glen on the road to Balhaire, the sprawling coastal fortress where he'd been born. It looked almost mythical when the mist rolled in from the sea and shrouded its walls and crenulated parapets. The village just outside the walls was bustling with Mackenzies, and today was no exception. This place was as familiar to him as his own head. He'd been raised here, had learned to fight here, had learned to sail here. Had learned to be a Highlander.

He and Odin trotted in through the gates of the fortress; Cailean leaped off his horse and handed the reins to Sweeney the Younger, who, like his father had before him, captained the house guards.

A gust of wind scudded across the courtyard, lifting the hem of Cailean's plaid. He strode inside, into the din of voices coming from the great hall. It would be full of Mackenzies as it was most days, a sea of first and second cousins having their fill of ale.

Cailean marched into the room and through the

throng like a crown prince—he was the heir to this seat, the future laird of this clan. He responded enthusiastically to those who greeted him and scattered lazy dogs in his wake.

He jogged up the steps of the dais to where his parents were sitting. His father, Arran Mackenzie, the laird of Balhaire, smiled with delight at the sight of his firstborn. "Cailean, lad," he said, reaching his hand for his on. "What brings you?"

"It's a bonny day to ride, *Athair*," Cailean said, leaning over his father and kissing the top of his head. "How is the leg?"

"*Och*, it's still attached to my body," he said with a shrug.

His father's leg was concerning. A few years ago, he'd broken it while attempting to train a mount. It had healed, but it had never been the same again. And now it pained him more often than not. Nothing seemed to ease him—he'd seen doctors in England and in Scotland, and even the old healing woman who still treated some of the clan with herbs. Nothing worked—short of a daily dose of laudanum, which the laird refused to take.

Earlier this summer, he'd told Cailean it was time to prepare to lead the clan. "My mind is too much on this leg, aye?" he'd said, rubbing it.

"You donna need me yet," Cailean had protested. He was in the midst of building Arrandale, his own seat, on the lands his father had given him. He was sailing frequently with Aulay. He wasn't ready to take over the responsibilities of the Mackenzie clan.

"Aye, but I do," his father had said. "I'd no' ask you were I not certain of it, lad. I canna go on as I have. I'm no' a young man, and the pain wears on me. We'll be slow about it, we will. A wee bit more each month, then."

So it had been settled. Cailean would assume his father's responsibilities at the end of the year. Most weeks he came to sit with his father, to receive clan members and hear their complaints and their requests, to receive their news. He reviewed the accounts with his father, learning just how much was required to maintain Balhaire and their trade. The responsibility would require his full attention, every day, when the time came.

His mother was seated beside his father. She was still the most regal woman he knew, even more so now that her hair was more silver than blond. "Where have you been, darling?" she asked Cailean, her voice still very British even after all these years.

He leaned down to kiss her cheek. "At work, *Màthair*. An estate doesna build itself, aye?"

"What of the cargo?" his father asked.

There was no shame among the Mackenzies of Balhaire when it came to their "free trade." Since the union of Scotland and England, the burden of taxation had been increasing to such an extent that many of their clan struggled. Arran Mackenzie's goal had always been to keep their clan close to Balhaire by giving them means to earn a living and reason to stay in the glen. They believed that good wine, good tobacco and good tea, sold at reasonable prices without usurious taxes were reasons to stay, and they were determined to see that they had those things.

Cailean filled his father in on the cargo and the progress he'd made on his estate since he'd last seen them a fortnight ago. It was not finished…but it had come along well enough that Cailean had taken up residence in a room with his best stalking dog, Fabienne. It was a meaner living than he was accustomed to, but he didn't mind it. He rather liked being alone, the only man for miles about. He liked surviving by his ability to hunt and fish.

"Cailean! Do you mean to ignore us?"

He glanced over his shoulder at his sister, Vivienne, as she waddled toward the vacant chair beside him. She was round with her fourth child, and sat heavily, sprawling her legs before her, her hand protectively on her belly. Vivienne was the second oldest sibling, eighteen months younger than Cailean. Then came Aulay, the sea captain who was away just now, and then his brother Rabbie. He took a seat beside Vivienne. The youngest of them all, Catriona, joined them as well, fidgeting with a string in her hands and propping herself on the arm of her father's chair.

"So you've met her, aye?" Vivienne asked, catching his hand. "The lady of Auchenard?"

Cailean shrugged. It was no surprise to him that word about her had spread quickly through the glen. It had been a week since he'd last seen her in that curious morning meeting outside the walls of Auchenard.

Vivienne's eyes fired with delight at his silence. "Did you find her bonny, then?"

"I—"

"She means to bag a husband!" Catriona eagerly interjected.

Cailean laughed at that.

"Aye, it's true!" Vivienne insisted.

"Why in heaven would a woman of her means and connections seek a husband in the Highlands of Scotland? Where do you hear these barmy tales?"

"MacNally," Rabbie said matter-of-factly. "She released him from service and he's had quite a lot to say. He's told anyone who will give him half an ear that the lady must marry in a year's time or forfeit her fortune."

"Aye, it's true," Catriona insisted as she shouldered in beside Cailean. "It was so said in her husband's last testament. She must marry within three years of his death or lose her *entire* fortune. It's quite large, aye? I've heard as much as fifty thousand a year."

"Who has said this?" their father asked.

"Mr. MacNally *and* Auntie Griselda. She's heard it all the way from London."

One of Arran Mackenzie's salt-and-pepper brows rose. "Zelda has said?"

"She said it was so large a fortune that any man in Scotland who had as much as half a head on his shoulders would be climbing the walls to have a look at her, then. Her husband has been gone more than two years now, and she's less than a year left to settle on a match and marry. *That's* why she's come to Scotland. To settle on a match!" she announced, sounding triumphant, as if she'd solved a mystery.

"*Diah*, are there no' men enough in England?" Rabbie scoffed.

"No' the sort a lass would want to marry," Vivienne said, and the Mackenzies laughed.

"There are men enough in England," Cailean said. "It's nonsense."

"Unless..." his mother said thoughtfully.

"Unless?" Vivienne asked.

"It is possible that she seeks a Scot for a husband. She might think to install him at Auchenard for an annual stipend, then return to London and live as she pleases."

Lady Mackenzie's children and her husband stared at her.

"Mamma, how clever you are!" Catriona gasped. "That's *precisely* what she means to do! And she's *bonny*," she added in a singsong voice. "*You* saw her, Rabbie. You could put her fortune to good use, aye?"

"And what would Seona have to say about that?" he responded, referring to the young woman to whom he'd been attracted of late. "The lady is a *Sassenach*, Cat. There is no fortune great enough to tempt me to tie my lot with the English."

"Mind your tongue!" Vivienne scolded her younger brother. "Your mother is English!"

"My mother is no *Sassenach*. She merely happens to have come from England," Rabbie said, inclining his head toward his mother.

Margot Mackenzie shook her head at her youngest son. "You've been too much in the company of Jacobites, Rabbie," she warned him, to which Rabbie shrugged. "I should like all of my sons to marry and give me the grandchildren I deserve, but I'd rather none of them become entangled with a woman whose motives are not true."

She didn't look at Cailean, but he knew she was thinking of Poppy Beauly...a woman whose motives had not been true.

Poppy was the other Englishwoman Cailean had known who was as adept at flirtation as Lady Chatwick. She had destroyed any notion that he might have had about complicating his life with a wife and children.

Aye, his world had narrowed considerably since that wound was opened.

He'd only just reached his majority when he met her. He'd spent that unusually cool summer in England, at Norwood Park, his mother's familial estate, under the less-than-watchful eye of his uncle Knox. The winsome, beautiful Poppy Beauly was the daughter of his mother's very dear friend, and Cailean had been truly and utterly smitten.

Over the course of that summer, he'd wooed Poppy and professed his esteem to her more than once. For that, he'd received her warm encouragement. He'd been so green that he'd even dreamed of the house he would build for her, of the children they would bring into this world.

Poppy had given him every reason to believe she shared his feelings. "However, I am sure you understand that I must come out before I will be allowed to receive any offers," she'd warned him. "I won't come out until my eighteenth birthday." Then she'd proceeded to assure him with a passionate kiss that had left Cailean feeling as if he might explode with need.

Cailean had waited. He'd spent another year aboard his father's ship, and the following summer he'd returned to Norwood Park. Poppy had been happy to see him. She had made her debut, and while he knew she had other suitors, she still encouraged his pursuit of her, and quite unabashedly, too. He was her prince, she said. He was so kind, she said. She held him in such great esteem, she said.

At the end of that extraordinary summer, with Uncle Knox's blessing, Cailean had offered for her hand.

Much to his surprise and humiliation, Poppy Beauly had been appalled by his offer. She'd snatched her hand back as if she feared contagion. "I beg your pardon, Mr. Mackenzie," she'd said, reverting to addressing him formally. "I must beg your forgiveness if I've given you even the *slightest* reason to believe that I could *possibly* accept an offer."

"You've given me every reason to believe that you would!" he'd exclaimed, horrified by his stupidity.

"No, no," she'd said, wringing her hands. "I have enjoyed your company, but surely you knew I could *never* marry a *Scot*, sir."

As if he were diseased. As if he were less than human.

The rejection, the realization that Poppy Beauly did not love him as he loved her had devastated the young man Cailean had been. He had loved her beyond reason, obviously, and had limped back to Scotland with his broken heart.

He'd taken a solitary path away from that wound, away from privileged young women with the power to slay him. His tastes ran to widows and lightskirts and, if he was entirely honest, he enjoyed his own damn company above most.

"Leave him be, Margot," his father said, chuckling. "Cailean follows his own path."

His mother knew this very well, and yet she never gave up hope. "He could just as easily follow his own path to the altar," she said, her attention locked on her oldest child. "He's not as young as he once was, is he?"

"Màthair!" Cailean said and chuckled at her relentless desire to see him wed. "I will thank you to mind your own affairs, aye?" He leaned back, glancing away from them, smiling smugly at their inability to affect him.

He did not mention that he'd seen Lady Chatwick in her bedclothes, had seen her bare shoulder, had seen the swell of her breasts. Or that she had the blondest hair he'd ever seen—the pale yellow of late summer, which, when he thought of it, was the only color of hair that could possibly complement pear-green eyes. He didn't admit that he had noticed her small nose with a scattering of freckles across the bridge, or the wide, full lips that ended at a dimple in her cheek.

Cailean was not meant to marry and provide heirs, obviously. He was five and thirty, for God's sake. He

was happy to let the reins of Balhaire and the Mackenzie fortune pass to his brothers' children someday. He would carry on as he had these last fifteen
years, bringing in the occasional hold of illegal wine
or tea or tobacco and building his house. He would
not concern himself with an Englishwoman foolish
enough to come here. No amount of cajoling from
his mother would change it.

But his mother's theory about his new neighbor
stuck with Cailean, and when he happened upon
Lady Chatwick a few days later, he couldn't help
but see her in a wee different light.

A very suspicious light.

He was walking up from the loch with four trout
on his line. Fabienne had raced ahead, chasing after
a scent she'd picked up. He watched her disappear
through the break in the wall around Auchenard,
and a few moments later, burst through again, racing across the meadow, her tail high, alert to something in the woods.

Just behind her, Lady Chatwick pushed through
the opening, stumbling a bit as she squeezed through
the wall, batting away vines of clematis, then catching her wide-brimmed straw hat before it toppled off
her head. She put her hands on her hips and called
after the dog. She hadn't yet seen Cailean—and
didn't until he whistled for Fabienne.

Both dog and woman turned toward him. Fabienne obediently began to lope toward him. Lady
Chatwick folded her arms across her body and

shifted her weight to her hip with the attitude of an inconvenienced female.

Cailean continued walking through the meadow toward her, his plaid brushing the tops of the tall grass, his fishing pole propped on his shoulder. When he reached her, he jammed the end of his rod into the ground. The fish swung near his shoulder.

"What do you think you are doing?" she asked imperiously.

What had happened to the flirtatious little chit? The husband hunter? The color in her cheeks was high, the shine in her eyes even brighter in full sun. And there was a curious smear of blood on the back of her left hand. "What would you think, then?" he asked, gesturing grandly to the fish hanging from the pole.

"You have not been invited to fish my lake! Sir Nevis warned of poachers—"

"Poachers?" He snorted with disdain as he withdrew a handkerchief from the pocket of his waistcoat. "I donna need an invitation to fish the loch. It is no' yours. It couldna possibly be. *Your* land lies beyond that wall and to the east."

"What?" She turned to look behind her with such force that her thick braid swung around and over her shoulder. "No, you are mistaken. My uncle said my land extends from the point where the lake empties into the sea," she said and pointed.

"Aye, your uncle is correct. But the loch meets the sea there." He covered her outstretched hand with his and moved it around so that she was pointing in the opposite direction. Her hand felt delicate in his, like a child's, and he felt a jolt of something quite warm and soft sluice through him.

Her brow creased with a frown. "Are you certain?"

"*Diah*, as if I could possibly be wrong. The loch belongs to no one. We may all fish there. You're bleeding."

"Pardon?" She looked back at him, startled.

"Your hand," he said, and turned it palm up. "May I?" he asked, holding up his handkerchief.

She glanced at her hand, nestled in his. Her frown deepened. "Oh, that wretched garden! It is my greatest foe. You need not fear being invited to a garden party after all, my lord, for it would seem that with every weed or vine I cut, another lurks behind it." She squinted at her palm, sighing, then glanced up at him through her long lashes. "My hands are quite appalling, aren't they?"

"Aye, they are," he agreed. They were surprisingly roughened and red. She looked like a crofter in her worn muslin gown and leather apron, with the tiny river of dirt that had settled in the curve of her neck into her shoulder. He watched a tiny bead of perspiration slip down her collarbone and disappear between her breasts.

He had an abrupt but strong urge to swipe that bit of perspiration from her chest with the pad of his thumb.

"I hadn't realized how bad they are," she said, gazing at her hand.

He looked at it, too—at the long, tapered fingers,

the smooth stretch of almost translucent skin across her inner wrist. He had another puzzling urge—to lift her wrist to his nose and sniff for the scent of perfume.

He wiped away a bit of dirt from her palm. "Your eyes are very blue," she said.

He looked up; she was observing him with a softness in her eye he didn't like. "Aye," he said warily and ignored the shiver her slow smile sent rifling through him.

Cailean turned her hand over to examine the back of it. "Have you no gloves, then?" he asked, staring at the many pricks and scratches.

"None that are suitable for that damnable thicket."

He turned her hand over once more to examine her injured palm. She sported a callous and several pricks here, too, he noticed. "You've been hard at work, aye?" He traced his finger across her palm; she immediately tensed, shifting from one foot to the other.

"I think I've never worked as hard as this. I know what I should like the garden to be—a square of green and roses surrounding an old fountain…if my uncle can make it function once again. And I'd like benches for sitting and arbors for shade. But I have begun to believe none of it possible."

Why would she want all that? Gardens required attention year-round. Surely she didn't intend to stay so long, the little fool. "Is there no one to help you?"

She shook her head. "All hands are needed to finish the repairs to the lodge. Nevertheless, I am determined to return the garden to its former glory."

He was beginning to wonder if she was truly daft. "There's never been any glory to Auchenard," he said flatly.

"Pardon?"

"Since I was a wee lad," Cailean said, pausing when she sucked in a breath when he dabbed at the cut in her hand, "it has no' been properly kept, aye? MacNally was no' entirely responsible for its decline."

She stared at him, clearly not understanding, eyes framed with lashes light in color but quite long. "Then who is?" she asked.

"The *Sassenach* who claimed it, that's who. Your husband, his father before them—they didna care for Auchenard, much less a bloody garden."

"Really?" She looked disappointed, as if she believed if she kept digging and cutting, kept rooting out the weeds that choked the life from all other vegetation, she'd discover some secret garden underneath the growth.

He returned his attention to her palm. "Did no one tell you, then? Auchenard has no' been inhabited in many years."

"Oh, I don't know," she said with a weary sigh. "Someone may have told me. In fact, I am certain someone did. But I didn't listen."

What a curious thing to say—why wouldn't she have listened to wiser heads? Ah, of course—because that pretty head of hers was filled with cake. He dabbed at her palm again and she sucked in her breath, wincing.

"You've a bit of a thorn or wood embedded in your flesh," he said. "Shall I remove it?"

She looked uncertainly at him. "I, ah…yes, if you would be so kind?"

He wasn't that kind, but he pulled a dirk from his belt. She gasped loudly and tried to pull her hand free.

"Be still, lass."

"I'd rather—"

He didn't wait for her to refuse. He made a tiny nick. It startled her and she cried out, then bit down on her lip as he carefully worked out the bit of wood. "Oh," she said, once he had removed the bit of thorn. *"Oh."*

He watched her closely a moment to assure himself she wouldn't faint. Her bottom lip was red from where she'd bitten it, and he was suddenly and annoyingly filled with another unwelcome urge—he wanted to bite that plump lip. Suck it in between his teeth and thread his fingers through her gold hair.

"Thank you," she said.

He removed his gaze from her lush mouth and moved his hand to her wrist, holding it lightly but firmly as he began to wrap her hand with the handkerchief. "You should have it looked after, aye? There is a healing woman in Balhaire."

"Where?"

"What, then, did you put yourself on a boat and a coach knowing nothing?" he asked.

"Well, yes," she admitted. "Oh, of course. *Balhaire.* Where is it?"

"Follow the loch to the sea," he said. "*That* way," he added, pointing. "Ask for Marsaili. And when she's treated it, ask after passage to England. Enough ships come round—someone will take you."

She seemed momentarily confused by that, but then something sparked in her eyes. "Why would I do that?" she asked.

"Because you donna belong here," he said. "It's only a matter of time before you admit it, aye?"

Her gaze narrowed. "So you've said, more than once. But I *like* it here."

Barmy and daft and stubborn to boot. He didn't believe for a moment that a lady of her obvious stature enjoyed rough hands and living without all the comforts her title brought her in England. "This sort of life is no' for refined ladies," he said.

"How would you know that? Are you some sort of master of refined ladies? I really don't care for your opinion, sir, for *I* think it's starkly beautiful here," she said emphatically, surprising him somewhat. "It's rugged and strong and...vast," she said, nodding as if she'd found the right word. "With a bit of hard work, we might be very happy here."

"With no society?"

Her face darkened. "*Society?* You cannot know what a relief it is to escape London society."

He was ready to question her about that, but she continued. "I like everything about this place, with perhaps the exception of the mist."

"The mist," he repeated.

"The mist," she said, gesturing with her free hand

to the sky. "I keep dreaming that I've lost my son in it. There he is, and the next moment, *poof*, he's disappeared into it," she said, her fingers fluttering toward the forest.

Cailean might have laughed, but when he was a child, Vivienne used to fear the mist. It rolled in quickly, covering everything. "What color was the mist in your dreams?" he asked as he continued wrapping the handkerchief around her palm.

"The color? White."

"Sea mist," he said, and recited an old schoolroom poem. "'When the mist comes from the hill, foul weather doth it spill. When the mist comes from the sea, fine weather it will be.' You son will be quite all right in the mist, aye? Many Scottish children before him have found their way home in it."

Lady Chatwick didn't immediately respond to that; she kept her intent gaze on him, and Cailean could feel heat spreading in him like a spill of water. It was the sort of heat that stirred all things male. He wanted to kiss her, to lick the perspiration from her breasts. To take them in his mouth, one by one. The heat wended its way down to his groin, and Cailean felt another heat—anger.

He dropped his gaze to her hand. He was angry with himself for having such lustful thoughts for this Englishwoman. He wondered how long it had been since he'd felt lust stirring in him in quite this way, but he couldn't recall it. He quickly finished tying the handkerchief across her palm. But when he had tied it, he impulsively, cavalierly, lifted her hand and kissed the back of it before letting go. Her fingers slid lightly across his palm, then fell away.

"I beg your pardon, my lord, but are you now trifling with *me*?" Her gaze slipped to his mouth, and that bothersome heat in Cailean flared again. "Have you forgotten that you do not *roundly* esteem me?"

"No' for a moment," he said and peeled away a bit of her hair that had glued itself to her cheek. "Mind that you clean the wound, aye? A cut to the hand is slow to heal." He picked up his fishing pole and propped it against his shoulder. *"Tiugainn,"* he called to his dog, commanding her to come, and walked on from the Lady Chatwick.

"My lord!" she called behind him.

Against his better judgment, Cailean paused and looked back.

"I've been—I mean to invite my neighbors to dine. Not a garden party, mind you, but a proper supper. Will you come?"

She was gripping the side of her apron, he noticed, the leather bunched in her hand. "Your neighbors," he repeated, uncertain just whom she meant, as the sort of neighbors who would be invited to dine with her were quite far from Auchenard and few between besides.

"Yes, my neighbors! I should like to make their acquaintance, naturally. You are my neighbor, are you not? You wouldn't say, but as you are walking with your fish, I assumed."

Did she mean to make the acquaintance of the poor crofters? No. She meant to parade eligible

bachelors before her. Perhaps she might invite a few
of the Jacobites to her table and determine their suit-
ability while she was at it. Or perhaps she meant to
start a war.

Cailean abruptly retraced the few steps he'd just
taken. "I will speak plainly, madam. You are no' welcome in these hills. Aye, there will be those enticed
by the promise of your fortune, but I've no interest in
it. I willna vie for your hand if that's what you seek."

Color flooded her cheeks. Her brows dipped into
a dark V above her eyes. "You flatter yourself quite
incomparably, Arrandale! You presume too much!
You may think you know something of my situation,
but whatever you've heard, I assure you, it is not ac-
curate. I invite you only as a neighbor. I thought you
might even be my friend!" she exclaimed, throwing her arms wide. "Now I shall be just as plain—
no matter if you come or not, you need not remind
me of your lack of desire for me ever again. You've
made it *quite* clear."

Cailean didn't flinch at her dressing-down of him.
"Donna look so astounded," he said. "A *friend*? Most
women who *befriend* men they scarcely know mean
to attach themselves to his purse. Or, in your case,
attach him to yours."

Her mouth gaped open. Something sparked in
those green eyes, something hot and glittering, and
Cailean could not look away—or ignore that the hot,
glittering thing was waking something just as hot
in him.

"Ah, I *see*—you are the prize catch of the Highlands, are you? You must be utterly exhausted from escaping the clutches of so many women. You need not fear my clutches, my lord, for I would *never* join the chase," she said and leaned forward, her gaze narrowing slightly. "Never," she articulated, her voice deadly in its softness. "I live as I please, and it pleases me to trifle with gentlemen—with *all* gentlemen. Don't flatter yourself that you are the only one. Don't imagine that your *purse* is so fat that I should be tempted by it, for I assure you, mine is much fatter, and I don't wish to attach anyone to it. If that scandalizes you, then perhaps you should stay away. But if it doesn't?" She settled back and shrugged insouciantly. "You will be most welcome in my home."

Cailean was surprised and a wee bit impressed with her admonishment. He couldn't help but chuckle.

That inadvertent chuckle seemed to vex her even more. "You shouldn't put so much stock in gossip," she said, and angrily whirled around, marching away from him, her chin up, her braid bouncing above her derriere with the force of her stride. She stopped at the wall and shouted over her shoulder, rather crossly, "Thank you for tending my hand!" and then disappeared into the break in the wall.

It was perhaps the first time in Cailean's life that he'd found indignation in a woman so wholly appealing.

CHAPTER SIX

TWO DAYS LATER, Daisy folded Arrandale's freshly laundered handkerchief and tucked it in her diary beside the two crushed rose petals and the letter from Rob.

She dipped her quill into the inkwell.

The garden at last has been cleared, though sadly nothing salvaged. I shall bring on someone to see it through the winter with the hope that a viable garden will emerge next spring, God willing. I should like to see it one day, but I suspect a husband shall divest himself of a Scotch Highland lodge, particularly one so terribly far from England.

Ellis has not yet found Auchenard to his liking. He is without humor and very pale and does not sleep well, as he has heard tales of creatures in the forest that have frightened him. Mr. Tuttle informs me that Ellis no longer has any desire to venture beyond the wall around the lodge.

A nest of mice was found in the settee in Belinda's bedroom. She is convinced that there

*is an infestation the likes of which cannot be
contained but with fire.*

Daisy looked at the handkerchief. She touched it,
her finger tracing lightly over the fine linen.

*Arrandale is a brute. He is given to be-
lieving gossip and speaking to women in his
acquaintance with a decided lack of decorum.
He voices what thoughts are on his mind with
little thought for my feelings. It vexes me terribly, but all in all, I rather appreciate it. I
am at least assured that he is speaking true.
Nevertheless, as he does not know me, he might
have extended me the courtesy of believing the
best of me. Not every woman is in search of a
husband! Well... I suppose I am, but he must
realize I'd not search for one here! I shall invite him and my other neighbors and give the
rooster quite a few more assumptions to make.*

*I have not yet broached the subject of a sup-
per party with Belinda and Uncle. I think they
shall not be favorably inclined.*

She touched the handkerchief again, thought of
the man who had bandaged her hand. She closed her
eyes, imagined him taking her hand that day, pulling her to him, removing her hat and kissing her.

*God help you, Daisy. You're such a little fool,
dreaming of intercourse with him when you've only
months to find a husband.*

She opened her eyes, closed her diary. She felt as if a clock were ticking inside her, relentlessly counting the moments until she was under the rule of a man again. She thought of Robert—her memory of him a bit hazy now—and sent up a silent prayer that he would reach London in time to save her.

Her writing finished for the day, Daisy wandered out to the garden to survey it under an overcast sky. It was not a beautiful garden. It was a desolate one, with scarcely any adornment, and a fountain that could not be made to work, no matter what Uncle Alfonso and Mr. Green had tried.

She put her hands to the small of her back and arched backward, closed her eyes and listened to the breeze rustle the treetops. It was so peaceful at Auchenard. So blessedly removed from the bustling world of London, of even Chatwick Hall in Nottinghamshire. How she wished her family would come to see Auchenard as she did, but alas, they did not.

They'd done all that they could to the lodge without benefit of builders and masons. Daisy was proud of the work they'd done, and the idea of the supper party, blurted in a moment in which she'd sought a reason to keep that wretched Arrandale about, had taken firm root in her. Perhaps her family might find Auchenard more to their liking with a bit of society. Daisy would very much like to meet her neighbors. She would like them to see what they'd done to the old lodge.

And she would very much like to see the fine pair of blue eyes of her least hospitable neighbor again.

She brought it up at supper that night, between the fish stew and the cake Mrs. Green had made. "I have an idea," she said brightly as Rowley cleared their supper plates. "I think we ought to invite our neighbors to dine so that they may see for themselves that Auchenard has been restored."

Four wide pairs of eyes—Uncle Alfonso, Belinda, Ellis and Mr. Tuttle—turned toward her.

"Oh dear," said Belinda instantly. "I cannot advise inviting *Scotsmen* into your home. They are not the sort of company you should entertain, Daisy. They scarcely speak English! And so many of them are *Jacobites*," she whispered.

"The few we've met speak English," Daisy said. "They are our neighbors, Belinda. Their complaint with England is not with me, and I should like to extend the welcome. I don't mean to invite the entire glen, but only those from neighboring estates."

"What neighboring estates?" Uncle Alfonso asked. "There is scarcely anyone about, love. There is Balhaire and Killeaven, but those are at a distance."

"There is also Arrandale," Daisy pointed out.

"That estate is inhabited by only one man."

"He is our neighbor nonetheless," she said, looking down at her soup and avoiding her uncle's shrewd gaze. "Perhaps we might go farther afield if the lack of immediate neighbors concerns you?"

"What, then, just ride about until we happen on something other than a croft or hovel?" Uncle Alfonso shook his head. "It doesn't seem prudent."

"Why must prudence be the measure of things?

Life is not meant to be lived prudishly!" Daisy complained. "Coming to Auchenard wasn't prudent, either, but we're here, are we not? And look what we've done. Look at all we've accomplished! I've rather enjoyed the weeks we've spent here."

Everyone avoided her gaze.

What an intractable lot. Daisy sat up straighter. "Look here, we can't hold ourselves out as superior. Isn't it better to know our neighbors than to fear them? These lands were once the most desired hunting grounds in the Highlands. I should think our neighbors would welcome the idea that it's been restored."

Belinda grimaced and glanced around the table. "We might expose Ellis to some very primitive people."

Sometimes Daisy wanted to slap words from Belinda the Doomsayer's mouth. As if she would endanger her own son! As if the world outside London was unfit for humans. Why was it that Belinda saw only the worst possible outcome in every situation? How did one live in eager anticipation of calamity?

And yet, when Belinda wasn't predicting disaster, she was an extraordinary help to Daisy, particularly with Ellis. She was also quite artistic. She had created some of the most beautiful paintings and pieces of pottery Daisy had ever seen, many of which graced Chatwick Hall. It was quite odd that a woman who created such beauty could find it in her to gloomily remark on every aspect of Daisy's life, unwilling to let pass any opportunity to predict disaster. Even more curious was that Belinda was never the least bit put off by the fact that her predictions of doom never came true. Daisy's mother had once said that Belinda's tutor was a Christian man who had struck the fear of God in her sister's children, but he seemed to have struck the art of pessimism in Belinda.

Before Daisy could say something she might regret—a sound *shut up* seemed in order—her uncle said thoughtfully, "Perhaps that is precisely what the boy needs. He should be acquainted with different people and situations. One day, he will rule his estate and will have cause to encounter many different persons."

Belinda looked horrified. "Uncle! Need I remind you that the Reverend Cosgrove and his wife exposed their young daughter to savages in the islands, and she engaged in an illicit affair with one of them?"

Ellis looked up from his plate at that. "What's an illicit affair?" he asked.

"It means…it's something like when Cousin Belinda admires the butcher beyond what is reasonable," Daisy said.

"What?" Belinda asked, confused.

"Now, what do you think, Ellis? Shall we meet our neighbors?"

Ellis looked around at the other adults. "Have they any children?" he asked timidly.

Thank the heavens! She might have convinced at least one of them. "We won't know until we've met them, will we?"

"I think we ought to invite them, Mamma," he said.

She beamed at her son and one true ally, then turned that smile to the rest of them. "I think we ought to, as well."

She could plainly see that Belinda and Mr. Tuttle didn't agree with her, but Daisy had made up her mind. There was no opportunity like the present— she was fast running out of time as it was. A young widow of a wealthy viscount and the mother of an heir to a substantial fortune could not remain free forever. Daisy would, out of necessity for her son, be under the thumb of a man again. But for now, she was free to do and act as she pleased. She answered to no one, and if she wanted to travel to invite her Scottish neighbors to dine, she could bloody well do it.

The invitations were sent out the next morning.

There were eight in all, a number determined after some consultation with Mr. Munro, an elderly gentleman who lived somewhere on the lake and brought hares around to sell. He knew who lived where, and agreed to deliver the invitations. "No' a man in these hills I donna know," he'd bragged.

But the replies were slow to return. By the end of the week, they had only four favorable replies from the eight they'd delivered—from the MacDonalds of Skye, the Somerleds of Killeaven, the Murrays of Moraig, and the Mackenzies of Balhaire. The others did not respond.

Among those who failed to respond was Arrandale.

"I see Arrandale has not replied," Daisy said casually to Mr. Munro when no one was about. "Was he not at home?"

"Aye, that he was. Setting a window as I recall."

Daisy considered his lack of response to be quite rude, but she was not the least bit surprised. The poor dear probably feared he'd have to fend off any ladies in attendance, who he surely believed would latch on to him like leeches, being the prize catch of the Highlands as he was.

But what of the other invitations that went unanswered? All their guests would be expected to stay the night, as the distances they would travel were too great. Was that it, perhaps? Did they fear Auchenard would fall down around their ears and didn't know precisely how to say so?

Belinda was, predictably, less optimistic in her reasoning. "They must know of your situation," she said. "Those that are coming mean to gawk."

Gawk. At her? At Ellis? Did they think her fortune dangled from her waist like a set of chatelaine's keys? Daisy deflated. Was there no one on this earth who desired to know her for no other reason than she was a new neighbor? "I think they are interested in Auchenard," she said stubbornly. "And those that didn't respond? Well…they must have their reasons."

Belinda shrugged and returned her attention to her painting of a tower ruin on a hill near Auchenard. Daisy couldn't help but notice the stormy sky her cousin had painted.

Preparation for the dinner was daunting, particularly with a smaller staff than what Daisy generally employed for such an evening. Nevertheless, they managed to prepare the food and the lodge for guests, and she was quite pleased that the meal would be sumptuous, owing primarily to the availability of vegetables in Balhaire. Moreover, Rowley had been dispatched and had returned with several bottles of French wine and enough Scotch whisky to fill the lake.

"French!" Daisy had trilled with excitement.

"Indeed, madam, and had for a song," Rowley reported excitedly.

"Well, of course," Belinda said. "It's been smuggled." Nevertheless, she exclaimed at the fine quality of the wine when she drank it.

The day of the supper dawned cold and quite wet, but Daisy didn't despair. The lodge was warm and dry, which was an improvement since their arrival. That afternoon, she dressed in her best gown, a soft green-and-gold brocade silk with a gold petticoat and embroidered stomacher, trimmed in satin ribbons and Belgian lace at the sleeves. It was the height of fashion, sewn for her just before she'd left London. Daisy also piled her hair high, then festooned it with summer flowers. She wore emerald earrings that matched the emerald she wore on a ribbon around her neck. If they'd come to gawk, let them see her in all her finery.

The guests had been invited to arrive by four o'clock. At a quarter to, Daisy made one last walk through the lodge, then went to the great room to wait with Uncle Alfonso.

Four o'clock came and went with no sign of anyone.

"It's the roads, no doubt," her uncle said, pacing the room with her. "They're bloody well impassable."

At five o'clock, Mrs. Green inquired if she should put the soup on. "They're not coming," Daisy said to her uncle.

"Patience, love."

At six o'clock, Daisy was dejected. She began to imagine it all a cruel joke, and she could picture all the Scots in their strange dress sitting before a hearth somewhere, laughing at the Englishwoman who had come to the Highlands to open a nearly abandoned lodge. Arrandale was right—no one wanted her here.

Ellis, restless and hungry, was as confused as Daisy. "Why do they not come, Mamma?"

"It's raining, darling," she said absently.

"But not very hard at all," he said, staring out the window.

Daisy stood up and held out her hand to her son. "Come. Let's go and ask Mrs. Green if we can save any of the supper, shall we?"

She took his hand and turned away from the window, but before she could take a step, Belinda shouted, "Here comes someone!"

Ellis and Daisy gasped. Belinda suddenly appeared in the great room, having run from the foyer. "It's a coach," she said frantically.

"All right then, be calm," Uncle Alfonso said, ushering her to a seat. "It will not do to appear overly anxious. Daisy? Perhaps you ought to be on hand to greet them."

"Yes, of course," Daisy said. She fluffed out her gown and straightened Ellis's neckcloth. With a wink at her son, she glided to the door to receive her guests.

Rowley opened the door and shot open an umbrella, then marched out into the rain to greet her first guests as the coach rolled to a halt. A coachman in a soggy livery jumped down from the back runner and quickly set out a stool before opening the coach door.

A man whose shoulders were so broad he could scarcely fit through the opening emerged. He wore a tartan plaid belted around his waist, and the tail of it draped over his shoulders. Behind him, another man emerged, just as large as he. They had ruddy cheeks and tufts of ginger hair sprouting from beneath their caps. The first man strode forward, ignoring Rowley completely, and when he reached the entrance where Daisy was standing, he bowed. "Lady Auchenard."

"Yes, I—"

"MacDonald. Irving MacDonald, that is, of Skye. My brother, Fergus MacDonald," he said, jerking his thumb over his shoulder to indicate the other man.

Daisy was confused. She had not invited these men. She had invited Mor MacDonald and his wife. "Ah...how do you do?" she asked and curtsied quickly. "Please, come in from the rain," she said, stepping back so the two massive men could enter. "You must have come for Mr. MacDonald and his wife?" she asked uncertainly as they crowded into the foyer and removed the plaids from their shoulders as rain dripped from their hair.

"Aye," said Irving MacDonald. He offered no further explanation, no reason why the affirmative reply she'd received from Mr. MacDonald had been passed to them. Neither of them spoke as they stared at her.

"But you've come from Skye," she said, her gaze going from one to the other.

"Aye," said Irving MacDonald.

"Well." She couldn't very well turn them out for being the wrong MacDonalds. "Well!" she said again. "It seems you are the only ones to have ventured out in the rain. Would you like a whisky?"

"No," said Irving MacDonald.

Dear God. "Then perhaps some wine?"

"No, we are no' alone," he said gruffly. "More's coming, they are. Rocks on the road up the way, aye?"

"If I may, madam." Rowley had come in behind the men, unnoticed by Daisy as they were so large. "Perhaps they will be more comfortable in the great room?" he asked as he managed to squeeze in around them.

Daisy followed Rowley and the gentlemen into the great room and introduced them to Alfonso, Belinda and Ellis. The gentlemen responded with greetings that sounded more like grunts, then stood silently.

"It's quite a deluge, is it not?" Daisy remarked.

"Eh? *Duda?*" Irving MacDonald said.

"Ah…" Daisy cleared her throat. "I thought perhaps we'd take a tour of the lodge."

The men looked at her as if they found that suggestion strange. Ellis, Daisy noticed, was sitting so tightly beside Belinda that her gown all but covered him.

Daisy looked helplessly at the windows. "Would you care for whisky?"

"Aye," the men said in unison.

Rowley went to fetch it. Daisy sank onto the settee beside Belinda but avoided her cousin's gaze. This was a disaster, and she didn't need to see it on Belinda's face. She watched the two giants toss back a whisky like water and hand the empty tots to Uncle Alfonso for more.

"Madam," Rowley said softly behind her. "A carriage has arrived. A rider, as well."

"Oh!" She sounded far too relieved, she realized, but hurried from the great room nonetheless.

"Mamma!" Ellis cried and ran after her, clutching at her hand as if he was afraid to be left alone with the Scots.

Again Rowley stepped out with the umbrella. A young couple emerged from this carriage and introduced themselves as the Murrays. After the exchange of pleasantries, Mr. Murray explained that their two children had been left with their nurse. Ellis was visibly disappointed.

"Milady, Mr. Ewan Somerled of Killeaven," she heard Rowley say, and she turned to meet a tall, slender man with blond hair. He was wearing trews and smiled warmly. "Lady Chatwick, it is my great pleasure to make your acquaintance."

Daisy held out her hand. "Thank you, Mr. Somerled."

He took her hand and bowed elegantly. "You will forgive me for coming in my parents' stead," he said. His voice was not as heavily accented as some the Scots she'd met thus far; he sounded more like Arrandale. "It is too wet for them to travel and bid me to come on their behalf and welcome you to the Highlands."

Ah, yes, the excuse of weather. She could imagine the scene in some rustic highland dining room, this man with his aging parents, both of them wrapped in plaid before a fire. *Go and see what sort of fortune it is, lad.*

"Thank you for coming," Daisy said. She invited him inside with the Murrays. Her head was spinning with the fact that men she'd not invited had come to her supper. Belinda was right—they'd obviously heard of her predicament, and with the exception of the Murrays, the rest of her favorable replies had sent their best prospects for tapping into her fortune.

It was maddening, disheartening—she thought she'd escaped that constant bother! But there was no escaping it. Not even as far away as the Scottish Highlands.

All the guests were gathered in the great room, and she'd have to make the best of it. Fortunately, Daisy was an accomplished hostess; she made sure that they all had drinks, that their wet cloaks were taken to be dried, that the fire in the hearth was roaring to chase the chill from their bones and that there was quite a lot of chatter about the condition of the road to Auchenard.

"Madam?" It was Rowley at her elbow again. "More guests."

"Are there?" Daisy turned about, and warmth waved through her—*Arrandale*. She tried to hide her ridiculous level of pleasure. She tried not to ogle his commanding figure in trews and boots and the dark blue superfine coat. And while he stoked salacious thoughts that fluttered through Daisy like dandelions, she was determined the bloody rooster would not know of her admiration.

Besides, he'd come with a lovely young woman with blond hair. Now she understood why he was reluctant to engage in the art of trifling. She had to admire him for staying true to the girl.

Daisy smiled at her popinjay of a neighbor. Naturally, he did not smile, but he inclined his head. "My lord Arrandale," she said. "You have *surprised* me. I had not received your favorable reply."

His companion glanced up at him, but Arrandale didn't seem to notice her at all. "My apologies, Lady Chatwick. I had no' intended to burden you with my presence, but my sister, Miss Catriona Mackenzie, would no' be put off of it."

His sister! Daisy almost tittered with delight. Now that she had a look at the girl, she did seem awfully young for what she assumed was Arrandale's terribly advanced age. "Miss Mackenzie, it is my pleasure to make your acquaintance. You are most welcome at Auchenard."

"Thank you," the young woman said and curtsied. Her eyes fixed on Daisy's tower of hair; she seemed

impressed by it. But then her gaze slid past Daisy to
the others in the room.

"Please," Daisy said, gesturing to the others.
"Shall I introduce you?"

"No, thank you," she said. "I am acquainted,
aye?" She smiled and curtsied to Daisy once more,
then flit into the room, her head high.

Daisy glanced at Arrandale sidelong as they
watched his sister greet the MacDonalds. "You
came," she said simply.

"Aye, I was coerced by my sister. She has set her
sights on Edward Fraser and there appears naugh'
that will stop her."

"Edward Fraser never responded to my invitation.
Perhaps, he, too, will suddenly appear at the door."

"I doubt it," he said. "He intends to offer for Nan
Gordon. Cat has no' yet accepted her fate in this. As
you have undoubtedly noted, the Highlands are no'
teeming with bachelors."

"I've noticed no such thing," she said primly.

"Nevertheless, I see you've left no stone unturned."

"Meaning?"

"Meaning you've gathered the local bachelors in
dire need of a fortune, have you no'?"

She frowned. "That was not my intent."

He chuckled softly, the sound wrapping around
her. *"Sealbh math dhuit."* At her look of confusion,
he leaned closer and whispered, "Good luck." He
gave her an enigmatic smile—but a smile all the
same—and stepped away, accepting the offer of
whisky from Rowley.

Daisy gaped at his back. That man was *astonishingly* rude. Granted, he was right, most of the bachelors had been sent by their mothers to sniff out her fortune, but he didn't have to be so gleeful about it. With a sniff, Daisy moved into the crowd of guests with her back intentionally set to Lord Arrandale and the tiny little pleasure that she had, at last, made him smile.

CHAPTER SEVEN

THE BONNIEST WOMEN were always the most dangerous.

In his life, Cailean had trained men how to fight, he'd sailed ships through rough seas, he'd out-maneuvered English ships and run for a hidden cove with smuggled cargo. Aye, he was a strong man…but he was damnably weak when it came to the fairer sex.

He'd meant to keep himself at a safe distance from Auchenard, but here he was, in Lady Chatwick's great room, in the midst of fawning idiots.

Little wonder why they were fawning. She was dressed in a gown the likes of which Cailean's mother often wore when she returned from visiting England: polished silk, highly embroidered. Her hair was artfully adorned and her face was not powdered as so many men and women in France were fond of doing. Personally, Cailean didn't care for all the powdering, and he never wore wigs as Englishmen did—he had quite enough of his own hair, thank you, which was presently tied into a queue.

A hint of a smile played across her lips as Somerled tried to impress her with God only knew what. Cailean guessed that Lady Chatwick was quite accustomed to men babbling like simpletons when they first met her.

Aye, she was bonny; he'd not deny it. Bonny enough that some unoiled, unused part of him had wanted to come to dine. It helped that he'd been browbeaten by his oldest sister and his mother into escorting Cat. The lass had been beside herself with elation when Cailean had at last agreed to see her to this soiree. She had thrown her arms around his neck, whispered a fevered "Thank you," then grabbed the hand of her cousin Imogen and tugged her along as she began to complain about the choice of gowns she had to wear to such an important event.

Cailean had groused about it, naturally, but privately he was not unhappy he had an excuse to come and witness how the barmy Englishwoman would conduct herself with the fortune seekers in attendance tonight.

Mr. Kimberly, her uncle, was conducting a tour, as if none of his guests had ever seen the inside of a hunting lodge. Cailean hung back, idly listening, his gaze wandering often to their glowing hostess.

How different she appeared tonight. Regal. Wealthy. *Boidheach*—beautiful. Quite different from the last two times he'd seen her. Gone were the bedclothes, the cheeks pink with sleep and the hair tousled about her shoulders. Gone was the soiled gown and leather apron, the bit of vine stuck in her braid, the smudge of dirt on her cheek. She wore a gown that shimmered when she moved and an embroidered stomacher so tight that her breasts all but spilled from her bodice. He was clearly not the only man to have noticed—all the bachelors looked as if they were teetering on the verge of enchantment.

That was what she wanted, he supposed.

They meandered through the hallways, taking in this or that. Mr. Kimberly was apparently the sort to keenly study the history of mundane things—he was determined that no part of the lodge go unmentioned. Yes, they'd done a remarkable amount of work in the last weeks, and, yes, the rustic nature of the lodge held a certain charm. Clearly, a good amount of money had been put into the work. But it was a bloody lodge all the same.

With the tour completed, they were once again in the great room. Cailean fought a yawn. Thus far, the evening reminded him of many interminable evenings he'd spent at Norwood Park. He might have at least looked out at the stunning view of Lochcarron, but on this dreary, wet evening, he could scarcely make out the loch at all.

He idly surveyed those gathered. Men were pathetically simple creatures—they were all of them slaves to feminine allure, stumbling through life like a herd of cattle while images of naked ladies and the burning hope of actually seeing one danced about their heads.

In her circle of admirers, Lady Chatwick suddenly laughed, the sound of it light and airy, and the gentlemen shifted closer to her. Ah yes, a mere smile, coyly given, could compel them all to daring acts of chivalry.

He looked away from that group and happened to catch sight of Catriona. She and Finella Murray had their heads together as if they conspired against nations instead of unsuspecting gentlemen.

Cailean glanced at his pocket watch and wondered how long before supper would be served. Someone moved beside him, and he turned his head, saw a woman he knew to be part of Lady Chatwick's household. He nodded politely, and she squinted her brown eyes at him.

"I know you," she said. She did not sound pleased; she sounded a wee bit accusatory.

"Pardon—I am Mackenzie of Arrandale," he said. "And you are...?"

"I beg your pardon. I am Miss Belinda Hainsworth," she said, and offered her gloved hand to him. "I am cousin to Lady Chatwick."

Cailean took her hand as she sank into a curtsy so stiff that he wondered if she was perhaps not in the habit of it.

"The weather is wretched, is it not?" she asked as he pulled her up. She folded her arms over her middle as if warding off a chill. "I fear it is too damp for Lord Chatwick." She leaned closer to Cailean and whispered loudly, "A nun once told me she had to leave Scotland, for all the dampness had given her a permanent ague!"

Cailean's brows rose with surprise.

She nodded with great verve, as if she'd just imparted some vital news to him. "Fortunately, I rather suspect we shall not be here long." She sighed, leaned back against the wall.

"And why is that, then? Your lady has gone to the trouble of repairing Auchenard." And restoring a garden to its "former glory" for all the garden parties she threatened to have.

"Well," she said, shrugging lightly, "her ladyship will marry again by year's end."

Something in Cailean hitched. He glanced down. "I didna know she was affianced."

"Well...not officially, mind you," Miss Hainsworth said and then smiled pertly. "But she knows who she will marry."

Cailean swallowed down a disturbing bit of disappointment. *Already?* "Is he here, tonight, then?"

"Here!" Miss Hainsworth laughed. "I should think not!"

"A Scotsman?" he asked.

"No, of course not," she said, as if that was a ridiculous question, and a wee bit of light shone on an old, deep wound in Cailean.

"I'm really not to say, but I suppose there is no harm in telling you. After all, you're not acquainted with the gentleman." She straightened her shoulders and said proudly, "My cousin will marry Captain Robert Spivey of the Royal Navy. When his commission ends, that is. We do not as yet know when that shall be."

It seemed to Cailean as if everything around them slowed, the sound receding as he reeled at the mention of that name. It was impossible. *Impossible.*

Cailean knew Spivey—he was an adversary, had been in pursuit of Aulay and Cailean for more than a year. They'd outrun him on at least two occasions and the last time had been terribly close. Their ships had passed so closely as Spivey's ship, the *Fortune*, tried to turn starboard to fire at them, that Cailean and Spivey had seen each other through their spyglasses. Cailean had seen Spivey very clearly when Aulay's first mate, Wallace Mackenzie, fired his musket and killed a sailor on Spivey's deck. Aulay had maneuvered their unmarked ship expertly, and they'd outrun the royal rig. But the *Fortune*'s cannon had clipped their foremast. They had barely escaped.

The ship had to be sent to Skye for repair. And the Mackenzies had continued on with their trade.

It was an impossible coincidence that Lady Chatwick would be marrying one of the few men on this earth who would gladly see him hang.

"But who among us is a farmer?" Miss Hainsworth said.

Cailean realized she was still talking to him.

"Certainly not I!" she said with a snort. "I can't be long in the sun as it gives me a wretched headache—oh, there is my uncle. Pardon me, sir," she said and stepped away.

Cailean stared at Lady Chatwick, stunned by this news. He had the sudden thought that Captain Spivey had sent her here to ferret him out. But he quickly dismissed the idea—Spivey would need to catch him in the act of smuggling to bring him to justice, and he was presumably so far from the Highlands that it was an impossibility. So was it just a bad coincidence? A peculiar, absurd twist of fate?

Fergus MacDonald startled Cailean, accosting him, whisky in hand. "Mackenzie, lad," he said with much jocularity. Apparently, it was not his first whisky of the evening. "I wagered I'd no' see you among us."

"I'd have thought the same of you, MacDonald." That was not exactly true—shipbuilding was not entirely profitable, particularly when one built a ship for a Scotsman who promised to pay, then watched that Scotsman sail away and never return.

"How did you gain an invitation, then?" MacDonald asked. "Had to wrangle it from the *da*, we did. He was right crabbit about it, too."

"You've come in your father's stead?" Cailean asked, not understanding.

"No' in his stead, lad. Left him tied to that bloody shrew of a wife, aye? Ach, donna look at me in that way, Mackenzie. He's his own fortune, he has. He doesna need another." He threw a companionable arm around Cailean's shoulders. "Like you, we've an interest in the lady's affairs," he said low, and waggled thick ginger eyebrows at him. "You've heard, have you no'? She's a bloody fortune to her name and must marry a Scotsman by the end of the year."

Cailean hadn't heard it quite in that way, but nevertheless he shrugged MacDonald's heavy arm off his shoulders. "I've no interest in her affairs. I've come only as escort to my sister."

MacDonald laughed and clapped Cailean on

the back. "Aye, of course you have, Mackenzie! Of *course* you have." He was still laughing as he wandered away.

Diah, Cailean could scarcely abide it, watching these men jockey around the lady, working to gain her attention. And worse, assuming he was working for the same.

But he'd rather see one of these men prevail than *Spivey*.

Somerled had attached himself to her side, he noticed. The rumors of his debts must be true, then. Lady Chatwick was enjoying his attention, obviously—she was quite animated when Somerled said something. She laughed, tossing her head back, her hand going to her belly as if to contain her glee.

He shifted his attention to the windows that overlooked the loch and the gloomy vista of never-ending rain. But he could see the reflections of the people behind him, could see Lady Chatwick's hair towering above the men. *Spivey*.

What a tragic waste of a beautiful woman.

He moved away, unwilling to look at her just now, and nearly stumbled over a lad seated in a chair.

Cailean paused. Lady Chatwick's son had either not noticed him or was refusing to acknowledge him. He had his hands braced against his knees and his head down, staring at the floor. The child seemed to be in abject misery. Well, then, they'd make good bedfellows.

"Good evening," Cailean said. The lad would not lift his head, so Cailean nudged his foot. "My lord?"

The lad spoke then, but in a tone so soft that Cailean couldn't understand him. "Pardon?" he asked, and squatted down on his haunches beside him, dipping his head to see the lad's face. At last, the young lord looked at him. *A Diah*, what a despondent lad he was.

"Would you like some company?"

The lad shook his head, pressed his lips together and averted his gaze.

"No?" Cailean asked. "A pity, then. I had hoped you might share what you think of the Highlands and Auchenard." He didn't really care, but the lad did look as if he could use a friend about now.

"I hate it," he whispered.

"Hate?" Cailean repeated. "What could you possibly hate?"

"There's nothing to do here."

"*Och*, you donna know what you say. There is much for a lad to do here, aye? Hunting and fishing, stalking and birding. And you canna argue that there is a better diversion than the summer *feill*."

That earned him a glance from the corner of the lad's eye. "What's a *feill*?"

"A festival. It's held at Balhaire every year, then. You know of Balhaire, surely."

The lad shook his head.

"The Mackenzie stronghold. An old castle with a village and whatno', aye?"

The lad said nothing.

"All the Mackenzies and more come round for the weekend. There is food and ale, games of chance and strength. Musicians, too, and enough dancing to make a lad a wee bit dizzy. And the men—they play men's games to challenge their strength and cunning. It's the likes of which you've no' seen in England."

Still the lad said nothing.

"I suppose you know that the strongest man on earth hails from these very Highlands."

"He does?" the lad said, turning his head slightly toward Cailean.

"Oh, aye," Cailean said, nodding. "They call him the Mountain, for he's as big as one and twice as strong."

"How can he be stronger than a mountain?"

"You've no' seen a man as big as this. He's as tall as an elk," he said, lifting his hand well above his head. "And he's as broad across as two grown men." Cailean leaned forward. "He can toss a caber farther than you might throw a stone."

"What's a caber?" the lad asked timidly.

"*Diah*, do my ears deceive me? Have you no' seen a caber?" he asked with feigned incredulity.

Young Lord Chatwick shook his head.

"Why, it's the trunk of a tree, It's whittled down and sanded, aye?" he said, miming the process. "It's as long as this room and as wide as you. It's an important part of the games we play in the Highlands."

Lord Chatwick twisted a bit in his seat so that he could see Cailean. "But how can a man throw the trunk of a tree?"

"With two hands," Cailean said, turning his hands palms up. He made a shoving motion. "He tosses it up in the air and hopes it lands on its head and falls forward." He smiled and came off his haunches, settling into a chair next to the bairn. "How far do you think you might toss a caber?"

He shook his head. "I couldn't."

"What's this? Of course you could," Cailean said. "With good Highland air and perhaps a wee dram of ale, you could do it. You need only try."

The lad shook his head again. "My mother won't allow it. She doesn't want me to be harmed."

What coddling! Boys could not become men if they were coddled. "Heed me—you canna grow to be a man if you donna earn a few bumps and bruises along the way. A caber toss will no' harm you, will it? On the morrow, if we have clear weather, I'll show you if you like."

"Yes," he said, nodding.

Cailean extended his hand to him. "I'm Cailean Mackenzie, by the by. You may call me Cailean."

"Cay-lin," the boy repeated carefully.

"What's your name, then?"

"Ellis Bristol, Lord Chatwick," he said, as if he had uttered those word a thousand times today.

"Well, then, Ellis Bristol, Lord Chatwick, I look forward to demonstrating the toss of a caber on the morrow." He stood up and winked at the lad. He intended to move on, but he very nearly collided with Lady Chatwick.

"Oh my," she said, folding her arms. "That worries me. What is to happen on the morrow?"

Cailean could detect her perfume. It was light and

clean and reminded him of fresh oranges. No, not oranges, exactly—but something so enticing that he wanted to lean closer to her to smell it.

"He means to show me how to toss a caber," Ellis said.

"A what?"

"It's a tree trunk, Mamma," he said as if it were quite common knowledge.

"A tree trunk," she repeated and glanced at Cailean. "You might show him how to toss something a bit more manageable, mightn't you?"

"A Highlander doesna toss things that are manageable—we leave that to the lassies and the *Sassenach*. Lord Chatwick and I have discussed it, and we have decided that we shall toss a caber or be damned trying. Is that no' so, lad?"

"It is," Ellis said, looking suddenly and fiercely determined.

Lady Chatwick smiled and put up her hands. "Far be it from me to interfere with the work of men. Ellis, darling, it's time you had your supper. Will you go and find Mr. Tuttle?"

"Aye, Mamma," he said. He stood up, bowed stiffly to Cailean and made his way across the room.

Lady Chatwick watched him go, then glanced up at Cailean, her eyes wide with surprise. "*Aye?* He said aye!"

"There is hope for him yet, then."

She smiled warmly, and Cailean felt it swirl through him. "Thank you," she said. "And I mean that quite sincerely. He's been despondent, really.

The landscape is intimidating so he doesn't venture far. He's charted all the stars so—"

"He's what?"

She laughed softly. "He's developed an interest in navigation."

Because of Spivey?

"And, curiously, rocks," she said with a lopsided smile. "He's collected several. I'm very happy that he has something to look forward to. Although, I am a bit concerned that he might harm himself tossing tree trunks about."

"Milady?"

Lady Chatwick shifted her smiling green eyes from Cailean to the butler.

"Supper is served."

"Yes, thank you." She turned back to Cailean and stepped a little closer, tilting her head back to look him in the eye. "My son has a delicate nature. Please remember it."

Cailean leaned slightly forward, bending his head over hers. "And he'll be a delicate man if you donna let him away from your side."

Her smile deepened. "Are you now advising me how to raise my son?"

"I'm advising you to allow him to toss a caber or two."

She lifted her gaze from his mouth, her smile sparkling in her eyes and in Cailean's blood. "Have you any further advice for me, Arrandale? Or have you delivered it all?"

His looked at her, at her smooth skin, her cheekbones. And her mouth, painted red for the evening. He tried to imagine the faceless English captain kissing those lips and felt a slight hitch in his gut. "Aye, I do. Keep close watch of your purse."

Now the dimples appeared. "Why, *thank* you, sir. I cannot imagine how I've carried on as I have without you to direct me."

Cailean couldn't help his smile. "Neither can I."

She smiled with amusement. Cailean could feel a draw of energy from somewhere deep within him, which was broken the moment she looked away. "Please excuse me—I must play the part of gracious hostess now." She glided away from him, her skirts brushing against his legs as she passed, the scent of her perfume lingering in her wake. Her fingers trailed over the back of the settee as she moved to her uncle's side to announce supper was served. Oh, this woman—she knew very well how to tease a man without as much as lifting a finger.

"Astonishing, is it no'?"

Cailean looked to his left. Mr. Murray had sidled up to him and was eyeing Lady Chatwick shrewdly. "What is?" he asked.

"That she has come to the Highlands at all, aye? Seems passing strange to me that a lady of her means and situation would waste as much as a day in these hills. I suppose she means to negotiate a devil's bargain and trade Auchenard for a husband." He sipped smugly from his whisky. "It meets all the stipulations of her husband's will."

How was it that everyone in the Highlands knew

of this woman's predicament? Did they have nothing to occupy them but to guess at what she was about? "Perhaps," he said with a shrug.

Murray chuckled. "It's common knowledge, Arrandale. I myself have heard it from Ned Burns, just returned from London. The lady caused a right scandal, she did, when she upended her house and brought it here."

Cailean shifted his gaze from Mr. Murray to Lady Chatwick again. "And what sort of man, do you suppose, would make a bargain that gives control of the purse to his wife?" he drawled.

"A desperate one, aye? Look around you," he said. "Look at how they smile."

Cailean's gaze landed on Somerled across the room. His smile was simpering. He would feel like a fool when Lady Chatwick took her leave to wed a captain in the Royal Navy.

"Any man with a need for fortune might strike a bargain here tonight," Mr. Murray said. "Mark me, the lady will no' remain in Scotland for long. These young men, smitten as they are by her fine looks, will be tricked into a situation in which she has the upper hand. I'd no' be happy with a wife who instructed me," he muttered.

"I'd no' be happy with a wife," Cailean said, and the two men laughed.

CHAPTER EIGHT

In HINDSIGHT, AS much as Daisy hated to admit it, the meet-her-neighbors evening did not appear to be one of her better ideas.

She looked at the guests around her dining table. Mrs. Finella Murray and Miss Catriona Mackenzie had their heads together, talking in low voices, ignoring everyone else. Daisy had tried to engage them, had asked Mrs. Murray if she'd ever been to Auchenard before.

Mrs. Murray shook her head. "Only in passing."

Daisy didn't know what that meant, precisely—they were at the end of a road, and one could hardly pass by Auchenard without splintering a carriage wheel. But she'd said, "I hope now that we have refurbished it, our friends will come often."

The two young women exchanged a look. "Well… in the winter, it's right hard to reach Auchenard, aye?" Miss Mackenzie said.

"Is it?" Daisy smiled and absently looked down at the table, wishing someone else would join the conversation. No one was paying them any heed. When she turned back, the two women were whispering to each other. About her? No, no—they whispered

about a man, surely. At that age, Daisy herself had
been quite single-minded about men.

She wished Belinda was here, but her cousin had
retreated as soon as she was able, citing a headache
from the damp.

The men poured their own whisky now, having
brushed aside the attentions of Rowley. Their plates,
scraped clean, had been pushed away, so that Rowley and Mr. Green had to lean far over the guests
to clear the table. Gone were the polite formalities
her guests had shown upon arrival, and Daisy heard
more than one belch. They were all of them laughing
uproariously at one another, slipping in and out of
their native tongue and English. Uncle Alfonso sat
at the other end of the table, as far into his cups as
some of the others, laughing louder than anyone else.

At least he was enjoying himself.

Arrandale didn't seem to be enjoying the company
at his end of the table. He sat stoically, his empty
whisky tot pushed away, listening impassively to
Irving MacDonald, who had commanded the floor
with yet another tale of a shipwreck. To hear him
tell it, it seemed as if ships were wrecked in droves
near Skye.

Daisy had thought this would be a proper supper
party like those she'd hosted in London. She should
have known it would be impossible here. Now she
wished they'd all go home.

She couldn't suppress her second sigh, and she
quickly straightened in her seat, hoping that none of
her guests had noticed. Naturally one of them had,

and that one arched a brow, as if silently chastising her. Daisy gave Arrandale a withering look.

"Beg your pardon, madam, but is there more of Arrandale's fine French wine?" Mr. Murray asked jovially, and the others laughed roundly.

Arrandale? Did they think he'd brought the wine to this supper? "Of course," Daisy said. "Allow me to bring it."

With a look of horror on his face, Rowley rushed to her chair to stop her from rising.

"It's quite all right," she muttered to him. "I really need to take some air."

He nodded. The poor man looked as if he could use some air, too. He pulled back her chair, and Daisy stood.

No one else stood. It surprised her, and she hesitated a moment, waiting for the gentlemen to rise, as they ought to have done in deference to her. As gentlemen across London did at the mere suggestion she might rise. Arrandale seemed amused by her look of astonishment. Her uncle didn't notice her at all. Was there no one in the Highlands with a proper set of manners?

With a slight roll of her eyes, Daisy quit the dining room and moved down the hall toward the kitchen. As she neared the kitchen, she could hear the banging of pots and the slosh of water as Mrs. Green and her girl cleaned up. She stopped a few feet from the kitchen entrance at the door of the larder and took a candle from the sconce on the wall. She heard someone coming down the hall, and assumed at first it was Rowley, whose years of training would not allow his lady to fetch wine herself. But that was not the footfall of Rowley.

Daisy held the candle aloft and peered into the shadows. She couldn't make anything out and lifted her candle higher. Then she sighed. "What are you doing here?"

"Looking for you, aye?" Arrandale said. "Your uncle had a wee bit of apoplexy for want of a cheroot. I promised I'd return with the tobacco with the speed of an angel, lest he perish before us." He smiled.

Daisy must have had more wine than she realized, because she was thinking how his eyes seemed almost gray in the light of a single candle.

"What, then?" he asked, his brows dipping.

"Pardon?"

"Why do you look at me in that manner?"

A warm blush crept into her cheeks. "Ah…" She gathered herself. "The cheroots are here. Would you mind?" she asked, and held out the candle for him to take. She opened the larder door, then retrieved her candle from him. "I'll be only a moment." And with that she disappeared down the short flight of stairs into the storeroom.

Arrandale didn't remain behind to wait like an obedient puppy. She heard him and turned to see his boots. Then his trews. Then the rest of him, ducking down beneath the slant of ceiling before reaching the floor. The larder was scarcely large enough for two people, and he stood awfully close to her as he looked around at the food they'd stored.

"*Now* what are you doing?" she asked with more exasperation than she felt. "There's not enough room—"

"I couldna bear another long-winded tale." He smiled conspiratorially, and when he did, it seemed as if the entire larder was illuminated with it. Daisy *felt* illuminated with it. Oh, but that was a beautiful smile, a smile that could tempt Daisy to do any number of things she really ought not to do.

"You're doing it again," he said, shifting closer to her.

"Doing what, pray?"

His attention moved to her mouth. "Looking at me as if I'm a piece of cake that you'd very much like to eat."

He'd seen through her completely, and Daisy didn't care. "Still flattering yourself, are you?" His lips were so...*lush*. She imagined the touch of them—wondered if they would be firm or soft on her lips. Firm or soft on her skin? On her thighs? On her breast? She hid a small shiver. "You accuse me of trifling with you, and yet you are the one following me into the larder to seduce me."

"Hmm," he said contemplatively and shifted so close to her that Daisy had to move backward so that she was standing with her back against the shelving. "You donna know me, Lady Chatwick, but if you did, you would know that if I meant to seduce you..." He paused, allowed his gaze to waft over her and down, to her décolletage. "You would have no question of it."

Daisy ardently wanted to know how this man

would seduce her. "You mistake me for a woman with no knowledge of the world, sir, but I know a notorious bachelor when I've met him. I know how he seduces."

He grinned. "Notorious, am I?" He braced his hand against the shelf at her head, and Daisy's heart began to race as he wolfishly devoured her with his eyes. "Aye, you're right, I am. I'm no gentleman, *leannan*, and I've a very strong desire at the moment to show you what has made me *notorious*."

She had an equally strong desire to see it. Daisy couldn't help herself; she reached up and brushed a tress of hair that had fallen over his eye. "Do you mean to show me now?" she asked and lifted her face slightly, so that there was no question of the invitation to kiss her. *Show me! Show me, Arrandale. Show me before it melts away.* Blood rushed in her veins, pooling heavy in her groin. Maybe she'd drunk too much of the wine, but she'd like it very much if he lifted her skirts and slid into her now, pumping his body into hers, taking her like a night's fevered dream. She could all but feel his hands on her skin, the warmth of his body against hers. She could all but taste those succulent lips and smell the scent of his skin.

Arrandale shifted closer, his hand sliding into the shelf near her head. He was so close now, his lips a mere breadth from hers, and Daisy's blood rushed harder, making it difficult to breathe.

"Do you think every man you meet lusts after you, Lady Chatwick?" he asked in a rough whisper.

"Most," she admitted.

One of his dark brows floated above the other. "You are so full of conceit it's a wonder you donna explode, aye?"

It was a wonder she'd not exploded, but not because of her conceit. Because every nerve, every muscle pulsed with want. "Shall I pretend it's not true? Shall I pretend to be an innocent? Would that please you?"

He laughed softly, the sound of it rich and silky, caressing her from head to toe. *Kiss me. Just kiss me.*

"On the contrary," he murmured. "I'd be disappointed if you pretended to be anything but who you are."

Daisy sucked in a breath to steady herself. He was going to kiss her, and every bit of her shimmered in anticipation. She'd gladly follow him down any path he led her. Waiting for it, she closed her eyes.

She felt him shift closer, and now she felt the fabric of his coat against her bosom. She parted her lips…

"But even a woman who is often lusted after ought to have a care for whom she seduces. Men are vile creatures and will take advantage."

What? Daisy opened her eyes. Arrandale smirked with triumph. He faded back from her and held up the box of cheroots. "I believe this is what your uncle wants, is it no'?"

She gaped at him. *The dirty, rotten bounder!* He'd baited her, and she, like a green little debutante, had taken it. "That was badly done," she said darkly.

Arrandale chuckled. "Who was it, then, who said she would trifle with whomever she pleased, and if I was offended, I should stay away?"

"And who was it who said he had no intention of engaging me in a flirtation?" she shot back.

"Lass, you play with fire—"

Daisy didn't allow him to finish. She caught his lapels and jerked him forward at the same moment she rose up on her toes and kissed him. She planted her lips on his, and she felt the shock of her behavior and the softness of his lips reverberate down to her toes. *Soft.* In spite of his strength, his lips were *soft.*

Arrandale did not resist her, oh no—his hand was on her breast, his arm around her waist, pulling her into his body, pressing her backward as he kissed her. Whatever Daisy's intention had been, it was swallowed and forgotten in the wake of his ferocious response. She opened her mouth to his, felt his tongue slide in between her teeth. He cupped her face, his thumb at the corner of her mouth as his tongue tangled with hers.

Her heart pounded a frantic rhythm as he pressed a length of hardness against her. A delicious and salacious image of her legs open as he slid that hardness into her, her breasts exposed and straining for him, filled her mind's eye. She moved against him, arching into him, sliding her pelvis against his hip. It was a wild kiss, full of unacceptable pleasure, full of craving and anticipation, full of the sort of thirst that could not be slaked.

And then, just as suddenly as Daisy had begun

it, Arrandale ended it. He let go her waist and drew back from her. He picked up the box of cheroots from the shelf where he'd dropped it when Daisy kissed him, and ran his hand over the top of his head as his gaze skated over her, from the top of her head to the tips of her jeweled slippers. He studied her as he swiped his forefinger across his bottom lip. "Was it worth the risk, then?" he asked, his voice deep and rough. He pointed to the open door, to the people, she presumed, that could have found them there in the midst of that torrid kiss.

Daisy couldn't think about that—she was still trying to find her breath. Still feeling his lips on hers. She shakily pushed away from the shelving and ran her hands down the sides of her waist. "You tell me."

In the dim golden light of a single candle, she saw a glittering in his eyes that she felt very much in herself. Lust and pleasure. Surprise. Fascination.

"As I said, you play with fire," he said softly. "You are to be married soon—you risk too much."

"I know," she said simply. There was no argument for her behavior. There was only need. Raw, monstrous need.

Arrandale moved toward the steps leading up to the hallway. He paused there and glanced back at her. His eyes still gleamed with the spark of that kiss…or rather, Daisy imagined that they did. "If you do that again, I'll no' be responsible for my response, aye?"

He meant that to shock her, to shake some sense into her. But it thrilled her. She looked at this man, this bewitching man, and thought she could very well take flight with all the desire she was feeling for him at the moment. "I understand."

He disappeared up the stairs.

When he'd gone, Daisy leaned back against the shelving and closed her eyes, releasing the breath she hadn't even realized she was holding. *That man, that man*...he stoked such a fire in her! No man had ever affected her so, not even Clive. She luxuriated in the tingling in her body, the memory of his mouth and hands on hers, the feel of his body pressed against her. She ran her hands up her arms trying to re-create that feeling, but it was no use.

Daisy sighed and opened her eyes. Good God, she had just kissed the Scotsman. Uninvited, she had kissed him like a woman with few morals and a complete disregard for her reputation. She had lost her fool mind. But to answer his question, it had been well worth the risk.

CAILEAN WAS A man of experience, and yet he feared the pleasure of that surprising, stunning kiss was evident in his expression somehow, if not in his trews. For that reason, he delivered the cheroots to the butler, then made his way to the room he'd been given for the night.

He was lost in thought and sensations he'd not felt in months. Women were such strange creatures, always fluffing their wings and smiling as if they knew a secret.

He was unsettled by that kiss. It had moved him, had made him want...*something*. Was that boldly flirtatious, devil-may-care widow likewise un-settled? Was it possible that she wasn't as daunt-less as she fancied herself to be? Could she really be contemplating marriage with one man and kiss him like she just had?

Cailean was annoyed with her for having kissed him and kicking up the storm that was raging in him. He was annoyed with himself for having succumbed to it so quickly and so completely.

And yet he knew it was absurd to be vexed. What did any of it matter to him? He was not her keeper. He was not in the hunt. He was not the judge of her character. The woman had a peculiar dilemma and perhaps she was addressing it as well as anyone could in her circumstance. What did he care, then?

He didn't care. He *wouldn't* care.

He readied for bed in that meager room with a sin-gle, narrow window overlooking the loch, and a bra-zier for warmth. The bed was too short, and his feet hung off the end of it. The pillow was little more than a square of cloth stuffed with a few goose feathers. Cailean punched it several times, but it was useless.

He lay on his back, his hands pillowing his head now, staring up in the dark at the bare ceiling. Aye, he was vexed. *Nettled.* This wasn't like him—he never felt so out of sorts. It was this blasted bed and pillow, that was what...

Or perhaps it was simpler than that. Perhaps, having discovered that he was now unpolished in the art of flirting, he realized he'd spent too much time with no other company than a dog and a horse.

Cailean had been well-occupied building Arrandale and working with his father. He'd had no time for unpredictable women. And he'd been perfectly content, too, by God.

Or, had he convinced himself of that? Because it had taken nothing more than a kiss to untether that unfed, untrained beast of desire in him.

Damn her, but this was *her* fault. He'd not asked to be kissed, especially not in a way that suggested the lady wanted more, *much* more from him, and goddammit, he'd wanted to give her more, there in the larder.

His ill humor, this feeling at sixes and sevens, was her fault.

But what, exactly, he intended to do about it, Cailean had no idea.

CHAPTER NINE

"I DON'T APPROVE of Mr. Fergus MacDonald swearing before Ellis," Belinda said to Daisy the next morning as she helped her dress. "That sort of talk will unduly influence a child and may very well lead to risqué behavior."

"Risqué behavior? What sort of swearing?" Daisy asked as Belinda finished lacing her gown.

"He took the Lord's name in vain at least twice," Belinda whispered.

Daisy didn't think that would lead to risqué behavior, but she knew when to argue with Belinda, and this was not the time.

Belinda stood back to admire her handiwork. "There you are, pretty as a painting."

"Thank you." Daisy took a seat at the small vanity to brush her hair.

"I'm *exhausted*," Belinda said and fell onto Daisy's bed, draping herself across the pillows. "Now that it's said and done, what do you think of your neighbors?"

Her neighbors? She could think of only one. She could think only of that kiss. "Unfortunately, I think very few of them can properly be termed neighbors,"

Daisy said. "It would appear you were right, dearest," she said, sighing with defeat. "Our neighbors have sent their prospects for a match, just as you suggested."

"None that you'd consider, I should hope," Belinda said.

Daisy laughed. "Of course not."

"Thank God for it," Belinda said softly. "I had begun to fear that you might have changed your mind about your best prospect."

Daisy glanced at Belinda's reflection in the mirror. "Pardon?"

Belinda flushed and averted her gaze. "I saw you speaking to the Scotsman, and I... I fretted that you had forgotten Captain Spivey."

"For heaven's sake, Belinda," Daisy said and turned about on her bench to face her cousin. "I don't know if I can be any plainer. My marriage, or lack thereof, is not your worry. You should think of your own prospects and not mine."

Belinda laughed. "My prospects? You know very well I could never marry, Daisy, on account of my hips being far too narrow for delivering a child. Mrs. Brendan, God rest her soul, died in childbirth because her hips were too narrow. I've explained to you more than once that no gentleman will have me if I cannot bear him a child, and certainly I can't risk my life for the sake of marriage."

Well, it was certainly true that Belinda had explained it more than once. It was just that there were times that Daisy feigned listening to Belinda. She turned back to the looking glass so she could resume brushing her hair.

"But even if I could bear a child properly, I don't have an edict from beyond the grave hanging over my head as you do, Daisy. You *must* marry, and really, dearest, shouldn't we return to London as soon as possible? We've been here for weeks now. Surely the captain has come. You've not seen him in years! Won't you need time for a proper courtship? Mustn't you reacquaint yourself with him before any talk of a match can happen?"

"Belinda—"

"I bring it up only because of Ellis," Belinda said quickly. "I would never forgive myself if I did not warn you of squandering his fortune."

Daisy didn't mean to bring the brush down on the vanity as violently as she did, but the ivory handle cracked, and Belinda gasped, sitting up, her eyes wide as she looked at the brush.

"I will *not* squander my son's fortune!" Daisy said sharply. "The arrangement will be made with or without me, and voilà, I will be married! Ellis will keep his fortune, and I will… I will manage somehow. But please, for the love of God, stop accusing me of squandering my son's inheritance."

"Oh, Daisy," Belinda said sadly. "I didn't mean to. I know you would never intentionally do such a thing. But I don't understand why we languish in Scotland. I only wish you'd find a bit more romance in your situation."

"*Romance?* Are you mad? My first marriage was

made without the benefit of *romance*," she said, biting out the word. "My situation now does not provide
for any romance. That is a young girl's dream, Belinda. It's not the truth of things." She picked up the
brush to examine it. She'd broken the handle. Now
what would she do? It wasn't as if she could send a
footman out to fetch her a new one.

"But…" Belinda sighed. "Never mind."

"Never mind what?" Daisy asked absently as she
tried to fit the broken piece onto the brush.

"It's none of my affair—"

"No."

"You do still hope to marry Captain Spivey, do
you not?"

"Yes!" Daisy said, terribly exasperated with her
cousin. She didn't want to think of Rob today. She
was still thinking of another man's kiss. Could she
not have that one small pleasure? "That's why we've
come all this way, remember? The bishop was so
eager to make a match that I feared he'd have done
it before Rob could reach me. You *know* this."

"Yes, I know. But I saw the way you looked at
Arrandale."

Daisy sighed. She came to her feet and began to
pace. "I have trifled with him, Belinda, that is true.
But it has been a harmless flirtation. I am a grown
woman and I *miss*—" She stopped herself before
she said too much. *I miss intercourse. I miss a man's
hands on me. I miss being desired and wanted in
that way.* Belinda would not understand these things.

Daisy looked at her cousin, her expression full of

despair. She sighed again and moved to sit next to her on the bed. "I hope to marry Rob. I *do*. Arrandale is…he's diverting, that's all. I am merely amusing myself—nothing more. Because he is the one man on this earth who cares nothing for my fortune," she added bitterly.

Belinda nodded. She took Daisy's hand in hers and squeezed it, then looked her in the eye. "Be careful of amusements, Daisy."

Daisy smiled wryly. "Why? Did something dire happen in the course of someone's amusement?"

Belinda's face darkened. "*No.* Because I am concerned for you and Ellis. I am allowed that. I am allowed to be concerned about what you're doing." She stood up and went out of the room without another word.

"Blast it," Daisy muttered and fell back on her bed, exhausted and torn and sort of distantly aroused—there were so many things in her head that it began to ache.

DAISY EVENTUALLY FINISHED dressing on her own and then reluctantly made her way down to breakfast and her guests.

On her way to the dining room, she detoured to her son's rooms.

Ellis was at breakfast with Mr. Tuttle. The books for his lessons were stacked neatly on a small desk near the window. Ellis was in the midst of a rather animated tale when she walked in. Mr. Tuttle came to his feet and bowed his head.

"I'm to learn how to toss a tree today, Mamma," Ellis said. "Cailean means to show me. Not Collin, Mamma—it sounds a bit different than that."

"Thank you for alerting me," she said, smiling. "But do you think it wise to call him by his given name?"

"He said that I should. Do you know what else he said? He said I looked quite strong."

Daisy exchanged a look with Mr. Tuttle, who said affectionately, "His lordship is most adamant that the tree be tossed, madam."

"Then by all means, it shall." She couldn't imagine how this tree tossing might be done, but she knew one thing—Arrandale had best live up to his promise to her son, or he would have an angry viscountess to address.

Daisy kissed her son on the top of his head. "If you mean to toss trees about, darling, you best eat a hearty breakfast," she said, pointing at his plate.

Her son obediently picked up a toast point. He leaned back in his chair, his gaze on the window, his feet swinging above the ground. It was remarkable, really—Daisy hadn't seen him this cheerful in weeks. All for the toss of a tree?

She stayed a moment to hear about his lessons, then continued on to the dining hall. The rain had cleared and left in its wake a cloudless and brilliantly blue sky. She paused at the window to look at the stunning landscape. The sun had cast a soft golden hue over the garden and lawn leading down to the lake. She could see a few people there, pulling the small rowboat, that Uncle Alfonso had purchased from a boat maker in Erbusaig, from the shore.

She found the dining room empty and Rowley clearing the sideboard. "Has everyone dined?" she asked, surprised. It was only nine o'clock.

"Yes, madam. Most of them were rummaging about for something to eat at half past seven. Shall I fill a plate?"

"No, thank you." Daisy gathered her shawl around her. "I should go and see what my guests are about."

She made her way out onto the terrace, pausing to turn her face up to the delicious warmth of the sun.

"A bonny vision you are," a man said.

Daisy lowered her head to see who'd spoken. "I'm not," she said laughingly at Mr. Somerled as he strolled across the terrace to her. "I was up far too late last night."

Mr. Somerled glanced toward the lake and the others, who were now piling into the boat.

"You didn't want to join them?" Daisy asked.

Somerled shook his head. "Too many people in a boat may sink it, aye?"

Daisy laughed.

"The weather has turned in your favor, Lady Chatwick."

"Indeed it has," she said, turning her face up to the sun once more. "It's glorious."

"I quite enjoyed our talk last evening," he said.

Their talk? She'd had so many conversations.

"You've a keen wit," he said, smiling at her.

Somerled had lovely brown eyes…but nothing

compared to Arrandale's vivid blue. "You give me too much credit, sir. My talent lies only in repeating stories I've heard."

"Nonsense. And you are to be commended on the meal. It was exquisite. It was a treat, it was, that you availed yourself of Arrandale's wine. You'll no' find that quality anywhere else in the Highlands."

That was the second time someone had referred to it as Arrandale's wine. "Did he make it?" she asked.

Somerled laughed gaily. "No, but he's brought it to the Highlands." At Daisy's blank look he said, "The laird Arrandale is a frequent visitor to the port of Calais, then. You must ask after his brandy, aye? It's exceptional."

France? She thought trade with France was forbidden, given the tensions between the two countries. Was he implying that Arrandale was a *smuggler*? No, he couldn't be. Arrandale was too…sophisticated. Too strong, too in command of himself. She had the idea that smugglers were weak, desperate men.

"Lady Chatwick…will you walk with me?" Somerled asked, startling her back to the present.

She was wary of gentlemen who invited her to walk, as there was always something of great importance they wished to say. "Shall I show you my garden?" she suggested. It was a quick walk, and she could do most of the talking. "I've brought it back from the brink of death."

They walked down the terrace steps and onto a well-worn path, headed for her garden, to the weathered wooden gate that marked the garden's entrance. She proudly opened it. "My garden," she said.

It was a bit muddy, but the garden looked fresh to Daisy's eyes. She was delighted that her sad little roses had held their ground against the rain, and the vines—all of them cut back now—seemed particularly lush.

"'Tis bonny," Mr. Somerled said as he paused to look around. He bent over one of her better rose-bushes and picked one of the open buds before Daisy could stop him. He held it out to her with a smile, and she tried not to look appalled that he'd just reduced her crop of roses by one. "A rose for a rose," he said.

Not very original, but Daisy appreciated the sentiment all the same. "Thank you." She smiled sweetly and took it from him, touching the velvet petals to the tip of her nose. Her roses were so small and lifeless that they scarcely emitted any scent.

"Have you a potting shed?" he asked, looking about.

"No," she said. "It's much too small a garden for that."

"You ought to have one." He glanced at her and said timidly, "You ought to have all that you desire."

Oh yes, and Mr. Somerled would next posit that he, of all men, was best suited to give her all that she desired. Daisy forced a smile. "I'd be rather spoiled, then, would I not?"

"May I speak plainly, then, Lady Chatwick?" Somerled asked and rubbed a leaf between his finger and thumb.

No! Go home now—go home! "Of course," she made herself say.

"I pray you will no' think me too bold...but you have been the bonniest surprise of summer. When I heard the Viscount Chatwick's widow had come to open Auchenard, I rather pictured an old woman with graying hair. What a delight to find you here, aye?"

She blushed a little and avoided his gaze by tucking the rose into her bodice.

"I should like to inquire, if I may, after your intentions."

She glanced up, not understanding. "My intentions?"

"Do you intend to stay on at Auchenard, then? Or will you soon be returning to London?"

"I've—"

"It would be my great pleasure to come to know you," he nervously interjected.

Would it really be such a great pleasure? Had he seen even the slightest thing in her that spoke to compatibility? Or did he see only a fat purse when he looked at her? "Aha...well." She cleared her throat. "That is terribly kind of you to offer—"

"I should like to be the one to introduce you to Scotland, aye? It's a bonny land—there are many stunning vistas in these Highlands."

"Yes, it seems there are," she said as her mind raced through all the things she might say to discourage him without harming his feelings. She glanced at the gate and pictured herself walking around him and out of the garden. She pictured herself walking all the way to the lake and throwing herself in, hoping the lake would carry her out to the sea.

"Many stunning vistas and…many romantic ones, as well."

Lord, it was worse than she suspected. "Mr. Somerled—"

"What's this? A garden?"

Daisy and Mr. Somerled turned at the same moment; the gate swung open with some force and through it strode Arrandale. He was dressed in buckskins and a dark coat, and his boots were muddied, as if he'd been hunting.

Arrandale glanced around the little garden, his gaze appraising. "You are clearly in need of a gardener, Lady Chatwick."

She gaped at him. "I beg your pardon, *I* am the gardener here. I would think you'd recall as such from our previous meetings."

"Was that what you were doing, then?" he asked as he looked around again. "I imagined you engaged in something else entirely." He gave her a pointed look.

Daisy's cheeks began to burn as he sauntered forward and looked at the rose she'd tucked into her bodice. Her skin burned beneath that little rose. "*Diah*, if this is a rose you have grown, I would highly recommend you attempt other endeavors, aye? Perhaps pottery."

"I beg your pardon, but I picked that flower for her," Mr. Somerled said, straightening up a bit. "You insult the lady, Arrandale."

"*You* picked it?" Arrandale said with a chuckle. "I might have left that on the vine if it were my best offering."

Daisy bit back a laugh of shock. Mr. Somerled looked truly affronted.

"Please, pay him no mind, Mr. Somerled," she begged.

"I pay him no mind at all, madam. He is of no consequence to me. I will leave you now so that Arrandale might impress you further with his wit, aye?" he snapped. He bowed, then stepped around Arrandale without another word and strode from the garden.

Arrandale watched him go, then looked at Daisy and smiled smugly.

"You're a wretched, wretched man. You needn't have teased him," she said, taking the rose from her bodice.

"What sort of man is he that he canna bear a wee bit of teasing?" he asked jovially. "Look at you, Lady Chatwick, with a gift from your admirer. You enjoy the attention, aye?"

"I do," she said breezily. "As I'm sure *you* would enjoy the attention if any was ever paid to you."

"Oh ho," he said cheerfully, "the lady doth challenge me. I've had a fair share of attention paid to me, I have. Quite a lot in recent days, I will boldly remind you. At least I've no' presented you with spindly blooms eaten by insects."

"You can't fault Mr. Somerled for the selection," she said, casting her arm around her.

"Aye, but I can fault him for being tiresome."

Daisy tried not to smile…and bowed her head so he'd not see it.

Arrandale clasped his hands and stepped around her, venturing deeper into her little garden.

"You sound rather envious, in truth," she said. "And yet I know that cannot *possibly* be true as you do not hold any great esteem for me."

"Aye, you are correct—it canna possibly be true," he said and cast a smile over his shoulder at her.

It was a pity he stood a few steps away—she couldn't kick him as she suddenly wanted to do. "Then what is it that vexes you?" she demanded, annoyed with him now.

"Oh, I'm no' vexed, madam. But I would no' like to see you set your sights on him."

"I'm not setting my sights on anyone."

"If you say so."

"Why should you not take me at my word?" she said, her vexation growing. He was maddening! "Have I been anything but unfailingly honest with you? You want to believe the nonsense that comes from the mouths of gossips and rogues."

He glanced at her again, but his smile was gone. "I know the men here. I know what they want."

Daisy bristled at the insinuation. It was one thing for her to believe it, but entirely another for him to say it aloud to her. "You can't possibly know their intentions—"

"I know the brothers Fergus and Irving Mac-Donald are shipbuilders and suffered the loss of a ship in the spring," he said, moving toward her. "I know Murray's brother lost his cattle to bovine plague, and now he canna keep his clan fed."

Daisy's eyes widened. Mr. Murray had indeed mentioned that his older brother might like to see Auchenard.

Arrandale moved closer. "And I know Somerled, aye? We attended Saint Andrews together. He's the son of an important Scotch statesman and barrister, a man whose fortune rose in defense of the king when Scotsmen raised complaints against the Crown, and whose fortunes fell with the rise of the Jacobites. Rumor has it that Somerled has significant gambling debts that his family can no longer cover."

Daisy gaped at him. Her blood was heating with rage. It was humiliating—the Highlands had sent their men running to Auchenard with the hope of catching her, the pot at the end of their rainbow.

She tossed down the flower. "I am weary of talk," she said. "Someone is always talking, always advising me what they think I am too blind to see."

"I donna mean to offend you, on my word I do no'. But I canna stand idly by while a woman as bonny as you are is pursued by gentlemen who donna honor you."

"I am well aware what they honor," she said hotly.

"Aye, I know that you are. Does Captain Spivey honor you, then?"

Daisy's heart stopped beating. "How do you know about him?"

Arrandale said nothing.

Belinda, of course. Daisy whirled away from him. "It is none of your concern. *None*."

When he didn't speak or move, she whirled back to him. His gaze bored into her. "Aye, it is no'," he agreed. "But if he does honor you... I'd no' like to see you harm him."

Her anger soared. How dare he tell her how to behave? She walked up to him, pushed his chest. "I don't need your advice, of *all* people. Perhaps I ought to give *you* some advice."

"By all means," he said, casting his arms wide.

"Don't smuggle," she snapped. She'd meant it to shock him, to put the shoe on the other foot. Arrandale's brows lifted with surprise. And then he laughed.

"Excellent advice," he said jovially. "But donna think you can intimidate me. I'm no' ashamed of it," he said and abruptly caught her face in his hand. "When the Crown's tariffs make it impossible for our clan to thrive?" He shrugged. "I will take that risk."

"Neither am I ashamed," she said angrily. "By the same token, when a husband's edict makes it impossible for me to live my life as I please, then I, too, will take some risks."

She glared at him. But then he tenderly stroked her cheek. "I understand," he said quietly, acquiescing.

"Do you?" she asked angrily. Her skin was tingling where he'd touched her.

"Aye, I do." He slipped his hand around to the nape of her neck, then bent so they were eye level. "You donna want my advice, then. But if you should ever decide you want it, you need only ask. I will always be truthful with you, on my word."

She was suddenly swimming in a pool of desire, the longing there again, pressing against her edges, threatening to erupt at the seams. What had happened to her? When had she become so lustful? When had she needed a man's pledge of honesty as desperately as she seemed to need it today? When had she begun to throw all caution to the wind in pursuit of her own pleasure?

This could not be her. As much as she wanted it to be, she had a son to think of. Daisy slowly reached up and wrapped her hand around his wrist. "I will keep my own counsel," she said evenly and pulled his hand from her neck. She knew a moment of indecision, when she thought that she might perhaps kiss him again. But his admonishment of her behavior still stung, and she dropped his hand.

Arrandale stepped back. He bowed. "As you wish," he said, strolling out of the garden with such insouciance that it was a wonder he didn't whistle as he went.

"Where are you going?" Daisy asked.

"To teach a lad how to toss a caber," he called over his shoulder. "Go see to your guests, Lady Chatwick."

"Thank you for *advising* me on how I might host my guests!" she called irritably after him.

She heard his chuckle as he went out the gate.

Mr. Somerled found Daisy again, on the shores of Lochcarron, where she was watching Mr. Murray row his wife and Miss Mackenzie about. Miss Mackenzie was having a grand time of it, shrieking with laughter every time the boat dipped to one side or the other.

Somerled handed her a parasol. "Miss Hainsworth is concerned about your complexion," he said, his eyes shining with amusement.

Daisy smiled. "I think she counts my freckles daily." She and Somerled sat on a bench that someone had installed quite some time ago—the wood was weathered and splintering, and he'd very gallantly put down a handkerchief for her.

No matter what Arrandale had said of him, Daisy rather liked Somerled's company. He was solicitous, and he didn't look at her as if he wished to devour her. He laughed at everything she said and complimented her too much. Her hair, her eyes, the smoothness of her complexion, with or without the benefit of the parasol. Her son was well mannered, and therefore she must be a wonderful mother. Auchenard had been turned quite completely around, and therefore she was a competent house manager.

Daisy could take no credit for the color of her hair or her eyes or her complexion. She was a middling mother at best and was not the house manager at all—she couldn't imagine the shambles Auchenard would be were it not for Uncle Alfonso. But she enjoyed his compliments all the same.

And he helped her forget about Arrandale for a bit.

Rowley came down to summon her. "Lord Chatwick requests you presence," he said. "He has something he should very much like to show you. He is just outside the garden walls," Rowley said and took the parasol she handed him.

Somerled and Daisy made their way up the grassy slope—now mercifully mowed by a pair of goats her uncle had purchased—and around the garden wall to the field where Daisy had twice encountered Arrandale.

The MacDonalds had joined Arrandale and Ellis, and they were tossing tree limbs that looked freshly cut. Fergus MacDonald was attempting the throw, arching his back and leaping at once to catapult it into the air. The limb soared in an arc, then bounced once before disappearing in the tall grass.

And Ellis... *Ellis*...laughed and raced across the meadow to where the limb had come down, gesturing for the men to follow. He was ebullient, and Daisy's heart soared with gratitude.

"It must seem passing strange to you, aye?" Somerled said. "'Tis a game played among Highlanders."

"A bit," she agreed.

It was Ellis's turn, and Arrandale had selected a smaller limb for him. He helped Ellis hold it correctly, and with some encouraging words Daisy could not hear, he urged Ellis to throw. Her son's throw went awry and very nearly struck Arrandale. Had it not been for his quick reflex, he might have been hit squarely in the head.

Ellis tried again. This time, the thing scarcely left his hands, but the men applauded all the same. "Did you see, Mamma?" he called out to her.

"I saw!" Daisy said. "A fine throw it was, darling!"

There was some discussion between the Mac-Donalds, and Arrandale handed the limb to Ellis again. Then came more instructions and even a re-positioning of Ellis's grip of the limb.

"Milady?"

Daisy turned away from the limb tossing as Rowley walked into the field. "Shall I serve luncheon?"

"Yes, I think—"

"Ow!" Ellis cried out.

Daisy whipped around; her son was on all fours, and then he rolled onto his hip to examine his knee. His face began to crumble, and Daisy picked up her skirts, dashing the short distance to his side. "What happened?" she asked, falling to her knees beside him.

"I fell," Ellis said, his bottom lip trembling. Daisy gingerly touched his knee through the rip in his breeches. Blood was smeared across his knee, and she could see what looked to her like a gash.

"Oh dear God," she said. "Rowley? *Rowley!* We need a bandage! Oh dear, Ellis—"

"Allow me to help you," Mr. Somerled said.

"Yes, thank you," Daisy said. "Come, darling, let's take you in and have Belinda clean it."

Ellis nodded. He didn't speak; he bit his lower lip to keep from crying.

Somerled helped Daisy to her feet as Arrandale lifted Ellis to his. "It's naugh' but a scrape, lad," he said jovially. "You'll be no worse for it, aye?"

"But it's bleeding," Ellis said, dangerously close to tears.

"Blood is the mark of a champion," Arrandale said.

Daisy put her arm around Ellis's shoulders and pulled him away from Arrandale. He limped as they walked out of the meadow.

"You mustn't fret, darling. Belinda knows precisely how to bandage knees," Daisy said, soothing him.

"Mamma...did you see how far I threw the caber?" Ellis asked. "I threw it quite far."

Daisy glanced down at Ellis. This was not the boy she knew—the boy she knew shied away from play, was fearful of other boys and of being hurt. And in the event he was hurt, he moped. But the boy limping beside her now was smiling, his thoughts obviously on something besides the gash in his knee.

"Perhaps you ought to wait for the toss until you're a wee bit bigger, aye?" Somerled suggested.

No, he should not wait—could Somerled not see how happy Ellis was? Daisy tried to erase the image of Arrandale's frown as she'd led Ellis away. As if she were doing something wrong! She supposed he would rub the boy's knee with grass and have him go again.

But she couldn't deny that she had never seen her son quite as happy as he was now, with his bloodied knee and dirt on his coat and the glory of having thrown a part of a tree.

CHAPTER TEN

THE FOLLOWING DAY, Cailean met Aulay at Balhaire and the two of them sailed to Newark on the River Clyde to sell some of their misbegotten wine and tobacco.

Hamish Gib, the "agent" they generally bargained with, was a stout Glaswegian with ears that looked like a pair of sails on either side of his head. "Have you any gin, then?" he asked as he counted the gold pieces he owed them, having made quick work of the negotiation over their cargo.

Aulay looked at Cailean. Aulay very nearly had been apprehended on his last trip to Calais, as the cove they'd used to hide from passing ships had been discovered and raided by the Royal Navy. But as Cailean had explained to Lady Chatwick, they would take their chances. They were Highlanders—they did not act from a place of fear, and even now, with the stakes mounting, a look of understanding flowed between them. Aulay said, "We can get it, aye."

"I can sell as much as you can carry," Hamish Gib said.

When they'd been paid, they walked outside the ramshackle office and onto the busy dock. They paused there, shoulder to shoulder, and looked down at their ship. "Abbot's Cove is lost to us," Aulay said in Gaelic.

"Then we'll sail to Inverness and take it over land. Rabbie can meet us with ponies."

"Our ships are known to them. Perhaps we ought to let the route cool for a time." He glanced at his brother. "I've found a man willing to trade from Bergen."

"Norway?" Cailean asked. The Norwegians were notoriously proprietary with their trade.

"Lumber and salt," Aulay said. "Glasgow is building at such a pace we could make a nice profit. In the meantime, the English think they've won."

It was a good idea, Cailean agreed. It was at least worth going to Bergen to have a look.

The brothers carried on—there were things they needed to transport back to Balhaire, such as wool, and furnishings for Arrandale. Cailean was thankful that he had something to occupy his hands and his mind. Anything to take his thoughts from the lady of Auchenard.

If his brother noticed his distraction, he didn't say so, but Cailean felt almost as if he had an ague, in spite of being as fit as any man. He knew what ailed him, because he'd felt this way once before in his life—it was his bloody rotten luck to have been bedeviled by his neighbor. Only this time, the bedevilment by a woman didn't fill him with anxiety and restless thoughts. He was too old for the un-

checked desires of a young man. This time, the bedevilment merely haunted him.

He couldn't keep the barmy woman from appearing in his thoughts. Images of her, with that
fiendish little sparkle in her eye, or a memory, such
as the creaminess of her skin, or the way she felt
against him when he'd kissed her, would creep up
on him at the most inopportune time. He kept hearing her laugh, particularly in crowds, and once he'd
even turned about, certain she'd somehow found him
in Glasgow.

Or course she hadn't.

That laugh and those green eyes were for Spivey,
however, and that knowledge raged in Cailean's
heart. It was entirely irrational—it was not as if he'd
lost her to Spivey. And he didn't *know* Spivey. What
he knew was that it was likely Spivey's desire was
to see Cailean and Aulay in a dungeon somewhere,
and probably hanged, if rumors of what happened to
smugglers was true. But for all Cailean knew, Spivey
could very well be a decent man.

And still, that did not ease him. He was quite
cross with himself for dwelling on it. Disgusted,
really—this was not the sort of man he was. He did
not occupy his thoughts in this manner. But God
help him if he could quit it.

They'd been gone ten days or so when Cailean
collected Fabienne at Balhaire, and with Rabbie's
help, drove two wagons of furnishings to Arrandale, which they stored in one of the finished rooms.
Cailean was bone weary and ravenous, and he'd

come home to an empty larder. When he'd seen Rabbie off, Cailean picked up his fishing tackle, whistled for Fabienne and walked down to the loch to catch his supper.

The air was thick and heavy that afternoon, and a bank of clouds had formed over the hills. Cailean guessed he had an hour, maybe less, before rain fell.

He was not having any luck. He kept moving along the shoreline, casting his line again and again, hoping for a nibble, and receiving nothing for his trouble.

The first distant rumble of thunder frightened Fabienne, and she darted away, bound, in all probability, for the dark corner of the kitchen where she generally waited out storms. *Damn fish*—would none of them be attracted by his lure? Cailean kept moving, kept casting, his focus on the water, on any sign of movement beneath the surface. He was startled by the sound of voices and glanced to his right. A boat was coming around a tree-lined bend in the loch's shore. There were two people on board, one of them a woman holding a parasol. He groaned—there was only one person that could be.

He watched as the boat glided toward him. The man rowing the boat had his back to the shore, rowing blind like a fool. Who rowed her about like a queen? She was lounging on pillows, he noticed, the parasol dipping with the occasional breeze.

As his boat glided closer to shore, he saw it was Somerled who rowed her about. *Diah*, the man must have debts up to his ears. There was something else—Somerled was wearing a wig. A *wig*.

"Lord Arrandale!" Lady Chatwick called out to him, waving as if he hadn't seen her.

The small rowboat was moving too fast, Cailean realized. "Have a care, man! You're headed for—"

The boat slammed into a rock outcropping. Somerled must have realized it a moment too late, for he leaped to his feet and tried to stop their collision with an oar to the rock. It snapped cleanly in two, and Somerled toppled out of the boat and into shallow water. Lady Chatwick shrieked. She dropped her parasol and grabbed onto both sides of the boat, somehow managing to keep from tipping out herself.

Somerled gained his feet, the water being only thigh deep where he stood. Lady Chatwick took one look at him and laughed quite gaily.

Somerled did not.

Cailean moved to pull the boat onto shore with Lady Chatwick in it. "Oh dear, the oar has broken," Lady Chatwick said as he helped her out of the boat. "Will one suffice?"

"You have none," Cailean said as he helped her onto higher ground, then pointed to the loch, where the second oar was floating serenely with the current, on its way to the sea if it was not caught by the shore.

"We'll have to carry it," Somerled said stiffly as he splashed out of the loch. He avoided Cailean's gaze, his cheeks flushed with the shame.

"What good fortune that we would find Arrandale here to help us," Lady Chatwick said and smiled up at Cailean. "It's a great surprise," she said sunnily. "I thought perhaps you'd fallen off a hill or had been eaten by wolves for we haven't seen you at Auchenard in an age."

"I've no business at Auchenard," he reminded her.

"No one has *business* at Auchenard," she said, "and yet Mr. Irving MacDonald and Mr. Somerled have been kind enough to call." She glanced at Somerled, who returned a tight smile.

"Then you've been well occupied and didna need my call at all, aye?"

"Oh, I have been *very* well occupied," she said pertly, her gaze narrowing slightly. She turned away from him. "We were just rowing in," she said. "Mr. Somerled says it will rain. Will you come and join us for tea?"

"No."

"No?" she echoed over her shoulder, clearly surprised someone might possibly refuse her invitation.

"I need to fish."

"But Mr. Somerled can't carry the boat on his own. And we've plenty of fish!" she exclaimed. "My uncle is quite obsessed with it, and every morning he returns from the lake with a string of them."

Did her smile have a hint of challenge in it?

"Perhaps the laird has other things he must attend to, aye?" Somerled suggested.

Well, then. Cailean slowly turned his head to Somerled, who stood soaked from the crotch down. "No, I've naugh' to attend."

"Wonderful!" Lady Chatwick said happily. "Shall we, gentlemen?"

Somerled clenched his jaw and turned around. "I'll take this end," he said, gesturing to the boat.

They hoisted the small rowboat above their heads and walked around the bend and through the trees the short distance to Auchenard. They stored the boat in the small inlet where it was kept. By the time they'd secured it, Mr. Kimberly was striding down to the water's edge.

"Uncle, look who has come!" Lady Chatwick said brightly as she dabbed at her chest with a handkerchief. "We had a bit of an accident. The oars were lost."

"The oars were lost!" her uncle echoed loudly.

Another rumble of thunder sounded closer, and a gust of wind lifted the hem of Lady Chatwick's gown.

"Oh, and Lord Arrandale wasn't able to fish," she said, ignoring the worsening sky. "Surely we've enough to share with our neighbor?"

"I salted some very fine trout this morning," her uncle said proudly. "Come up, then. The sky looks as if it will open at any moment."

Lady Chatwick looped her arm through her uncle's and began to walk up the lawn to the lodge, chattering about the boat, the loch, the crash and broken oar as if she'd read the tale in a novel, while the two men trailed behind.

Somerled stalked along behind her like a sullen lad. Cailean mentally kicked himself for having let his pride get the best of him, but he was enjoying Somerled's pique so much that he carried on, bringing up the rear.

Rowley met them on the terrace with Lord Chatwick, who stood shyly with his hands behind his back. Somerled ignored the lad altogether, but Cailean smiled down at him, put his hand on his shoulder. "Have you practiced your caber toss, lad?"

Lord Chatwick shook his head. "I've no one to help me." He glanced warily at Somerled, who was speaking to Mr. Kimberly, almost certainly explaining how it was not his fault the oars were lost.

"Mr. Somerled had an unexpected swim," Cailean muttered, and Lord Chatwick smiled.

Miss Hainsworth emerged from the lodge then, hanging out the door as if afraid to step onto the terrace. "Come in, all of you! It will storm at any moment and you'll all catch your death!"

They wouldn't catch their death, for heaven's sake. One did not live in the Highlands of Scotland and escape rain or water. Nevertheless, Cailean followed the others, and as he closed the door behind him, thunder cracked so loudly over their heads that it shook the rafters of the lodge.

Mr. Kimberly stoked the fire in the great room's hearth. A brilliant flare of firelight was followed by another deafening crack of thunder, and Lord Chatwick grabbed his mother's hand.

"*That* was very close," Miss Hainsworth said. "How fortunate we are to have these hills surrounding us, as that would have surely struck the lodge. Lightning is one of the most common causes of fires, you know."

Cailean tried to recall even one home lost to fire caused by lightning.

"Bring whisky, Rowley," Kimberly said as he settled onto the settee. "That will settle the nerves."

As they waited for the butler to pour, the rain began to fall. As he passed the drams of whisky around the room, the storm began to rage in earnest; winds whipped the tops of the trees and the rain came down in a deluge, torrents of it running down the windows. "We must have something to pass the time," Lady Chatwick said nervously.

"It willna last long," Cailean said. "Storms that crop up in the late summer are ferocious, but almost always short-lived. It will pass quickly enough."

"She's right," Somerled agreed with Lady Chatwick. Unsurprisingly. Predictably. *Pathetically.* "Shall I read, then?"

"Read?" Lady Chatwick sounded surprised by his suggestion. No doubt she had in mind something far more diabolical, something that would pit her two callers against each other. "We've very few books—"

"Aye, but you have a Bible," he said, pointing to a desk and the two books there.

She blinked, looking almost as if she'd never noticed it before. She gave Cailean a quick, sidelong glance, and then said with an enthusiasm he knew very well she did not feel, "*Thank* you, Mr. Somerled. We will all be made the better for it. Won't we, Arrandale?"

He gave her a withering look. She smiled pertly.

Somerled picked up the Bible. He turned several pages, found something that he deemed suitable and began to read. "From Exodus, nine two four. 'So there was hail, and fire flashing continually in the midst of the hail, very severe, such as had no' been in all the land of Egypt since it became a nation...'"

Cailean listened politely for a few minutes—he was not an utter heathen—but his mind began to wander, and he mentally listed the things that needed to be done at Arrandale when he was not frowning at Lady Chatwick, who kept flashing tiny, pert little smiles at him. He watched Rowley and Mr. Kimberly slip from the room. He watched Lord Chatwick doze off, his head propped on his mother's shoulder. He watched the lad's mother's lids grow heavy, too, because she *was* an utter heathen, and this sermon, or whatever it was Somerled was attempting to do to impress her, served her right for being so coy.

The only one who seemed to be enthralled with Somerled's droning was Miss Hainsworth, who sat on the edge of her seat, rapt with attention, as if she had never heard the tale of the Israelites' exodus from Egypt.

Cailean didn't know how long Somerled read, but his droning did the trick—it got them through the worst of the storm. Sun began to break through the clouds just as the Israelites reached Mount Sinai—or somewhere in the desert, as Cailean had lost track—and he said quickly, before Somerled could draw a breath, "The storm is done, then," and nodded at the window.

"Hmm?" Lady Chatwick said, rousing from a nap. "Oh! Look, Ellis," she said, and shook her son awake. "The storm has passed. Let's have a look— there might be a rainbow." She hopped up and led him to the window, thereby signaling the end of the Sermon on the Mount.

Mr. Somerled seemed slightly wounded that she offered no commendation for his reading. He put the Bible aside.

Miss Hainsworth was happy to offer it. "Thank you, Mr. Somerled," she said gravely. "I was comforted by your reading during that dreadful storm."

"Oh, look! It's blue sky," Lady Chatwick said. "How fortunate, Mr. Somerled," she said and turned about. "You've such a long ride home, do you not? But with the sun now, you should reach your home by nightfall. Won't you?"

Somerled looked confused. "Ah...aye," he said uncertainly. The man didn't know which way to turn because he was a poor little mouse and Lady Chatwick was a cat. A cat that had just chased the mouse away.

"Oh, good, I'm so relieved! I'd not like to think of you riding in a storm. Belinda, dearest, will you take Ellis and inform Mr. Green that Mr. Somerled's horse should be brought round?"

Of course Cailean followed them out onto the drive. Of course he took pleasure in watching Somerled shuffle about, clearly wanting a private moment with Lady Chatwick, which Cailean refused to grant him.

Somerled began to realize he was defeated. He mounted his horse. "Good day, Mr. Somerled!" Lady Chatwick said brightly.

"Good day," he returned curtly and spurred his horse on.

Cailean and Lady Chatwick stood side by side and watched him ride away. "Well," she said. "Thank goodness that is done."

"Aye. *Latha math*, Lady Chatwick."

"What?" she exclaimed, spinning around to him. "You're leaving?"

"Aye. I've carried your boat. I've waited out the storm, and I've heard enough scriptures for the day."

"But there's something I want to show you!"

Behind her, Mr. Kimberly wandered out onto the drive. "What's this?" he asked.

"Lord Arrandale means to take his leave, but I want to show him our new potting shed."

"Don't waste the man's time," Mr. Kimberly said gruffly. "It's not worth the attention. The man has no talent for it."

A potting shed? What man?

"It was very kind of Mr. Somerled to have come all this way to build it. *That's* a good neighbor for you, for I hadn't realized how desperately I needed it until he appeared to build it."

"You did realize it, Daisy. I told you," Mr. Kimberly pointed out.

Daisy? Her name was *Daisy?* She was named for a sunflower? *Diah*, but the English were barmy.

"Well, yes, you did, Uncle. But Mr. Somerled arrived with the materials."

Cailean's head was telling him to walk on, but he couldn't help himself. "He built you a potting shed?"

"He did!" she said, as gleefully as if Somerled had brought her a pony. "Come and see."

"Go on, then. I've seen that upright coffin too many times as it is," Mr. Kimberly said, and, with a flick of his wrist, he retreated into the lodge.

Lady Chatwick—*Daisy*, the sunflower—clasped her hands behind her back and rose up on her toes. "Well?" she said, sinking down again.

Cailean groaned. "Aye, go on, then—make haste, make haste," he said, gesturing for her to walk.

They rounded the corner of the lodge, where Cailean nearly collided with a barrel.

"I forgot it was here," she said. "Therein lies my uncle's fish, all properly salted and bundled," she said, gesturing to it. "We've no room to store it in the larder, and he has not yet decided where he will keep his treasure."

They carried on, turning another corner, when Lady Chatwick suddenly stopped and swept her arm grandly. "Here it is!"

There it stood, a rough-hewn shed that, as Mr. Kimberly had said, looked only slightly larger than a coffin. "It's a bloody box," Cailean said. He stalked forward, threw open the door and stepped inside. Lady Chatwick stepped in behind him and closed the door. Somerled had cut an opening in the door and in one wall, presumably to use as windows. "It's ridiculously small," Cailean muttered, annoyed with Somerled.

"Mr. Somerled said it's cozy," she said, smiling up at him, always smiling, as if she knew that spark in her eye made him uncomfortably, acutely, dangerously aware of her.

"All right, I've seen it, aye?" he said. "What else have your many admirers given you?"

"Only this," she said, glancing around. "Mr. MacDonald showed me a drawing of a ship he'd like to build. He's very talented."

"A ship he wants you to fund," Cailean said. "*Och*, it's worse than I thought. You donna seem to know a thing about fending off fortune hunters."

"Of course I do!" She laughed. "I've been surrounded by them for nearly three years. You must think me a silly little fool, Lord Arrandale."

"I'm no' a lord. I'm a laird. Laird of Arrandale. And I'm no' a dandy in some London drawing room that you must address by his title, aye? I'm Cailean."

"Yes, but I—"

"If we are to be friends, you may use my given name. It is Cailean. Say it."

"Cailean," she said obediently. "Does this mean we are to be proper friends? I rather thought you were quite firmly against it." She lifted her chin.

"I'm quite firmly against a courtship. And I donna offer friendship lightly, but you are clearly in need of it. *Tiugainn*, open the door to the box you charmed Somerled into constructing for you, aye?"

"*I* didn't charm him—he quite insisted," Daisy said, making not the slightest move to open the door. "I still maintain you are jealous of him."

"That is preposterous," he said gruffly.

"You *are*," she said, her hands finding her waist. "I clearly saw the envy in your expression today."

He brushed dirt from the sleeve of his coat with a vengeance. "Are you barmy? I didna look at him at all, aye? I scarcely kept my eyes open during his sermon."

"You must at least admit he has a fine voice," she said. Toying with him, another mouse. He knew what she was doing, and it rankled that he was powerless to walk away from it. "And then you accuse him of fortune hunting."

"Aye, that he is," Cailean said flatly. "You're a bloody fool if you donna see it."

Her smile only deepened. "Perhaps *you* are the one who seeks my fortune and you mean to have it by maligning others."

"Look at me, *leannan*," he said, gesturing to himself. "Do I seem to you a man in need of a widow's fortune?"

"I'm looking," she said, her voice suddenly very seductive—or did it just seem so to him? Her gaze casually slid down the length of him, then just as casually came up again, taking in his buckskins. His coat. His neckcloth, which he'd untied and had allowed the ends to hang down his chest. "No," she said at last. "But the lust for power and fortune is not always evident in one's countenance." She quirked a brow.

Ah this woman, this barmy woman. How had she taken hold of his senses as easily as she had? One corner of his mouth tipped up, and he slowly shook his head. "You're a wee *diabhal*, aye? You seduce with your eyes, with your words…and your bloody bonny smile," he said, his gaze drifting to her mouth. "But are you fully prepared for the consequences of your games?"

He thought she would laugh in that sultry way she had. But her expression turned cool. "Games?" she repeated, sounding offended. "Men are drawn to my fortune. What am I to do with that attention? Swoon?" She snorted and folded her arms. "You want to advise me? Then please, sir, shower me with your sage advice," she said irritably. "Tell me what I am to do with the vultures that surround me. Tell me how to find a man to marry when I can't trust anyone, because I must choose someone."

Cailean was startled by her frankness. "So it's true, then? The rumors?" he ventured. "Your husband's last testament has decreed—"

"Ah so you've heard all of my humiliating secrets," she said and pressed a hand to her stomacher. "Of course it's true. Do you think that sort of gossip is completely fabricated? If you want to know the truth about me, you shall have it. My dear late husband left my fate in the hands of Bishop Craig. He feared I would squander my son's inheritance if left without a firm hand to guide me, and therefore made allowances that I would lose all of my son's inheritance if I did not follow the bishop's celestial advice and remarry in three years' time."

Cailean didn't speak right away—he was too taken aback.

"And now, because more than two years have passed, and I have been quite unable to separate the fortune hunters, as you call them, from the gentlemen who might truly esteem me, Bishop Craig is increasingly determined to settle a match on me, for clearly I cannot be trusted to choose one myself!" she said bitterly. "Have you any idea how difficult it is to try to discover some fond feelings for someone when you've only just buried your husband? Or when you know what everyone else in all of London knows— that every gentleman is in want of a fortune?"

She twisted away from him and rubbed her nape.

Cailean felt how this pained her in his own heart. "Did you love your husband?" he asked with quiet curiosity.

"Did I *love* him?" she repeated angrily, then sighed. "I came to care for him," she admitted. "Before he took ill, he was a good man, a good father." She paused, running her fingers over the rough wood of the single shelf in the shed. "But I never loved him the way I loved Robert Spivey," she said in a voice only scarcely above a whisper and glanced at him sheepishly. "Will you think even less of me if I tell you I was in love with another man before I married my husband? Robert Spivey was my one and only true love."

That admission struck Cailean like a soft blow. He didn't think less of her—he knew that women born into her situation had little say in who they would marry. His own mother had been a political pawn in her marriage to his father. What struck him was that her feelings for Spivey were so...*deep*. "Why did you no' marry him, then?"

She shrugged. "He wasn't suitable."

Those words twisted in him, seeping into a wound that had been made nearly fifteen years ago.

"Does that astonish you? My father was a baron, and, therefore, I was destined to marry a man of standing, and certainly not a parish vicar's son. I understood my duty, but when I was seventeen, a proper match seemed desperately far away, and Robert was so very handsome," she said, looking down at her hands. "I could have used a bit of your advice then, for I was quite naive. And so...blind," she added, frowning.

"And he loved you?"

"Oh yes," she said. "He loved me deeply. In my memory, our love was beyond reason."

"What happened?" he asked, not fully understanding. Perhaps he was naive, too.

"Oh, utter disaster, naturally. I rather thought I might convince my father that a match with Rob would be ideal...but before I could do so, my father announced to me that he'd agreed to a match with Lord Chatwick, and all there was left to do was for me to consent. The match I thought so far away was upon me."

"Aye. What did you do?"

"What did I do? I married Lord Chatwick."

"But—"

"Rob understood, you know. He said that perhaps we'd reached too far into our dreams. He understood," she repeated, her gaze still on her hand as she stretched her fingers apart. "He was a gentleman, and he let me go as he ought to have done."

She dropped her hand and looked up at him, and for the first time, Cailean saw uncertainty in her eyes. Spivey might have been a gentleman, but what sort of man was he? "I donna understand a man who doesna have the brass to fight for what he wants, aye? For who he *loves*. No' a word of protest from him?"

Daisy colored.

"Your cousin said you were to marry him," he said flatly.

To that, she laughed. "I hope to. He wrote me recently. He had heard of my husband's death and hoped to reunite. That's why I came to Scotland. Not to find a husband, but to give Rob time to reach London before the bishop is pounding on my door."

Cailean stared at her, trying to imagine this tale of two young lovers reunited after all these years. Something about it seemed a wee bit off.

"Please don't think ill of me," she begged him. "Haven't you ever been in love?"

"Aye, of course I have."

Her countenance suddenly changed. "You *have*?

Just as I was beginning to believe you a heartless scoundrel. Who was she?"

"A *Sassenach*, aye? Like you."

"Like me?" She beamed, pleased with that. "Why didn't you offer for her?"

"I did," he said. "I courted her in earnest for two summers, but when I made my offer, she refused me."

He said it so dispassionately that Daisy giggled. Cailean didn't smile. "Oh," she said quietly. "I beg your pardon. I thought you... I'm sorry, Cailean."

"No," he said brusquely. There was nothing more demeaning to him than her pity. "It wasna meant to be."

She reached for his hand and squeezed it affectionately. "And there has been no one else," she said. "Is that why you've never married? You love her still?"

Cailean chuckled and interlaced his fingers with hers. "No, I donna love her. *Och*, lass, there have been many others. I'm a man, no' a priest. Never mind me—if you mean to marry this Spivey, why then did you kiss me?"

"Because my husband was ill for many years." She toyed with the end of his neckcloth. "And neither am I a priest." She smiled ruefully.

He understood her completely, and his skin began to tingle with anticipation. "You are no'," he agreed, his hand finding her waist.

"I want... I *need* diversion. Do you understand?"

Her words shot through him, lighting him up, setting him on fire. The lady needed him, and he was helpless to deny her. He moved forward, pushing her back against the wall. "I understand. What sort of diversion?" he asked, cupping the back of her head, then sliding his hand to her nape. "Attention? A kiss in the larder?" He moved his hand to her collarbone. "Tell me what you need."

"I've already had a kiss in the larder. And *my* name is Daisy," she said.

"Daisy," he muttered. "Aye, it suits you to be named for a silly, sunny little flower," he said, and touched his nose to her temple.

"Do you mean to divert me?" she asked, lifting her face to his.

"That would depend," he muttered and moved his hand to the swell of her breast, his fingers dipping into her décolletage.

She leaned back and pressed her hand lightly against his chest. "On what?"

"On how you behave."

Her smile of pleasure deepened into the dimples, and Cailean felt his corruption was complete. He would give whatever this woman wanted from him. He dipped down to kiss her.

She slid her hand up his chest and around his neck, pulled him into her body, and kissed him back, arousing him instantly. Cailean squeezed her hip, then gathered her gown in his hand, reaching for the hem. When he touched her bare leg, Daisy gasped as if touched by ice and bit his lower lip. "Am I behaving?" she asked breathlessly.

Cailean responded by silencing her with another kiss as he slid his hand up her leg. Her skin was lightning to him, singeing every nerve.

She pressed against him. "Scoundrel," she whispered, and bent her neck so that he might kiss it.

"Diabhal," he murmured against her skin.

Her breathing shortened; he could feel her body warm, as if she was melting into him. He himself was hot with lust. He moved his hand again, now to the inside of her thigh, soft and smooth, and a shudder of ardor snaked through him.

"A Diah, resist me, Daisy," he said into her hair. "Think of your future and *resist* me."

"I won't. I refuse," she said, and drew the lobe of his ear between her teeth. It was a small thing, but it pushed Cailean over the edge. He slipped his fingers in between her legs.

She gasped, her body trembling at his touch. Cailean tried to hold himself above the desperate, urgent desire that was ballooning in him, but it was no use. He craved her body, craved the release he would give her, and when she sank against him on a sigh, he craved the release he wanted from her.

He slipped his fingers deeper in between the folds of her body as he caught her face with his hand so that he could look in her eyes, to assure himself he hadn't gone too far, hadn't taken this liberty without her consent. There was a prurient shine in her eye, unfocused with passion, a shine of sheer longing. He pushed the skirt of her gown up higher. He could detect the scent of her desire, and like an animal, his mouth watered.

"You don't esteem me," she reminded him. "You shouldn't look at me as if you do." She sank her fingers into his hair.

"I donna esteem you. No' in the least," he agreed.

Her laugh was throaty and hoarse; she pushed on his shoulders, pushing him down. "No, I can see that you don't," she said as he went down on one knee at her urging.

She couldn't have possibly made him more ravenous than he was at that moment. It was incredibly stimulating to the man in him for a lady to know what she wanted and boldly ask it of him. He pushed her gown with both hands above her hips, and put his mouth on her sex.

Daisy gasped again. He slid his tongue into the folds of her sex, and she grabbed his head between her hands, falling over him, moaning loudly as he laved her.

"*Uist*, lass," he said. "You donna want help to come running, aye?"

"No, no," she whispered. But she whimpered as he moved his tongue on her. She clutched at his head, draped one leg over his shoulder, and Cailean's senses filled with the prurient sensation of her body. He had her at his leisure, deliberately and torturously slow, giving her what she desired. Every slight spasm of her body shot into him like white light, feeding the fire raging in him. His heart, beating wildly, was almost deafening in his ears, and he was torn between the desire to abandon all pretense and take her completely and his real fear of having them discovered—all of it mixing into a volatile swell of pleasure in him when she began to buck against him, desperate to reach her end. He closed his lips around her bud and drew it between his teeth, and Daisy was lost in a spasm of ecstasy, sobbing with her release, and stoking the fire in him to a white-hot pyre.

He was throbbing, aching with his own need now. But he was satisfied in the way of a man who'd given a woman what she had craved from him. He took her arms and lifted her off him to stand. He was grinning like a victorious warrior as he removed a handkerchief from his pocket and dabbed at his mouth. He bent over her, kissing her cheek. "Who is the good neighbor now, *leannan*?"

She smiled at him as she brushed the back of her hand against his cheek. "You are undoubtedly the most cocksure man I've ever met."

He laughed, and she slid her arms around his neck and rose up on her toes to kiss him. "Do you esteem me now?" she asked.

"No' for as much as a moment," he said and kissed her lips softly before pulling her arms free of his neck. "Now I must go, aye?" He didn't want to go. He wanted to remain in this ridiculous shed with her all afternoon. But Cailean also knew that if he stayed, if he indulged in the bond they had created, it would be difficult to break free. He tenderly stroked her cheek, then opened the door of the shed. *"Feasgar math,"* he said and stepped outside.

He walked around the back of the house and started down the grassy lawn to the loch.

He still had to catch his supper.

But he heard Daisy call him, and he paused, glancing back. She was running after him, in her hands a clothbound bundle. "The fish!" she said breathlessly when she caught up to him. "Please, you must take some with you. We have more than we can possibly eat." She shoved the bundle at him, forcing Cailean to catch it with one hand.

"Thank you," he said uncertainly.

"Will you come to dine tomorrow?"

He eyed her. "Daisy, I—"

"You are our neighbor," she said. "Have you been without good neighbors for so long? We have too much fish and need all the help we can summon to eat it. Please say you'll come."

He glanced at the bundle in his hand.

"Please?" she asked and touched his arm.

With his body still thrumming with desire, Cailean was incapable of refusing. "All right," he said. "But only this once. I donna care for so much fish."

"Of *course* it's just once," she said and laughed. She let go of his arm, turned and dashed across the terrace, pausing at the corner of the house to look back at him. She raised her hand and waved, then disappeared around the corner.

Cailean looked down at the bundle. Somewhere he heard a door close. He felt another door quite deep inside him open a wee bit.

CHAPTER ELEVEN

Blue skies and a warm breeze met us this morning after yesterday's dreadful storm. Though it passed quickly as Arrandale said it would, the storm laid down some of my herb seedlings. Uncle said that our next caretaker will need to do without bog myrtle through the winter, but that it might be bought at Balhaire.

B now holds Mr. S in great esteem, and has proclaimed him a right good Christian man. I do wonder if we shall see Mr. S again given the apparent disappointment with which he rode away. At the very least, it would seem I discovered an unconventional use for his little potting shed.

Arrandale's hands are large and rough with use, but they are quite strong, which he demonstrated without conceit when he lifted the boat from the lake. Mr. S's hands, by contrast, are fine and slender, and seem better suited for the harp.

DAISY TOOK A late luncheon with Belinda, who nattered on about her apparently rampant fear that with all the rain they'd had, the roads would be utterly impassable when it came time to return to London.

Belinda managed to mention their departure almost every day, as if it were imminent. Daisy hadn't thought of leaving quite as seriously as she ought to have done. She'd grown into Auchenard, at least for the time being. She wasn't ready to go back to London yet. There was still time.

As Belinda continued on with her studied lecture on the state of country roads in general, Rowley appeared in the dining room with a silver tray, the sort that generally held calling cards. He bowed at Daisy's side.

"What's this?" she asked, looking at a bundle of folded parchments.

"It is the post, milady. A messenger has reached us from London."

Daisy glanced at the bundle of letters. "The post? Here? But how?"

"I can't rightly say, milady. I know only that he came up the lake from Erbusaig."

She took the bundle of letters and removed the twine. One, she was delighted to see, was from her good friend Lady Beckinsal, who had promised to keep her informed of events in London, and was the only person with whom Daisy had left instructions on how to reach her. Daisy decided to leave that missive for later, when she was alone and could laugh freely.

The second was from her estate agent. She read it aloud to Belinda. "The roof at Chatwick Hall has suffered some damage. The repairs are expected to be fifty pounds." Daisy looked up. "Fifty pounds! Did they lose the roof altogether?"

"Roofs are almost always the first thing to fall in disrepair," Belinda said as she spread jam over a toast point. "Once the roof begins to decay, the rest of the house will likely follow." She glanced up from her toast. "You best ensure you set aside a bit for more repairs."

The last letter was addressed simply to Lady Chatwick, Auchenard, Scotland. But the familiar handwriting made Daisy's heart skip.

"Who is it from?" Belinda asked.

"Rob," Daisy said. "How does he know where to find me?" she asked as she broke the seal of the letter.

"What does he say?" Belinda asked excitedly.

Daisy unfolded the letter.

My dearest Lady Chatwick,
I hope this letter finds you and your son in
good health. I pray this letter reaches you so
that you might know I have arrived in London.
Upon my arrival I went directly to your house
but discovered, to my great consternation, that
you had recently gone. Your staff, possessing a
great sense of loyalty, refused to tell me, who to
them presented a perfect stranger, where you
had gone. One fellow relieved my suffering and
said that I might find your direction with Lady
Beckinsal. I was certain she'd not receive me,
but as my name was not unfamiliar to her, the

dear lady did take me into her salon. She did indeed take pity on me as she told me where you'd gone. She did acknowledge that you had received my earlier letter, but would not say more than that. However, she kindly offered to see that a letter was dispatched to you now.

Daisy, if I may speak very plainly so that my intentions are clear, I have come to present myself to you. Perhaps I presume too much in saying that, but I have resigned my commission from the navy in the hope that I can resume our friendship. It's been too long since I last laid eyes on you, and I pray that you still feel as you once did for me. Please know that my feelings are unchanged by all these years. I have held you in the highest regard in my thoughts and my heart since we were forced to part, and now I have given up all that I am for you. I can only hope that fate has led us to the place where we may realize the dreams we once had, together. My greatest fear is that your feelings have changed, and as you have left London after receiving my last letter, I fear that perhaps they have.

"What does he say?" Belinda insisted. She was leaning eagerly forward, as if she were trying to read Robert's words through the back of the parchment.

Daisy slowly lifted her gaze. "He's in London," she said.

"In London!" Belinda repeated. "His commission has ended so soon?"

Daisy nodded. "And he still feels the same as he did all those years ago. And he doesn't understand why I left."

"Oh no!" Belinda said.

Daisy stood abruptly. "I shall write him straightaway and put his mind at ease. I'll explain why I came, that I didn't know how to reach him, or how long it would be before he arrived in London, and how the bloody clock followed me here."

"Shouldn't we just go home?" Belinda asked. "A letter might take too long."

"It would take us at least as long," Daisy said. "But yes…we ought to go home."

Belinda gasped. Such a look of relief washed over her face that Daisy's gut soured. What was wrong with her that her cousin felt the weight of time passing so much more urgently than Daisy did?

"If you will excuse me now, darling, I shall go and think on my reply," she said and swept out of the room before Belinda could say anything more to add to Daisy's sudden burden of guilt.

She walked almost blindly from the dining room to the great room and the writing desk there. But instead of seating herself at the desk, she went to the windows and stared out at the world, at her private little world, her belly churning with many conflicting emotions. A sense of urgency first and foremost— she couldn't lose Rob. She couldn't. It was *Rob*. She had loved him so completely and without qualification, and was there a better prospect? But yesterday...yesterday there had been a moment when she'd felt something so strongly for someone else that she couldn't quite dismiss it.

"Daisy?"

She whirled around from the window; she hadn't heard Uncle Alfonso come into the room. He was without a coat, and his shirtsleeves were rolled up to his elbows. "Is something wrong?" he asked as he walked across the room to join her at the window.

"No, nothing. Actually, something is right," she said, trying to make herself smile. "I've received a letter from Captain Spivey."

"Did you!" he said, clearly surprised. "And what did the good captain write?"

"He's in London. And he feels the same for me as he did eleven years ago. He has come to make his case, and he is worried of my affection since he found me gone."

Uncle Alfonso studied her face a moment, his expression inscrutable. "What do you want to do?"

"I suppose we should plan to return," she said without equivocation. Of course they would. Anything less would be to risk her son's future. She managed a smile. "My prayers have been answered, have they not?"

Uncle Alfonso frowned slightly. He slipped his finger under her chin. "If this is the answer to your prayers, then why do you look so forlorn?"

She wasn't forlorn, really. She was...indifferent. She should have felt elated by this letter. That Rob went to such lengths to get word to her. That he confessed his feelings for her, which had been her most ardent hope from the moment she heard of him. "I'm not forlorn—I'm happy," she said. "But I... I just finished the garden." No, no, it wasn't the garden that made her hesitate. It was her imprudent infatuation with Cailean and her very real desire to feel his rough hands on her skin again.

Uncle Alfonso put his arm around her shoulders and hugged her to his side. "We'll build another garden, darling," he assured her.

"But it won't be the same, Uncle. Someone else will do the digging. Someone else will determine what to cut and what to plant and where to plant, and I shall be as useful as a statue."

Her uncle squeezed her shoulders. "Darling... have you perhaps developed an affection for someone other than the captain?"

Daisy's breath caught in her throat. She could feel her shame flood her cheeks. She *knew* it—when she'd returned to the lodge yesterday, no one had seemed to notice a thing about her, but she *knew* it must have been quite evident what she'd done.

"I know Mr. Somerled has called a few times—"

"Somerled!" Daisy suddenly laughed with great relief. "Oh no, Uncle. *No.* You misunderstand me. I've enjoyed my freedom. I suppose my lack of enthusiasm is because I realize it is at an end."

"But Captain Spivey is what you've hoped for," he said. "He will be good to you."

"He will. I know he will," she said. "I do want to marry him."

Uncle Alfonso smiled. "The bishop cannot settle a better match on you."

Daisy snorted. "I'm sure he'll try."

"He does seem partial to his choices," her uncle agreed. He dropped his arm and leaned forward, looking at something out the window. "I'll begin to make the arrangements for our departure."

Daisy followed his gaze. "Is that Ellis?" she asked, squinting at two figures on the shore.

"It is," her uncle said. "Arrandale brought the escaped oar around today. He asked for Ellis."

Daisy watched as Cailean's dog plunged into the lake, then turned around, paddling back to shore. "I should thank him," she said and pulled her wrap closer around her.

She left her uncle and made her way down to the shore to Cailean and her son. As she neared them, she heard Ellis's laughter. She drew up, watching.

They were throwing rocks, she realized, skipping them on the lake's surface. Ellis was throwing as hard as his young arm would allow...something Daisy had never seen him do. She watched how Arrandale stepped behind him and held his arm, showing him how to throw the rock so that it would skip across the lake's surface.

Daisy and her sister, Marybeth, used to do that, too, when they'd played behind their grandmother's dowager house. Marybeth had died of scarlet fever many years ago, and the sudden memory of her made Daisy feel quite nostalgic. She dipped down and searched the sand beneath her feet for a suitable rock. When she'd found one, she joined Ellis and Cailean.

She reached them just as Arrandale threw a rock that skipped five times on the lake's surface before it sank. As Ellis admired the toss, Cailean noticed Daisy. His gaze seemed to soften, the blue eyes spilling into her. Daisy smiled.

"Look, Mamma!" Ellis cried gleefully. "Look what I can do!" He picked up a rock and hurled it. It didn't go very far, and it sank without skipping. Ellis didn't seem to mind—he was irrepressible, his face shining with pleasure. She was shocked by this boy. Her somber son didn't laugh easily, and he didn't take to physical activity.

"Remember, lad, you must throw it with a bit of a hook, aye?" Cailean stepped around behind Ellis to mimic the throw with him again.

"Watch!" Ellis said gleefully and threw it. The rock skipped twice. He whirled around. "Did you *see*?"

"Yes, I saw, darling. It was a magnificent throw!"

Ellis squatted down and began to look for more rocks as Daisy moved closer. She frowned playfully at Cailean.

"Why do you look at me as if I've stolen your dog?" he asked amicably.

"How did you come to be in the company of my son?"

"He and his keeper were wandering about like

two pilgrims when I returned the oar Somerled sent sailing out to sea."

"That's not his *keeper*—that's his tutor."

"His *tutor*, then," Cailean said with a shrug. "The man is no' inclined to throw rocks and returned to his books, I suppose. Fortunately, your uncle sees the value in it."

Ellis threw another rock, too hard, and it plunked into the lake, sending big circular ripples out across a glassy surface of the water.

"Try again, lad," Cailean said and handed Ellis a rock, reviewing with him the proper mechanics.

Ellis threw the rock, and it skipped twice. He laughed with delight. "Cailean knows how to sail a ship," he said. "He uses the stars. Do you want me to teach you how to skip a rock, Mamma?"

"I happen to know something of it," Daisy said confidently.

"You *do*?" Ellis asked, eyeing her skeptically.

Daisy laughed. She reached into her pocket and withdrew a rock and showed it to Ellis. "Now watch," she said. She braced her feet apart and then threw the rock. It splashed into the water and sank without a single skip.

Ellis burst into laughter. "That's not how it's done at all, Mamma!" he cried. "Don't be sad. My first rocks sank, too, aye?"

Aye? There it was again, that word coming from her son.

"Here, Mamma. Here's one for you," Ellis said, holding up one of his rocks.

"Aye, a bonny one," Cailean said and took it from Ellis. "Shall I instruct your mother, then?"

"Yes!" Ellis exclaimed.

"Thank you, but I don't require instruction," Daisy said pertly.

"Ah, lass… I've yet to meet a woman who didna require a wee bit of instruction," Cailean said with a wink as he stepped behind her. He slid his hand down her arm, to her hand, and then held it out. "When you throw, turn your palm up, like this," he said and mimicked throwing as he held her hand.

Daisy nodded. Her son was watching with keen interest. She was very aware of the hard, broad man at her back, his hand dwarfing hers. He put one hand on her hip, and Daisy stifled a gasp. He was too bold! But she dared not call attention to it in front of Ellis.

"When I give you the word, throw the rock," he said. He swung her arm back, then thrust it forward. *"Now."*

Daisy released the rock from her fingers. It sailed perhaps a foot and splattered into mud a foot short of the water.

"Aye, I see that you are indeed quite the expert," Cailean said softly in her ear. "Here, then." He put a rock into her hand and shifted closer to her back.

"You are too familiar," Daisy whispered.

"You didna think so yesterday, aye?" he asked with a chuckle, and this time, instead of his hand going to her hip, he put his arm around her waist and drew her into his chest.

Daisy's gaze flew to Ellis, but he seemed not to notice at all.

"*Och*, breathe, then."

"I *am* breathing."

"You're as stiff as a new bride, aye?"

Daisy could feel the heat crawling up her neck; she couldn't bear to look at Ellis, certain he was scandalized beyond repair.

"Hold out your arm, Mamma!" her son said encouragingly.

So he was not scandalized. He was interested only in the rock.

"Bring your arm back like this," Cailean said, pulling her arm back. "As you release it, turn your hand up, like this. Do you see?"

"Yes, yes, I see," she said curtly—her heart was beating so hard that she was certain he could feel it, and she wanted nothing more than to let go of the blasted rock. She elbowed him in the chest. With an *oof*, he let go of her and Daisy threw the rock as hard as she could. It skipped three times before it sank.

"You did it, Mamma!" Ellis shrieked.

"I did it!" she cried, throwing her arms into the air.

Cailean laughed at her glee, and his smile sent a rush of desire through Daisy.

Ellis was speaking to her, explaining, she thought, the nuances of rock throwing, but the blood was pumping so loudly in her ears that Daisy couldn't hear him at all. She couldn't seem to think of anything but yesterday, and how she'd felt in Cailean's arms. Safe. Cherished. So exquisitely female. She couldn't seem to think of anything but how she wanted to be there again.

"I've promised to take Lord Chatwick up to the bluff to the bonniest view of the glen. Would you care to join us, then?"

"Please, Mamma!" Ellis said excitedly.

"Yes," she said, and held out her hand to her son. "I would like that."

They walked for a half hour, meandering along a trail that had been forged by generations of wild-life. Cailean was patient with Ellis, answering his many questions about things ranging from stars to rocks to how one went about learning to shoot a bow and arrow. Ellis seemed to stand taller, and instead of speaking with his head down as he often did, he looked Cailean in the eye when he asked his ques-tions, and he laughed at the things Cailean said.

Daisy was moved by it—even her uncle couldn't elicit this from her son. Cailean had somehow seen past her son's fears and timidity, and, as a result, Ellis was blossoming before her eyes.

Cailean led them up a rocky path, catching Dai-sy's hand to help her up over some of the larger rocks. At the top of the bluff, they looked out over the lake and the hills beyond it, the landscape dappled with the shadows of the puffy clouds overhead, the tiny dots of sheep on one hillside and then the shimmer-ing line of the sea beyond the loch.

The view was breathtaking. It felt as if they were the only people in the world here, rulers over all they saw. *This* was freedom. This landscape, these hills, this life—all of it freedom. Daisy could feel in her heart how much she would miss Auchenard and her freedom. It didn't matter that she hoped to marry her first love. Her life would never be hers again.

Cailean was the one who broke the spell by suggesting they return to the lodge. It was time for Ellis to be at his supper.

They made their way back down the hill and around the edge of the loch to the lodge. As they walked up the lawn, Daisy had a look at her son. His shoes were muddied, his breeches stained. He'd lain in the grass, and the elbows of his coat were stained, too. "Belinda will have an apoplectic fit when she sees you," she said, tousling his hair. "You best find Uncle Alfonso first," she told him with a wink.

When they reached the terrace, Ellis brushed his blond hair from his eyes and beamed up at Cailean. "Might we do it again?" he asked.

"I donna know," Cailean said gravely, and Ellis's face fell. "We best be about stalking the red stags first, aye? The season will be upon us soon."

Ellis grinned. "Do you mean it?"

"Aye, of course I mean it," Cailean said.

Ellis whooped with joy and bolted away from them, running for the lodge.

"Uncle! I'm to learn to stalk!" he shouted, as if Uncle Alfonso could hear him from somewhere inside.

"He's too young to hunt," Daisy said as she watched her son bound into the lodge.

"You mother the lad to death, aye? He's what, twelve years?"

"He's nine years!"

"*Och*, all the same," Cailean said, grinning. "A lad should be about the world, learning how to be a man."

"Yes, well, I'm to be the judge of that."

"Beg your pardon, but you canna be the judge of that," he said cheerfully. "You're a woman."

Daisy wanted so badly to touch him, to put her hand against his face, rough with the beginnings of a new beard. "I thought perhaps you might not return to Auchenard."

He arched a brow in surprise. "Aye, of course I have. I said I would, did I no'?"

She smiled sheepishly. "You must think me beyond redemption," she murmured.

"Aye, that I do," he said, and touched his fingers to her chin. "You're bloody incorrigible, Daisy."

Daisy's smile sank deeper. "Then do you forgive me? Will we still be friends?"

"No, I donna forgive you," he said. "For there is naugh' to forgive, *leannan*." He winked at her. "Aye, we are friends yet, in spite of my better judgment, and only because you need a friend, quite obviously. But that willna happen again." He smiled, his eyes sparkling with mirth.

"No, of course not," she said. She felt lighter than air. "Because you don't care for me."

"No' in the least," he said, and with his hand to her back, nudged her to continue toward the lodge.

"Is it true you live at Arrandale with no one else?" she asked.

"Aye, for now," he said. He began to tell her about Arrandale, of the house he was building there, stone by stone, timber by timber. She was enthralled, imagined him working, lifting beams by himself, hammering them into place. She didn't look away from him at all until he said, "Who has come, then?"

"Pardon?" She turned her head and looked to the terrace. Her heart instantly seized—Daisy knew who it was. The way he stood, the color of his hair—she would know him anywhere. She stopped moving, rooted to the earth as she stared in disbelief at the ghost from her past. "Rob," she said. "My God, it is *Rob*." It was a dream; it had to be a dream. She stepped forward cautiously, trying to make sense of his being here. Rob lifted his hand.

Daisy glanced up at Cailean. The light in his eyes had changed. Gone was the shine—they had shuttered, his thoughts hidden from her. "It's Rob," she whispered.

"Aye," he said, as if he knew, as if he'd been expecting him. "Go on, then, lass. Donna let your one and only true love wait."

Daisy ran. She picked up her skirts and ran for Rob, bringing herself to a halt at the edge of the terrace, out of breath, out of her mind. "Is it really you?"

Robert Spivey, *her* Robert, smiled. "Yes, it's really me," he said. He was older, naturally, but still the same tall, handsome man with sandy-gold hair and beautiful brown eyes. He moved forward, his hand extended for hers, smiling. "How happy I am to see you, Lady Chatwick."

"But I only just received your letter! You made no mention of coming here. How did you know where to find me?"

He laughed. "Lady Beckinsal finally relented and told me where you were. I followed the letter not two days after I'd posted it. I beg your pardon if I was wrong to have come, but I couldn't wait to see you."

Daisy was too stunned to move; he took her hand, bowed over it, kissing the back of it. "You are a very difficult woman to find," he said softly. "How grateful I am that I have."

Oh, so was she. For many reasons, *so was she*.

CHAPTER TWELVE

CAILEAN GAVE THEM time to greet their guest, of course. And he needed to collect himself before he met Spivey face-to-face. He retreated to Daisy's garden and idly looked around as the happy reunion took place, pretending to examine a wind chime that had appeared since the last time he stood there. His mind was racing, a thousand thoughts slamming through his head at once.

He could not understand what the man was doing at Auchenard. While it was possible Spivey had somehow heard of Cailean here, had somehow used Daisy as an excuse to pursue him, it really made no sense. It was too much of a coincidence. But he slipped his dirk into the waist of his plaid all the same, prepared to defend himself if necessary.

When he could stand it no more, when his curiosity threatened to choke him, he walked out of the garden and onto the terrace. Miss Hainsworth had joined them, and the four of them—Daisy, her cousin, her uncle and Spivey—were laughing, all of them happy, all of them acting as if the great problems of the world had just been resolved and there would be no more war or famine.

They didn't notice Cailean at first, but after a moment, Daisy caught sight of him. "Arrandale!" she said, reaching out her hand to him.

Arrandale. Not Cailean. Not friends, then.

He walked toward them, his gaze on Spivey. He was as tall as Cailean, but younger and fitter. His hair was dark gold, and his clothing looked as if it had been recently sewn; the collar of his coat was too stiff to lie down properly, his knee breeches shiny. He did not wear the uniform of a captain in the king's navy. He looked like a country gentleman.

"I, ah... Mr. Spivey, allow me to introduce my neighbor, Lord Arrandale," Daisy said. She was smiling, but it was not as bright as he'd come to know it. She seemed slightly ill at ease.

"Laird," he said. "I am laird of Arrandale."

"How do you do," Spivey said and walked forward, his hand extended to greet Cailean. But as he neared Cailean, something flickered in his expression. He shook Cailean's hand enthusiastically, as if meeting the vicar who would perform his marriage to Daisy here and now...but his gaze was shrewd.

"Mr. Spivey has come all the way from Cornwall," Daisy said.

"*Captain* Spivey," he said, and smiled indulgently at Daisy.

"Oh yes, I beg your pardon. *Captain* Spivey." She laughed. "I'm not yet accustomed to it."

"Pardon, sir...have we perhaps met?" he asked Cailean. "You are somewhat familiar to me."

"Aye, I suspect I am. I am Cailean Mackenzie of Arrandale."

The color drained from the captain's face. He jerked his hand free of Cailean's and put it on the hilt of his sword. "What are you doing here?" he demanded sharply. He looked all around them, as if he expected more Mackenzies to appear.

"I live here," Cailean said calmly. "I am a Highlander, aye?"

"What you *are*, sir, is a smuggler!" Spivey said and abruptly pulled his sword. But Cailean had been trained by his father and had trained Highland guards. He moved quickly, knocking the sword from the man's arm and at the same moment drawing his dirk. He twirled him around, putting the knife under the man's throat.

Miss Hainsworth screamed.

"Arrandale!" Mr. Kimberly shouted. "The captain is our guest! Put down your knife!"

Cailean kicked the sword and heard it scud across the terrace. When he was certain it was out of reach, he pushed Spivey out of his grip, but held on to his dirk. "Have a care, Captain," he said, pointing the dirk at him. "You are in Scotland now, and unless you've brought an army with you, keep your sword in its sheath, aye?"

Spivey's hat had been knocked from his head. He bent down and swiped it up, then yanked at his waistcoat. He looked at Mr. Kimberly, who held his sword and nodded curtly. "I do not understand how you have welcomed this smuggler into your home," he said coolly.

"Smuggler," Mr. Kimberly said angrily. "He is not—"

"Aye, I am, Mr. Kimberly," Cailean said. "I am indeed a free trader."

Mr. Kimberly swung his gaze to Cailean. "You're *what*?"

"A free trader."

"Meaning?"

"Meaning the tax the Crown has imposed on goods we need to survive here has exacted a toll on our clan. We've had to seek relief—we bring in the goods our people need without paying tax."

"In other words, a thief," Spivey said. "I've chased him and his ilk for years," he said, his voice full of disgust.

"Some would argue the Crown is the thief," Cailean said with a shrug. "But you didna come here to debate with me, aye?" He glanced at Daisy, but she was not looking at him. She was looking down, her expression calm and slightly distant. She had adopted the demeanor of a proper English viscountess. Detached. Polite. Emotionless. Was she shocked? He'd told her the truth, just as he'd promised. Always the truth.

"Smuggling is punishable by death, Mackenzie," Spivey said. "You could very well hang for your crimes. These good people could be charged with offenses for harboring you in their home."

"No one is harboring me," Cailean said sharply.

"And I willna hang here in the Highlands, so again, sir, unless you've brought a bloody army with you, donna make trouble."

Spivey clenched his jaw and exchanged a look with Mr. Kimberly. "I may not be able to bring you to justice today, but if you ever step foot in England, there is no one who will protect you. I will personally see to it."

Cailean smiled wryly. "I know that, man. Just as you know there is no one to protect you here. It is perilous in these hills for any Englishman, much less a captain of the navy."

"Please," Daisy interjected, holding up her hands. "Please let us have no more talk of hanging and… this." She looked at Cailean, her eyes pleading. "Mr. Spivey—beg your pardon, *Captain* Spivey—has heard of my husband's death and has come to me straightaway after all these years. He didn't come to root out smugglers. And the laird," she said to Spivey, "has been our friend. I don't know what he has done, but he has been our friend. Please… I should not like to ruin your welcome here."

Straightaway? Did Daisy realize that *straightaway* would have been upon the occasion of her husband's death? Cailean didn't believe that for a moment—the word of this widow's fortune had spread like a plague in the Highlands, and he'd wager there wasn't a man in all of bloody England who hadn't heard it. Including this man.

Spivey lifted his chin, as if he knew what Cailean was thinking.

"He's come all this way," Daisy said, her eyes still pleading.

"What a comfort he must be to you now, madam," Cailean said. "After more than two years since your husband's death."

Miss Hainsworth gasped softly and gripped Daisy's hand, while Daisy stared with disbelief at him.

Spivey actually looked surprised by Cailean's lack of decorum. "I hope to be of some comfort, of course, as any decent gentleman would do. I am well aware that Lady Chatwick is without family."

"Without family? Her uncle and cousin are with her now."

"Look here," Mr. Kimberly said curtly. "Enough of this."

"I'll take my leave," Cailean muttered.

Daisy didn't try to dissuade him. "At least let me see you out." She held out her arm as if to show him the way to the door.

Her stride was brisk; she said nothing as they walked through the lodge to the front drive. When they reached the portico, she paused, turned to him and put her hand to his arm. "You didn't tell me you knew him," she said, her voice accusatory.

"I donna know him. I know of him."

"You drew a *knife* on him!"

"Before he put his sword through my gut, Daisy."

"Why didn't you tell me?" she demanded. "I told *you* the truth. Why didn't you tell me?"

"*Diah,* I didna expect to ever encounter the man

face-to-face, aye? I didna see a reason to distress you. Why is he here?"

"I *told* you," she said, clearly annoyed with him.

"No, I mean *here*. Do you no' think it a wee bit strange that he would take the risk of coming into the Highlands, where he might assume he has enemies?"

"No!" She pressed her fingers to the bridge of her nose. "I don't know," she said. "How can I possibly know? I've only just been reacquainted with him, Cailean."

He sighed and ran his hand over the top of his head. This was not his concern. He ought to be happy that she had found someone to marry, someone she could accept. He ought to go, be happy he was leaving with his throat intact. But he felt only the air shattering around him like a thin sheet of ice, falling into nothing. This…affair? Friendship? It had come to its inevitable end. He started to move, but he paused and glanced at her, at the pear-green eyes, the shine gone from them at the moment. "Donna make a hasty decision, aye?" he said softly. "Heed me— there is something peculiar about his appearance."

"Don't advise me," she said, throwing her hand up. "Don't tell me what I should do."

He said nothing. So many things were flitting through his head that he couldn't actually grasp any coherent thought, except one—he did not want to leave her with Spivey.

They stood in awkward silence a moment, lost in their own thoughts. Daisy clasped her hands before her, and she kept her head down, as if she were truly interested in the pebble she was toeing about.

What was he to do? Whisk her away from Spivey? And then what—return her to England to find someone just as… English? And a noose waiting for him? What alternative for her was there? He couldn't put it to rights, and his presence had made it worse.

Cailean had let this go too far between them, had allowed himself to delve too deeply into their acquaintance. He groaned—the time had come for him to leave it be. A swell of disappointment, tasting of bitter dismay, rose to the back of his throat.

He touched her face, his fingers lingering, forcing her to look up at him. Her eyes swam with regret that he couldn't make sense of. Did she regret him? Spivey? The unfortunate altercation on the terrace? "Be happy, Daisy," he said. "Now and forevermore."

She pressed her lips together. He dropped his hand and turned away from her, walking briskly across the drive, headed for the path through the woods that would take him to Arrandale.

As he stepped into the shadows of the wooded path, he realized that as the trees had swallowed the sunlight, so would her departure swallow the bit of sunshine over Auchenard. And in its place, a dark cloud would hang.

THERE WAS A small fishing hamlet on the road to Balhaire, and on the edge of that hamlet was a cottage in the forest where every man in the Highlands knew he might slake his thirst. To the outside world, the women who inhabited that cottage were sisters, drawn together by some familial tragedy.

They were not sisters, but no matter, their stories were a mystery to Cailean. They lived on a patch of land with a wee bit of livestock and a robust garden. They were hardy women, too, all of them big-boned and strong, accustomed to the sort of Highlanders who came down from the hills to call on them.

Against his better judgment, Cailean stopped there on his way to Balhaire. He felt in desperate need of a distraction—anything to take his mind from Daisy. He'd been at odds with himself for two days now, since Captain Spivey had come to Auchenard. Cailean's imagination had gotten the best of him, holding him captive and torturing him with unwanted images of Daisy in that bloody wooden box of a potting shed with her one and only true love.

They were images that could be tamped down with hard work and determination.

In those moments Cailean managed a small victory over those thoughts, his own desires rushed to the forefront of his mind. He found himself remembering the moment she'd found her release, the feel of her fingers digging quite painfully into his shoulders. She was with him in every moment of the day. Her mouth, ripe and wet from his kiss, accompanied him to fish in the mornings. Her hair, braided and fragrant, filled his nostrils as he cleaned a hare.

Everything he did to try to ignore her only made the images of her grow and bloom and press against his flesh and bones, reminding him of just how bloody long it had been since he'd been in the company of a woman.

Cailean had finally determined he had to do something or lose his fool mind, if it hadn't been lost already. He commanded Fabienne to wait and strode into the cottage in the woods, prepared to release the demons from his body.

Unfortunately, he knew the moment he stepped across the threshold into the low-ceilinged room with the smell of burned peat and unwashed man permeating the air, and the women flocking around him, cooing over his physique, that he would find no relief here. Not for this fever.

One of them lifted her skirts so that he could plainly see her sturdy legs and the dark patch between them. Another cupped her breasts with her hands and bit her lower lip.

But not a single one of them had spirited green eyes or a bloody seductive smile. *Not one.*

Cailean didn't speak; he tossed some coins on the table and left, even as the women taunted him and called him back, one of them promising a remedy for his failed masculinity. He was mortified by that, of course—if there was one thing on which he could depend, it was his bloody masculinity. In fact, it was pounding hard in his veins as he rode away.

He was soon enough at Balhaire and the village that surrounded the fortress. Everyone was in the throes of preparing for the *feill* to celebrate the end of summer. The Mackenzie tradition was an annual affair, and it brought dozens, even hundreds, to Balhaire for market, games and dancing. The *feill* was particularly important during trying times—Balhaire was a true stronghold, and Arran Mackenzie wanted his clan and other Highlanders to know it and depend on it.

The inner bailey and the old keep were teeming with people when Cailean arrived. He walked down the long, narrow corridor that led to his father's study, sidestepping two footmen who carried a sideboard between them.

At the end of that hall, Cailean walked into his father's study in such a stew that at first he did not see his mother until she cried out with delight.

"Cailean! I am in astonishment!" She hurried across the room with her arms outstretched. Cailean reached for her hand, but she pushed his hand away and threw her arms around his neck, rising up on her toes to kiss his cheek. "I'll not be greeted like a distant cousin." She hugged him tightly, small thing that she was, then let him go. "I thought at first you were a vision—I have so rarely seen you of late, and particularly when the day is fine."

"Aye," he said. "Business has brought me in from the sunshine for a word with *Athair*."

"Ah yes, good, then. We men must speak of cargos and prevailing winds," his father said from behind his desk.

"What matters?" his mother asked.

"You'll no' want to hear it, *leannan*," Cailean's father said and fluttered his fingers at her. "Best you go and occupy yourself."

"Are you asking me to leave, dearest? Don't you want my advice? Cailean, darling, you will attend the *feill*, won't you?"

Cailean couldn't help but smile—after all these years, his mother's English accent weighed down any word she tried to speak in Gaelic. "Aye, of course I will."

"I'd like you to invite your neighbor."

Cailean's heart stilled. "Who?"

"Your *neighbor*," she said, enunciating the word. "Lady Chatwick."

"Mathair—"

"Her family, as well," she said before he could object. "She has a young son, does she not? He will be delighted."

"Aye, she does, but I—"

"I should like to meet her," his mother said quickly. "She is English after all, and there are precious few of my countrymen in the Highlands."

"Aye, with good reason," her husband reminded her.

"You sound like a Jacobite, darling. Cailean, please do extend the invitation."

"If you mean to try your hand at matchmaking *again*," he said, leveling a pointed look at her, "you're too late."

His mother gasped. "She's made a match so soon?"

"No' with a Scotsman. An old love has come from England to fetch her."

His mother gaped at him. "Who? Who would come all this way?"

"Captain Robert Spivey."

His mother stared at him blankly, but his father's brow furrowed. "The name is familiar."

"Aye, it is. Spivey is or was captain of the *Fortune*."

His father frowned darkly. "Is that no' the ship whose gun nearly brought down our foremast?"

"It is the ship that lost a sailor to Wallace's gun, aye," Cailean said.

"What in bloody hell is he doing here, then?" his father demanded.

"He's come for her. They courted before her marriage to Chatwick."

"No' bloody likely," his father began, but Cailean shook his head.

"He didna know me, aye? He was surprised. Drew his sword."

His mother gasped. "Oh my. Why has he come?" she repeated, sinking down onto a settee. "I don't like it, Cailean, not at all. Why would a captain of the Royal Navy suddenly appear so very close to Arrandale?"

"Lady Chatwick believes he has resigned his commission," Cailean said. "I think his appearance is a war tactic—"

"A war tactic!"

Cailean held up his hand. "In the war of fortunes. What I mean is that I think he has come, has inserted himself between a woman he loves and open sea— that is to say, between her and any other suitor, aye?"

"Between any other suitor and her fortune." His

mother snorted. "A man in search of a fortune plays to win, doesn't he?"

"Aye, that he does," his father said thoughtfully.

"Invite him, then," she said to Cailean.

"Pardon?"

"Invite him to the *feill*."

"*Màthair*, think of what you are saying," Cailean calmly suggested. "Any number of people at the *feill* would gladly slit his throat."

"They'd no' do it at Balhaire," his father said.

"No, never," his mother agreed. "Your father and I learned a very long time ago that it is better to keep your enemy close. Otherwise, one cannot know what he is about. And if there is even the slightest chance that he might be sending English troops down Loch-carron for Arrandale—" She shuddered, then vigorously rubbed her arms. "They won't come near Balhaire," she said firmly.

"No' unless they mean to start a war," his father agreed.

Cailean didn't disagree. To attempt any retaliation in the midst of so many Scots—many of them Jaco-bites—would be grounds to take up arms.

"And have a pair of guards with you, darling," she said. "I can't bear the thought of you at Arran-dale alone with someone like him so close. I'll speak to Rabbie and Cat about it. We'll need to welcome them here, which will take a bit of persuading with the clan." She stood up to leave, but before she went out, she put her hand on Cailean's cheek. "Do have a care."

"Aye," he said and kissed her cheek.

He watched his mother leave, then turned to his father, who moved as if he meant to stand. With a sudden grimace, he caught himself on the edge of his desk and bowed his head.

"Athair," Cailean said, alarmed, starting for the desk, but his father waved him off.

"It's naugh' to worry over," he said and rubbed his leg.

Cailean could see the pain etched into his father's face. "I'll ring for—"

"No," his father said curtly. "I donna want to upset your mother, aye? She worries enough as it is. I'll need you on hand to start the games," he said and eased back in his seat. He sighed, leaned his head back a moment, then opened his eyes and smiled at Cailean. "Now then," he said. "Let's discuss the *feill.*"

Cailean listened to his father, but he couldn't stop his thoughts from rushing. It was clear that he would be needed at Balhaire in his father's stead sooner rather than later. He was beginning to feel as if his life had been tossed into the air by a fierce ocean wave and then smacked back down onto the deck, scattering into pieces he would have to quickly gather before he lost them all.

CHAPTER THIRTEEN

I cannot describe the joy in my heart upon see-
ing Robert after all these years. He is of course
older, as am I, but still very much himself, as he
proved to me by embracing me and kissing my
cheek in earnest happiness at finding me well.

Our acquaintance has been very much re-
newed and in many ways, it is as if the years
have melted away and meant nothing. We have
talked of everything. He asked if my husband
was good and honorable, and I assured him
that Clive was a good husband. Robert never
married as I had supposed he might have done,
but said rather that after he was forced to let
me go, he had married the sea. I don't remem-
ber it in precisely that way, but then again,
many days have passed since then and memo-
ries do fade.

Robert had heard various and sundry things
about me over the years. He knew of Ellis's
birth. Of Clive's illness. Of my mother's death.
But he'd not heard of Clive's passing until only
recently, and he said he dreamed that night
that an angel told him to come straightaway,

all the while knowing that a journey into the Highlands would be particularly perilous for a captain in the king's Royal Navy.

I cannot fathom how Robert came to pull his sword. He admitted he reacted poorly, but only out of concern for me. Perhaps he thought A had come up from the lake to rob us at that very moment, although that seems rather impossible. He was quite insistent that I tell him how I have come to know A. He has warned me he is a dangerous smuggler. He would not tell me what A has been accused of smuggling, but he did insist that I should not consider him friend or invite him into Auchenard again.

Robert has surprised me with a gift of a gold necklace, one that he purchased in India. It is quite lovely, and I wear it proudly. I did understand him to mean that he made the purchase with me in mind, but at supper that very same evening, he regaled us all with tales of his daring sea voyages, and related that he'd sailed to India more than a year ago. As he didn't know of Clive's death as long ago as that, I must assume that perhaps he bought the necklace for someone else he admired.

Mr. S called yesterday. The poor man could not seem to find his tongue at the sight of the captain, and took his leave very shortly thereafter, refusing my invitation to bowl with us on the newly shorn lawn.

Uncle has taken to fishing and may very

well take barrels of them to Balhaire. I suggested he set up a booth and sell them. He said I would thank him on the long journey back to London. We are to leave in a fortnight, and all arrangements have been made. Rob is to escort us home, as is Rowley, and uncle and the rest of the servants will follow once they have closed Auchenard.

Rob has not asked to speak with my uncle, or me, and I therefore cannot know his intentions, although he has given me every reason to believe he intends to offer. Perhaps he means to wait until we are in London again.

Mr. Munro has told us the preparations are being made for the festival at Balhaire, to be held at week's end. I think E would very much like to go, and he informs me the world's strongest man shall be in attendance. He asks when A might come round again. I thank the Lord that he did not see what happened on the terrace.

I, too, should like to know when A might come round again. Whatever he has done, I would not like to think I've seen the last of him. I would not like to think that at all.

I saw the strangest, most colorful bird in the garden this morning, pecking at the petals that have fallen from some of the roses. It looked like a blue chicken, the likes of which I have never seen.

DAISY DID NOT care much for lawn bowling, but Ellis seemed to enjoy it, and Robert suggested they amuse him. "Fresh air and his studies are what the boy ought to be about," he'd said.

Daisy had bowled the last two rounds—her balls going quite astray—and was staring absently at the loch, wondering why she'd not seen any boats gliding past in the last two days. Not a rowboat, not a single sail. Not a man fishing on the edge of the lake. Not a Highlander in sight.

"Madam?"

She started and turned toward the sound of Rowley's voice.

"Arrandale, madam, and two riders, as well."

Cailean. Her heart fluttered madly, and she touched the lobe of her ear in a vain attempt that Robert not see how the news affected her. "Thank you. See him to the great room, please."

"I invited him to do so, milady, but he refused. He asks you meet him on the drive."

"Oh," she said and felt the disappointment rush through her. He had given up on her after Robert pulled his sword; she was certain of it.

"Who has come?" Robert asked, drawing up from what would have been his turn at bowl.

"Ah…our neighbor," she said carefully.

Robert immediately dropped his ball. "I'll accompany you," he said firmly.

"I'm sure it's nothing—"

"Lady Chatwick," he said, in a habit he'd forged of addressing her when he was quite serious, "as I have said, you should not receive him at all. He is a traitor to the Crown. A common criminal. You must not tarnish your reputation by association."

"No he's not!" Ellis said angrily.

"Darling," Daisy said, warning him. Perhaps Robert had forgotten that she was, indeed, Lady Chatwick and still mistress of this house. Perhaps he'd forgotten that they were in the Highlands without society, and there was no reputation for her to tarnish.

"I knew he'd come, Mamma!" Ellis said pleadingly. He ran before she could stop him.

"The boy needs to learn to be presented," Robert said curtly as he put his hand on Daisy's back to guide her around the lodge.

"Ellis! Ellis, darling, wait for us!" she called to him, and Ellis reluctantly slowed his step. She grabbed her son's hand and ran with him around the lodge, Robert walking briskly behind them.

When they reached the drive, Ellis broke free of her hand and ran to Cailean, throwing his arms around his waist. "I thought you wouldn't come," he said breathlessly, and Daisy's heart caught in the vise of her son's need.

Cailean looked at Daisy over the top of Ellis's head, and her heart quickened. Cailean was magnificent, as magnificent as the day she'd first laid eyes on him. He wore plaid, his hair in a queue, and his eyes, crystal blue, seemed to leap out of his face, breathing new life into the fire that had smoldered in her since the last time she'd seen him.

He didn't smile; he didn't speak—but didn't she

see a flicker of longing in his eyes? Or had her own longing filled her vision?

"*Diah*, lad, you donna know you own strength—you all but put me on my arse, you did," he said, tousling Ellis's hair.

Ellis beamed up at him, his grin as broad as a horizon. *Oh my son, my dearest son.* She could see the adoration in his face, and it broke her heart that he likely would not see Cailean again once they left Scotland.

"Arrandale!" she said, forcing cheer into her voice, her attempt to pretend that there was nothing between them.

She picked up her skirts and hurried forward, with the pretense of pulling Ellis from his grip of Cailean, but truthfully so that she might stand closer to him. "I'm afraid you've come too late to bowl. We were just finishing our match."

"I didna come to bowl," he drawled. Daisy slid her gaze to the two men on horseback behind him. They were stoic, but she realized both of them wore swords, and both of them had their hands on the hilts of those swords, as if they expected to draw them. She glanced over her shoulder at Robert; his gaze was also on the two men, wary and watchful.

"Are we to stalk?" Ellis asked eagerly.

Daisy realized Ellis had not yet released his grip of Cailean. She put her hands on his shoulders and pulled him back, forcing him to drop his embrace.

"No' today, lad. The bucks are no' out yet, aye? It's a wee bit early yet."

"But…but we are going back to London soon," Ellis said, sounding slightly panicked.

Cailean's gaze instantly met Daisy's.

Before she could say a word, Robert answered for her. "In a fortnight, we will depart Auchenard."

If Cailean heard Robert, he gave no indication. He kept his focus steady on Daisy. She could feel it, could feel how deeply it penetrated her.

"What business have you here, sir?" Robert asked, stepping up beside Daisy and putting his hand on Ellis's shoulder.

Cailean slowly shifted his gaze from Daisy to Robert. "What *business* I have is business with the Lady Chatwick, aye? No' you, Spivey."

"Whatever you will say to her, you may say before me," Robert said, and drew Ellis back, forcing him behind Daisy's skirts. He braced his legs apart, as if preparing to fight.

"What is the matter?" Daisy whispered sharply. "He has not threatened—"

"A lady does not receive gentlemen on her own," Robert said and stepped in front of Daisy, ignoring her displeasure, standing almost toe-to-toe with Cailean.

Indignation flared in Daisy—how could he possibly know what a lady did or did not do? "Captain Spivey, I must—"

"You've naugh' to fear, then…for I am no gentleman," Cailean said casually and smiled.

Daisy felt short of breath, her fear that this could result in another confrontation ratcheting. "Ellis, darling, go and fetch your uncle," she said, pushing Ellis toward the lodge. "Quickly!"

"But I want to stay here!" Ellis complained.

"Do as your mother tells you!" Rob snapped.

Cailean's gaze narrowed darkly, and Daisy frantically, impetuously, stepped in between the two men. "That is enough!" she said frantically. "I will speak with Arrandale, Captain Spivey, and I will ask you to please see Ellis into the lodge."

Robert turned his heated gaze to her.

"If it is business for Auchenard, it is business for me," she said, trying to breathe.

Robert's gaze bore through her, and Daisy flinched at the coldness of it. "It is not *safe*, madam," he said through clenched teeth.

"It is perfectly safe."

He considered her, flicked his gaze at Cailean, then reached for Daisy's hand, bowing over it, kissing the back of it. And then he squeezed it so tightly that she winced. "Do not be long," he said quietly. "I'll just inside."

Daisy pulled her hand free.

He turned about, gestured for Ellis to go ahead of him and strode to the lodge.

The moment he disappeared through the door, Daisy grabbed Cailean's hand.

"Daisy—"

"Come," she insisted, tugging on his hand. "A bit of privacy, please, Cailean."

He sighed, then said something to his men. He reluctantly followed her onto the path that led through the woods. She pulled him along until she could not see the drive, could not see the lodge, then dropped his hand and turned to face him.

His jaw was clenched, his expression stern. But his eyes, his eyes—she could see how painful this was for him.

Confusion began to swirl in her, kicking up dirt and feelings that felt tight and on the verge of erupting. Her heart was beating too hard for her to find her breath, and she pressed her hands to her belly, as if trying to keep her breath in her. "What business?" she asked.

His eyes moved over her, as if he was reminding himself of her. "I've a message from my mother."

"Your mother!"

"Aye. She'd like to extend an invitation to you and your kin to attend the *feill* at Balhaire—the festival—at the end of the week. She will, of course, make accommodations for your household."

"That's your business?" she asked sharply and folded her arms. "How kind of your *mother* to invite me," she said coolly.

Cailean frowned impatiently. "Do you think I ought to have extended the invitation? Do you think your friend would allow it?"

"You might have extended the invitation to him," she said.

Cailean snorted. "You donna know him as I do. Has he told you about me?"

"Yes," she said, lifting her chin. "He told me you

are a dangerous smuggler and that I shouldn't associate with you."

Cailean smiled. "Dangerous to him, perhaps. No' you, *leannan*."

"He asked how I might have possibly made your acquaintance. I told him. I told him everything."

Cailean's gaze narrowed. "Everything?"

Daisy flushed. "No, not *everything*." She tried to look past Cailean, to see if anyone had followed them on the path.

"Do you fear him? Donna fret now—the lads will kill him before they'll allow him up this path."

Daisy gasped. "How can you say such things! I don't know what has gone on between the two of you, but he is a kind man, Cailean. He cares very much for me."

Cailean looked away from her as if he didn't want to hear it, his jaw working. "Then he's made his offer," he said flatly.

"No...not yet." She put her hand on his arm. He flinched as if her touch singed him. "We are reacquainting ourselves. You know my situation," she said.

"Aye, I know it. And I know he'll have your fortune yet, Daisy," he said, removing his arm from her hand and turning his back to her, almost as if she were repulsive to him.

"No, he won't!" she said, frustrated now. "Why do you think he's come all this way?"

"To cut off your defenses, aye?"

"Pardon?"

Cailean shook his head. He put his hands on his waist and turned his head to look at her, frowning as if he thought her addled. "You donna understand, lass—"

"I understand!" she said angrily. "Don't condescend to me, Cailean. Robert wouldn't have come so far if he didn't hold me in high regard!"

"Are you certain of it? Of his affections?"

There was an almost imperceptible hitch in her thoughts, a tiny shard of doubt. "Of course I am," she said, furious that he would question Robert's devotion. "I'm not cake-headed."

"Then you donna want my advice. Aye, then, do as you will." He began to stride down the path.

"Are you jealous, Cailean?" she called after him. "Has jealousy caused you to end your friendship with me?"

He stopped. He stood with his back to her, his shoulders flexing, reminding her of a hawk readying to take flight. But he slowly turned back to her, and with his eyes locked on hers. He deliberately walked back up the path to where she stood. "Are you so certain of him?" he demanded, his voice dangerously soft. "For if you are, you might put his true intentions to a wee test."

What was left of her patience evaporated. "Oh, how you amuse me, Laird Arrandale," she said hotly. "How perfectly ridiculous you are! There is no need to *test* him."

"No? Then tell me, how and when did he learn of

your husband's death? How is it that all of England knew of it, and no' him?"

Daisy flinched. That question had already been raised in her mind when he'd given her the necklace.

"Then you might inquire as to what he means to occupy him now that he's resigned his commission, aye? Surely a *captain* of the Royal Navy would no' resign a commission without some thought as to what he meant to do."

She hadn't asked him. She'd just assumed they would marry. "Everything happened so fast. I'm sure he's not had to time to think of it."

Cailean smirked. "Watch how he will flatter you, Daisy. So much that others around you might expire of the treacle he spills all around."

Daisy clucked her tongue.

"Aye, he will flatter you," Cailean said, slipping into the tiny sliver of space her doubt had left in her heart. "But he willna give a damn about your hopes or fears. It's all part of his scheme—"

Daisy suddenly shoved him in the chest, pushing him back a step. "Why are you trying to ruin this for me?"

Cailean remained silent, and it infuriated Daisy. Her frustration with him, with her situation, with the simple fact that she had no control over her destiny was mounting, exploding. She shoved him as hard as she could again.

He didn't move.

"What do you want me to do? *Refuse* him? Marry

the stranger Craig presents? Why are you *doing* this?" she shouted, dangerously close to tears.

His face softened. "*Och, leannan*, I gave you my word I'd be honest, aye? I donna trust him."

"And I don't trust you," she said, her voice shaking. Her whole body was shaking, she realized. With grief, with fear, with such raging disappointment that she feared she might collapse into it. "How shall I know if a man truly esteems me?" she asked, throwing her arms wide.

Cailean looked at her as if she were daft. "You know."

"I don't! *All* men are very flattering. Should they be any other way? Should they disdain me? *All* men are helpful and solicitous. Should I look for a man who cares nothing for me? Is *that* how I am to judge?"

"*Diah, leannan,*" he said and caught her face between his hands. "You will know it in the way a man looks at you. In the way that he touches you. You will know it in the way he wants to know even the smallest thing about you."

Daisy's heart slammed hard in her chest. "That's odd," she said softly. "For the one man who has looked at me in any meaningful way, or has touched me, or has wanted to know anything about me at all is only my *friend*," she said. "And he doesn't esteem me."

Something changed in Cailean's expression. His gaze turned dark. "I am no' your friend," he said. And he kissed her. Hard. He kissed her with such ferocity that Daisy began to dissolve into an appallingly and equally ferocious wave of desire. Nothing had changed—she still craved him, still wanted to feel his body in hers. His lips were succulent, his body hard and supple at once. She was lost in that kiss, lost in her desire and the way her heart seemed to beat so strongly whenever he was near.

Cailean twisted her about, put her back to the tree and muttered something in his native tongue before dipping to kiss her neck, her chest. This was madness, utter madness, and she was careening down a dangerous path with abandon, with no regard for her future. Robert could find her at any moment. She would risk everything, and yet she couldn't tear herself away from him. She wanted Cailean so violently that it confused her. She *wanted* Robert. These feelings for Cailean were to have dissipated the moment she saw Robert on the terrace.

And yet…*and yet*.

Was it so wrong? Was it so wrong to want him as she did? To wish this man would fill her up? Was it wrong to feel such passion for him when she would make a match with another?

He crushed her to him, holding her tightly in his arms as he kissed her, nipping at her bottom lip, his hand kneading her breast. Daisy returned the kiss with the physical hunger that had been gnawing at her since the moment she had met him, and the pressure kept building, kept pushing, kept seeping into every fiber.

Cailean slipped his hand into the bodice of her

gown, his fingers cool on the hot skin of her breast, her nipple rigid between his fingers. She gasped with pleasure and clutched at her gown, trying to pull it up, around her waist.

But just as suddenly as he'd kissed her, Cailean stopped. "No," he said, his breath short. "I canna give you that."

No. She tried to kiss him, but he leaned back.

"Daisy, no," he said. "What you want—what *I* want—I canna give you, aye?"

"Cailean—"

"*No*, Daisy," he said. He took her face in his hands and forced her to look at him. "You donna want to do this. No' like this," he said. "The moment will satisfy you, aye, but on the morrow, you will no' like what you've done."

"That's not true."

"Then I know I will no' like what *I've* done."

The pressure in her suddenly evaporated, and in its place, overwhelming sorrow rose. She innately understood the sorrow, because she'd felt it once before in her life. She knew that the sorrow she felt was the sort that came from the loss of something or someone she loved.

Daisy folded her arms defensively across her middle. Cailean's expression was cool now, his emotions hidden behind the mask of the mighty Highlander who had ridden down from the hills that warm summer day.

"You'll return to London soon. You'll marry as you must, and, God willing, you'll have more children, aye? I willna allow you risk it all, here on this path."

"It is not for you to allow or disallow," she said coolly, her sorrowful fury so utterly consuming she was afraid she might put a fist in his mouth. "It is for *me* to allow or disallow. I've had a father and a husband and an uncle and a bishop to command me and advise me. I don't need my friends to do it, too, Cailean."

"Daisy… I am no' your friend, aye? I am a threat to you, just as your captain has warned you. Go to him now. Marry him. Be happy."

She couldn't look at him another moment. She hated him in that moment, almost as much as she loved him. She pushed away from the tree and started walking, uncaring if he followed her or not. She could scarcely see the path before her, so volatile were the thoughts and images mixing dangerously in her head.

She wished she'd never met Cailean Mackenzie. Her heart had gone out to him, and now she wanted it back.

She couldn't face Robert just yet, not with her thoughts swirling and building in a bank of clouds as towering as those building overhead. A gust of wind caught her; she gathered her wrap around her and walked around the lodge for her garden. The wind had picked up, and the temperature had dropped since yesterday.

The summer was truly at an end.

"There you are!"

She turned her head, saw Robert striding to her

across the terrace. "I've been very worried," he said and shrugged out of his coat, draping it over her shoulders.

"I'm quite all right," she protested.

"What business did he have?" he asked, peering at her with concern. "You shouldn't have resisted me, Daisy. You should have allowed me to speak with him. You don't understand the sort of man—"

"He is my friend," she said. Or at least, she had believed him to be. She shoved the gate of her garden open with such force that it banged against the hedge.

"He is no friend of yours," Robert said. "Undoubtedly, he would like you to think that is true, but he is no friend. I will be right glad when we've gone from this den of thieves and traitors."

Daisy halted in her walk and whirled around to him, looking into those brown eyes, so familiar to her after all these years, and yet unrecognizable in some peculiar way. "You do realize that Auchenard is Ellis's legacy, do you not? He likes it here. And he clearly admires Arrandale."

Robert made a sound of disgust. "Do you really wish for your son to admire a smuggler?"

Daisy winced and looked at her feet.

"Lord Chatwick is better suited to Chatwick Hall. He'll be quite happy there, as well."

"Chatwick Hall?" she repeated, distracted by the sprout of weeds she saw beneath the wild orchids.

"Yes, Chatwick Hall," he said, looking at her strangely. "I assume you will reside there when you return to England."

She hadn't lived at Chatwick Hall since Clive's death. "Why do you assume so?"

Curiously, Robert blushed slightly. "Well, I...that is where you resided when you and I were forced to part. It's quite large, room enough for a family and what have you."

What have you? Did that mean a husband, too? Daisy turned her gaze back to the weeds.

"You do want a large family, don't you?"

"I have Ellis," she said simply. "And I've lived in London since Clive's death."

"But surely you want more children. Another son, perhaps?"

Another son? Why? In case something happened to Ellis? The very idea made her shiver. Daisy didn't know if she wanted a large family—she hadn't thought of it in so long now that she wasn't entirely sure. She knelt to pull the weeds.

"Daisy..." Robert was suddenly on one knee beside her as she pulled weeds from beneath the wild orchids. He took her hand, brushing the dirt from it. "You shouldn't do this."

"What?"

"Pull weeds," he said, grimacing slightly.

"But I like—"

"You are a great lady with other responsibilities. You need someone to care for you as you have for your family. Someone upon whom you can lean and look to for advice and guidance."

She didn't feel as if she needed that at all. "You?" she asked softly. She was struck with the memory that she'd tried to lean on him once before and his guidance had been to accept her fate.

But Robert stroked her face, his gaze admiring. "Is it not obvious?" he asked. "Haven't I shown you my devotion by making this journey to find you? I've always loved you, darling. *Always.* Scarcely a day passed that I didn't think of you. I never dreamed I'd have another opportunity, but…" He hesitated.

"But?"

He boyishly bit his lip. "I can only hope you feel the same for me, or at least can find some affection for me that remains with you after these many years."

"Why haven't you offered?" she whispered, suddenly desperate to know.

"Daisy—"

"Isn't that why you have come?"

"Of course it is," he said flatly.

"Then why?"

He sighed heavenward, then met her gaze once more. She could see his affection for her. He was earnest; she could feel it in her heart. "Because I must speak with the bishop first. I have been a captain in the Royal Navy, and my situation is greatly improved…but still, I am not good enough for a woman like you. I have to prove to the bishop that I am worthy of your hand."

It was a declaration of esteem, and once Daisy's heart would have burst with love for him. But her thoughts, so many jumbled questions and doubts, raced. "How do you know about the bishop?" she asked. She hadn't told him about the bishop. She hadn't told him how Clive had betrayed her. She'd been too ashamed to admit that her late husband had not trusted her to care for her own son, and the only way he could know it was to have heard the gossip about her.

Robert blinked. And then his brows dipped. "Lady Beckinsal told me," he said. "She told me everything."

Daisy dropped her gaze to the weeds beneath the wild orchids, still there, stubbornly clinging to that tiny patch of soil. Was that why he'd come to Auchenard? Because Lady Beckinsal had made him aware of a deadline after which she would no longer possess a fortune?

"So now you see why I am so eager to return to London," he said, squeezing her hand lightly. "I will waste no time in speaking to the bishop. I hope to tell him that you return my affection."

Daisy felt a little as if she'd just taken a blow to her belly—she had no breath. None. She couldn't speak, couldn't think clearly. She hadn't told him of the bishop…and neither had he told her that he knew of her unique circumstances. Not until she'd pressed him.

"You don't have to answer just now, of course," he hastily added. "You will at least consider it?"

Daisy swallowed down the lump in her throat. She nodded. "Yes," she said. "I will consider it." She was considering it even now. But she didn't care for the suspicious thoughts rumbling around in her head as she did.

Robert studied her with some concern. He abruptly leaned forward and kissed her. It was a real kiss, not the chaste and proper sort he'd given her the last day or two. And yet he stopped the moment he began, shyly backing away. "We ought not to allow our emotions to overcome our good judgment," he said. He leaped to his feet and pulled her up. "Come, darling."

But she hadn't finished her weeding. Daisy looked down at the weeds as Robert put her hand in the crook of his elbow. The weeds were staying. They had rooted here; they were staying.

He led her out of the garden, and as they emerged onto the path, they were startled by a burst through the lodge door. Ellis was racing toward them. "Mamma!" he cried. "Is Cailean coming to dine?"

Robert stopped Ellis with a hand to his shoulder. "Hold there, lad. That is not the way you approach a lady."

"It's all right—" Daisy started, but Robert interrupted her.

"He needs to learn. The boy will never be the man you want him to be if you don't teach him properly." He dropped Daisy's hand, put both hands on Ellis's shoulders and turned him around, marching him away a few steps, then turning him back around to Daisy. "Now then. Approach your mother with respect. Bow your head. Ask her permission to address her."

Ellis looked as confused as Daisy felt. He looked mortified as he took two tentative steps forward, woodenly bowed, then said, "May I speak now?"

Daisy's heart ached. She sank down onto her

knees before him and took his hands. "Of course, darling. You may always speak to me. You need not ask my permission. *Never*," she said.

He nodded.

"The laird is not coming to dine, darling. But he came round to invite us to a festival."

Ellis gasped. "May we?"

She smiled. "We'll speak to Uncle Alfonso about it. Go and find him, will you? Ask him what he thinks." She kissed his cheek. Ellis darted away, cutting a wide berth around Robert.

Daisy stood up before Robert could help her. "That wasn't at all necessary. I have taught him *properly*," she said, struggling to control her temper.

"I have not implied otherwise. But there are some things only a man can teach a boy. I know you've done the best you could under the circumstances."

Daisy opened her mouth to argue, but he shook his head and put up a hand. "I don't expect you to understand, darling. You must trust me when I tell you that if you want him to be a respected viscount one day, he must possess the proper manners and demeanor. I'm only doing it for his sake."

Her son possessed very good manners. And he had the demeanor of a nine-year-old boy, just as he should.

The bank of dark clouds in Daisy's thoughts grew thicker.

"You cannot mean to attend this…festival," Robert said with a dismissive flick of his wrist.

"I do," Daisy said. "For Ellis's sake, I do."

"For God's sake, Daisy," Robert said. He pivoted away from her, his hands finding his hips, shaking his head to the heavens. "Will you not heed me? He is a dangerous man. A *criminal* in the eyes of the Crown. Your...association with him not only tarnishes your reputation, but it is destructive to your son's future prospects!"

"I don't believe it!" Daisy argued. "How can anyone know of the summer he has spent here?"

"Because people come and go between Scotland and England every day. Because tongues wag. Because all it takes is one mention," he said, shaking his finger at her, "of the Lady Chatwick at the home of a known smuggler, and talk *follows.*"

He was angry with her, brimming with it. There was some truth in what he was saying, she knew—but she had seen her son flourish here in a way she'd never seen. She wanted to give him this. And she couldn't bring herself to believe that someone would hasten back to London to tell where she'd been.

"I'll speak to my uncle," she assured him, but Robert was not mollified.

"I don't want you to go," he said sternly. "I can't force my will on you," he added.

Daisy thought, *Yet.*

"But I am asking you to consider my wishes," he finished.

"And I am asking you to consider mine," she said. "I have been in the man's company on several occasions. If there are tongues to be wagged, it is too late for it."

"That is not—"

"I beg your pardon, Robert, but I am unwell," she said. "My head is hurting so."

He pressed his lips together as if he was biting back what he would say to that. "Perhaps you should rest," he said curtly.

"Perhaps I should," she agreed and left him standing on the path, his dark gaze boring through her as she retreated to the lodge and her room.

She lay down on her bed and stared up at the ceiling.

Her head hurt, but it was the exhaustion of her emotions that had felled her and caused the tears that welled in her eyes. Robert was the man she thought she'd always wanted, a good man. She didn't care for the way he'd corrected Ellis, but she was also painfully aware that it could be worse. It could be the edicts of a complete stranger with no regard for her at all. And if that stranger was indifferent to Ellis, or worse, cruel, she couldn't bear it. She may not care for the way Robert spoke to Ellis, but at least she knew that he cared for her, and surely that devotion would carry over to her son. Wouldn't it?

There had been only one man besides her uncle who had shown Ellis even the smallest amount of regard, and that was Cailean. And oh, how Ellis adored him.

A tear escaped her eye and slid down her cheek. Daisy swiped angrily at it. She had only herself to blame for turning an impetuous physical spark with a handsome man into something more than it was or could ever be.

It was time that she stopped daydreaming. It was time she faced her future. But by God, she was going to allow Ellis the pleasure of that festival before she did.

Another tear slipped out, and this time Daisy not only swiped at it; she got up, determined to cease all feminine displays of disappointment. She had a son to think of, a future to get on with.

She moved to her writing desk and opened her diary. She removed Cailean's handkerchief and touched it to her nose. It didn't smell of Cailean; it smelled of lavender. She returned it to the book and closed it, then restlessly stood up and moved to look out the window at her garden. It was in full bloom now, brought back to life with a little care, some rotting fish and a lot of rain. She would miss it so.

With a heavy sigh, she gazed out at the lake and the heavy clouds overhead. There, in the distance, she could see a boat. The first boat she'd seen in days. She watched it glide along until it finally disappeared around the bend in the lake and she could no longer see it. That single, solitary boat reminded her of Cailean. It was like he was gliding away from her, disappearing in the distance, just...drifting away from her, carrying her heart with him.

She loved him. She knew that she did. It wasn't the infatuation she'd felt the first time she laid eyes on him, and it was wrong, so wrong, and impossible, but she couldn't deny that she loved him desperately.

She loved the way he treated her, with respect. As an equal. She loved the way he cared for Ellis. She loved everything about him...except that he was a smuggler, and an unrepentant one at that. That, she found maddening.

DAISY AT LAST came out of her room to join the others for supper.

Robert and Uncle Alfonso were already in the great room, staring out the windows as they sipped from drams of whisky. Robert was talking about the navy, and Uncle Alfonso looked a bit glassy-eyed. The clouds overhead had turned everything quite gray. Even the light of many candles and the hearth could not chase the shadows from the room.

When Rowley announced supper was served, Robert instantly held out his arm to Daisy, as if it were his place, and not that of her uncle's, to escort her into the dining room. Her uncle seemed not to notice, remarking on the weather to Belinda.

As Rowley served the first course, Uncle Alfonso said that Ellis had told him of the festival to be held at Balhaire. "Mr. Munro tells me it's quite the event," he said. "Dancing and demonstrations of strength and wares to be sold."

"A festival held in a den of smugglers—" Robert snorted "—does not sound like an appropriate *event* Lord Chatwick should attend."

Uncle Alfonso nodded thoughtfully. "There are indeed smugglers in these hills. But good people, too. I think the boy would enjoy it."

"I would like to attend," Belinda said uncertainly, earning a look of surprise from her cousin and her uncle.

"You *would*?" Daisy asked.

"Mr. Munro saw my painting of the Dinwiddie keep," she said. "It's a ruin on the hill," she explained to Robert. "He seems to think it might fetch a good sum."

"That settles it, then," Uncle Alfonso said. "We will attend the festival."

Robert looked around, clearly unhappy with the lot of them. "I will not allow Lady Chatwick and her son to go alone," he said. "I shall attend, as well."

It was curious that not one of them exclaimed how happy they were that he would deign to accompany them.

Uncle Alfonso changed the subject entirely as Rowley served plates of fish and potatoes. "You'll be quite proud of this meal, I should think, darling," he said to Daisy as Rowley spooned sauce over the fish. "Ellis caught it. It was a pollack the size of a cat."

"Ellis caught it!" Daisy said, delighted.

"I shudder to think of Ellis on the shoreline with a large fish on the other end of his string," Belinda said and actually shuddered. "That's precisely how Master Cavens died, you know."

"Oh, Belinda, please don't mention it," Daisy said, pressing a hand to her breast.

"He had a fish on his line that pulled him right into the Thames. They found him a full day later."

"This is not the Thames," Uncle Alfonso said

brusquely. "The lake is calm. He would not be pulled away by the waters."

"Well, no," Belinda agreed. "But the danger is present all the same."

"That is quite enough," Robert said and laid down his fork. "Miss Hainsworth, you will kindly cease with your untoward talk at this table. You have a way of putting everyone off their otherwise exceptional meal and I, for one, will not tolerate it."

Poor Belinda's cheeks turned crimson.

"Rob!" Daisy said, aghast.

Tears sprang to Belinda's eyes, and she pushed away from the table before Rowley could reach her, tipping her chair over in her haste. "I beg your pardon," she said and fled from the room.

Robert sighed. "She certainly has a sour view of the world." He picked up his fork to continue with his meal, seemingly unconcerned that he'd just sent Daisy's cousin fleeing in tears. "You were saying, Mr. Kimberly?"

Daisy and her uncle exchanged a stunned look. "That's simply the way she is," Uncle Alfonso said darkly. "She doesn't know better."

Robert nodded but offered no apology.

As soon as the meal was done, Uncle Alfonso politely declined the port Robert suggested with the excuse that he had some work to do. Robert escorted Daisy into the great room and seated her on the settee near the hearth with her needlework. Needlework that had gone untouched for weeks now. Robert produced a book and sat down across from her, his legs crossed, and proceeded to read.

Daisy made several stitches, but she had to remove them. She was exasperated, her work careless as a result. It wasn't what Robert had said to Belinda—Lord knew they'd all lost patience with her at one time or another—it was his complete disregard for her feelings.

She lowered her embroidery and stared at him.

Robert glanced up from his reading. "Is everything all right?"

"Belinda has no one else in the world but us."

"Pardon?" He lowered his book.

"Belinda has no one else," Daisy said again. "I know she can be quite difficult, but she is a member of this family, and we accept her as she is."

Robert looked confused. "Have I given you reason to think I want differently?"

"You treated her ill this evening, Robert."

"Oh." He nodded. "I agree I was a bit harsh. My apologies." He put the book aside and came to the settee to sit beside her. "My *sincerest* apologies," he said, taking her hand. "I vow to do my best not to criticize Cousin Belinda."

Was he sincere? Or was he saying what she wanted to hear? "Perhaps you might apologize to her."

"The first opportunity, you have my word," he said. He frowned lightly. "You are cross with me." He leaned forward and kissed her tenderly. "Forgive me, darling. I would never consciously wound you or your family—you know that I wouldn't."

She believed that was true. Or rather, she wanted to believe it was true. He was new to them, new to her life now. Naturally it required accommodations from both of them. And patience—she had to be patient, had to see that this new relationship between her and Robert worked, for the sake of them all.

Daisy moved her hand to his thigh, and he immediately deepened his kiss, his tongue slipping in between her lips. She moved her hand higher up his leg—

Robert suddenly lifted his head and snatched her hand from his leg. "Daisy! Have a care!" he snapped.

"It's all right," she tried to assure him. "I was married for many years—"

"What has that to do with it?" He stood, his cheeks blooming. "That sort of behavior is very unbecoming, madam. You are too immodest!"

She was too *immodest*? He'd spoken of marriage this afternoon, but he feared her touch?

"Look now, I've displeased you," he said irritably and sighed. "I was surprised. Forgive me for speaking so harshly." He sat down again, took her hand in his. "I love you, Daisy. But I… I forget how much time has passed. You must allow me to grow accustomed to you as you are now."

"As I am now," she repeated. "I am the same as I've ever been. Only a bit older and a bit more experienced." She leaned forward and kissed him tenderly. Once again Robert broke away. With a nervous laugh he stood. He was acting like a boy, like a virgin…

"Robert? Are you…have you never…?"

He seemed confused at first, but then his face darkened. "I beg your pardon!" he said low. "That is hardly something after which a proper lady should *ever* inquire."

Daisy sighed with impatience and sagged against the back of the settee.

"I am quite shocked by your behavior this evening, Daisy. I never took you for a wanton."

"Shocked," she repeated. There was a time she might have been mortally wounded by such a claim, but she was too old, too widowed, too uncaring to deny it. She shrugged and picked up her embroidery. "I am not a wanton, Robert. I am a widow."

He watched her resume her needlework, waiting for her to say more, then rubbing his chin uncertainly when she did not. He suddenly went down on his knee before her, pushed the embroidery aside and grabbed both her hands. "Listen to me, darling. You must have a care for appearances. But…but when we are wed, I promise you will find every imaginable delight in my bed."

Ah, but it would be *her* bed, wouldn't it? Hadn't he already mentioned Chatwick Hall? Moreover, she rather thought she could imagine the delights in bed very clearly, and they did not excite her. Daisy smiled dully. "Do you promise?" she asked sweetly. Like a proper chaste virgin, precisely as he wanted. Like a woman who was dead inside but playing her part.

He stroked her face, then kissed her tenderly. "I do." He stood up and looked around the room, as if he was uncertain what to do next. He picked up his book. "I should like to retire now. Perhaps you should, as well."

To end this perfectly dreadful evening, he would also tell her when she ought to go to bed, as if she were a child. "Of course," she said, carelessly tossing aside her embroidery. "Good night, Rob." She walked from the room, acutely aware that there was no fire between them, no flames to engulf them. And for some peculiar reason, she was glad for it.

CHAPTER FOURTEEN

THE TRIP TO Balhaire was as hard as Daisy suspected it would be. She, Belinda and Ellis were in the coach they'd hired when they had arrived in Scotland, and Uncle Alfonso and Robert rode borrowed horses. The road was very narrow, disappearing in parts, pitted in other parts. They made wretchedly slow progress down the glen. At one point, Belinda remarked that the people walking toward Balhaire through the meadows with bundles on their back or pulling carts behind them were moving faster than the coach.

Daisy forgot her discomfort when they neared Balhaire and passed another meadow where men erected tents.

"What is it for?" Ellis asked, crowding in beside her at the window to have a look.

"I don't know," Daisy said.

From there, the coach moved into a sizable village, teeming with people and animals that wandered in the lanes, jostling past wagons loaded with wares for the squat buildings that lined both sides of the high road. The entire village was shadowed by the fortress up on the hill, toward which they slowly wended, until they reached the gates.

Daisy had seen many castles in her life, but this one was quite imposing. It had towers and wings jutting off this way and that. She supposed someone could very easily get lost in there, and unthinkingly she put her hand on Ellis's.

As they pulled through the massive wooden gates, someone shouted, and the coach rolled to a stop. A moment later, the door of the coach swung open, and a beefy, ginger-haired man with a heavy beard put his head inside. *"Madainn mhath,"* he said.

"Ah...good afternoon," Daisy responded.

The man looked startled by her English and squinted at her as if he wasn't certain what he'd heard. He suddenly disappeared, and the door shut behind him.

Daisy and Belinda exchanged a look of confusion.

The door swung open again, and another man glanced disapprovingly around at the three of them. "Good afternoon," he said, his voice deep. "Lady Chatwick," he said, and inclined his head. "Rabbie Mackenzie." He held out his hand to her.

Daisy allowed him to help her out of the coach and waited as he helped the others. She was astounded by the activity in that bailey—there were more people and animals and so many dogs. One sniffed at her hem and her shoes now.

When they had all climbed out of the coach, and Uncle Alfonso and Robert had come down from their mounts, the ginger-haired man said something to the driver, and the coach lumbered on.

"Welcome to Balhaire," Rabbie Mackenzie said.

"Thank you," Daisy said and tried, unsuccessfully, to wave the dog away.

"*Sguir dheth!*" Mackenzie said sharply to the dog. The dog's ears flattened, and it slowly sank down onto its belly.

"Ah…may I introduce—"

"I'll take you in to my mother, Lady Mackenzie, then," he said curtly, cutting her off before he would have to exchange pleasantries with Daisy's family and gesturing to the massive door of the castle. He began to stride toward it. Daisy grabbed Ellis's hand and hurried to catch up. Belinda, her uncle and Robert followed behind.

In the foyer, Daisy could scarcely take in all the armaments hanging above their heads before she was ushered along, down a darker corridor and into a room the size of a ballroom. In here, three long and highly polished tables stretched almost the length of the room. They were anchored by hearths on either end, and there, in the middle, was a platform on which a smaller table faced the others, with ten or so upholstered chairs along one side. Above the tables hung iron wheels full of candles that had not yet been lit. And dogs! More dogs wandered about in here, and three of them curled onto mats in front of the hearth.

Ellis had an iron grip on Daisy's skirt, she realized, and she didn't blame him—she would very much like to cling to someone's skirt, too. Her uncle, on the other hand, was enthralled. "Look there," he said, pointing to the stained glass window high overhead, and the stone arches that crisscrossed the ceiling. "Marvelous architecture, is it not?"

Daisy never answered—there was a burst of activity behind them as two women and three young children appeared through a door near one of the hearths. The children, two girls and a boy, skipped forward, stopping just before Daisy to eye Ellis with curiosity.

Her son pressed into her side.

"Welcome, welcome!"

A regal woman wearing a mantua glided toward them. Behind her were two young women, one of them heavy with child. The other, Daisy was relieved to see, was Miss Catriona Mackenzie.

"You are Lady Chatwick," the woman said with an English accent. She sank into a curtsy. "You are our honored guest."

"Thank you," Daisy said.

The woman smiled, and when she did, she looked remarkably younger than the sixty or so years Daisy guessed her to be. "I am Lady Mackenzie. My daughters, Mrs. Vivienne Mackenzie," she said, indicating the pregnant one, "the wife of Marcas Mackenzie. And, of course, you've met Catriona."

"Thank you for your invitation. May I introduce my family?" Daisy asked. She made the introductions. Lady Mackenzie did not look at Robert.

When Daisy introduced him, she chose that moment to squat down so that she was eye level with Ellis. "Lord Chatwick, I am so glad you have come," she said. "My grandchildren are desperate for playmates. And I have heard that you enjoy the caber toss."

Surprised, Ellis looked up at Daisy.

"I told her," Catriona Mackenzie said. "I've seen it with my very own eyes, have I no'?"

"I am rather good," Ellis unabashedly agreed.

"Perhaps you might like to have a look at some of Egan's toys?" the pregnant Mrs. Mackenzie asked and put her hand on her son's shoulder. "I think he possesses a toy caber."

"Aye," the young boy said.

Ellis glanced uncertainly at Daisy. "May I?"

"Yes, of course!" Daisy said, thrilled and stunned that he wanted to go, that he was not clinging to her and begging to stay at her side.

"I'll go along and watch after him," Belinda offered.

Belinda and Ellis followed Lady Mackenzie's daughters and grandchildren from the room. Lady Mackenzie smiled at Daisy and Alfonso...but still did not look at Robert. "You must forgive the dreadful decor. My husband clings to tradition as if it were the air he breathes," she said laughingly. "This room has remained virtually unchanged for centuries."

"The architecture is quite impressive. I guess it to be twelfth century?" Uncle Alfonso asked.

"Thirteenth, I believe," Lady Mackenzie said. "At least this room. Various parts of the castle have been added on over the centuries. Would you like a tour, Mr. Kimberly?"

Uncle Alfonso's face lit with delight. "If it is not a bother, I should very much like to have a look about."

"Not a bother in the least!" She walked to a bell-pull and gave it a hearty tug. Moments later an elderly man, stooped in the shoulders, appeared. "Seamus, our guest Mr. Kimberly would like a tour of this old pile of stones. Would you be so kind?"

"Aye, mu'um," he said.

"Perhaps you should accompany him, Captain," she said and glanced at Robert for the first time, her gaze gone cool.

"Thank you, but I prefer to stay with Lady Chatwick—"

"Oh, I'm afraid that won't be possible. She'll be in good hands." Her smile was thin.

Robert was clearly taken aback. "Ah…" He nodded curtly, his expression inscrutable, and followed behind Uncle Alfonso and his escort, who were already engaged in a discussion of architecture.

Lady Mackenzie's warm smile returned. "We've put you in a suite of rooms, and your guest will have accommodations as well, but perhaps in a different part of the castle."

"Thank you."

"Let's go to the study, shall we? It's much more inviting than this hall." She looped her arm through Daisy's and led her out of the hall. "Vivienne is expecting her fourth child at any moment," she said. "I shouldn't be the least surprised if the child comes during the *feill*. I myself was at a wedding when Vivienne decided to make her appearance. Lord Chatwick is your only child?"

"Yes."

"You were widowed at such a young age," she said sympathetically.

"Yes," Daisy agreed.

"Tell me, how do you find the Highlands? I will confess I was quite intimidated when I first arrived. The landscape was so stark and lonely."

"Oh, I wasn't intimidated in the least by the landscape," Daisy said. "I found it quite beautiful. I wish I didn't have to leave it."

Lady Mackenzie paused. "*Must* you leave it?" she asked pointedly and watched Daisy closely for her answer.

Goodness, she'd said too much. The lady no doubt had heard much about the Chatwick purse. She said vaguely, "Eventually."

Lady Mackenzie smiled and resumed their walk. "Have you ever attended a *feill*?" she asked, politely changing the subject.

Daisy laughed. "No, never."

"You will be astounded," Lady Mackenzie assured her. "We'll go down this afternoon to watch the games. You might have seen the tents on the edge of the village? That is where the games will be held. Tonight, there will be dancing here and card games if you like. Are you a gambler?"

"A poor one," Daisy admitted. "I've surely lost more than I've won."

They came to a closed door in the corridor. Lady

Mackenzie knocked softly, opened the door and led Daisy into a room swathed in sunlight so bright it was almost blinding. But she did see a man who looked very much like Cailean, but with graying hair. He stood up from behind his desk and limped around it, heavily favoring his left leg.

"Mackenzie, may I introduce Lady Chatwick of Auchenard?" Lady Mackenzie said. To Daisy, "My husband, Laird Mackenzie of Balhaire."

"How do you do," Daisy said, sinking into a curtsy.

"Aye, what is said of you is true, is it no'?" Lord Mackenzie said, smiling broadly. "You are bonny, you are," he said as he limped forward. Daisy reflexively held out her hand, and he took it, bowing over it. "I trust the travel was no' too hard, then?"

"The roads are a *bit* rough," she said, smiling coyly. "But we've arrived in one piece. Thank you."

"There is naugh' but Auchenard and Arrandale in that direction, no one to pack down the road and make it hard, aye? Have you settled into Auchenard, then? I've no' seen it in many years."

"Yes, actually, I have. More happily than I expected."

"Pardon, but I've no' allowed my son a word," he said and looked over Daisy's shoulder.

Daisy turned slightly; her heart leaped at the sight of Cailean. He was standing across the room, his back to the wall, one ankle crossed over the other, his arms folded across his chest. And his blue-eyed gaze bored through her. "I, ah… I beg your pardon,

my lord," Daisy said. "I didn't see you there." Her
pulse fluttered madly, and she wanted to grip her
hands together to keep them from shaking. Were they
shaking? They felt as if they were shaking.

"Madainn mhath," he said, his voice low and
calm. He did not share her nervousness, clearly.

"Cailean, will you not come forward and greet
her properly?" Lady Mackenzie asked, sounding a
bit perturbed.

Cailean responded to that in the Scotch tongue
in a low voice.

Whatever he said caused his mother to smile. "I
don't speak Gaelic," she said to Daisy. "Since my
son was a wee lad, he has expressed his displeasure
with me in Gaelic."

"I could never be displeased with you, *Mathair,*"
he said and insouciantly pushed away from the wall
and ambled forward. When he reached her, he flicked
his gaze to her hand, then to her face.

She supposed he thought she should offer it. But
Daisy did not offer it to the popinjay. So he reached
for it, without taking his eyes from hers, and lifted it
up, bowing over it, kissing the back of it. "Welcome
to Balhaire, Lady Chatwick."

She snatched her hand free. Perhaps a little too
forcefully. A little too obviously.

"Shall we sit?" Lady Mackenzie asked and
showed Daisy to the settee.

Cailean, she noticed, remained standing.

"Perhaps you might pour our guest a whisky,
Cailean," his mother said.

Cailean moved lazily to the sideboard.

Lady Mackenzie sat beside Daisy. "Now, you must tell me what brings you all the way to Scotland. It is so very rare for an Englishwoman to appear in our little glen."

"Auchenard is my son's heritage," Daisy said. "I wanted him to see it. Unfortunately, my husband was too ill to bring him."

"And your friend?" Lady Mackenzie asked, still smiling.

Her friend? She thought of Belinda, then realized she meant her escort. "Captain Spivey?" She noticed how they all looked at her, very still, waiting for her answer. Warmth crept up her neck—she felt almost as if she'd done something wrong in bringing him. But the invitation had clearly been extended to him, as well. "He...he surprised us all," she admitted, searching for the right thing to say. "I had known him a very long time ago. He went to London to call on me after resigning his naval commission, and when he discovered I had gone away for the summer, I suppose... I suppose he thought to follow."

"What a dear friend," Lady Mackenzie said, but she didn't sound very sincere. "How did he know where to find you?" she asked. "Auchenard is not on any known road, is it?"

Lord Mackenzie watched her like she was a mouse and he a hawk. Cailean's gaze was locked on her, too, as he leaned over to hand her a dram of whisky. Did they think Robert had come here for Cailean? "My friend Lady Beckinsal told him where I'd gone," she said. "Pardon, but why do you ask?"

"Oh, no reason at all," Lady Mackenzie said quickly and lightly. "We are not accustomed to strangers and it's so very unusual to have a captain of the Royal Navy *here.*"

"Yes, well, he's no longer in the navy."

"Ah," Lady Mackenzie said. "What will the poor man do without a ship to captain?"

Marry me, Daisy thought, and felt a tiny swell of misery. But she smiled and shrugged. "You must ask him, I'm afraid."

"Indeed I will," Lady Mackenzie said, putting aside her untouched dram of whisky. "Arran? Perhaps we ought to go and have a look at the field."

"At the what?" her husband asked, startled.

"We discussed it earlier today," she said, giving him a pointed look.

"But the games willna start for two hours more," he said, sounding confused.

Lady Mackenzie rose from her seat. *"Arran."*

Whatever the laird saw in his wife's face made him change his mind. "Aye. The field," he said.

Lady Mackenzie smiled and put her arm around his waist. "Cailean, you will see Lady Chatwick safely returned to the hall, won't you?"

"Of course," he said pleasantly.

"Please take your time with the whisky, Lady Chatwick. It is quite good," she said as she and her husband began the arduous walk to the door. "We will see you shortly." The two of them went out.

When the door closed softly behind them, Cailean looked at Daisy and smiled a little lopsidedly, and her pulse began to flutter all over again. "You may no' have guessed it, but my mother is in the midst of matchmaking."

"You must be terrified," Daisy said smartly and stood up. She was still annoyed with him. Still loved him. Still felt so at odds with herself about everything, but most of all, she could not look at his eyes, at his smile, and not want to melt into him.

He chuckled. "There have been many attempts in the past. I've grown accustomed to it."

"I can rather imagine that at your advanced age there have been *many* attempts. I would do the same were my son still unmarried as he entered his dotage."

Cailean's smile deepened, and he slowly raised a brow. "What has you cross, *leannan*?"

Good God, the man was insufferable. He knew very well what had her cross. "It doesn't matter," she said and turned away from him, crossing her arms as she moved aimlessly across the room. "How long must we remain here before your mother is convinced she's done her duty?"

"Five minutes ought to suffice," he said. "The impropriety of leaving you alone with a notorious bachelor will undoubtedly trump her desire to see me wed."

Daisy groaned. She moved to the window and peered out at the bailey. Cailean joined her there, standing shoulder to shoulder with her. His fingers touched, then tangled with hers. The spark shot up her arm, and she sighed inadvertently. Daisy leaned her head against his shoulder. She ought to slap his fool hand away…but she didn't. She ought not to rest her head on his shoulder…but she did. Her desire for his touch tugged at her heart more than her exasperation with him.

He touched the small of her back, then slid his hand around to her waist and drew her into his side. No, it was too much—it only served to ratchet up her longing to make it unbearable. Daisy pushed away and turned to face him. Cailean turned, too, his blue eyes moving over her face, lingering on her lips.

"What do you *want* of me?" she whispered.

His gaze moved lower, to her décolletage, and he traced a knuckle over the swell of her breast. "That is a dangerous question and one I canna answer."

"I don't understand you, Cailean," she said plaintively.

He winced. "Aye, it's complicated."

She expected him to explain himself, or to try to convince her that there was nothing to understand. *"Complicated,"* she said irritably. "You say things that make me want to despise you, and yet I think you want to kiss me right now."

"I do," he murmured. "In the most violent way. I am, in fact, besieged with want."

She tilted her head back and lifted her chin, so that her mouth was a breath from his. "Then why don't you?"

His breath was warm on her lips. He cupped her

face with his hand, caressed her lip with his thumb, and she could feel her heart softening. "For the love of God I donna know why no', but I willna kiss you, Daisy. I want only to help you…but I canna help that I desire you, as well."

She couldn't bear this. She couldn't bear all the longing for him when he wouldn't reciprocate, when he wanted her to marry Robert and be done with it. She jerked her face from his hand and stepped back. "You are tiresome, Cailean. Help someone else." She walked across the room and opened the door, sweeping out of it. She'd only taken a step or two when she realized she had no idea how to return to the main hall. She stepped back inside the room.

Cailean was still at the window, still standing where she'd left him. His head was down, and he'd folded his arms tightly across his chest.

"Cailean?"

His head jerked up, and for the slender wisp of a moment, he looked incredibly hopeful. But Daisy would show him no mercy—she was too angry, too frustrated. "Will you please show me back to the great room? I want to find my son."

Something flickered in his blue eyes and the hope disappeared, buried under the insouciance, the casual indifference that took its place. "Aye, of course," he said.

CHAPTER FIFTEEN

CAILEAN HAD WANTED to kiss Daisy—more than wanted, had burned with that desire—but something had shadowed his thoughts, something he couldn't quite grasp.

Was it duty? No. It wasn't his duty to protect her. He did not answer to duty.

A resentment of his mother's never-ending attempts to see him wed? No. He didn't begrudge his mother that natural desire.

What bloody arse didn't take a kiss when offered? This was the second time he'd failed to act, and he was a man who *never* failed when such an opportunity presented itself. Nor had he failed to keep his sensibilities and feelings far above the fray of his physical wants since that day fifteen years ago when Miss Beauly had refused him.

What had happened to that man? And what in damnation was that thought in his head he couldn't quite drag into consciousness?

Aye, he *did* feel himself under siege with irreconcilable thoughts and feelings. It was troubling—a kiss in his father's study was certainly not as inflammatory as what he'd done in that potting shed. He'd taken great liberties with Daisy, clearly—and now suddenly he was concerned with *what*, pray tell?

He had no time to study this unexpected alteration to his conscience, thank the saints, for he might have hung himself from the rafters. He might yet. But he was needed to open the games in his father's stead.

Cailean did not see Daisy that afternoon. He was surrounded by clan and fellow Highland guard members as he joined the caber toss and the stone throw. The physical exertion and camaraderie of men he knew and admired helped him to push down the troubling thoughts of Daisy. The lingering feeling of discomposure was successfully drowned with several tankards of ale.

He didn't see Daisy, but he did stumble upon Ellis. There was an area in the meadow set aside for children to play games that emulated those in which the adults engaged. Ellis watched from the side in the company of Miss Hainsworth. He was dressed formally in spite of the heat, and was clearly not a participant.

Cailean squatted down beside Ellis. The lad's face lit with a smile. Cailean clapped him on the shoulder and asked, "Why do you no' participate, then?"

Ellis's smile faded. "I don't..." He looked at the other lads. "I don't know how," he said.

"You'll no' learn if you donna play. Come," he said and took Ellis by the hand, walking into the field where boys were lined up to participate in the stone put, whereby they launched a smooth stone from their palm and measured the distance of their throw. He asked the other lads to allow Ellis to participate.

"But he's a *Sassenach*," a ruddy-faced ginger-haired lad said in Gaelic. "My da said I'm to stay away from them."

Cailean squatted down before that young man and said quietly, "You may tell your da that Lord Chatwick is our guest, *Sassenach* or no', and if he doesna welcome him as he ought, I will rip him from limb to limb."

The color drained from the lad's face. "Aye, laird," he said.

Cailean stayed to ensure that they did indeed include Ellis. One of them was kind enough to instruct him how to throw the stone. Ellis was wretched at it, but he didn't seem to care—his face was awash in happiness, and he was eager to please. He congratulated each throw to the point Cailean laughingly told him that their throws couldn't all be as good as that.

He moved to the other side of the field while keeping a watchful eye on Ellis, and was watching him have another go at the stone put when he saw the flash of light blond hair. He turned and saw Daisy standing between her uncle and Spivey, watching the men at their stone toss. Spivey rested his hand on the small of her back, and he leaned over her shoulder and said something that made her smile brightly. Maybe she even laughed.

Cailean felt a strange constriction in his chest. He turned away from the sight of her. He had no right to feel anything. Cailean walked in the opposite direction and away from her, in search of something that could silence his thoughts.

He found himself at the games once again and noticed that the backhold wrestling event was about to commence. *Wrestling*. That was it, that was exactly what he needed. Let him release his frustrations by slamming a man or two into the ground. All in good fun, of course, or at least he'd tell the unlucky lads he beat that was so.

He joined the men lining up to compete. There were ten in all, vying for the prize of a kiss from Aileen Ramsey, a bonny young woman. The last man standing would have the pleasure of receiving her kiss. Aileen stood on a platform, swinging her skirts this way and that, calling out encouragement to the men who stepped in line to wrestle.

Cailean was pitted against men he'd trained— all of them quite good if he was allowed that bit of self-commendation. As he waited for the game to begin, another man entered the competition—the one they called the Mountain. He was a head taller than Cailean and a good bit wider. Cailean almost smiled when he saw him. His mood was not precisely competitive—it was more lethal than that.

The first matches went quickly; Cailean pinned his opponents in a matter of seconds. Round they went, winnowing the number of contestants down to the last few men who consistently managed to keep their feet. Each round, Cailean brought his opponent to the ground with a roar, but with each successful win, the roots of his agitation only sank deeper.

The competition finally came down to two men—Cailean and the Mountain, who had dispatched his opponents like small children. A large crowd had gathered around them now, and someone had thrown a hat onto the ground to collect the wagers.

They were called to the center of the ring. Cailean moved to take his position, and he happened to catch sight of Daisy with Spivey standing apart from the crowd, watching. Her gaze, cool and distant, met his. Unaffected. *English.*

Cailean ignored her and turned to his opponent. "I mean to win," Cailean said to the Mountain.

"Aye, but you will no'," the Mountain said, grinning.

They locked their arms around each other's back, and the warden of wrestling called for the start.

Cailean expected to lose, and he hardly cared if he did. He only hoped it was a painful loss, that his battered and bruised body would be slow to get up, but that this swelling of infatuation, or whatever the bloody hell it was that had taken up residence on his chest, would be gone. He wanted the Mountain to squeeze the air from his body, to knock the infatuation from his veins.

But something miraculous happened.

The Mountain began to struggle against *him.* Cailean's strength, stoked by old and new frustrations, poured out of him. With a guttural cry, he managed to knock the Mountain off his feet and pin him to the ground.

The crowd roared with delight.

The game warden called the match in favor of Cailean. He stood up, offered his hand to the Mountain.

"Aye, you've won, lad," the Mountain said congenially, and he slapped Cailean so hard on his back that he very nearly went down to his knees.

The gathered crowd was frenzied now, shouting his name. He turned his back to them and marched up to where Aileen Ramsey stood on a box. He couldn't say why he did what he did, but he lifted the woman off the box, threw his arm around her back, dipped her backward and bloody well kissed her.

The crowd cheered wildly.

Cailean felt nothing for it, but when he lifted the lass upright, she looked at him with a stunned expression. And then a glorious smile.

Aye, then, all was not lost. He was still a man after all.

In the late afternoon, fires were lit around the meadow ahead of clouds thickening in the east. The musicians picked up their pipes and began to play, and the country dancing commenced for those who had traveled to the *feill*. Arran Mackenzie's clan and Highland nobility retreated to the castle—they would dance in the great hall.

Cailean dressed formally for the evening in a coat and waistcoat, a plaid sash across his chest pinned with the clan's emblem, and a sporran around his waist. The hall gleamed with the light from two hearths and dozens of candles. A long line of Mackenzies and guests had already formed at the sideboard, which was laden with roasted beef and traditional Scottish pots, such as haggis, turnips and potatoes. Servants wandered through the crowd, carrying ewers of whisky and ale, refilling cups.

Cailean made his way to the dais and sat next to Rabbie, who'd had a wee bit to drink, judging by the way he sat, slung over a seat like woolen blanket. He looked sourly at the crowd.

"What has you cross?" Cailean asked, sitting next to him.

Rabbie lifted his chin as if to indicate something; Cailean followed his gaze and saw Daisy, her uncle and Captain Spivey. They were seated at a table with Somerled.

Diah, she looked brilliant tonight. The edges of her bodice had been embellished with silk rosebuds that matched those on the ribbon around her neck. Her gown was the color of her eyes. Somerled was leaning toward her, as if sharing a secret with her and her uncle. Spivey looked as sour as Rabbie.

"What then, do you no' see?" Rabbie snapped. "His musket shot is in your flank yet."

Four years ago, Cailean had been grazed by a musket ball fired from the gun of an English sailor. He'd been moving a ship through a particularly dangerous part of the French coast, trying to slip past the naval ship in heavy fog while Aulay sailed north. It was a dangerous thing to do, as Cailean and his men couldn't see more than a few feet in that soupy fog. But they had sailed that coastline for years, and had crept along, knowing that if they didn't, when the fog lifted, they'd be a sitting target for the English naval ship.

As they could not see the Scottish ship, the English captain had decided not to fire a canon, probably thinking he'd waste good ammunition. Later, Cailean and Aulay had reasoned that one ambitious sailor had fired blindly, hoping to hit something to inform the English ship where they were. It was a miracle that Cailean and their crew had remained silent when he'd been grazed, and had managed to slide past undetected.

Cailean shrugged. "It was no more than a burn, aye? And it wasna him."

Rabbie snorted. "Does it matter?"

"Aye, it matters," Cailean said calmly. "He's harmless. He seeks his own fortune now."

Rabbie looked at him with surprise. "Do you really believe it? Will you believe it until a ship arrives in our cove, if no' at Arrandale as we sit, waiting like fat geese?"

"We've men there," Cailean pointed out.

Rabbie rolled his eyes at his older brother. "They may no' come today, Cailean. But they will come. One of theirs is dead, aye? They'll no' allow you to rest now that they know where you are." He signaled one of the servants by lifting his empty tankard. "He is a spy. Mark me."

Cailean wasn't as pessimistic as his brother. Of course they had to be careful. They always had to be careful. But this was a long way for the English to come for one man. They'd not take ships from the seas between England and France for a free trader. But neither was Cailean naive. He looked toward the table again, and he inwardly started when he caught Spivey staring at him.

He suddenly stood, kicking his chair out of his way and startling his little brother.

"Where are you going?" Rabbie asked.

Cailean didn't answer. He didn't know, precisely. Why in God's name had that barmy Englishwoman come to Scotland at all? She'd succeeded only in making trouble for them and saddling herself with the likes of Spivey. *Diah*, was he the best she hoped to do? It angered him. A woman like Daisy Bristol deserved much better than Spivey.

Cailean walked through the crowd, pausing to speak to people who intercepted him. Pressing on, he reached the table where Daisy was apparently having a bloody grand time of it, judging by the way her head tilted back with gay laughter at something Somerled had said.

"Mackenzie!" Somerled said grandly.

Daisy stopped laughing and turned, glancing up at him with a shine in her eyes that he recognized. The lady had imbibed a wee bit of whisky.

Not Spivey—he surged to his feet, glaring at Cailean.

"Feasgar math," Cailean said curtly. He held out his hand to Daisy. "Lady Chatwick, will you dance with me?"

She blanched. "Oh, I…ah… I'm not familiar with the style of dancing."

"It's simple enough," he said and impatiently gestured for her to take his hand. "Naugh' more than a wee bit of skipping about."

Daisy stared at his hand, clearly debating how she might blatantly refuse him.

"The lady does not wish—" Spivey started, but Daisy suddenly came to her feet.

"Yes," she said and put her hand in Cailean's. She smiled at the captain and said, "He is our host."

As if she needed his permission.

Spivey smoldered…but in a very different way than Cailean was smoldering inside. He closed his fingers tightly around Daisy's, lest she have any notion of changing her mind. Without another look at her companions, or before Spivey could challenge him to a duel—as Cailean guessed he very much wanted to do, and would have, had he not feared for his own life among so many Mackenzies—he led Daisy to the part of the hall cleared for dancing.

"I must warn you that I am not a very good skipper," she said.

"You will survive it." He noticed how many in the hall turned to look at them. Some of the expressions were disapproving—there was no love of English here, no matter that Lady Mackenzie was herself English. Some of the looks were admiring—she was beautiful; anyone could see that she was. All of them were curious, suspicious and cool.

He escorted her into the line of dancers, put his hand to the small of her back, held her other hand overhead and said, "You're still cross, are you?"

"Quite," she said emphatically. "I'd not have danced at all had it not been for..." Her voice trailed off.

Had it not been for what? "How long do you intend to be cross, then?" Cailean demanded as they waited for the music to begin.

"I don't know. At least a fortnight. Quite possibly forever."

"Aye, but that is too long. I will allow a few days of it, no more."

Someone brushed past her, and Daisy stumbled. Her heel mysteriously connected with his ankle, and rather hard at that. "Oh. *Pardon,*" she said dramatically. And then, "You do not have the privilege of decreeing how long I am allowed to remain cross, and now that you have, I am determined to be cross even longer."

"Diabhal," he muttered.

She tossed her head. "I haven't the slightest idea how to perform this dance."

"Follow my lead," he said gruffly.

"I don't want to," she said, glancing at him sidelong.

He was unable to take his gaze from her slender neck, the color in her cheeks. He couldn't bear to think of Spivey's hands on her. Cailean shrugged as the music began. "I donna care if you do." He startled her by skipping twice and twirled her away from his body. She cried out with surprise as he did, and when he twirled her back, she clumsily slammed into his chest, wide-eyed.

"Skip," he said.

"Skip!" she echoed with alarm, but she managed to do it. He repeated the steps, then dropped her hand, passed behind her, came around again. And this time, he lifted the opposite arm in the air.

"Again," he said.

After several missteps, and one unfortunate heel to the top of his foot, and some swaying that was not in time with the music, she seemed to understand the dance and began to move with him. But she refused to look at him.

Around and around they went. Daisy began to smile. She laughed, the sparkle returning to her eyes. She kicked up her heels a little higher and seemed to truly enjoy the dancing.

When the music came to a close, the dancers began to set up for a reel. Cailean held out his arm to Daisy; she put her hand on it and wobbled beside him out of the dancing area. He tried to escort her in the opposite direction of Spivey, but Daisy removed her hand from his arm and sank into a curtsy. "Thank you. Your duty is done."

Cailean sighed. "Verra well then, lass. Would you prefer if I said only the things you want to hear and then kiss you in dark corners?"

"Yes!" she said, then groaned and shook her head. *"No."* She sighed. "You shouldn't ask me what I want, Cailean. You'll not like the answer."

She turned from him, started to walk away, but Cailean caught her hand. "Pardon?"

She tugged her hand free of his. "You heard me."

She tried to go forward, but there were so many people, her hasty exit was thwarted.

"Aye, I heard you, but it doesna make a wee bit of sense. Why donna you tell me instead of making me guess?"

"No," she said as she slipped between two couples. "I won't confide in a hardened scoundrel."

"Oh, I'm a hardened scoundrel now, am I?" he said, exasperated, and barreled past the two couples.

"So I've heard," she said over her shoulder.

"I can well imagine that you have. And I can imagine you were quick to point out, to whomever might have had your ear, that we are no longer friends, aye?"

"Yes, I hinted at that to Mr. Somerled."

Somerled! "He's a fool," Cailean said. "And no doubt he assured you that his friendship is superior to mine, aye?"

"Well," she said airily. "He might have implied it."

Cailean paused to let two loud men with their arms around each other pass before them. "Did your admirer say more?"

"Hmm," she said, pretending to consider it. Then said, "Yes." She walked on.

And Cailean followed the woman like a hopeless puppy, unable to stop himself. He caught her again, his hand on her arm. "You will listen to me, woman—"

She whirled around, her brows dipping into a V over eyes glittering with vexation. *"Listen* to you?"

She meant to say more, but they both heard someone call Cailean's name.

He looked over his shoulder to see Catriona darting through the crowd toward him. "I've been looking for you!" she said. "I want to play whist, and Rabbie refuses. Partner with me, will you, Cailean?"

"*Och*, lass," he said and glanced back to where Daisy was standing. Or where she had been standing.

But she had disappeared into the crowd.

And in her wake, the smoldering inside of Cailean turned to glowing embers. One waft of a breeze, and he would be consumed with the fire.

CHAPTER SIXTEEN

DAISY WAS STILL very cross with Cailean, and not
because she was slightly inebriated, which she defi-
nitely was, as whisky seemed to flow with the force
of a river through Balhaire.

It wasn't because he'd refused to kiss her and had
made her feel incomparably foolish for that desire,
the bastard. Yes, all right, she supposed she might
perhaps consider that his actions were noble and that
he had more of a care for her virtue and place in society than she did.

He was maddening. So was her desire for him,
which raged beyond her control and only deepened
when she watched him take his victory kiss from
that beautiful young Scottish woman. And again,
when he made her dance with him and she enjoyed
it as much as she had.

Rake.

But she wasn't cross with him because he was a
rake. She was cross with him because he didn't love
her. If he loved her…*if he loved her*…he would kiss
her, and he would take her and Ellis from here. He
would save her if he loved her.

Oh, but she was bereft. There was a gaping wound

in her. She was reminded of a chemise she'd once had, in which she'd somehow managed to put a small hole in the fabric. Without her notice, the hole had begun to stretch and grow into something much larger and quite noticeable in that inferior piece of cotton. Daisy felt a hole just like that had opened inside her. A tiny one, at first unnoticed, but now stretched and pulled by her desires and her duty into something much larger and painful.

"Daisy?"

She hadn't realized how far away from the dancing she'd wandered until she felt Robert's hand on her back. He'd appeared at her side like a sentry while she tried to make desperate sense of her feelings. "Rob," she said and smiled with a bit of relief. "There you are."

"It's time that we retired. They are all deep in their cups," he said, glancing around them. His hand held her elbow, as if he thought she might flee.

"It's not very late, is it?"

"Daisy, please," he said and pulled her around to face him. "We are not welcome here. Perhaps you haven't noticed, but they look at us as if we are the enemy. It's your safety that concerns me."

He looked truly concerned. She looked around them—the crowd was growing more raucous. And it was true that Daisy had noticed some vaguely hostile looks cast her way today. "Yes, all right," she acquiesced.

Robert sighed with relief and instantly began to

move her along, exiting the hall as quickly as he could maneuver her through the crowd.

He escorted her through the maze of hallways, and when they reached the wing of rooms the Mackenzies had so graciously granted her family, Daisy slowed. "I want to look in on Ellis." She paused at the door of her son's room and knocked softly. Hearing no response, opened the door quietly and looked in. She could just make out Ellis's form on the bed, and from somewhere deeper in the room, she could hear Uncle Alfonso's heavy snoring.

She pulled the door closed. "They are sound asleep."

The next door was Daisy's room, which adjoined Belinda's. They paused there, and Daisy tried to think of something to say, something encouraging or, at the very least, kind...but her thoughts were miles from that door. "Thank you," she said. "Thank you for agreeing to come."

She couldn't read Robert's expression in the dimly lit hallway, but he said, "I am still of the opinion that this was a foolish thing to have done. I shan't sleep at all tonight, for fear of foul play."

Foul play? She didn't believe that for a moment. Her hosts had been gracious, and Ellis had enjoyed it so. "You are too suspicious," she said and caressed his arm.

Robert sighed wearily, as if he'd explained this to her dozens of times and she still didn't understand. "I can't fault you for not understanding the darker side of men, darling. But I shall be quite relieved when we take our leave in the morning." He leaned forward and kissed her cheek. "Good night," he murmured, then reached around her and opened the door at her back. "I'll wait until I hear the latch."

"Good night," Daisy said and stepped inside. She closed and latched the door, likewise feeling relief— the relief of being free of him this evening.

She turned about and started. Belinda was in her room.

"I beg your pardon, did I frighten you?" Belinda asked cheerfully as she laid out Daisy's bedclothes. "I rather thought you'd be quite late to bed."

Daisy waited for Belinda to continue with some dire warning of some horrible fate that had befallen someone who had stayed too late at the dancing. But she didn't. She was humming. *Humming.*

"Belinda? Is everything all right?" Daisy asked. Belinda smiled, and Daisy gaped at her.

"I sold my painting," she admitted excitedly. "A nice gentleman from…oh, I don't know where. I could scarcely understand a word he said! But he paid me fairly and carried it away." She held up a small pouch and shook it so that Daisy could hear the coins clicking. She beamed, her face illuminated with happiness.

"Darling, that's marvelous," Daisy said.

"Yes, it is, isn't it? I can't think of a single reason I should be unhappy." She made a sound of delight and laid Daisy's slippers at the end of the bed. "There you are, all ready," she said. "Shall I help you undress?"

"No, thank you," Daisy said. "Go to bed, Belinda. Sleep well. Dream of your next piece of art."

"Oh, I don't think I'll sleep a wink," Belinda said excitedly. She hugged Daisy on her way to her room, jingling the pouch of coins in her hand as if it was a toy.

Astonished, Daisy sank down onto the edge of her bed. Robert feared the worst, but no one could deny that Ellis and Belinda had *changed* here. They had found a piece of themselves at Auchenard and had grown from it. Shouldn't that count for something?

The window behind Daisy rattled with a gust of wind, and rain began to patter against the panes.

Daisy had found something here, too, hadn't she? She'd found love, something she'd never expected to experience again, not like this. It was unrequited, but it didn't matter—she felt it in every bit of her, and she wasn't ready to let go of it just yet.

She stood up, smoothed her gown, pinched her cheeks, and with only a twinge of conscience, knowing that Robert would be very unhappy with her, she left her room.

She followed the sounds of the merrymaking and managed to negotiate the maze of hallways to find the great hall. Now that it was raining, the people from the meadow were coming inside, crowding into the hall, making the crush of bodies even greater than before. There was scarcely room to move about.

She tried to find the table where Mr. Somerled had been seated, but people were looking at her, some of them leering. This had been a mistake. She scarcely knew anyone, and she hadn't realized how vulnerable she felt without a man at her side.

She pushed through the crowd to a door and went out. But she found herself in an unfamiliar corridor that was so crowded, she was forced up against the wall. She looked down the hallway, to her left, then to her right, searching for an escape, not realizing at first that two men were towering over her, speaking to each other as they leered at her. Their glassy-eyed expressions made Daisy's stomach clench. She was suddenly reminded of all the things she'd heard about Scots and Englishwomen, and tried not to panic. It was so loud—would anyone really notice if she screamed?

One of them was speaking to her in Gaelic. She shook her head, and the two men, now joined by another, laughed.

"Lost?" she heard a familiar voice say, and her relief was so swift and great that she sagged against the wall at her back.

"Yes," she said, finding him now.

Cailean stood beside the two men. He was taller than the others and glowered down at them. One of them spoke, and Cailean responded heatedly. Dear God, she was safe. Daisy pressed her hand to her heart to quiet it.

"Lady Chatwick," he said, leaning over her. "They mean no harm, aye?"

"I didn't… I didn't know what they were saying."

"It doesna matter," he said as the two men dispersed into the crowd. "There is gaming here—do you mean to play?"

"No, no… I was looking for my room," she said

vaguely. Her blasted heart was racing again. Not
from fright as it had been only minutes before, but
from his nearness. From that cauldron of emotions
that mixed and stewed in her whenever he was near.

"Aye, I'll show you the way." He picked up her
hand, slipped it into the crook of his elbow. He proceeded to escort her from that corridor, calling for
people to step aside and let them pass, turning into
this corridor, and into that one, in that never-ending
maze.

At last the crowd began to thin, and with the exception of a servant or two, they were alone in the
corridor that led to the suite of rooms where Daisy
was staying.

"Where is your guard?" he asked as they moved
at a slower pace.

"He thinks I have retired for the evening," she
admitted.

"Why have you no'?"

Because of you. "There will be time enough for
retiring when I return to England."

He chuckled and squeezed her hand. "Sounds a
wee bit like death."

"It feels a wee bit like it," she said and glanced
up at him.

He was looking at her, his gaze sympathetic. "Had
you come looking for me, then?" he asked.

The man understood her better than he should
have. "I don't know. Perhaps," she admitted.

He smiled. "I thought you were cross."

"I *am* cross," she assured him, then sighed heavenward. "But it's not your fault. I can't fault the one man on earth who refused to take advantage of me, can I?"

Cailean didn't answer. She glanced up at him again. The space between them was magnetic, the lure irresistible and heated.

They had come to her door, Daisy realized. She opened the door and pushed it open. She glanced back over her shoulder; Cailean leaned insouciantly against the wall behind him, his head lowered, his gaze dark and riveted on her.

"I must apologize," he said.

Daisy took a step backward. "For what? You owe me no apology."

"Aye, I do. For disappointing you," he said.

Daisy took another step backward; Cailean pushed away from the wall and walked to her door. "It could not be helped," she said softly. "I was destined to be disappointed." She took another step backward. He moved to the threshold. In the low light of the corridor, and in that pleasant state of being between a dram or two of whisky, he looked almost dreamlike. "You shouldn't come in."

"No," he agreed. "I shouldna kiss you, either."

She stepped back again, so that she was now very much in her room. "You keep saying that," she said and lifted her arms, pulling the pins from her hair.

Cailean watched her hair tumble down around her shoulders. "I keep meaning it," he said quietly.

"Do you mean to torment me?" she asked.

"No, never, lass. If I have, you must tell me what

I might do to ease you," he said and stepped just inside her room.

Daisy's heart was in her throat. "There is only one thing that will ease me, Arrandale, and you know perfectly well what it is. But I think you are too fearful."

"I'm no' fearful, *leannan*. Donna mistake my reluctance for fear. What of the man you mean to marry?"

"He is asleep in another room. And he has not yet offered. I've not yet accepted."

"You are dividing your words now, aye?" he scolded her. His expression was predatory, as if he were assessing the prey he would soon devour.

Daisy's pulse raced in her veins; she was breathless, anticipating what would come, her body straining for it. "Not my words. My life," she said. "I want to be here now, with you. Is that so wrong? Is it so wrong to have been widowed and feel desire again? Is it so wrong to separate my true desires from my duty as a mother?"

Cailean shook his head. "I'll no' be your conscience, *leannan*, any more than I'll allow you to be mine, aye? I willna be your diversion. If I touch you now, I willna kiss you. I will possess you. You've gone too far down this path and now you've awakened the beast in me. Do you understand?"

What she understood was that her heart was racing so hard that she feared it might burst. She nodded.

His gaze turned even darker. Prurient. "Shall I close the door, then?" he asked, his voice low and calm. It sent a shock through her.

She nodded.

With his boot, he shut the door behind him. He locked it shut, then began to advance on her, his approach slow and catlike. When he reached her, he sank his hands into her hair, whispered, "How mad you are, *leannan*. How mad you've made me," and kissed her.

All rational thought vanished with that kiss. She slid her arms around his neck and kissed him back with the demand of the many years she'd endured simply wanting.

Cailean twisted her about, pressing her against the wall, his mouth hungrily devouring hers. His need was just as evident as hers. She could feel it in his touch—demanding yet restrained. In his body—hard and long against hers. In his kiss—insistent and reverent. *This*, she realized, would happen. She was almost frantic for passion. *True* passion. The sort of passion she would rush headlong into and then abandon herself in the pool of it. She wanted to savor every moment. She wanted to feel his body against hers, in hers.

Cailean's mouth was warm and wet and agonizingly pleasurable. He slipped his tongue into her mouth, and the fire of desire spread so quickly there was nothing that could douse it. She clung to Cailean, felt his muscles moving beneath her hands, felt his erection pressed against her belly. This was what she wanted; these were the arms she wanted around her.

He was moving her backward now, his hands working the ribbon ties that fastened her gown around her. He threw the mantua aside. Her stomacher came off next, discarded on the floor. She wore a coral petticoat and a corset over her undergarments. Cailean paused, his hands sliding delicately down her shoulders as he took her in. *"Boidheach,"* he said and untied the waist of the petticoat, helping her step out of it. He then began to work the laces of her corset while Daisy tried frantically to free him of the neckcloth and plaid sash.

But Cailean pushed her hands away and gathered her up in his arms once he'd freed her from the corset. He picked her up, put her on her back on the bed and put himself on top of her. He kissed her mouth ravenously, then the hollow of her throat, fluttering his kisses there. He moved to her collarbone and down. Daisy soundlessly cried out when he took her breast in his mouth. He held her hand pinned to the bed, as if he feared she would disappear as he suckled her breasts, kissed her skin, touched his tongue to her nipples.

His touch unleashed a monstrous storm of yearning in her, and Daisy was lost in the maelstrom. She clutched at him, caressed him, freely explored his rugged, almost rocklike body as he shrugged out of his shirt.

He tossed his shirt aside and kissed her breast again, murmuring something about her galloping heart. She began to pant on a white-hot river of anticipation that ran down her spine, then spilled between her legs. When Cailean pressed his erection against her leg, she cupped his face, rising up to kiss him.

"What have you done to me?" he asked gruffly. "I donna ken myself."

Daisy pushed a lock of dark hair from his brow and stared into his eyes. This was different. This was unique and exotic, and there was something flowing between them and seeping into their skin and filling the space around them, wrapping them in its cocoon.

He groaned, kissed her tenderly, then latched two fingers into the strap of her chemise and pulled it over her shoulder, sliding it down her arm, until the garment was gone and she was bare. He removed his plaid and hovered above her, powerful and thick. Daisy closed her eyes and pressed against him, teasing his lips with the tip of her tongue. He slipped his hand into the soft, warm flesh between her legs, and Daisy whimpered with unapologetic desire. She was ready for this moment; she'd imagined it since their first meeting.

Cailean was patient and deliberate, stroking her slowly as he kissed her face and neck. She sank into the moment, gave in to the sensation of his touch, to the feel of his body against hers. She gave in to her heart, beating so wildly in response to him. She gave in, she capitulated and finally she surrendered.

She closed her eyes and bit down on her lip as he began to stroke her, his fingers sliding over the wave of pleasure that was building, gathering itself from every corner of her body, swelling and nearing the point of bursting. She kissed him, tried frantically to memorize every plane of his body. He was intoxicatingly robust—beneath her fingertips she could feel the nicks and scars of his life, which made her want him even more.

She sank her fingers into the flesh of his arms, pressed her knee against him as he swirled his fingers around the core of her pleasure, sliding deep inside her, moving faster. He anchored her with one arm around her, his eyes on her face, watching her succumb to his touch and to the pleasure he was giving her.

"Now, Cailean," she said, her voice ragged with passion and emotion. With a deep growl of approval, Cailean moved between her legs and pushed into her, filling her up.

Daisy was instantly transported. It was so exquisite that it was nearly unbearable. She moved with him and against him, urging him to abandon. Their eyes were locked on each other, a powerful current of mutual desire between them, each silently daring the other to crest the wave first, until Daisy shattered.

With a strangled cry, Cailean yanked free of her, spilling his seed on her thigh.

Daisy slowly floated back to earth. She threw an arm over her eyes and fought for breath. She could feel the heat coming off Cailean, could feel his heart pounding against his breast. He slowly fell onto his side beside her and laced his fingers with hers. "Are you still cross, then?" he asked raggedly.

Daisy smiled. She rolled onto her side, cupped his face and kissed him on the mouth. Her heart exalted in the sensation of having been freed of the prison of her desires after all these years.

"I will take that as a no, then," he said. He kissed her cheek, her forehead and her mouth before gathering her in his arms and holding her to him.

An intangible bond, warm and shimmering, formed around them and seeped into Daisy's bones. Her blood still flowed hot in her veins, and she wanted to remain like this forever. She wanted to keep the two of them in this bed, with the rest of the world held behind an invisible dam. She wanted to be with him, only him. She loved him. Oh, but she loved him. She realized that this was what true love felt like, heavy and fluid, wrapping itself around them, holding them together, enveloping them in this moment. No one could touch them here.

They lay that way for a while as the storm raged outside and flashes of lightning lit the room. It was odd how the the storm seemed close to them and yet so far. They were safe here, with each other.

Cailean stroked her hair, twined it through his fingers as he made her laugh with observations of her dancing. They talked about their childhoods. Their favorite pets. Their horses. Their tutors. Their sorrows, their joys.

They made love again when Daisy climbed on top of him. They moved slowly as they explored the suddenly verdant landscape between them.

Daisy didn't know when she fell asleep in his arms, but she was awakened in the dark by the movement of someone in the room. She sat up, propping herself on her elbows and blinking into the dark. "Cailean?"

"I'm here," he said low. The bed sank to one side with his weight. He touched her face and smiled tenderly. "I must go, aye? The servants will be moving about soon."

"Don't go," Daisy said sleepily and reached for him. Cailean hugged her to his chest; she pressed her cheek against his shoulder, her head filling with his masculine scent. She closed her eyes, wanting to relive every moment.

"*Och*, but you make it hard to take my leave, *leannan*," her murmured against her hair. He kissed her mouth and stood up, pushing his arms into his coat.

She sat up, wrapped her arms around her knees. "When will I see you?" she asked. She had a sudden, girlish image of the two of them, riding horses in flower-strewn meadows with the sun shining overhead...but her little fantasy disappeared when she saw Cailean run his hands over his hair and then hesitantly turn toward her. He didn't speak immediately...but he didn't have to. The look on his face said it all—sorrow. Regret. Apprehension.

The feeling of sweet warmth Daisy had felt all night disappeared under a wave of disappointment. She said nothing. *Let him say it. Let him say he'd given her what she wanted and there could be no more.*

"Naugh' has changed, aye? You donna believe that I...that *we*—"

"Good God, Arrandale, did you think I expected

you on one knee offering for me?" she asked irritably and drew her knees tighter to her.

He put his hands on his waist and gazed down at her. "I am fond of you, aye? You know that I am, *leannan*. But you will take your leave of Scotland and I will…" He paused, seeming to look for the right word.

"Sail off and smuggle wine?" she asked coldly.

He winced slightly, as if that pained him. "Aye," he said.

She responded with silence.

"I'll always be your friend, Daisy. If you are again in Scotland—"

"I won't be," she said curtly. He thought he could make love to her like he had and then continue on as a friendly neighbor?

But what *had* she expected? She was the one who had initiated this affair. She was the one who had all but begged for physical release, and now she would take offense once he'd given it to her? She hated herself for hoping for something different. She was no blushing debutante; she knew the rules of this game. So why, then, did it feel so wretchedly heartbreaking?

"I rather thought we understood each other," he said quietly.

"I understand very clearly, Cailean," she said. "But I had hoped I was wrong."

He sighed sadly. He moved back to the bed and leaned over it to kiss her, but, like a spoiled child, Daisy turned her head. She could feel the tears of humiliation burning in her eyes. She was a fool, an utter fool. Of course she hadn't thought she'd *marry* him. But she'd thought...she'd thought—

"*Leannan*—"

She leaned away from him. "Cailean... I *understand*. Will you please go?"

He didn't move immediately, but Daisy refused to look at him. She couldn't look at him, for fear of breaking into sobs that welled from a place so deep in her that it felt almost foreign to her. A dam had burst somewhere, and at this moment, with the feel of his hands and his mouth still fresh on her skin, she couldn't see him, couldn't staunch the flow of ugly, bitter disappointment. And *loss*. She was losing him, losing herself. She was losing everything. Her freedom. Her garden. Her heart. Everything was lost.

She heard the door open, then quietly close. She held her breath—was he gone? Should she call him back? She looked to the door—he had left her. Daisy groaned and fell back into the pillows, ashamed of the way she'd treated him and irrationally infuriated with him at the same time. It made no sense, not even to her.

Daisy got up, found her chemise and donned it. She picked up the room without thought, as reality began to seep back into her head like black smoke, curling in around the joy she'd felt during the night and suffocating the life from it.

She wanted gone from Balhaire. Gone from Scotland. Gone from him, that beautiful, exasperating, sinful man. Whatever she'd been seeking when she'd dragged her family here, she had not found it.

CHAPTER SEVENTEEN

CAILEAN MADE HIS way up from the meadow of the *feill* and to the great hall at Balhaire, taking his place on the dais along with his family for the midday meal. He sat next to Vivienne, who was in extreme discomfort, squirming in her seat as her husband tried to make her more comfortable.

"What's wrong?" Cailean asked, frowning with concern.

"What's wrong? This child will no' be born, that's what," Vivienne said irritably.

Cailean glanced at her husband, Marcas, over the top of her dark head; Marcas shook his head in silent warning.

"Cailean!"

He turned from his sister's discomfort to his mother, who stood above him, frowning down at him.

"Feasgar math, Màthair," he said, coming to his feet.

"Yes, yes, good afternoon," she said impatiently. "Why were you not here to send off Lady Chatwick?"

Gone? He hadn't expected her to leave so soon. "She's gone?"

"Yes, darling, she's gone, all of them back to Auchenard."

"But the *feill* continues on today. I'd assumed they'd remain for it." He'd assumed there would be opportunity to…to soothe ruffled feathers. Or perhaps…

His mother's look of exasperation softened. "Well. Perhaps you might call on her when you return to Arrandale. You can explain that you were occupied when she left."

"I donna know if that's wise," he said.

"Of course it is. Someone needs to have a look about. We don't want the captain wandering about unattended, do we?"

"What lass occupied you?" Rabbie asked, playfully grabbing Cailean's shoulders and leaning around him to waggle his brows at him. "Aileen Ramsey, aye? Everyone is talking about the kiss, lad."

Cailean shrugged Rabbie off his back.

"Aye, all right. Where you've been, then?" Rabbie asked.

"What does it matter?" Cailean asked gruffly. Why did they have to question him at all? Wasn't a man of his age and stature in this clan allowed a morning to himself? He did not need to explain to his overly curious family that he'd gone down to the meadow early this morning before people were milling about, and had thrown his dirk at a target, over and over and over again, trying to rid himself of the impotence in his heart. He could not be what she wanted; it was that simple. *He could not be what she wanted.*

After his dirk had chewed up the wood of the target, Cailean had drunk a tankard of ale. Or two. Or three or four.

"We'd no' wonder at all if you didna answer in that manner," Vivienne said. "Why will you no' say?"

"I was in the games meadow," he said. "I had a wee bit of ale, aye?"

His brother and sister laughed.

He'd needed the morning, had needed the space to think. Cailean was at sixes and sevens, bewildered and angry with himself for the way he'd left things with Daisy, for letting things progress so far with that barmy little flower. *Diah*, but his response to her had been quick—he had, for years, been quick to put up a defense against women, erecting a barrier so high that no one could possibly misconstrue his intentions. There was never affection, never any hope of it; he made certain of that. But Daisy was different. Daisy had managed to break through that barrier, and there *was* affection.

Deep affection.

And then he'd seen her crestfallen face and how his words had wounded her, and he'd abhorred himself for it.

Now he didn't know what to do with himself. She was gone. He couldn't explain to her that he was only now coming to grips with the idea that he actually *felt* something, after fifteen long years. Or that no matter what he was feeling, there was naught he could do for it. She had Ellis to think of. The lad was an English viscount, and he needed to be brought up in England. Even in a perfect world, he could never have Daisy—he was a smuggler. A Highlander. A firstborn son of a clan that needed him here. Not to mention he would be six and thirty soon, and the laird of Balhaire in a matter of months. His time for love sonnets and courtships and the promise of a married life with children had passed long ago.

It wasn't necessary to say these things to Daisy. She was brilliant and amusing and full of wants and desires. She knew what she wanted. And she knew what she had to do. In fairness, she hadn't been asking for the obligation he now felt. She'd simply asked to see him again.

CAILEAN RETURNED TO Arrandale the next day with three Highland guards and a gift he'd purchased for the Chatwick lad.

The guards took turns watching Arrandale and Auchenard from the hills for any sign of espionage from Spivey. But after a day or two, his men reported that Spivey seemed to do nothing but loiter there.

Cailean didn't ask about anyone else.

After several days of watching, Cailean sent the guards back to Balhaire and proceeded to putter about the rambling house he'd built. The work was near to done; the head mason had assured him they'd be done at month's end. One wing had been completed, and Cailean began to furnish the rooms with the things he'd stored this summer. When he wasn't working on his house, he and Fabienne fished and hunted for small game. It was life as he knew it, as familiar to him as the stubble on his chin. But the days were growing shorter and the nights longer, and at night, where Cailean might have once read, he brooded.

It kept coming back to him like a bad stomach— he should not have left things with Daisy like he had. He owed her an apology at the very least. An explanation at best.

One morning, he wasn't completely dressed when he heard voices on the front lawn. He pulled on a pair of buckskins beneath his lawn shirt, picked up his musket and, barefoot, walked outside, half expecting to see troops on his lawn. He set the musket aside, however, when he saw Catriona and Rabbie along with some of the Mackenzie guards, their horses prancing impatiently around his lawn.

"It's a wee bit early for social calls, is it no'?" Cailean asked.

"Have you finished the work?" Catriona asked, hopping down off her horse.

"No."

"It looks finished," she said, ignoring him, removing her gloves as walked past him, uninvited, into his house. "You must invite us all!" she called over her shoulder before disappearing into the interior.

"Why are you here?" Cailean asked Rabbie as he came down from his mount.

"My mother has sent me, aye?" he said and winked

as he followed Catriona inside. "We're to look in on you and report if you are dead or alive, aye?" He glanced back at Cailean with a grin. "Which is it, then? Dead? Or alive?"

That was an excellent question. Cailean waved to the guards, then followed his siblings into his house.

Catriona was in the salon, looking up at the plasterwork. "When will it be finished?"

"A fortnight. Perhaps a month."

Fabienne had been asleep near the hearth, and now she stretched her lanky legs before trotting over to dip her head beneath Catriona's hand. Catriona cooed to the dog, then said, "We've heard an English man-of-war was seen near Tiree."

"Pardon?" Cailean asked, startled by that bit of news.

Catriona turned around to face him. "You've no' heard?"

Cailean's heart hitched—what was a man-of-war doing so far north on the eastern coastline? "No," he said and signaled for his dog, squatting down to hide his despair behind scratching her ears. "Who has seen it?"

"The MacDonalds," Rabbie said. "They claim to have chased it away with their mighty fleet of three." He snorted. "Whatever might have happened, the ship came no farther north and turned about, headed south. *Athair* believes it's the English captain's doing."

Cailean mulled that over a moment. He didn't see how that was possible. Spivey didn't know what he'd find when he came here. He couldn't have possibly sent word back so quickly. Even if he had, an English man-of-war was not something one could dispatch with ease. "They'll no' find the cove," he said.

"Aye, perhaps no'," Rabbie agreed. "But if they come round again, they might find the captain hanging from the tree on the cliff above the rock. Good riddance, I say. The fewer *Sassenach* in our glens, the better we are for it, aye?"

"Rabbie!" Catriona scolded him. "You speak so ill of the very place our mother was born."

Rabbie shrugged. "She's a Scot now," he said unapologetically. He paused to examine the woodwork around the mantel. "She is loyal only to us."

Catriona snorted. "Donna be barmy, Rabbie. Come on, then. We'll go, Cailean," she said cheerfully and moved to quit the room, Fabienne trotting behind her. "Our mother bids you come to supper soon!" she shouted back at him.

"Aye, I will," he muttered. He scarcely took notice of his sister's departure. His mind raced—Daisy and her family had to go. At once. Rabbie would never hang a man, but Cailean wouldn't put it past half the men in these hills.

"What ails you?"

Startled, Cailean looked at Rabbie. He hadn't even noticed his brother had not followed his sister. "Pardon?"

Rabbie's eyes narrowed. "You donna look yourself, Cailean."

"No. It's early yet," he said.

Rabbie smiled wryly. "I rather thought it was too late," he said.

Cailean looked at him in bafflement.

"Forget her, lad. She's no' one of us," Rabbie said, and with a slight shake of his head, he walked out, following after Catriona.

When Cailean reluctantly followed, Catriona was already on her horse. Rabbie mounted his, then lingered a moment, studying Cailean before spurring on after his sister and the guards.

Cailean stood at his door and watched them go, until their horses had gone over the rise and he could no longer see them. Then he turned his head and looked to the east, in the direction of Auchenard. He didn't know what he'd say—all he could think of was kissing her, in truth—but they had to go. *Now.* As soon as possible.

He whistled for Fabienne and went inside.

He could just as easily send a messenger to Daisy, for what was the point of prolonging their acquaintance? It served only to torment him.

And yet there was a stronger part of him that couldn't let her go without seeing her one last time. It was a part of him that felt strangely unsettled and disturbingly wistful.

In the end, he determined he must go for the sake of the lad, if for no other reason.

His decision made, he rambled about his house, changing coats and neckcloths, studying his waistcoat and buckskins and plaids. It was barmy, all this dithering. Quite unlike him.

At last, with the gift he'd purchased for Ellis at the *feill* tucked under his arm, Cailean put himself on Odin's back and headed for Auchenard.

It was interesting how a bright day could cast a light on a neglected hunting lodge and make it seem almost bucolic, what with the smoke curling out of the chimneys and the lawn cut and tidied. On Odin's back, Cailean trotted down the drive, slowing to a walk when the butler came out to greet him. He came down from his horse and handed the man his reins. *"Tapadh leat,"* he said. "Is your mistress about, then?"

"Yes, my lord," he said. "They are on the lake just now. If you'd like to wait in the great room, I will send Mr. Green—"

"No, thank you," he said. He didn't want Daisy to find him anxiously waiting for her like a suitor. "I'll walk around, aye?" he suggested and walked on, going around the side of the house to the garden. He was surprised to see so many blooms—he'd not have thought it possible to bring it back after a few short weeks, but the roses seemed to be flourishing. *Fish*, she'd said that night she lay in his arms. Her roses liked to feed on fish. Roses, blue thistle, catchfly and wild orchids had shown their heads, nestled in beside the wild-growing primrose. From the branch of a crab apple tree hung wooden chimes that tinkled in the afternoon breeze.

It was strange how present she seemed in this garden, even now. He could see her in her soiled dress, that long braid of tangled hair and the grimy wide-brimmed hat. Never had she looked lovelier than she did in here.

Cailean touched the fragile petals of a rose; a few of the petals fell into his hand. He rubbed them between his fingers. She'd been here only a short time, but he couldn't imagine Auchenard without her now.

The sound of laughter awoke him from his ruminations. He dropped the petals and lifted his hat, running a hand over his hair, then went out to meet them.

His appearance on the terrace as they climbed the steps startled them all. Daisy's eyes sparked, and she smiled tentatively. *Diah*, but why must she look so ravishing? Her gown, a rich red, was not as overly adorned as some of her others, but framed to perfection a body so familiar to him now. She was as bonny to him as any woman had ever been, and he couldn't take his eyes from her, uncaring if anyone else noticed.

In fact, he hadn't even bothered to see who accompanied her, but when Mr. Kimberly discreetly cleared his throat, Cailean noticed that the entire family, as well as Spivey, was assembled. Ellis had in his possession a very large stick.

"My lord," Daisy said and walked forward, her smile deepening now, her eyes shining at him. Cailean would never understand the workings of a woman's mind—one minute cross, the next disappointed, the next vibrant and happy. Perhaps she'd made her peace with her situation. Perhaps she and Spivey had come to their understanding. All the more reason for them to go.

"Arrandale! Good to see you," Mr. Kimberly said, striding forward, catching up to Daisy, his hand extended. "Very good of you to come. You are welcome sir, most welcome."

"Thank you," Cailean said. He looked at Daisy and swallowed. Something sharp sliced through him. "Lady Chatwick, how bonny you are this afternoon."

"Thank you," she said. "I had not expected to see you again, my lord. What a surprise."

"You've no' managed to rid yourself of me yet," he said and let his gaze slip over her before turning to her cousin. "Miss Hainsworth," he said, inclining his head. "You are to be commended, aye? I saw the painting Alpin McBee purchased. You are a skilled painter, you are."

"What? Oh! Thank you," she said, blushing furiously as she sank into a curtsy.

He glanced at Spivey, who stared coolly in return and offered no greeting. "Captain," he said and turned his attention to the lad, who was eagerly waiting his turn.

"*Feasgar math,*" he said, offering his hand. "Good evening, Lord Chatwick."

Ellis took his hand and gave it a hearty shake, so vastly different from the one he'd given Cailean the first time he'd met him. "Look," he said, reaching into his pocket and withdrawing two stones.

Cailean peered down at them. "Ah, the bloodstone, is it?" he said. "Do you know that Highland warriors once marked their bodies with it? They believed it made them invincible."

"They did?" Ellis said and stared down at the stones. "Have you come to stalk?" he asked. "Might we find the red stags now?"

Cailean forced a smile and put his hand on Ellis's shoulder, squeezing lightly. "You're too eager, lad. The stags will no' come down from the hills before the verra end of summer."

His face fell. "But...we'll be gone soon."

"We canna hasten the natural progression of things, can we? You must come again, aye?"

Ellis didn't answer; he looked down at his rocks, hiding his disappointment.

Cailean squatted down beside him. "Look here, now," he said softly. "I've brought you something."

"You have?" Ellis asked.

"Aye," he said and held out the bundle to him. Ellis didn't take it immediately. "*Och*, have you no' received a gift, then?" Cailean said laughingly. "Take it, lad. Open it."

"Is it a dirk?" he asked suddenly, taking the bundle from Cailean.

Cailean laughed. "No. You'll have no need of a dirk in London, will you?"

"Come in, come in," Mr. Kimberly said, his hand on Ellis's back. "We'll have a look at the gift and indulge in some fine brandy I purchased at Balhaire," he said, ushering them all inside.

In the great room, Ellis went down onto the floor with the package and untied the twine that held it together while the butler poured brandy. Spivey, Cailean noticed, refused his.

Ellis folded back the cloth and picked up the first item: a sporran made from a hare's skin.

"What is that?" the captain asked.

"A sporran," Cailean said.

Ellis put it aside and picked up the next item—a small plaid. He gasped with delight and scrambled to his feet, holding it up, then trying to wrap it around his waist.

"I'll show you how it's done," Cailean said and demonstrated how to fold the plaid, how to don it. "You'll need a belt, then. And it's a wee bit long, but you'll grow into it."

"I rather doubt he'll have need of that in London, either," Spivey said dismissively.

Daisy looked appalled. "It's wonderful," she said to Cailean. "Thank you. Isn't it lovely?" she said to her son, pushing him toward Cailean.

Ellis looked at Cailean, and his lower lip began to tremble. Clutching the plaid to his chest, he suddenly launched himself at Cailean, throwing his arms around his legs and burying his face in Cailean's side.

Bloody hell, the bairn was weeping.

"Stop that," Spivey admonished him. "It's unbecoming."

"I've one last thing for you, lad," Cailean said quickly, and he put his hand on Ellis's back, patting him. "A wee secret shared only among Highlanders. But I must offer it to you in private…if your mother doesna mind?"

Daisy shook her head. He turned Ellis around to

the door and moved him briskly along, out of the great room.

Thankfully, no one followed.

He marched Ellis down the corridor and out into the portico, and there he knelt down and looked him in the eye. "Let's have it, then. What ails you?" he asked, squeezing Ellis's shoulders. "Highlanders donna cry unless they have good reason."

Ellis looked to the ground. "I don't want to go," he said miserably. "I want to stay here, at Auchenard. With you!"

A Diah. "That would be my wish, too," Cailean said. He put his arms around Ellis and hugged him tightly. He was surprised by the amount of affection he held for this child. He felt sympathy for his shyness, sympathy for his uncertainty about where he stood in the world.

He slowly pushed Ellis back. "Do you know what keeps me, then?" he asked.

Ellis shook his head.

"That I know you'll come back, aye? I hang all my hopes on that, I do. You'll come back to Auchenard. You will, Ellis Bristol."

"I won't," Ellis said tearfully into Cailean's shoulder. "Mamma will marry him, and I will be in England."

Cailean closed his eyes for a moment, feeling the same sorrow that Ellis felt, along with a generous dollop of regret seeping into him, filling him up.

"You'll be back, lad. I feel it in my bones, aye? You'll reach your majority before you know it, and then Auchenard will be yours. And then you might come whenever you please."

"But…" Ellis lifted his face from Cailean's shoulder. "But what about you?"

"Me?" He smiled. "I'll be at Arrandale until I die, will I no'? I'm a Mackenzie, and did you know, then, that I'll take over for my da as the laird of the Mackenzie clan? I'm a Highlander, a Scotsman, and there is no other place for me but the Highlands. Just as there is no other place for you but England. But we are neighbors. We will always be neighbors. Rest assured that when you come back, I'll be right here, just over those trees, waiting for you to come round and tell me of your adventures."

"Do you swear it?" Ellis whispered.

Cailean held up his hand. "I give you my word as a Highlander and a Mackenzie."

Ellis nodded. He rubbed his hand under his nose. "Thank you, Cailean," he said. "For my plaid and…" He gulped down his tears. "And for being my friend," he said, his voice breaking.

Cailean rather thought it was he who owed the boy his thanks. He would never have children of his own, but Ellis had given him a brief glimpse of what might have been, and for that, Cailean would be eternally grateful.

He stood up, roughly wiped the tears from Ellis's upturned face, and then leaned back to look him over. "Aye," he said, nodding approvingly. "A strong highland lad if ever I've laid eyes on one." He patted

Ellis on the back. "We best return to your mother lest she think we escaped."

Ellis drew a breath so large that his shoulders lifted with it, and then he clutched Cailean's hand in one hand, his plaid and sporran in the other, as they reentered the lodge and made their way to the great room.

All eyes turned toward them as they entered the room, and Ellis went straight to his mother, who wordlessly held out her arms to him. He walked into them, his head down. Over the top of her son's head, Daisy smiled gratefully at Cailean.

"Will you stay to dine, Arrandale?" Mr. Kimberly asked.

"No, thank you," Cailean said. He could hardly sit about and watch Daisy and Spivey dining as if they were already married. "But I'll have a word with you and the captain, if you please."

"A word?" Spivey snorted. "I can think of nothing you might have to say to me."

For a moment, Cailean reconsidered warning the pompous bastard that his hide was in danger. But he glanced at Ellis and smiled. "You might be surprised, then," he said.

"A word about what?" Daisy asked, looking between the men.

"Ellis, go with Cousin Belinda now," Mr. Kimberly said, gesturing to the door.

"I don't want to," he protested. "I want to stay here, with all of you."

"You heard your uncle, boy. Do as he tells you,"

Captain Spivey said. He didn't even look at Ellis when he commanded it.

Had it already come to this? Was Spivey already dismissing Ellis from his sight?

"Come dearest," Miss Hainsworth said, taking his hand. "Would you like to try your plaid?" She put a protective arm around Ellis.

Cailean gave Ellis a smile and a conspiratorial wink as he moved past, and then he turned his back to the lad's exit and looked into the fire. He was astonished that he couldn't bear to see the lad leave. And he was appallingly and unduly bothered by that. He was not a sentimental man—he was the sort to say farewell and never look back. But watching Ellis leave the room, knowing he might never see him again, was much harder than Cailean could have anticipated. He had a sense of foreboding for the lad, an unease that he would crumble under the scrutiny of a man like Spivey. Ellis needed a man to see him, to really *see* him, to help guide him. Cailean feared he'd be shunted aside, sent off to school, left in the shadows, and there was nothing he could do about it.

"Madam, perhaps you ought to accompany your son and allow the gentlemen to speak," Spivey said.

The captain aggravated Cailean. He acted as if he owned Auchenard, as if he were already married to Daisy and was her lord and master. However, he did wish Daisy would leave the room. He didn't want to frighten her.

But the Daisy he knew was not one to take instruction from men. "No," she said defiantly. "If it has to do with Auchenard, I must hear it."

Spivey pressed his lips together and looked at Cailean. "What is it, then?"

"An English man-of-war was spotted near Tiree just south of here," Cailean said, his gaze locked on Spivey's.

Spivey shrugged. "What of it?"

"A man-of-war never comes this far north on the eastern shore, aye? There are many in these hills that believe you might have something to do with it."

Spivey snorted. "Had I known of this den of thieves, I would have summoned them. But I didn't. I came here as a free man. Is that all you have to say?"

"No," Cailean said calmly. "It is my best advice that you all leave as soon as possible. That is, if you donna wish to hang."

Daisy gasped. Her hand flew to her mouth and she stared wide-eyed at Spivey.

But the captain merely chuckled. "That is a capital offense, Mackenzie. Would you add that to your other crimes?"

"I didna say me," he said evenly. "But there are other men who would see a Stuart on the throne and the *Sassenach* banished from Scotland. They wouldna worry so much about a capital offense, as there is no one here to catch them save their own, aye?"

"Oh my God," Daisy said. She pressed both hands against her abdomen.

"We've arranged passage on a ship that has not

yet returned to port," Mr. Kimberly said, looking concerned.

"Go to Skye," Cailean said. "See Irving Mac-Donald in Portree. He'll see you safely to England. Tell him I've sent you to him."

"But...but what of Auchenard?" Daisy asked. "We've not found a caretaker."

"I'll look after it," Cailean offered. "Until you come again."

"Do you really think Lady Chatwick will be free to return here?" Spivey asked. "She'll no doubt have more children, and her responsibilities to Lord Chatwick are such that she can't simply summer here."

Cailean looked at Daisy. She looked, he thought, a little ill. "We are different in the Highlands. If we want something, we reach for it," he said to Daisy. "Our...*circumstance* does no' prevent it."

"Daisy, dearest," Spivey said laughingly. "Don't listen to what this man says. He means to unnerve me, that's all. You're in no danger here. Personally, I find it impossible to take the advice from a free trader."

"Aye, so would I, were I you, Captain," Cailean said calmly. "But even a free trader would no' risk the lives of women and children, would they? You best heed me."

Now Spivey twisted about, his expression full of ire. "Is there more you wish to say, Mackenzie? Or have you delivered all the dire warnings you mean to?"

"I've said what I came to say," he said. "I'll take my leave now."

"Thank you, Arrandale," Mr. Kimberly said. "I can't thank you enough. You've been a good friend to us."

"Don't go, not yet," Daisy said. "At least finish your brandy?"

"No, thank you," Cailean said firmly. He offered his hand to Mr. Kimberly. "It has been a great pleasure, sir," he said. "I hope to see you again one day, aye?"

"God willing," Mr. Kimberly agreed and shook his hand effusively.

He next turned to Spivey. "Best you take the loch to the sea and avoid any travel over land."

Captain Spivey lifted his chin. "I am quite capable of seeing the family from here."

That remained to be seen.

Cailean had to face Daisy now, had to say goodbye. He felt sick, a little weak in the knees. He bowed over her hand, kissed the back of it, his lips lingering a moment too long on her soft skin. "You will come again." It wasn't a question. It was a command.

"I hope," she murmured.

He could see the tears beginning to build in her eyes, and he wanted to spare her that, particularly in front of Captain Spivey. Or in front of him. It was heartachingly difficult as it was. "You will be missed," he said tersely and let go of her hand. "Haste ye back," he said. And with the small smile he managed to muster, he began to walk out of the room.

"Wait...before you go," Daisy said behind him.

Cailean hesitated; he glanced back. Daisy moved

toward him, and behind her Captain Spivey was ambling closer. The captain was not a naive man—he knew better than to let his prize catch drift too far. "Lady Chatwick?" he called to her. "Is everything all right?"

She put out her hand, halting Spivey's advance. "Please, Captain, I should like a word with Arrandale. If he's to look after Auchenard when we go, there are things he should know."

She turned away from Captain Spivey and walked quickly to the door, as if she feared the captain would follow her.

Cailean followed her out of the great room.

In the corridor, she paused, glancing nervously over her shoulder. "I haven't… There is more I want to say," she said.

"No," he said and grabbed her hand, squeezing it. "Donna say more, Daisy. Donna say what you might later regret, aye?"

She looked exasperated, but he was quite earnest.

"*Och, leannan*, there is naugh' to be done for it, is there? You must keep your head about you now."

Her brows dipped into a dark V. "What about you? You are free to say what you like, Cailean. Is there nothing you will say? No word you will leave with me?"

What word would he leave? That he would miss her? That he was sorry he couldn't be the man she wanted him to be, no matter how desperately he wanted to? That his heart was breaking, that it felt as if she were already gone? "*Tha mi gad ionndrainn.*

Tha mi duilich." I'm sorry. I miss you. *"Tha gaol agam ort."* I love you. Oh, how I love you. He dipped his head and kissed her lips, lingering there, relishing the taste and feel of her mouth beneath his, fighting back the torrent of memories that were rushing in his veins. He caressed her cheek, then let her go and made himself walk on, walk out of Auchenard.

Cailean put himself on his horse, but held Odin as he pranced, eager to be on his way. He looked back to the door, where Daisy Bristol, his one and only true love, stood watching him.

He didn't believe that he would ever see her again.

CHAPTER EIGHTEEN

My heart has turned cruelly against me.

I have mourned R for so many years only to discover now that I don't love him at all as I believed I did, and I could never truly love him. He is much changed, or perhaps I am the one who is different, but we are no longer the least compatible. I cannot even believe he has come because he once loved me as he claims. I think he has come because of my fortune. It is only a feeling, but it grows stronger within my thoughts every day.

I have reached the conclusion that I should sooner marry a stranger than the devil I know.

I've not told anyone of my decision, as it seems premature. R has not formally offered for my hand after all. I will tell him once we are in London.

The news A brought is quite troubling and we all make haste in our preparations to depart. R believes A meant only to frighten him, but I believe A. He has been honest with me and I think he is now.

We are set to sail in a few days and Mr.
Munro said the weather looks very fine for it.

DAISY PUT DOWN her quill, picked up the wild orchid
she had cut that morning from her garden and put
it to her nose, inhaling the fragile fragrance. She
plucked two petals from the flower and pressed them
in between the pages of her diary.

The garden has grown so; it will be so beau-
tiful in the spring, and I shall not be here to see
it. I would not have thought it possible when I
first laid eyes on the terrible neglect. I am as-
tonished at how life will flourish with the least
amount of care.

She paused again, gazing outside, to her garden.
It was now a riot of color; yellow and red and pink
and blue and scarlet and white. She looked down at
diary and dipped her quill once more.

What did A say to me? Did he speak words
to pierce my heart or to hold it? It tortures me.

Torture. He'd left her with a constant pain, dull
and sharp at once.

Daisy put aside her quill, shut her book and stood
up from her desk. She needed an occupation. Anything to take her mind off her troubles.

She pulled a shawl around her and went out to her
garden. In the potting shed, she put on her apron

and gardening hat, and the gloves from which Uncle Alfonso had snipped the fingertips so that she might handle the more delicate plants. She picked up her trowel and carried on to the garden, where she got down on her knees and began to pull tiny little weeds from the dirt, one by one.

It was a glorious, sun-dappled late summer day, and yet Daisy had never felt so bereft. Her heart was heavy in her chest, and in spite of having her family with her, she felt quite alone. All of her burdens had fallen onto her, weighing her down, pressing the joy right out of her. Even her garden, with the soft music of the chimes and birds chirping overhead, did not soothe her.

She ached. Every muscle, every joint ached as if she had ague. But she was perfectly well. It was only her heart that ailed her.

After an hour or so, Daisy had cleaned her beds and pruned her bushes. She sank back on her heels and looked at her handiwork. A tear, surprising and unbidden, slipped from her eye. She swiped it away with the back of her hand.

"Daisy, my love."

She'd not heard Robert enter the garden.

"Look at you," he said, bending over to help her up. "Working with your hands." He made a *tsk* sound of disapproval as he held them up for inspection. "You'll ruin your beautiful hands with all this hard work."

She slowly pulled her hands free of his, perturbed

with his admonishment. "Hands are meant to be used, Rob."

"Not all hands are meant for labor, and a lady's hands are among them," he said sternly.

Daisy removed her gloves and wiped her hands on a handkerchief. She wished he'd not stand so close. She glanced up at his brown eyes, eyes she once imagined were vast oceans of esteem only for her. She squinted at that foggy memory and blurted, "Eleven years ago, we were very much in love, weren't we?"

"Yes," he agreed.

"Then why didn't you offer for me?"

"What?" He laughed.

"Why didn't you, Robert?" she asked again.

Now he frowned. "Daisy, darling." He reached for her, but she stepped back, just out of his reach.

"I want to know," she said.

He sighed, annoyed. "You know very well *why*. I was in no position to make a formal offer. I was the son of a country vicar, and *you* were the daughter of a baron."

"But you encouraged me. You said we would be together always. You said you loved me and wanted to be my husband, and yet you never went to my father to try and persuade him to our desire to wed."

"Well, naturally I didn't," he said, his exasperation clearly mounting. "What case would I have made? We were very young, Daisy. I would have gone in due course, when the time was right."

When the time was right. That phrase knocked

something from her past off a dusty shelf. She suddenly remembered that he had used those words with her then. He'd said he would speak to her father when the time was right.

Her gaze narrowed with suspicion. "And yet the time was never right, was it? I wonder, was it because you knew the Chatwick offer was in the making?"

Robert scoffed at that, but the color rose in his cheeks. "No," he said, sounding vexed. "How could I have possibly known it?"

"You did," she said softly. "You knew. Apparently everyone knew but me. You never intended to speak to my father, did you?"

"What rubbish. Of course I did," he insisted.

Daisy didn't believe him. She was filled with a clarity she'd never had about that part of her life until this very moment. It made perfect sense—all the clandestine meetings, the silly kissing…but the moment Daisy wanted more, Robert would back away, promising to speak to her father soon. He never did because he never intended to. He'd intended to seek the naval commission all along.

"For heaven's sake," Robert said. "It doesn't matter. What matters is that I intend to formally offer for you *now*, Daisy. I *love* you. I have always loved you. I want only to make you happy, and after all these years, I am able to do so." He smiled and caressed her cheek. "Let us vow to forget what happened many years ago. I was young and callow. I'd never been in love before, but on my honor as a captain in the

Royal Navy, whatever I did then was because I was thinking of you, Daisy. Only you."

She hesitated. She could believe his youth had played a role. Maybe he had loved her but had wanted to experience a bit of life before marrying. Maybe she was unfairly looking for reasons to doubt him, because her heart was somewhere else.

"We'll think only of the future," he said, smiling again.

The future? Daisy laughed with incredulity, but of course Robert believed her to be that stupid, stupid girl she'd once been. He smiled with self-satisfaction that he'd made her happy again. But Robert couldn't make her happy. He could *never* make her happy.

"That's better," he said. "My heart is always made glad by your sunny smile." He dipped his head beneath her bonnet and kissed her softly on the lips. "In a few days, we'll be on England's shores once again, where we belong. I will speak to the bishop straightaway, and I will be the happiest of men. And in turn, I will endeavor to make you the happiest of women."

"Yes," she said simply.

"Now then, your uncle and I are on our way to call on Mr. Munro about some provisions we will need for our voyage."

"Oh," she said. "Is that wise?"

He smiled charmingly, as if he were teasing a precocious child. "You put far too much stock in the words of a thief." He kissed her cheek. "We'll return before dark."

"Oh," she said again. Her thoughts began tumble and race.

Robert touched her chin. "Don't fret," he said and winked. He took her hands in his. "No more work in the garden—will you promise me?"

"Yes, I promise," she said sweetly. Anything to make him go.

He strode away, calling for her uncle.

Daisy followed well behind, walking onto the terrace and watching Robert and her uncle stride down to the water's edge, get in the boat and glide away from Auchenard. She watched them until she could no longer see them, then turned and hurried to the stables in search of Mr. Green.

When she found him, she said breathlessly, "A horse, please, Mr. Green. I mean to ride."

She then ran into the lodge calling for Belinda as she yanked the apron from her.

"What is it? What has happened? Is it the Highlanders come for us?" Belinda cried, running out of the great room.

"No, no, all is well. You must stay here with Ellis—there is something I must do."

"What must you do? Where are you going?" Belinda exclaimed, rushing after Daisy as she tossed her hat onto a chair.

"Riding!"

"*Riding!* You haven't been riding since we've been here. Where are you *going*, Daisy? It's unsafe! You must tell me!" Belinda frantically begged her as she followed Daisy out to the drive.

There was very little time. Daisy whirled around to Belinda and grabbed her arms. "Promise me you will not shriek."

"What? *No!*"

"I'm riding to Arrandale," she said and braced herself for the lecture she was sure would come, along with the warnings of riding too fast and the risk of breaking her fool neck.

Belinda's face darkened. She pressed her lips together a moment. "Have a care," she said simply.

Daisy blinked with surprise. "I will," she said. She impulsively kissed Belinda's cheek before hurrying on to the stables.

Mr. Green helped her onto a horse and pointed the way to Arrandale. "Just the other side of those trees, mu'um. A mile or so, not more."

She spurred the horse, shrieking with surprise when the feisty thing broke into a gallop.

In only a few minutes, Daisy saw the chimney tops and what looked like a spire above the treetops. The horse followed a worn path down to the house and when the tree line opened, Daisy gasped with surprise and pride for Cailean—the house was beautiful. It was built of limestone, with two wings and a spired turret anchoring one end. It was not as large as her house in Nottinghamshire, but it was larger than Auchenard.

But it seemed deserted. There was no one about, no animal, not even a chicken. Daisy's heart began to race erratically—she didn't know what she would do if he was not there. Ride on to Balhaire? No—

she couldn't even say what direction Balhaire was from there.

He had to be there. He simply had to *be* there.

In the front lawn—more of an untended meadow, really—she hopped down from her mount and walked up to the door, which, oddly, stood open. Daisy leaned inside and glanced around. "Good afternoon!"

There was no response. She noticed very few furnishings in one room off the entry, but nothing else. The house looked uninhabited. She stepped cautiously inside, glancing back over her shoulder to assure herself her horse was still there before walking into the foyer. She paused and glanced up at the simple, clean lines of the plasterwork, then down at the stone tiles at her feet. The house was elegant but not overly so. It reminded her of the lodge, only finer. She turned a slow circle, taking it all in. It was odd, a house of such beauty, peaceful and soothing, standing empty on the shores of the lake. When she looked out the front door, she could see the Highlands rising up around her.

She heard the sound of boots on the stone floor and whirled around. "Good afternoon!" she called.

There was a moment of silence, and then Cailean appeared at the end of the hall before her, stepping out from another room. He was wearing buckskins and a lawn shirt, open at the collar. His hair was in a loose queue. He was holding something in his hands, but Daisy couldn't see it and didn't care—her heart hammered in her chest, and she felt almost sick with

the thought that this might be the last time she ever
saw him, this man she desired beyond sanity.

"Daisy?" he said and took a cautious step forward.

"Cailean." Her voice shook when she said it, and
so did she. She suddenly broke into a run.

Whatever Cailean was holding shattered on the
floor when she leaped for him. He caught her in his
arms, his mouth landing on hers as he twirled her
around. "Are you barmy?" he asked, roughly pushing loose tresses of hair from her face. "What are
you doing here?"

"In the Highlands, if you want something, you
reach for it."

"Mi Diah," he muttered, and kissed her again,
carrying her into a room that was somewhat fur-
nished. He put her down on a settee and kissed
her décolletage, his hands sliding up her sides, his
breath warm and intoxicating on her skin. They
were fevered, both of them frantically clawing at
each other's clothing. Daisy pushed his shirt over
his head, pulling it off him while he caressed her
with his hands and his mouth. There was no need for
words between them; their ardent desire was mutu-
ally shared. But Daisy was impatient—she pushed
Cailean back, forcing him to sit on the settee, then
lifted her skirts to straddle him.

She kissed him as she slid her hands down his
chest, over his nipples, to his abdomen. She nuzzled
his neck, pressed her breasts against him.

"You bewitch me, Daisy," he said gruffly. "From
the moment I laid eyes on you, you have bewitched

me." He slid his hands under her skirt, to her thighs, and then between her legs.

The touch was startling, and Daisy released a breath she hadn't realized she was holding. Cailean watched her as he slipped his fingers inside her, then out, glancing against the tip of her pleasure, then sliding slow and long inside her again. Her eyes slid shut, and she clung to his shoulders as he buried his face in her breasts.

He began to unlace her gown. Their craving was equally potent, so ethereal, so in tune. It was love! Intense, burning *love*. His fingers slid into her again, and Daisy had to hold the back of the settee as he brought her to the edge of the abyss and then happily sent her into that seemingly bottomless cavern of pleasure. She cried out with her climax, gasping for air.

Cailean fumbled with his buckskins to free his arousal as Daisy pushed her gown from her body. He made a guttural sound of pleasure when she tossed it aside and sat up, holding her tightly on his lap to take one breast in his mouth, sucking the hardened peak into his tongue.

Blinded by desire and beyond redemption, Daisy wanted to give him what he had given her. She lifted herself up, then guided herself onto his cock as she covered his face with kisses, a mix of desire and adoration filling her body and soul, spilling out of her, enveloping him. It didn't seem possible that she could feel so profoundly for another human being, to want him and his touch so bad that nothing else mattered.

He was moving in her, driving her to the brink again. Daisy trembled with sheer anticipation; the fever between them overwhelmed her, and Cailean, too, because he suddenly yanked her up like a doll and twisted them around, so that she was on her back on the settee. His actions grew more urgent, and he slipped his hand between her legs and stroked her in time to his movements.

It was Daisy who plummeted first. Her release drew a powerful one from Cailean. He was spent, and he somberly gathered her in his arms and pressed his face to her neck. Daisy clung to him as the heat ebbed from their bodies, afraid to let him go. If she let go of her hold of him, she would lose him forever.

Cailean, however, did not feel that panic, for he pushed up from her, kissed her tenderly, then sat up, still trying to catch his breath. He grinned at her. "You hair will need a wee bit of tidying."

She laughed and sat up, reaching for her gown. She slipped it over her head and began to take the pins from her hair so that she might put it up again. There was an ease between them, a sense of comfort. Such compatibility, such harmony that Daisy said, without thinking, "I'm not going to marry him."

Cailean paused in fastening his buckskins and looked at her. "Pardon?"

"I won't marry Robert." She smiled, certain he'd think this happy news.

But Cailean frowned thoughtfully and motioned for her to turn around so he could lace her gown. "Why no'?"

"How can I possibly?" she asked. "As it happens, I'm in love with someone else."

The pulling of her laces suddenly stopped. And then Cailean put his hands on her shoulders and turned her about. "What did you say?"

"I said, I'm in love with someone else."

She expected his blue eyes to shine. But Cailean's frown only deepened, and Daisy's belly began to quiver with dread. He took her face in his hands. "*Diah, leannan*, what are you doing?" he asked plaintively.

The quiver turned to nausea. "I just told you I *love* you, Cailean."

But Cailean shook his head, and Daisy's heart, so full only moments ago, began to deflate. "It's impossible, Daisy, aye? You know it is. I've been honest with you, have I no'? From the beginning, have I no' said—"

"That you had no interest in my fortune," she said, shoving against his chest. "But you have interest in *me*, Cailean—you do! You obviously do!"

"Aye, of course I do!" He groaned, shoving a hand through his hair. He looked as if he was trying to impart something very important and she was refusing to listen. "Listen to me now. I want you with everything that I have," he said, knocking his fist against his chest. "But I canna marry you, lass."

"I didn't—"

He wouldn't let her speak. He took hold of her chin. "*Heed* me," he said. "I'm no' welcome in England and, in fact, I am wanted there. And frankly, you're no' particularly welcome here. Even if you were, *leannan*, I am five and thirty, well past the age for marrying and a family."

Not only was her heart completely deflated now; the queasiness was strong. She sank onto the settee and pressed her hand against her belly.

Cailean sat beside her and took her hand. "My duty is to take my da's place and lead this clan. And that I will do, before the end of the year. I canna leave Scotland now, no' when Spivey knows where I am and what we do. England would mean the end of me, aye? No, I willna leave Scotland, Daisy, but you *must* leave Scotland. For the sake of Ellis, you must leave. You know what I say is true."

Daisy couldn't comprehend how this man, this beautiful, perfect man, could make love to her like he had and then say such jarring and awful words.

"A Diah," he muttered, studying her. "You know I am right, *leannan*. Ellis must be in England. He's a viscount. He has property, and he will need the connections only England can give him, aye? He canna hide away in the Highlands with a free trader, and neither can you."

He was right. She knew he was right. But God help her, how she wanted him to be wrong. No matter what she felt, no matter who she loved, her responsibility to her son was far greater than her own wants. She knew this. She had always known this.

The weight of the truth was too much for Daisy. She pulled her hand free of his and sagged to one side, bracing her arms against the settee, breathing heavily, feeling as if she might be sick. All the wild hope she'd felt riding to Arrandale, all the hope she'd harbored that Cailean would somehow save her had been a foolish little dream. That dream was too much to carry now, and she felt as if she would collapse.

"Daisy," Cailean said, and he caught her up in his arms, cradling her against his body. Daisy thought of Ellis, her boy, probably wondering where she was, and pushed free of his embrace. She didn't need him. She didn't need anyone. She stood and unsteadily shook out her skirts, then tried, unsuccessfully, to tuck her hair back into some coif. She finally gave up and let it hang loose down her back. She took several steps toward the door, almost stumbling away from him.

"Daisy, for the love of Christ," Cailean said and put his arm around her shoulders, trying to pull her back, to keep her from leaving.

She held up her hand to make him stop. She swallowed hard, trying to gather herself, but her heart was still breaking, shattering into little pieces. She needed a moment before she could speak. Finally she asked, "What did it mean?"

He looked at her strangely, glanced at the settee, trying to understand her question.

"What you said when you left Auchenard," she said. "What did it mean?"

"*Och*, lass," Cailean said and gently stroked her hair. "It doesna matter."

"It matters to me."

Cailean stroked her hair. "I'd rather you no' know. There is enough heartache, is there no'?"

She laughed ruefully. "It is too late to spare me, Cailean. My heart is broken into pieces. What did you *say*?"

He grabbed her hands and held them tightly. "That I love you, aye? That's what I said, Daisy. I love you. I miss you. I am sorry for all of it." He roughly smoothed her hair. "I love you with all that I have," he said, his voice ragged with emotion.

A sob of despair caught in her throat. "I love you, too, Cailean. Dear God, how much I do." She was utterly defeated now. She felt like so many disjointed pieces, a broken toy trying to function properly. She pulled her hands free of his and turned away, blinded by tears and overwhelming disappointment. She heard him say her name, but she was already walking. And then she was running. Running out of the house, for her horse, away from Scotland.

He went after her, of course, calling her name, but Daisy scrambled onto the back of her horse before he could reach her, and she spurred him on, because she couldn't bear to hear another word. *Not a single word.*

It was unbearable and devastating to know that she'd found love—real, soul-searing love—and couldn't have it because of her wretched place in this world, and because of Ellis, because of what her son needed to thrive and what his title needed from him.

It was so horribly, wretchedly, heartbreakingly unfair.

CHAPTER NINETEEN

Of course Cailean knew she'd left—he saw the boats going by with passengers and crates and trunks. He'd been tormented by it, too, wanting for the truth of their lives to be different and feeling wholly impotent in his power to change it.

He had to believe it was best it had ended as it had.

A few days later, Cailean and Aulay sailed for Norway.

Cailean knew he was miserable company. His brother thought it a fever, but there was nothing physically wrong with Cailean. His complaint, acknowledged only in his private thoughts, was his heart—it wanted free of his chest. It felt tight, as if something were tugging on it, making him so uncomfortable that he remained in a foul humor.

They were gone longer than he'd anticipated—almost sixteen days in all owing to unfavorable winds on the return voyage—and by the time they arrived back in Scotland, he still hadn't rid his thoughts of her. It was like she had perched there, her eyes and devilish little smile taunting him at all hours of the day.

When he walked into Balhaire, he was immediately set upon by his mother. "Cailean, you must come!" she said, grabbing his hand. "Where is Aulay? Vivienne has been delivered of a boy!"

At long last, Vivienne's fourth child had arrived in this world, and from the look of it, the bairn was a strong, healthy lad. Cailean leaned over the bed where Vivienne suckled her son, marveling at his little fingers, his button nose.

"He arrived a week past," Vivienne said, stroking the lad's dark patch of fuzz. "He gave me quite a fight, he did, but look at him, Cailean. Go on, then—hold him," she said and unlatched the baby from her breast.

"I ought no'—"

"Donna be afraid of him." Vivienne laughed. "He's like all my bairns before him—he willna break." She slipped the baby into his hands. The bairn began to wiggle his legs, his rosebud mouth searching for his mother's breast. Cailean managed to get him into the crook of his arm—he didn't believe Vivienne that he'd not break—and stroked his cheek.

"We'll call him Bruce," she said.

Aye, a strong name for a strong lad. Cailean looked down at Bruce and thought of Ellis. He was suddenly overcome with a well of longing so deep and vast that he was startled by tears of old and new regrets that began to burn in his eyes.

"Cailean," Vivienne said softly, surprised. "*A grha*, what is wrong?"

Cailean swallowed back those blasted tears and handed the bairn back to his mother. "He's bonny,

Viv," he said. "Bonny Bruce." He smiled through
the sheen of tears, touched Vivienne's face and then
went out as his sister and her husband exchanged a
baffled look behind him.

Outside her chambers, Cailean paused, pressed
his back against the wall and looked heavenward.
For the first time in his adult life, he had no idea
what to do with his emotions.

He shook his head and carried on to his father's
study. He knocked lightly and went inside.

"Cailean, come in, then," his father said.

He did not rise from his seat behind the desk, a
certain sign his leg ailed him today.

"How did you find Norway? Aulay believes it
holds promise."

"Aye, that it does," Cailean agreed, although he'd
be hard-pressed to recall any of the details in his
current state. He walked to the hearth and looked
into the fire.

"We've a lot to discuss, aye? There's been a Jacobite uprising to the south of us," his father said, then
began to relate the news as he'd heard it. Cailean was
generally quite interested in such news, but today he
scarcely heard his father; his thoughts were miles
away.

"*Diah*, have you heard a word?" his father said.

Cailean snapped to attention and jerked around.
Somewhere in the course of the news, his father had
stood up from his desk and come around to a chair,
and Cailean hadn't noticed. He was sitting with his

leg stretched out before him. He studied Cailean as he rubbed his thigh. "What's wrong with you, lad?"

"Wrong?"

His father's ice-blue eyes narrowed, and he clucked his tongue. "I'm your father, am I no'? You look as if you lost your pup."

All his life, his father had seen past the facade Cailean presented to the world. He had never been able to hide when he was troubled. He sighed, walked to the settee and sat heavily, bracing his arms on his legs as he leaned forward. "It's far worse than losing a pup, aye?"

His father looked confused for a moment, but then he nodded and shook his head. "The Englishwoman, is it?"

Cailean's eyes widened with surprise. "How do you know this?"

"*Och*, I donna know it at all," he said with a flick of his wrist. "Your mother is the one who noticed. As has Rabbie."

It was even worse, then, if his family had determined what ailed him.

"Donna look at me like that, lad—you're no' the first one of us to be afflicted by a woman, are you, then? She's gone, is she?"

"Aye."

"It's good that she is. She'd no' be safe at Auchenard."

"No," Cailean agreed morosely.

His father said nothing for a long moment. Then, "You love her."

It was not a question. Cailean shrugged. "I do," he admitted.

"Well, well," his father mused. "Then there is naugh' to be done for it, is there? You'll go and get her." He shrugged, as if directing his son to go to the hall and fetch some ale.

Cailean laughed ruefully. "She's in London."

His father lifted his hands. "Your uncle has a town house there."

Cailean gaped at his father. "Have you forgotten that I am a free trader, then? That I was on the ship when the English seaman was shot by one of our muskets? Or have you forgotten that my grandfather was a known traitor? I'd no' be welcome there," he scoffed.

"Have you forgotten that it was your uncle who exposed your grandfather? They canna prove you are a free trader, lad. You'd be as welcome as any Scot. No' warmly, mind you. But you might move freely."

Cailean shook his head. It wasn't that simple.

"Go. Dress like them, speak like them. Your uncle Knox will help, aye? He's excellent connections."

"And what, then, knock on her door and…?"

"And offer for her hand," his father said, as if Cailean was thick.

Again Cailean shook his head. "She's no doubt married now, aye?"

"And if she is, she'll say no, and you'll ride like the wind away from there. But if she's no' yet married?"

Cailean grimaced. He rubbed his face with his hands. "She may yet say no."

His father smiled sympathetically. He reached across the space between them and put his hand to Cailean's shoulder, squeezing it. "You've been wounded before, you have. And if you are wounded again, it willna hurt any less. No, lad, it will hurt like hell. You will prefer the pain of a musket ball to that."

Cailean chuckled ruefully. "Do you mean to encourage me, then?"

His father grinned. "A man canna go through life without pain, aye? If she says no, you may console yourself with the knowledge that you were bloody well right, that women are more treacherous than the English, and you may never want for them again. You can live a life of misery and fall into drink and forsake your family." His grin broadened as he leaned forward. "But at least you will know, will you no'? Better to die a bitter man than an ignorant one."

"What of Arrandale? What of Balhaire?" he asked, gesturing to his father's leg. "I'm to assume your responsibilities."

"I'm no' dead quite as yet. I can manage well enough a few months more. And I have Rabbie. Cat, too."

A tiny light of possibility opened in Cailean's thoughts. He was almost afraid to hope. He stood up and began to pace. "What of the trade with the Norwegians?"

"Aulay," his father said, as if it were all so very simple. Cailean shot him an impatient look and his father chuckled. "*Diah*, Cailean—you'll no' be forever gone, will you?"

"I canna bring her here," he said flatly. "In the best of worlds, if she agrees to marry me, I canna bring her here."

"Aye, you can. No one will touch her at Balhaire. I'd no' go to Auchenard, no' while the Jacobites are about, and no' after the English captain has been there. But she may come here, and she and her family will be welcome."

Cailean's mind began to churn. He linked his fingers, ran his hand over his head. "There is the matter of her son. He's a viscount. His education, his connections must be made in England."

"Aye, they must. But he's a wee bairn, Cailean. Cat said his tutor has come to Auchenard with him. Will he no' come to Balhaire? When he's older, he might return to England for his training, aye?"

Cailean desperately wanted to believe there was hope. He glanced at his father, and a swell of love washed over him. "How can I leave you now, *Athair*?" he asked plaintively. "You need me, aye?"

His father smiled fondly. "I canna move as well as I once did, aye, it is true. But I've four other children besides you, Cailean. Any one of them might act in my stead. We'll do well enough without you for a time, and you need no' worry over me yet." Arran Mackenzie slowly came to his feet. "My advice is to go now, lad. Donna think too long or you will think your way out of it, aye? Go while the fire burns."

The fire, so to speak, was suddenly burning brighter than it had in days.

IT WAS ASTONISHING how quickly a man with determination could arrange things. Cailean gave no thought to the dangers he faced. He could think only of stopping Daisy before she married.

He sought out Aulay, who was preparing to sail back to Norway. "I need passage to England," he said.

"Are you mad?" Aulay demanded. "There's too much to be done to romp off to England."

"That I know, as well as you. But we're sailing south."

His brother groaned but instructed his first mate to off-load the goods they meant to trade.

Cailean next sought out Willie Mackenzie. The man was more than happy to look after Arrandale and Auchenard for the princely sum of ten pounds. Cailean brought Fabienne and Odin to Balhaire, and as he walked from the great hall that day after saying goodbye to his family, Fabienne, napping before the hearth with other Mackenzie dogs, scarcely lifted her head.

Remarkably, within a fortnight of speaking with his father, Cailean had arrived at Norwood Park, the northern estate where his mother had been raised and where her marriage to his father had been arranged. They all knew the story—his mother had fled Scotland soon after she'd married, but her father had sent her back to Balhaire three years later to determine if Arran Mackenzie was plotting against the throne.

The idea was laughable—there was not a better man than Arran Mackenzie. Which, thankfully, his mother had also realized. Unfortunately, her father, Lord Norwood, and her oldest brother, Bryce Armstrong, were not good men. Lord Norwood was the traitor, and he was convicted of conspiring against the Crown. Bryce Armstrong was stripped of his hereditary rights. His mother's half brother, Knox Armstrong, was made Lord Norwood and given all that entailed.

Cailean arrived at Norwood Park in the midst of a soiree, which, his mother had warned him, was not uncommon since Knox had come to assume the title. The ride from port to Norwood Park had not been an easy one, and Cailean was bone weary and covered with the grime of the road. He asked the butler to show him to a private room so that he'd not disturb the guests.

As he followed the butler to a private salon, however, he caught sight of a familiar face. Poppy Beauly—now Lady Prudhome—was sitting in a chair, talking to another woman. He knew her instantly, though this was the first time he'd seen her since the day she'd rejected his offer. Her face still clung to some of the beauty from her youth, but there were dark shadows under her eyes, and her hair was graying. She'd softened and widened with time.

Cailean ducked into the small receiving room, certain she hadn't seen him. He hadn't been to England since that summer, and now, having seen her, he felt like a fool. What had kept him from it all these years? *That* haggard woman?

Uncle Knox entered by throwing the door open and toddling into the room, slightly drunk and much rounder than the last time Cailean had seen him. "Cailean!" he exclaimed with his usual vigor.

Cailean had fond memories of Knox, the congenial uncle who had always been quick to hug and quick to shove ale into one's hand. Even now he threw his arms around Cailean and hugged him tightly, bouncing him around a bit. "You look well indeed! A grown man, are you, and a laird now—how about that? Soon to sit on the throne of the Mackenzies, I've heard. Well, I am very glad to see you. I thought you'd never come down out of those hills!"

"Neither did I," Cailean agreed.

Uncle Knox went to the sideboard and poured two drams of whisky, then handed one to Cailean. He touched his glass to Cailean's and said, "To old times," and tossed it down his throat. "Now then, your mother's messenger arrived only yesterday."

"My mother sent a messenger?" Cailean asked, unaware of it.

"Certainly!" Uncle Knox bellowed, smiling jovially. "She was resolved that I should understand her instructions explicitly and do as she bade me," he said with a courtly bow and laughed. "I sent the messenger back straightaway with one of my own. My dearest Margot, I said, you wound me with your distrust. Of course my nephew may have all that he needs in pursuit of whatever he is pursuing," he said with a flourish of his hand. "My guess is a woman?"

Cailean flushed.

His uncle laughed with delight. "To all things there is a season," he said. "Now then, I'd invite you in, but you look a shambles, and, besides, your last attempt at marital felicity attends me this evening."

"Aye, I saw Lady Prudhome," Cailean said.

"Her husband is a drunkard, you know," Uncle Knox whispered conspiratorially as he rummaged around a drawer in the desk. "Ah, here it is! The key to your kingdom, as it were. At least the key to my London townhome. I've not been there in an age, and I'm afraid you'll have to make do without a proper staff, but old Bussey is there, and he'll mind you. I'll just dash off a note of introduction. We have much to discuss, naturally. You'll need some letters of introduction, lest you encounter some corrupt business. There are those who don't care for Scotsmen."

"Aye, I am aware," Cailean said.

Uncle Knox handed the key to Cailean, then glanced down at Cailean's clothing. He wrinkled his nose.

Cailean looked down, too. "It's the dirt of the road."

"It's not that, my good man," Uncle Knox said. "It's your *dress*. You can't dress like a Highland savage here. Don't take offense. You're certainly not a savage, but they will *think* you are. I'm sure I've something that will suit you. Come along, then. My valet is probably diddling a maid downstairs. We'll go and have a bit of fun, won't we, make him pull up his breeches and outfit you properly? We'll make an Englishman of you yet!"

Cailean's head was spinning. He was hungry and fatigued, and he was not exactly besotted with the idea of appearing as an Englishman. He followed his uncle out of the room and forgot to notice Poppy at all.

Three days later, properly outfitted, with a fresh horse, and letters of introduction tucked into his coat pocket, Cailean started for London.

CHAPTER TWENTY

IT FELT TO DAISY as if the return voyage to England
had taken twice as long as the voyage up, when in
fact, it was two days shorter in length. Robert complained about the ship's navigation—it lacked the
finesse of the Royal Navy—but he addressed the
MacDonalds and their crew with restrained civility.
He kept his sword at his side and said he slept poorly,
as he expected to be set upon by the Scotsmen in
the night.

But he was attentive of Daisy and her family, and
as they neared England, Daisy tried, she really did
try, to rekindle the feelings she'd carried for him for
so long, to put aside her misgivings about his true
intentions. What did it matter? His intentions were
the same as every other man's in London. At least
she knew Robert. At least she knew what to expect
from him. What did it matter that his touch now left
her cold, or that he instructed Ellis at every turn? It
could be much worse with a stranger, couldn't it?

But it was no use—Daisy couldn't think of anything other than Cailean.

"Does the voyage make you ill?" Belinda had

asked her from the cramped cabin they shared aboard the ship.

"Ill? No," Daisy said, slowly shaking her head as if trying to dispel a heavy sleep.

Belinda didn't say more—in fact, she was unusually quiet during the journey to London—but she kept a fretful eye on Daisy. That only made Daisy's agony worse. She wanted only to wallow in her misery, unnoticed, uninterrupted. But she felt as if she had to maintain her composure so that her family, and Robert, would not worry, would not ask her at every turn if she was all right. She would never be all right. She would never be the same again.

It was a gusty night when they at last reached London and the Chatwick town house on Audley Street at half past eleven. Daisy was exhausted, and she allowed Robert to carry Ellis up to his room, where one of the chambermaids was on hand to put him to bed. Belinda excused herself, too, and wearily climbed the stairs.

Robert joined Daisy in the salon. He didn't show any signs of fatigue. It was as if he'd never journeyed at all and had been waiting in this salon for her for days. "You are fatigued, my poor little dear," he said. "Now, I want you to get a good night's sleep." He clasped her shoulders. "I'll call on you on the morrow, and we will speak of our future." He smiled, as if that ought to send her off to sweet dreams.

"Where are you going?" she asked curiously. He'd been under her roof for so long now that in some respects, it felt as if they'd already said their vows.

"To the club. It is one thing to be your guest in the backwater hills of Scotland, but it wouldn't be proper for me to remain under the same roof with you here."

She was too tired to argue and merely nodded, accepted his kiss and walked him to the door.

Daisy was exhausted, but she did not sleep well. Her bed felt too soft somehow, and she tossed and turned in it. She dreamed that she and Ellis were in her garden at Auchenard, and she was planting new roses. Cailean was there, too. But in that state between sleep and consciousness, she realized it wasn't a dream; it was a wish. She wasn't asleep at all—her sorrow kept her floating above the surface as her unspoken wish played out in her mind's eye.

She did eventually find sleep, however, because she was rudely startled awake by a shake to her shoulder. It was Belinda looming over her. "Dearest!" she whispered. "Are you unwell?"

"No. I don't think so," Daisy said groggily and pushed herself up, forcing Belinda back. She winced at the pain behind her eyes. "Why?"

"It's two o'clock. Captain Spivey is calling at two, and Bishop Craig sent word that he shall call at half past two."

Daisy opened her eyes. "What?" she exclaimed and scampered out of the bed.

"I hope it is only fatigue," Belinda said as she threw open Daisy's wardrobe and began to search for a gown. "And not some horrible foreign disease. Those ships carry them round like cargo."

"I'm not ill. I'm…" Daisy's voice trailed off.

Belinda paused what she was doing and glanced over her shoulder.

Daisy swallowed back a sob. "Resigned," she said softly.

She scarcely had time to dress and to eat a little something before Robert arrived. He had on a fresh set of clothing and had donned a periwig. He strolled into her salon with his tricorne tucked up under one arm. His smile was ebullient as he clicked his heels and bowed formally. "How do you do, Lady Chatwick? You look well," he said. "London agrees with you."

She thought she looked gaunt and weary. "Thank you," she said, peering at him uncertainly. "You look as if you've dined with the king."

He laughed. "Not the king. But I have been to call on Bishop Craig this morning."

Daisy froze. *So soon?* They'd scarcely set foot in London, and he'd already gone to Bishop Craig? "I beg your pardon?" she said, her voice betraying her panic.

Robert arched a brow. "Darling, you must realize that word of your return—in my company—will spread quickly. I took the liberty of telling the bishop of our journey and…our understanding."

Daisy's belly clenched. She caught the back of the settee before she collapsed, as she felt her knees might give way. "You shouldn't have done that," she said. "You shouldn't have, Robert."

He blinked. He laughed nervously. "Of course I should have. One does not share a voyage with a gentleman unless one has an understanding. And if she didn't have one before, she certainly has one when she returns to London."

"I shared a voyage with my family and with your protection—that is *not* an understanding. If it were so, I'd be affianced to Sir Nevis now."

Robert slowly put his tricorne aside. "Then allow me to offer my apology," he said carefully, treating her as if she were a crazed woman. "Would you like to know the bishop's response?"

She looked at him warily.

Robert smiled. "He was impressed with my connections and my letters of recommendation."

"Your letters of recommendation," she repeated, not understanding.

"Of course I have them—a man of my standing must come armed to offer marriage to a woman of your standing. I presented a letter from Admiral Kensing and Lord Woodhouse."

"Lord Woodhouse? Is that not the estate where your father resides as vicar?"

Robert nodded.

"You received these letters today?" she asked, trying to make sense of how he'd managed to procure them so quickly.

"No, darling. I received these letters before I embarked for Scotland."

"Before," she repeated.

Robert's smiling expression changed. He rubbed his forehead as if he was trying to work out a difficult puzzle. "I don't think you understand, Daisy.

Before I could speak to you, before I could even entertain the idea of *offering* for you, I had to make sure I would not be denied. I thought you would appreciate the lengths to which I went to give us a happy future."

Daisy pressed her hands to her face a moment, disbelieving the lengths he'd gone to. He was either entirely too presumptuous to call on the bishop without her knowledge, or he had knit together his plan to put his hands on her fortune. Whatever the reason, she couldn't prolong this any further. "I wish you hadn't done so, Robert. You presume too much."

His hopeful smile faltered. He folded his arms. "If you have something to say to me, then please do say it."

She gathered her courage. "I don't... I don't have the same feelings for you that I once did," she said simply.

Robert did not seem particularly surprised. In fact, he shrugged as if that were a trifling matter. "I am aware that your esteem lies with someone else. It has been obvious."

Stunned, she waited for him to say more. When he didn't, she asked, "Does that not change your opinion?"

He smiled a little and shook his head. "Quite obviously, I would prefer if you held the same regard for me. And if my offer for your hand was to be made solely on the basis of compatibility and esteem, then perhaps I should be offended. But an offer for your hand has more to do with your son, does it not?"

Daisy gaped at him. Quite clearly he didn't feel the same about her as he once had, either. "It has as much to do with me as it does my son. My feelings must be considered."

Robert laughed softly, and Daisy's blood turned cold. He moved toward her, a smug bit of a smile on his face. When he reached her, he touched her earring, then let his hand drop to her shoulder. "Lady Chatwick, if you believe that you will hie off and marry your Highland thief, you are mistaken. The bishop would never allow it. Certainly *I* will not allow it. I know where the worst of the free traders are. I know an admiral who would be much delighted to have the information. If you do not accept my offer, he will have the whereabouts of Mackenzie within a fortnight. Your...*infatuation*...will be brought up on charges of free trading and made to pay the price. If I were you, I would think carefully before you refuse me."

Daisy glared at him, her heart racing with fury. She saw Robert for what he was now, and very clearly at that. "How *dare* you," she said, her voice shaking with anger. "It is none of your concern whom I marry, and if you think your threats will persuade me to act differently, you are very much mistaken."

His expression turned darker, and he frowned at her as if she were an unruly child. "Is there a better alternative for you? Will you marry someone you scarcely know? Or will you pine away for a bloody *Scot*?"

"I won't marry someone I don't love," she said. "And I don't love you, Robert. Please go."

Robert snorted. "You are as naive as you ever were, Daisy. You will not marry for *love*—you will marry for advantage. Perhaps the bishop might put some sense into your head," he said and walked across the room, preparing to take his leave. "By the by," he said, pausing at the door. "You might want to know that I have made the bishop aware you might be a bit reluctant, due to your blatant and misguided admiration of a Scot free trader." He threw open the door and went out, slamming the door behind him.

Daisy trembled with rage as she slowly sank onto the settee, trying to catch her breath. She felt heartsick and furious. She didn't care who Bishop Craig would recommend to her now. She didn't care, but she would never marry Robert. He would never touch her fortune.

She wondered if there was some way she could get word to Cailean about his threats. She wanted desperately to speak to Uncle Alfonso, but he'd gone to Chatwick Hall to attend to some matters there.

As she tried to think of what to do, the door opened and Ellis's head appeared, peeking around it. Daisy managed a smile. "Come here, darling."

Ellis ran to her, throwing his arms around her to hug her. He was wearing a cloak, and Belinda walked in behind him, dressed to go out, as well.

"Where are you going?" Daisy asked as she nuzzled her son's neck.

"For a walk," he said.

"He needs to use his legs after spending such a very long time in a coach and on that wretched boat," Belinda added. "Mrs. Cooper's son lay in a bed for a full year with a fever and never was able to walk properly again after a long voyage."

Daisy smiled wearily. "Then by all means, you must walk," she said and straightened Ellis's neck-cloth. She winked at her son. "I hereby command you to have your walk with Cousin Belinda every day."

"Aye, Mamma."

Oh, how that expression made her ache for Ellis, too—Scotland had not yet left him, either.

"Unless, of course, you'd prefer I stay and receive the bishop with you?" Belinda asked.

"No, thank you," Daisy said. "It is best I hear his news alone. I'll need time to swallow it whole before supper, won't I?" She sighed and hugged Ellis to her, looking at Belinda over the top of his head. "I refused Captain Spivey's offer of marriage."

Belinda was stunned, her eyes widening. Even Ellis looked up at Daisy with an expression of astonishment. Daisy smiled and tucked a bit of his hair away from his face. "You do recall that I explained to you that I must remarry, don't you? It's what your father wanted for you."

Ellis nodded.

"Captain Spivey wanted to marry me and take care of you," she said, lying about the true nature of his intentions. "But I don't love him and I don't want to marry him."

"Then I want you to marry Cailean," Ellis said earnestly.

Her heart clutched, and tears sprang to Daisy's eyes so immediately that it shocked her. Her heartbreak was so deep that she felt it would burst out of her and flood the room with her tears. She hugged Ellis tightly to her. "Me, too," she said. "But it's impossible, pet."

"But why?" Ellis insisted. "I like Scotland!"

"Because you are an English viscount. You must be properly educated and introduced into the world you will someday oversee. You can't do that from Scotland. Auchenard is for hunting—not for living."

Ellis was crestfallen. He bowed his head and studied the carpet. "I am glad you won't marry the captain," he muttered.

Daisy kissed the top of his head. "Not if he were the last man on earth, darling. Go now—have your walk with Belinda. I have yet to speak to Bishop Craig. I'll see you before supper."

Ellis nodded and walked to the door, the skip in his step gone. Belinda held the door open for him and glanced back at Daisy. She smiled uncertainly and said, "I'm glad you refused him, too," then slipped out, as if she feared Daisy would admonish her for it.

When they had gone, Daisy stood up, dragged herself over to the sideboard and uncharacteristically poured herself a bit of whisky. She'd grown to like it. She winced at the taste—it was inferior to what she'd had at Balhaire—but she welcomed the warm slide down her gullet and the way the warmth spread through her limbs.

She put the dram aside and moved to the window. The day was quite gray, and clouds were heavy overhead, blanketing London. Just as they blanketed her.

Down below, she saw Belinda and Ellis walking in the direction of Hyde Park. She saw them pass Bishop Craig and his entourage of two. Seeing him made her feel ill, and she went back to the sideboard for another bit of whisky before she had to receive him.

Several minutes later, Rowley showed the bishop into the salon. He wore a black coat and starched collar, a black waistcoat and breeches and hosiery. It was as if the Grim Reaper had come calling. His two companions were also clad in religious clothing.

Daisy didn't know who they were, and she didn't care. She rose gracefully from her seat and curtsied to the bishop. "My lord."

He strode forward to greet her. He took her hand and then surprised Daisy by leaning in to kiss her cheek. He instantly swayed back, his eyes narrowing as he stared down at her over his hook nose. "Madam, I would welcome you home after your foolish flight to Scotland, but I detect the smell of spirits on your breath."

Daisy put her hand to her mouth. "Medicinal," she muttered.

The bishop frowned. "Medicinal, indeed. I don't know what to make of you. You have risked the life of the Viscount Chatwick with all your darting about in search of fancy."

Daisy bristled. She would never risk her son's life, and she resented him greatly for thinking so, for thinking that she was frivolous, when all she had ever done was care for her husband.

"Your husband was quite right in setting his terms. He clearly understood that your judgment could not be depended upon to see his lordship safely to his majority."

Would God forgive her if she put her hands around the man's throat and squeezed the stuffing from him?

"Captain Spivey has informed me of his intention to offer for you. He has also told me of your unseemly admiration of a Scot smuggler, Lady Chatwick." His bushy gray brows furrowed over his nose. "It is beyond my comprehension that you might have subjected your son to such a despicable being. Have you no care for him?"

She wished someone were here to keep her from launching her body at this man. She imagined tackling him to the ground and pummeling his face. As it was, she had to step away from him and clutch her hands together. "Of course I care for him, my lord, just as I always have. Captain Spivey has had quite a lot to say," she said, fighting to keep her anger from showing itself in her words. "I have refused his offer, as his unwarranted jealousy has proven itself to be a danger to me and my son."

The bishop squinted. "His what?"

"Unwarranted jealousy. He is a very jealous man and imagines esteem where it doesn't exist," she said.

"What do you mean?" the bishop asked.

"He came to my son's hunting lodge Auchenard without invitation from me," Daisy said, her mind galloping, looking for an answer. "I have not encouraged his esteem. Never have I, not even as a young debutante. I refused him then, too, for my heart was set on Lord Chatwick. I was quite surprised to find him on the drive of my son's hunting lodge, professing his affection for me after eleven years. Can you imagine? I've not heard a word of him in all that time, and he expects me to believe he has harbored a torch for me?"

The bishop clasped his hands behind his back, his expression wary. "He paints an entirely different story."

"Of course he does, my lord. He was refused. He had come all that way to make his case for my hand in marriage without the slightest hint that I might share his esteem. You may ask my cousin or my uncle if that is true. He mistakenly believed that I didn't share his esteem because I admired our neighbor, the laird of Arrandale. He is the son of the laird of Balhaire. The Mackenzies are a powerful Scots family. They are most certainly not *smugglers*," she said, as if that were impossible.

"How can you be certain of this?" the bishop asked. "Would not Captain Spivey have a sense of it? He claims to have encountered the man on the open sea."

"On the open sea!" Daisy said and laughed. "How could he possibly identify a single man across the bow of one ship to the other?" Daisy honestly didn't know if it was possible, but she laughed now as if it was madness, and the bishop...the bishop looked doubtful. "He has made some serious accusations against a good neighbor and a friend of my uncle's," Daisy continued, sensing that she was turning the bishop's attention. "None of them are true. I never saw a smuggler's ship or bounty. We were invited to Balhaire and treated with the utmost courtesy. Quite frankly, I suspect Captain Spivey will impugn anyone whom he thinks is a threat to his getting his hands on my fortune."

"That is a serious accusation in itself," the bishop said.

"But it is the truth, my lord. It's quite obvious, isn't it? He has resigned his commission from the Royal Navy. Where will he derive his income if not from Lord Chatwick's inheritance?"

The bishop glanced back at his assistants, uncertain now. He returned his gaze to Daisy and flicked his wrist dismissively. "It hardly matters. I would not advise a marriage to Spivey. He is *not* suitable."

"I agree," she said.

The bishop straightened. "We might debate the merits of your journey to Scotland and your choice of company another time." He yanked at the tails of his long waistcoat and then gestured to the settee. "Please be seated. We have much to discuss."

Daisy sighed. She sat.

"Now then," he said, and put his hands behind his back as he began to pace before her, as if preparing to impart crucial words of wisdom. Or a sermon. She didn't want to hear either.

"The issue of your hand in marriage is of utmost importance. You have dallied long enough. I have come to the conclusion that there are two men who are suitable and are willing to take your hand in marriage."

Willing!

"The first gentleman is somewhat older—"

"How old?" Daisy interrupted, earning a dark look from the bishop.

"He is in his fiftieth year," he said.

Daisy blanched.

"Lord Vanderberg is a widower and a devout Christian man. His Christian influence on Lord Chatwick would be, in my opinion, superior to any but my own."

That hardly recommended the gentleman to Daisy. She didn't know Lord Vanderberg and she didn't want to know him. Fifty years of age? She'd only recently turned nine and twenty! She thought of her shy, tender son in the hands of a devout Christian taskmaster. Would he be made to do penitence for some perceived sins? She didn't like it. Not at all.

"The second gentleman, Lord Yarbrough, is a bit younger than yourself."

Daisy almost moaned. She knew Lord Yarbrough—every woman in London knew him. He was a libertine who'd had as many lovers as he'd had years on this earth.

"He is young, and he can be brash at times, but he faithfully attends church services, and he has shown himself to be principled when managing his family's fortune. He would be a good steward of Lord Chatwick's fortune."

Daisy was a good steward of Ellis's fortune, and she had been for several years now. She didn't need a man to do that for her.

"Both men have excellent connections, which will benefit Lord Chatwick in the years to come. Now then, to the matter of formally making their acquaintance. I shall bring them around to meet you and Lord Chatwick. Naturally, I will be on hand to help assess your compatibility. I shall send a messenger with the details. Are we clear?"

"I am clear on everything you've said," Daisy said sweetly. "Thank you, my lord."

"Very good." He seemed to think his work was done. He glanced at his two assistants and signaled them to go out.

"Good day, Lady Chatwick," the bishop said.

"Good day, my lord."

He followed his assistants, but Daisy caught him before he could quit the room. "Pardon, my lord, if I may?"

The bishop glanced back, impatient now. He was done with this bit of business and eager to be on to the next soul he might direct and control.

Daisy took a step forward. "If I am not mistaken,

my husband's will does not specify that you must approve or otherwise assess compatibility with any gentleman from whom I might entertain an offer... Does it?"

The bishop stared at her.

Daisy lifted her chin. "His wish was that you help me find a match. But he did not ask you to make it for me."

The bishop slowly turned about and walked back to where she stood. He was scarcely taller than she was, but it felt as if he were towering over her now, his disapproval coming off him in waves. "You have an audacity that is unbecoming, madam. You know as well as I that your husband's wish was that I find a suitable steward for you and your son."

"It was his wish that you help me," she said. "I am a grown woman. I am capable of deciding for myself."

His expression darkened. "Do you find my selections for you objectionable? Do you not find them clearly superior to any *you* have entertained?"

Daisy lifted her chin. "I find the entire conversation objectionable."

The bishop's expression turned angry. He shifted closer, forcing her to lean back. "You may find it objectionable, Lady Chatwick, but you must agree that the will specifically states you will marry by year's end or forfeit Lord Chatwick's inheritance. You have enjoyed your *freedom*," he said, nearly spitting the word at her. "You have played the part of the merry widow quite well. Now is time to think of someone other than yourself and marry. And unless you have someone in mind who exceeds the qualities of the two men I have presented to you, I suggest you cease pretending outrage and indifference and get on with the business of raising your son properly."

He didn't allow her a response; he whirled around and marched from the room. She heard him barking orders to his two assistants, then the front door slam behind him as he went.

She did have someone else in mind. *A gentleman. A soldier. A hunter and woodsman, a lover and...* Her skin flushed.

She whirled around, looking for something, anything. Seeing the empty glass of whisky, she picked it up and hurled it with all her might into the hearth. The glass shattered against the stone. And then she shattered, sinking down onto her knees, her head bowed, reality bleeding into her, making her ache.

CHAPTER TWENTY-ONE

CAILEAN STOOD OUTSIDE the house on Audley Street in a new set of clothing, properly tailored, prepared to present himself to Daisy. Since he'd settled in London and moved into Uncle Knox's town house, he'd been to Chatwick House once. He had seen only servants coming and going on daily errands, and callers, dressed in fine clothing and elaborate wigs, going into the house and coming out again. Now he strode down the street with determination, but before he could reach the door, a carriage pulled up outside Chatwick House. Out of it emerged four men, three of them wearing the cloth of a church and one of them in a periwig, a silk coat and breeches, with lace dripping out of each sleeve.

Cailean's step slowed. He looked quite plain in comparison to the gentleman. He jogged up the steps with the church men, one of whom Cailean realized must be the bishop. They knocked, then quickly disappeared inside.

Cailean was suddenly struck with uncertainty. He began to question himself. She'd probably settled on a match. Of course she had—she'd been in London for what he guessed was about three weeks now.

She'd probably posted the bloody banns. He was a fool to think he could come out of the Highlands and offer marriage to an English viscountess.

Cailean felt a wee bit dejected as he returned to the Grovesnor Square, from which he could see the house. He took up residence on a bench there, leaning to his left now and again to view her house, debating what he ought to do now.

He was distracted by a wee lass in the square with her nursemaid, her arms spread wide, twirling around and around while her nursemaid warned her she would make herself ill. He smiled to himself and glanced back to Chatwick House—and his heart skipped a few beats. Miss Hainsworth and Ellis were walking. They turned away from him at the corner of Audley Street and the square and walked briskly on. Ellis had to skip to keep up with Miss Hainsworth.

Cailean surged to his feet and hastened after them, darting around people and carts and horses, almost losing sight of them when they turned onto another street. When he caught up to them, he saw the street led them to Hyde Park.

Cailean walked faster.

He was familiar with the park, having spent some time there as a young man, and he walked as quickly he could without seeming to run with the hope of intercepting them. He managed it, emerging on the path before them, quite breathless. He removed his hat.

Miss Hainsworth didn't notice him at first, but the lad saw him instantly. "Cailean!" he shouted, breaking away from his cousin's grip and running for him.

Cailean squatted down to catch him, hugging him tightly, astonished at how happy he was made by the sight of the lad. He kissed his cheek, set him back. "Aye, there you are, then, the Lord Chatwick on his daily walk."

"You came!" Ellis cried happily. "I prayed you would," he added excitedly.

"Did you indeed? God must have heard your prayers, aye?" He chuckled, and with a pat to Ellis's back, he rose and bowed to Miss Hainsworth.

She was staring at him with a decided look of panic. "You ought not to be here!" she said, reaching for Ellis and pulling him back. She glanced around, as if she expected someone to come running to apprehend them.

"I ought no' to be, aye," he agreed. "But I've a wee bit of unfinished business."

"Not now," Miss Hainsworth said, looking increasingly anxious. "The bishop, he's…he's with Lady Chatwick now."

"Is she to marry Spivey?" Cailean asked bluntly.

The blood drained from Miss Hainsworth's face; she opened her mouth as if she meant to speak but couldn't manage it.

"She's not," Ellis said. "She's to marry one of the bishop's men."

Cailean's gut clinched. He looked at Miss Hainsworth, hoping she would deny it. She didn't. "Has the agreement been made?" he asked.

Miss Hainsworth shook her head. "No. Not as yet."

Diah, there was no time. "Miss Hainsworth," he said and moved closer. "I need your help."

Miss Hainsworth immediately began to shake her head. She looked over her shoulder, as if someone were following her. "You really shouldn't be here. If anyone sees you—"

"Miss Hainsworth," Cailean said, ready to beg if he must. "You must help me, aye? If you donna help me, she might make a decision that will impact all of you for the rest of your days."

"But it is the *bishop*," she said fearfully. "I cannot commend my immortal soul to hell for defying him."

She was determined to make this difficult. "No," he agreed. "But if your cousin found her happiness on this earth because of you, would no' your immortal soul soar to heaven?" He was grasping, hoping that made even the slightest bit of sense.

"He's right, Belinda!" Ellis tried.

Miss Hainsworth bit her bottom lip. "No," she said to Ellis and to Cailean, "My lord... I beg your pardon, but I can't help you."

Cailean felt the jaws of defeat begin to close in around him. His shoulders sagged. His spirit was draining out of him.

"*I* can help you," Ellis said with determination.

Cailean smiled. "You're a bonny lad, but I donna think you can help me with this." No, he'd lost the battle before it was ever waged. "I'll take matters in my own hands, then," he said. "Have your walk, aye? Perhaps I shall see you back at Chatwick House."

"But you can't," Miss Hainsworth said frantically.

He could, and he would. With a bow to Miss Hainsworth and Ellis, he stepped around them and started back down the path, headed for Audley Street.

He'd not taken many steps when Miss Hainsworth shouted, "Wait!"

Relief swept through Cailean. He glanced heavenward with a silent prayer of gratitude and turned around.

CHAPTER TWENTY-TWO

THREE DAYS AGO, the bishop had brought around Lord Vanderberg. He had a poorly powdered wig that emitted a faint but unpleasant scent. His breeches gaped around his spindly legs, and his complexion— a shade of gray—seemed sickly to Daisy.

He greeted her with a warm smile and showed Ellis his Bible. He politely inquired of Ellis about his religious instruction.

"I attend church services with my mother," Ellis muttered.

"That's a good boy," his lordship said. "Now then, do be so kind as to run along to your governess so that I might have a word with your mother, will you?"

"Yes, my lord," Ellis said and dodged the man's liver-spotted hand as he hurried from the room.

Lord Vanderberg smiled at Daisy and invited her to join him at the other end of the room, away from the bishop and his men. He gestured for her to sit in the only chair there and stood above her—crookedly, with his hands clasped behind his back. "Now then," he said. "My lord bishop tells me you've enjoyed your freedom these last few years."

"Pardon?"

"By that I mean you have not attended church as often as perhaps you should have done—is that not so?"

Daisy glanced at the bishop, who pretended to be reading from his Bible. "I didn't realize my attendance was an issue," she said coolly.

"Yes, well…if I may, Lady Chatwick, if we are to come to terms, I must be able to count on you to be a willing and devout partner in our faith and service to the Lord."

Daisy was not afraid to pledge devotion and service to the Lord…but his request seemed so much more than that. As if she were pledging to be willing and devout in service to him.

Lord Vanderberg arched a gray caterpillar of a brow. "Do I sense hesitation?"

"You do not," she said. "I confess I am slightly taken aback, my lord, as no one has ever questioned my devotion to the Lord."

"No? I think we must question our devotion every day," he said and smiled, showing his yellow teeth. "It is doubly important that we do so for the sake of young Lord Chatwick."

She didn't hear what else he said; she was fighting off a swell of nausea. Lord Vanderberg ended his call by asking her to bow her head and join him in prayer for Ellis.

This morning, the bishop brought around Lord Yarbrough, who smiled salaciously throughout their meeting. At least he was handsome…but that was the only thing she could say for him. They had not stayed long; Lord Yarbrough begged her forgiveness with the excuse that he had a prior appointment.

She was surprised when he called again not an hour later, without the company of the bishop. When Rowley showed him into her salon, he bowed deeply and said, "I beg your pardon, madam, but I thought perhaps it might be more productive if we met without the watchful eye of Bishop Craig."

Daisy smiled. At least she agreed with him in that regard. He took her hand and then, quite surprisingly, licked her knuckle. "Mmm," he said, and glanced up at her through lashes so long that she wondered if they were real. "I had heard of your beauty, Lady Chatwick…but it was quite understated."

She pulled her hand free of his and said, "I am expecting my son to join me at any moment."

"A pity," he purred. "As to the boy… I was educated at Framingham. I would assume the same for him?"

Daisy started. She would not send Ellis away. "He has a tutor."

"Naturally. But he should be with boys his age." His gaze meandered over Daisy, taking her in. "I would think a new bride would want to send her son away, at least for a time." He casually touched the jewel at her throat. "She might be quite well occupied." He smiled salaciously. "As will his new stepfather."

"My lord—"

"A widow for nearly three years, isn't that so? You must be near to *bursting* with desire," he murmured and traced a line from the jewel at her throat to the top of her breasts.

Daisy pushed his hand away. "Is this your way of courting me?"

He laughed. "There is no need to *court* you, madam. It's simply a matter of coming to terms, and when we do, you will be my lawful wife with all the attendant privileges that conveys."

"And if I don't come to terms with you?"

He shrugged. "Then you will be sorry. Were I a woman, I should much rather lie in the bed of a man who still has his wits about him than one who sleeps with a Bible."

Daisy was beginning to quake. With rage, with frustration, with revulsion. "Please go, my lord."

He smirked as he touched her face. "If you wish," he said and bowed grandly before her. "Send word when you've come to your senses, and we will, as his lord bishop has suggested, assess compatibility." He winked at her and walked out of the room.

When the door closed softly behind him, Daisy began to shake. She fisted her hands at her sides, trying to tamp down her rage. She had done this to herself—if she had tried in earnest to find a suitable husband, she might have spared herself this agony now. She couldn't bear to think of either Vanderberg's or Yarbrough's hands on her.

"Daisy?"

She hadn't heard Belinda enter the room. "Not now, Belinda, please," she said and reached for the settee, falling onto it. "I am unwell."

Belinda closed the door behind her and hurried to Daisy's side. "What has made you ill?"

"Is it not obvious? I'm heartsick! I am utterly and completely heartsick, Belinda." She forced herself to sit up and took Belinda's hands in hers. "What am I to do?" she begged her cousin. "I can't bear the thought of either one of them."

"Neither of them, then," Belinda said.

"You know very well I must choose one, or I will lose everything! You've been warning me of my demise for an age! Why didn't I listen to you?"

"It happened to Mrs. Cully," Belinda said. "After her husband died, she discovered her great debt. She was forced to debtor's prison in his stead," she said ominously.

Daisy closed her eyes with a moan and sagged against the cushions.

"There is something I must show you," Belinda whispered.

Daisy shook her head, imagining a painting or a piece of pottery Belinda had completed. "No, not now. My heart is too heavy."

"It will help you, I swear it."

Daisy groaned again. Her cousin meant well. "Nothing will help me, darling. The only thing that would cure me is if I somehow, miraculously, became a man."

Belinda frowned. She worried a cuticle. And then she nodded, as if someone had spoken to her, and stood up. "I never ask you for anything, Daisy. But I am asking you this," she said. She went to the door of the salon and opened it, calling for Rowley. "Please bring our cloaks."

"What? *No*," Daisy said.

Belinda said nothing and waited for Rowley to return. When he did, she took the cloaks from him, marched across the room to Daisy and held hers out to her. "You've not been out of this house in days."

Daisy could not recall ever seeing such determination in Belinda before. She snatched the cloak from her cousin's hands. "Very well. But I best be helped, Belinda," she warned her.

She donned her cloak and refused Belinda's suggestion that she repair her hair—apparently a few locks had come undone. Daisy didn't care if they had. She didn't care about anything.

The wind whipped down the street when the two women stepped outside, but Belinda walked on, her head down. She kept firm hold of Daisy's hand, lest she mean to run back inside, and dragged her along behind her.

"It's wretchedly cold!" Daisy complained. "Where are we going?"

"You'll see soon enough," Belinda said staunchly. She turned down an alleyway onto another street. They were going away from Grosvenor Square, away from Mayfair and away from Hyde Park.

"Belinda! This is absurd. Where are you taking me?"

Belinda wouldn't answer.

They had walked for half an hour when Daisy yanked her hand out of Belinda's grip, forcing her to halt. "*Where* are we going?" she demanded.

Belinda pointed up the street to a small parish church.

Daisy gaped at it. "You forced me out in this wretched weather to escort me to church?" she all but shouted. "Are you *mad*?"

"Just *come*," Belinda said, sounding almost as angry as Daisy. Her jaw was set, her color high.

"No!" Daisy said petulantly.

"Can you not, for once, do something for me, Daisy?" Belinda shouted at her. "Just *once*."

The admonishment struck Daisy in her heart. Belinda was absolutely right—Belinda never asked for anything from Daisy. She was grateful for her room and keep and had been there for Daisy whenever she needed her. Daisy nodded meekly. "Yes," she said. "Of course I can."

Belinda seemed slightly surprised by her small victory but hardly mollified. She whirled about and continued on. And Daisy followed obediently.

At the church steps, Daisy complained at the sight of her muddied and wet hem.

Belinda opened the door to the church and sent Daisy inside before her.

An Anglican vicar with unkempt hair and rheumy eyes appeared in the narthex. "Welcome," he said, smiling as if he knew her.

"I beg your pardon," Daisy said apologetically as she removed her cloak. "We don't wish to disturb you."

The vicar nodded and disappeared into the interior of the church.

Daisy frowned at Belinda. "Did you bring me here to pray over me? The good Lord knows I need it."

"Go into the nave," Belinda said and took Daisy's cloak from her. "I'll be along."

Well, then. Daisy supposed at the very least she might sit in a pew and brood about her wretched situation. Maybe that's what Belinda thought she needed. Very well, she'd oblige her and pray with all her heart for a miracle.

When she stepped into the small nave, her gaze was drawn to candles flickering at the chancel. A man was standing there, and though it took a moment for Daisy to fully recognize him, her heart seized. And then began to beat wildly. *Cailean.*

It was him. It was really, truly him.

She couldn't believe it. She couldn't *understand* it. She couldn't seem to move, or even think, really, so hard was her heart beating—with anxiety. With love. With wonder.

He was dressed in a coat and waistcoat and breeches; his hair was combed and tied in a neat queue. He looked quite different from the last time she'd seen him, and she couldn't grasp the circumstances by which he was *here*. She was afraid it was a trick, or that if she blinked, he would disappear.

He didn't disappear. He began to walk down the center aisle toward her, his steps cautious. When he reached her, he took her hands in his, then gently drew her into his embrace.

"How?" she whispered into his coat.

"With Belinda's help, aye? It took all my powers

of persuasion, but she at last relented and agreed to help me."

She leaned back so that she could see his face, his lovely, handsome face and blue eyes shining with love. "Why are you here? Don't you know how dangerous it is?"

"Daisy, lass…is it no' obvious, then?" he asked. "I'm lost without you. My world was gray and plain… and then you stepped into it and made it bright again, aye? I was a fool to have let you go."

Her heart began to swell with love. And torment. Oh God, how this declaration would torment her all her life.

"I never expected to fall in love with you, aye? But I did, headfirst and irretrievably. I love you, Daisy. I ardently *love* you. And I'd sooner die than no' have you."

"P-pardon?" she stammered. She still didn't understand. All the reasons they couldn't be together still existed, and some of them had been made worse. Robert's threats echoed in her head.

"*Diah,*" he muttered, his gaze moving over her. "Tell me it's no' too late. For God's sake, tell me it's no' too late."

Of course it was too late. How could he think otherwise? "But what of Scotland? Of Balhaire and Arrandale? Of your…occupation," she whispered, looking furtively about. "What of Ellis? Nothing has changed, Cailean."

"Aye, it has. I'd as soon be English than lose you—do you no' understand? If a Highlander wants something, he bloody well reaches for it, but I've no' reached for anything in a very long time. And during the darkest and longest days of my life, I realized I didna reach when I had you in my arms. Daisy, *leannan*, my world canna exist without you. So I have come to offer for your hand in marriage," he said, sinking down onto one knee before her. "And if you accept my offer, the vicar will marry us now."

Daisy's mouth gaped open with shock. She was afraid to speak, afraid the emotions, the love and relief, would make her collapse. Her thoughts were utter chaos, because this didn't seem possible. He would wed her *now*? It was madness—but she wanted nothing more than to marry him. Ellis wanted nothing more than that, too.

She didn't realize tears were sliding down her face until she tasted them on her lips. "Dear God," she whispered. "Dear God."

Cailean gripped her hands. "Do you still love me, Daisy?"

Daisy was shaking with emotion. It seemed as if every trouble she'd ever had was lifting from her, making her feel almost weightless. That was absurd, for their problems were just as present now as they ever had been. But they felt lighter. In this moment, with her heart bursting, they felt insignificant.

"For the love of God, will you speak, then?" he asked.

She suddenly smiled. "I do still love you," she said. "More than anything, Cailean. You have answered my prayers." She sank down onto her knees, too. "I don't know how we will manage, I don't know what will become of Ellis, and Robert has threatened to see you turned over to authorities—"

"Pardon?"

"But I know that my son will have a good man to raise him, and I will have a good man to love. Yes, Cailean, I will marry you."

He sighed with relief and hung his head for a moment. *"Mo maise, mo muirninn,"* he muttered, and lifted his face to hers. His blue eyes were swimming in emotion. "Thank you," he said, squeezing her hands. "Thank you for making me the happiest man." He kissed her, then pulled her to her feet.

Daisy heard Belinda's sob, then laughed with surprise when Belinda threw her arms around her from behind. "Thank heavens!" Belinda said. "I'll fetch the vicar."

And so it happened that on that horribly cold afternoon, Daisy married her one and only true love in the eyes of God. She didn't care about the scandal that would surely follow. She didn't care that she would be made a pariah, or that the bishop likely would censure her. She cared only that she and Ellis had found someone to love them and protect them. And when the vicar pronounced them wed, she kissed Cailean with all the joy and hope and the promise of what was to come, and then nearly fainted from happiness.

BELINDA HAD PROVED surprisingly resourceful. Apparently, she'd instructed Rowley to send a portmanteau with some of Daisy's things to Knox's town house on Portland Street before she'd forced Daisy to come with her.

Daisy and Cailean retreated there after the wedding. It was best, Cailean suggested, since they had not posted banns or received special license, if they sealed their union with two or three days of conjugal bliss. "The marriage is done, aye? Our names signed on the parish register. But if the bishop has any notion of annulment, a few nights spent in the arms of your husband will make it difficult, will it no'?"

"Exceedingly," she agreed. "But what of Ellis?"

Cailean smiled. "I trust you'll no' mind that I sent a note to the lad with Belinda. She'll bring him round on the morrow." He drew her into his embrace. "But as for today, Lady Mackenzie, you must attend your husband."

"With great pleasure," she said and kissed him.

"The pleasure," he said as he swept her up in his arms, "will be mine, *leannan*." He carried her up the stairs to the master suite and deposited her on the bed. He climbed on top of her and gazed down at her, eyes shining with love and clear desire. "I have missed you, *leannan*," he said. "God, how I've missed you."

"Show me how much," she said, and she sighed with delight when he put his hand on her ankle and began to slide it up her leg.

EPILOGUE

One year later

THERE WAS A painting that Belinda had done of the of the little parish church that graced the Chatwick Hall in Nottinghamshire, just next to the door of Daisy's sitting room. It was the same church where Daisy and Cailean had said their first vows. The vows that Bishop Craig tried desperately to undo in the ensuing scandal created by the clandestine marriage of Lady Chatwick to a sinful Scottish laird, for which everyone said she showed absolutely no remorse.

Bishop Craig was a powerful man indeed, but he was no match for Cailean's uncle Knox, who, as it happened, had very recently been on a hunt with the archbishop of Canterbury. The two men had enjoyed each other's company immensely, apparently, so much so that the archbishop was persuaded to intervene.

Uncle Knox did insist, however, after the furor had died down, that Daisy and Cailean obtain a special license and take their vows again—from the archbishop himself. No one would question them then.

Daisy and Cailean were happy to do it, particularly as Ellis had not been present the first time. Ah, Ellis. If there was anyone happier about the marriage than Daisy, it was he. It seemed to his mother that the boy had shed an outer cocoon and had emerged a happy, joyful boy.

They'd retreated to the country and Chatwick Hall out of necessity. There was too much talk in London, too many who were vocally critical of Daisy's sudden marriage to a Scotsman. Most notably among the critics was Robert Spivey, who made some public accusations against Cailean, all of them quite true. But it was the captain's word against his, and Cailean and Daisy steadfastly denied it.

Nevertheless, Daisy and Cailean had feared that the authorities would come around at any moment to gather him up and try him for free trading. Daisy fretted so that she persuaded Cailean they ought to seek the advice of Lady Beckinsal's cousin, a barrister.

Mr. Barnabus Wilkins was happy to call at Chatwick town house on Audley Street, where he explained to Cailean that in spite of the many accusations against him, there was simply no proof. Without any physical evidence—a ship, or even a bottle of wine that the excise man had missed—no one could prove his guilt. "I would suggest, sir, that you leave London and don't come back," he'd said, gathering his things on his way out.

"What of the captain, then?" Cailean asked. "What's to keep him from making the same accusations?"

The man shrugged. "Nothing. I suppose he can

make life quite difficult for you if he likes with his aspersions against you. But Captain Spivey may be preoccupied. I understand he's been offered a position aboard the *St. Maria*."

Cailean looked at him blankly.

"She is a ship with the East India Company. I understand she sails frequently to India. He stands to make a great deal of money in the spice trade." He glanced meaningfully at Cailean. "It would behoove you to stay off the seas for a time."

"Aye," Cailean agreed.

Daisy was eager to take the barrister's advice and retreat to Chatwick Hall. Mr. Tuttle had developed a fondness for the boy, and had agreed to come along to the country and see after his studies until it was time for him to attend university.

They made plans to return to Scotland, perhaps the following spring. Cailean settled uneasily into Chatwick Hall with Daisy's help, although it was clear he never felt entirely at ease in England and in Englishman's clothing. And he confessed to her one night that he still waited for authorities to arrive on the doorstep one day to take him into custody.

"They would have come by now, darling," Daisy tried to soothe him.

"Aye," Cailean said. "But never turn your back on the *Sassenach, leannan,*" he'd said gravely. In spite of their happy marriage, it was clear deeply rooted suspicions would never die away.

Daisy liked it better in the country for Ellis's sake.

Every day, Cailean spent time with him. They fished; they hunted. They talked at length about stalking red stags until Daisy could bear it no more. They built a small fort in a tree in the forest, and Cailean taught Ellis how to shoot.

Ellis's appetite grew robust, and so did he. He never looked sickly now, and though he had suffered a fair number of bumps and bruises, Daisy had to agree with Cailean—she had coddled him, and now he was thriving.

So was she. She had never paid much attention to the gardens at Chatwick Hall, but they suddenly seemed wanting, and she was determined to create the most beautiful garden in Nottinghamshire. She insisted on doing the work herself, and no one thought to argue with her. Cailean once said he loved her best when she had twigs in her hair and dirt on her gown. Whether or not that was true, Daisy couldn't say—he seemed to love her best no matter what she was wearing…or not wearing.

Belinda's interest in painting had reached new heights, given that she had sold one at Balhaire. She had a reputation for fine art in the village, too, and one day, Mrs. Sudder asked if Belinda would be so kind as to instruct her daughter, as she had yet to show any great promise.

By the end of the year, Belinda had four students. She asked Daisy if she might use part of the old orangery as a studio. "Children must have something to occupy them, for without occupation, they might revert to criminal acts," she'd explained. "It happened to a young man in Alberwick. He had nothing to keep his hands busy and confessed to stealing a ham."

"Dear God, we can't have packs of ham thieves roaming the countryside," Daisy had said laughingly, and had helped Belinda convert the orangery for her use.

Uncle Alfonso had taken up residence at the Chatwick town house in London, where he could oversee Ellis's holdings until Ellis was grown. He visited Chatwick Hall often, generally with a tale or two, including one that featured Lord Yarbrough, who, by all accounts, was caught in the bed of a married marchioness and was very nearly shot while bare from the waist down.

But the news from Scotland was not good. Cailean's father wrote that the situation with the Jacobites in the Highlands had worsened. They were growing bolder, were plotting another attempt to put a Stuart on the throne, were aggressively recruiting men to their cause. Cailean's father suggested it was not entirely safe for Daisy and her son at present. "We can trust no one," he wrote. "Your wife and son are safer where they are for the time being."

He also wrote that he feared Rabbie might take up the Jacobite cause.

Scotland worried Cailean, Daisy knew, as did Rabbie's involvement. But mostly Cailean worried about his father. More than once, Daisy had awakened and found her bed empty; Cailean was restless and would pace.

One night, as they lay in bed, naked and still warm from their lovemaking, she touched his chest, drawing a faint line to his groin. "Do you regret it?"

"Lovemaking?"

She laughed. "No...do you regret coming to England?"

Cailean abruptly sat up and stared down at her. "Have you lost your mind, then?"

"I don't think I have. But I know how you worry. I know how you long to be home, with your family"

"Aye, you have lost your barmy little mind," he said gruffly. "Else you'd know how much I need you, *leannan*. I need you now more than ever, aye?" He suddenly grabbed her up in his arms, pressed her cheek against his shoulder. "I've said it before, and I'll say it again. My world was gray until you shone a light in it. I want to be there, aye. But I want to be here, with you, much more than that. You and Ellis and Belinda are my family. So never let me hear you ask again, Daisy."

She smiled into his chest. "Never, sir," she promised and kissed his chest. "I love you, Cailean."

"Aye, I know you do," he said and nuzzled her neck. "You can scarcely keep your wee hands from me." He kissed her shoulder. Then her chest. "Aye, you love me, you do, as well you ought. But you'll never love me as I love you." He took her breast in his mouth.

She wasn't going to argue with him, at least not now. She closed her eyes and descended into the sort of pleasure she'd never known in her first marriage. No matter how hard he tried, this Scotsman would never love her as much as she loved him.

But he did come awfully close.

* * * * *

*In 1746, the Battle of Culloden left scars
on the Highland landscape and its people.
Their losses were great, and the Crown's
punishment for their rebellion ruthless.
Rabbie Mackenzie's loss of the woman
he planned to marry cuts deep, and when
his parents suggest he marry the daughter
of an Englishman to save what they can of
Balhaire, it is the ultimate humiliation.
He is determined that no one will forget his
grief or the injustice done to the Highlands...*

*Look for Rabbie Mackenzie's story in
HARD-HEARTED HIGHLANDER,
available May 2017.*